NUEVA LUZ

C. J. PETIT

C. J. PETIT

TABLE OF CONTENTS

CHAPTER 1

The stallion's head whipped to his left and his nostrils flared when he recognized the scent of the most dangerous of his enemies. Somewhere nearby there were men.

He began to move, and his mares and the other, smaller herds, kept pace as he searched for the source of the dreaded odor. He had been bringing his herd to the canyon for four years now and it had always been a haven for the mares to foal with its plentiful grass and water. Until now, the only danger had been the occasional visit by a stray cougar, but that danger had been limited to the foals. But now, he could sense men, but he couldn't find them.

He broke into a fast trot and headed toward the mouth of the canyon; the only path out of the canyon. His herd followed, panicking as they also smelled men.

It was only a half mile to the canyon's mouth from where they had been peacefully grazing and the stallion knew he shouldn't hurry, lest the foals be left behind. If the foals strayed, then their mothers would stray, and he needed to keep his mares with him.

He kept moving toward the opening to the canyon that would give them the freedom of the open land, even as the scent of man was growing stronger as he approached its mouth; yet he had to bring his herd to safety and to make the dash out of the canyon.

————

It had taken Lee and Willie two weeks to set up the fence that prevented the horses from escaping. First, at both ends of the canyon mouth, they had built ten-foot-wide gates. Then, they had put in fence posts every five yards on the outer halves and put up barbed wire fencing but left a two-hundred-yard opening in the center, where they had seen the hoof prints from the herd's coming and going. In that opening, they had placed fence posts that were ten yards apart but had put up no fencing. They hoped that the horses, especially the wary stallion, wouldn't notice the posts. The big question was would they have enough time to string the last two hundred yards while the herd was still in the canyon, or would the stallion get wise to their plot.

Once they had set up the trap, they had had to wait for the herd to return, assuming it would.

It was a gamble to try to trap the herd. They had used a good chunk of their cash reserves to buy the wire and tools and only had $128 left; all of which was Lee's. When they had met on the trail, Willie had less than seven dollars in his pocket and Lee had almost two hundred and fifty dollars, just because of the difference in their personalities.

When Lee first had seen the herd the year before, he had hoped they would be back. He and Willie had explored the canyon and seen the lush grazing area and the spring that created the stream of water. It was ideal for horses.

When the herd had moved out of the canyon, Lee decided to gamble that they'd be back.

Lee had filed on a quarter section of land that encompassed the canyon's mouth. The eastern border at the back of the canyon still left a lot of land that he didn't own, but he didn't mind. Because it was a box canyon, access to the other land would have to be made through his property, making it only accessible to him. He owned another two hundred yards in front of the canyon and Willie had filed on the quarter section just west of Lee's claim, outside the canyon. That gave them a mile of property going east and west by a half mile across the north-south border. Now, the whole reason for filing for the land needed to fall into their trap.

And now they had done just that. The herd had arrived a little early but had ignored the posts as they would bushes or trees. The stallion simply led them into the trap without a care.

When they had first spotted the returning herd, both young men were excited. Lee and Willie had been almost a mile away, watching them approach from upwind so they wouldn't be spooked. When they had at long last entered the canyon, they couldn't believe their luck. Willie wanted to go rushing to the gap and start fencing the opening, but Lee preached patience and wanted to let the herd get deep into the canyon and get settled.

It had always been like that between the two eighteen-year-olds. Willie was impetuous and anxious while Lee was always calm and thoughtful. They had met on the trail just three months earlier after Willie had left his job as a drover and Lee was traveling south into Arizona from Colorado. When they had met on the trail, they hit it off and Willie decided to join Lee on his horse-finding enterprise. Lee had always loved horses and wanted to raise a herd of his own and had been told by a miner he met in southern Colorado that there were lots of mustang herds in Arizona, but it took him a lot more travel into southern Arizona to find what he was looking for.

Now he had found it, and more importantly, had it in his almost completely blocked canyon.

When Lee was satisfied that they were well into the canyon, he and Willie rode quickly to the gap and began laying wire. They strung the top string first; Willie running the wire along the fenceposts and looping them around each one. He had the entire first string done in ten minutes. Lee followed with the hammer and the u-shaped wire nails. One tap and a pound sealed the wire to the fencepost.

After reaching the end of the gap, Willie waited on Lee. When Lee arrived, he turned and began a slower ride back, with Lee walking behind slamming the retaining nails into the fenceposts. It took a little over an hour to get the opening sealed.

It wasn't ten minutes later when they could hear the approaching herd and soon spotted the large mass of horses with the angry gray stallion leading them. He approached the fence at the far end of the canyon and began his display of fury.

Angry at being caught unaware, the stallion reared up and thrashed the air with his hooves, screaming his defiance. He trotted along the fence, rearing and pawing the ground every few yards; the rest of the herd crowding against the fence. The stallion traveled the length of the fence twice before he ceased his ranting. There was no use any longer. The men had trapped him and his herd.

The stallion had then calmed and walked around the mouth of the canyon indecisively. After not finding an opening, the herd finally moved back into the canyon and the thick grass and water that lay inside, putting as much distance between them and the men who had cornered them.

"I can't believe we got the whole herd, Lee!" Willie shouted as he watched the herd trot away.

"Now, all we need to do is start breaking them, so we can start making some money. We're running a bit short. We need to build a cabin in the canyon, too, so we qualify for the homestead. We have a lot of work ahead of us, Willie."

"Why do you always have to spoil everything by bringing that up?"

Lee laughed and said, "Because, Willie, we can't keep sleeping out in the open, and we need to get some income before we go broke. The good news is that there are enough materials around to build what we need without going broke."

"I can tell you one thing, Lee; I'm not going near that stallion. You can break him if you want."

"No, sir. The stallion isn't going to be saddle broken. He's going to keep giving us foals, but he'll never have a saddle on his back. I'll cull another young stallion or two for breaking in that we'll use to start two other small herds. I figure we can break and sell about fifteen horses this year and after that, about twenty to twenty-five a year. The herd is just under seventy right now. We'll geld most of the young colts and let the fillies stay until they can join the new herds. We should be up to a two hundred horses in a couple of years."

"I thought we were just gonna sell the whole lot and be done with it," Willie said.

"Of course, not. Why do you think I had us file on the homesteads? I told you we were going to raise horses."

"Yeah, but I thought we'd sell this bunch and then get some more."

"We're sort of doing that. We're selling some of this bunch and then letting them make us more."

"Damn, Lee. That sounds like a lot of work!"

"Anything worth having is a lot of work, Willie."

Willie just grumbled and climbed back on his horse.

―――――

Over the next week, Lee selected and cut out sixteen horses and put them into a corral that they had built. Then came the dangerous job of breaking the horses. Willie was useless in this, which was surprising because he had been riding horses since he was six, but Lee was a natural with the animals. He took his falls, but because he spent so much time in preparation; getting the horse calmed down and then used to his presence, the breaking part wasn't so violent.

Lee then sent Willie to Fort Grant, a two-day ride, to see about selling the horses to the army. Usually, they were avid buyers of saddle broken horses. By the time he returned, Lee had broken all the horses to the saddle.

"So, what did the army say?" he asked when Willie approached.

"They'll pay forty-five dollars a head for broke horses."

"That's a surprise. I thought they wouldn't go for more than forty dollars. We could have made a killing during the war, though. Even green horses were selling for five hundred dollars."

Willie exclaimed, "You're kidding! That much?"

"They were killing horses and mules faster than they were men. But forty-five dollars is a good price."

"It turns out that they're in short supply right now. It seems the ranches in the area have been snapping them up."

"I think we'll run this bunch over to Fort Grant, and after that, maybe we should go visit Nueva Luz and see if any ranchers want to buy some in the future."

"I'd like to go to town. Haven't had a drink in a while," said Willie.

"Come on, Willie, you're not even nineteen yet. How long have you been drinking?"

"Hell, Lee, I can't ever recall not drinking. With you bein' Irish and all, I figured you'd be a heavier drinker than I am."

"My mother was a strong non-drinker. My father would sneak a nip or two every once and a while, but she never let me near it. Turns out when I finally tried it, I didn't even like it anyway. I had no cause to get drunk, either. When I was younger, we lived near Chinatown, so I spent a lot of my growing up days talking to Chinese. They taught me a lot, including how liquor clouds the mind. Did you know I can speak Chinese?"

"No kidding? It sounded like a bunch of gibberish to me."

"It's not too bad. Now Gaelic, on the other hand, is a disaster."

"What's Gaelic?" asked Willie

"It's the ancient Irish language. You can almost break your tongue with some of it, but my mother and father both spoke it a lot, so I used it every once in a while."

"I always thought the Irish language was things like, 'You'd not be fooling with me wee lassie, would ye?' and other things like that."

Lee laughed and said, "That's just a way they have with the English language."

"Can you speak any other languages?"

"Nope. Just three."

"One is enough for me."

————

The next day they herded the sixteen broke horses and trailed them down to Fort Grant. The supply sergeant, a good Irishman, who oversaw acquisitions, was very pleased with the horseflesh and paid them their seven hundred and twenty dollars. Lee immediately handed half to Willie whose eyes grew large at having so much money.

They rode back and stopped in Nueva Luz for some supplies, and Willie went off to a saloon called Phil's Place, while Lee stopped at the bank to open an account. He deposited three hundred dollars, leaving him with enough cash to start work on the cabin which would need more materials, supplies and tools.

He rode to the livery stable and bought a pack mule and saddle for sixty dollars. Then he led the mule to the dry goods store and bought some bacon, beans, coffee, flour, salt and baking powder. He also picked up two boxes of .44 ammunition for his Colt and Winchester. That set him back another $17.30.

Then he led the mule to the hardware store and picked up a double-bladed axe, a sharpening stone, a maul and wedge, a hatchet, pickaxe, and finally, a saw and shovel. That ate up another $22.40.

He was down to around eighty dollars when he finished, but he had what he needed to build the cabin.

Nueva Luz was a nice town compared to most towns of its size in the West. There was only one saloon but there were three churches, and one was a Catholic Church. It was Saturday, so Lee decided he'd head that way and go to confession. It had been a while, and he hoped the priest didn't give him too long of a tongue-lashing or so much penance he wouldn't be back to the canyon for a month.

He trotted Stonewall, his six-year old roan gelding and the mule down to St. Mary's church, tied the horse to the hitch rail and removed his Stetson as he walked in. As expected, it was dark inside and quiet. There were already three women sitting, waiting to go to the confessional, so he just genuflected and stepped into the pew.

The line moved slowly, which meant that either there were a lot of big-time sinners waiting to purge themselves of years of misbehaving, or the priest was a lecturer, perhaps both.

After about twenty minutes, he entered the confessional. Lee began with the traditional, "Bless me father, for I have sinned ...", and then waited for the first admonishment he knew he'd get when he said, "... it has been three months since my last confession."

He didn't have to wait long.

A healthy Irish brogue chided him, "And what's been keeping you so long from coming to the confessional, lad?"

Lee was taken aback by an Irish priest after having met only Mexican priests in Arizona but saw a possible way to escape too much penance.

He replied in his best Irish tongue, "Well, it's like this, Father. I've been riding cross country, heading from Colorado all the way here, and haven't found a single Catholic church. Not one. Now, I was thinking that surely, there'd be at least a Mexican Catholic church, but not a one did I find. I just arrived in the area two weeks ago and haven't even got a roof over my head but was blessed to see your church. I came right over, and here I am."

"Aye. I can understand it then. You sound like a good Irish lad. I'll be forgiving you for that, then. What sins will you be confessing to Father Kelly now?"

"Well, Father. I've missed Mass on the journey and I'm right ashamed of it, too. Aside from that, I've used profanity."

"This profanity, did you take the Lord's name in vain or blaspheme?"

"Oh, heavens no, Father. It's just that I sometimes get frustrated with those that don't work hard."

"Well, the good Lord will understand some level of improper language. Is that all, my son? No drinking or womanizing?"

"No, Father. I never took to drink and when I find myself a good young lady, I aim to make her my wife and have many babies for you to be baptizing."

"Well, miracles do happen. So, son, for your missing of the Masses, I'll be giving you three *Our Fathers* as penance. Now, I hope to see you in Mass tomorrow. It'll be at eight o'clock."

"I'll try, Father. My canyon is ten miles northeast of here. but I should make it if I leave at six o'clock."

"Bless you, son."

The priest absolved his sins in Latin and blessed him officially as Lee crossed himself.

He left the confessional and smiled at the next penitent, a red headed young lady. In fact, there was a row of red-headed folk in line; eight of them. Lee assumed they were all related, or at least he hoped so.

He walked up to the altar rail and said his three *Our Fathers*, and when he finished, stood, genuflected and walked down the aisle, smiling again at the line of redheads.

When he exited into the bright Arizona sun, he squinted as pulled on his hat.

He mounted Stonewall and trailed the mule down the main street, expecting to see Willie exit the saloon soon. After another ten minutes, without seeing him, he decided he'd get something to eat while he was in town and set the animals toward Winchell's Diner.

It was a clean place and almost half full, so he quickly found an empty table and sat down, removed his hat and set it on the nearby chair.

A waitress arrived shortly and simply said, "The special today is beef stew."

She was around forty and shaped like an apple.

"I guess I'll have the special, and some coffee," Lee said as he smiled.

She nodded and turned back to the kitchen. Because he had ordered the special, his meal showed in two minutes, complete with a pot of coffee and a plate of biscuits. The waitress may not have been overly pleasant, but the stew was tasty and filling, and the biscuits were excellent. The coffee was hot and black and that was just about all he needed it to be. Overall, it qualified as the best meal Lee had eaten in some time, which was a bit sad.

He finished his dinner, took the two remaining biscuits and left fifty cents on the table, then walked outside and climbed into the saddle.

He had just turned to go to the saloon to find Willie, when he saw a sight that would always stick in his mind. There was a wagon plodding along the street filled with redheads of various sizes. The entire family had left the church and must not have had many sins, he figured. The bright sun made the vision of eight bright red heads almost blinding.

Lee rode past the wagon with a smile, tipped his hat to the family and said, "Good afternoon!" as he passed. They smiled back, and the younger children waved, as did the older girl, who appeared to be around sixteen or seventeen.

He couldn't help but notice her. She was a pretty lass, and surely as Irish as they came.

But that was for another time, he thought. Lee rode on, not looking forward to rousting Willie. He'd had to do it twice before, but that had been in towns where they had just been passing strangers. This was the first time on home territory, and he was under the obviously mistaken belief that once they had found someplace to start their herd, Willie would modify his behavior. He felt a bit foolish for believing that he would change.

He dismounted, tied Stonewall to the hitching rail and entered the bar. Lee was tall and although he appeared slim, he packed almost two hundred pounds of solid muscle on his six-foot frame from the hard work that he enjoyed as much as Willie loved his liquor.

He scanned the room and couldn't see Willie anywhere, which he thought was odd. They'd been in town for less than two hours and he'd seen Willie enter the bar, so he must be here somewhere.

He looked more carefully, and still didn't find Willie. Finally, he walked up to the bartender to ask where his partner had gone.

He was an enormous man and must have been almost six and a half feet tall and weighed over three hundred pounds. Too much of his weight was fat, though.

"Excuse me, sir, I'm looking for my friend. I saw him come in about two hours ago. He goes by the name of Willie Thompson. He's a short, skinny guy about my age."

"I know where your pal is, mister. He's cooling his heels in the jail."

Lee sighed as he nodded his acknowledgement. This was a hell of a way to introduce yourself to the town.

He turned, left the saloon, mounted Stonewall and walked him and the mule down to the sheriff's office. This would be worse than dragging Willie out of a bar. He hadn't had to get him out of jail before, and wasn't even sure that he wanted to this time because it might become a habit.

He stepped down and looped Stonewall's reins around the hitching rail. After he dismounted, he hesitantly walked into the office, its door already wide open, unsure of what to expect. There was an average-sized man with dark brown hair sporting a long, flowing handlebar moustache and a star on his chest standing near the wall hanging some wanted posters. Lee judged him to be mid to upper forties.

"Sheriff?" he asked.

The sheriff turned and spotted Lee, his eyes revealing a personable nature.

"What can I do for you, son?"

"My friend was arrested down at the saloon. I hate to ask how much trouble he could have gotten into in just two hours."

"You'd be surprised. Can I get your name?"

"Yes, sir. My name is Lee Ryan. I'm starting a horse ranch about ten miles northeast of town."

"Well, Lee, your friend had been drinking pretty heavy for about an hour. Then he decided he wanted to sit in on a poker game. He had a bet of over a hundred and fifty dollars riding on a pair of fours, I guess he figured he could just buy the pot. But one of the other fellers was holding three queens and wasn't about to let him do it. When the other gent laid down his winning hand, he flew off the handle and accuses the man of cheating and goes for his gun. Luckily, Phil, the bartender, pulled his shotgun and threatened to blow him apart if he did anything. The kid stops dead, puts his gun back in the holster and then he goes and tries to take back his money. That's when he got cold-cocked by another player. I got called and we dragged him down here. He had ninety dollars on him when we brought him in. Was that legal money, son?"

Lee was stunned as he replied, "Yes, sir. We had just sold sixteen horses to the Army at Fort Grant. *I can't believe that he went through more than two hundred and fifty dollars in two hours!*"

Lee then shook his head and said, "I don't know what I'm going to do with him. He doesn't like to work, either."

"I'm not surprised. Did you want to take him? The fine will be ten dollars for drunk and disorderly."

Lee thought about it for a minute and didn't take long to decide.

"Sheriff, I'd appreciate it if you just kept him. When he wakes up, he can pay his own fine and if he wants to come back to my canyon, he can. It'll be up to him. He needs to grow up."

"Well, Lee, it seems you have your head set right. That's a smart thing to do. I'll tell him what you said, but don't be surprised if you don't see him for a week or so until he's flat broke again. What happens after that is up to you."

"Thanks, Sheriff. I never did get your name."

"Ernie Smith."

Lee shook his hand and said, "Pleased to make your acquaintance, Sheriff Smith. I surely won't be trouble like Willie over there. In fact, if you ever need any help, I'd be willing to offer it."

"Not too many do that when it's needed the most. I appreciate it, Lee. Have a good ride back."

Lee nodded, then turned and left the office, climbed aboard Stonewall then rode out of town leading the mule back to his canyon.

———

It was early Sunday morning when Lee was already aboard Stonewall and heading back down to Nueva Luz. He hadn't eaten as he was going to be receiving Communion later. It was a beautiful sunrise as he made his way down the long, gentle slope toward town, and he appreciated the beauty of the natural landscape as it almost glowed from the fresh sun.

He arrived at well before eight o'clock, hitched Stonewall to the post on the opposite side of the church and walked up the steps. He removed his hat and again adjusted to the darkness. He chose a pew at the back of the church as he usually did, then sat and waited for the Mass to begin. The regular churchgoers began arriving, including the family of redheads. They took the third pew across the aisle from Lee and he noticed that all the females, the mother and her young daughters wore identical light green hats, probably fashioned by their mother from a single bolt of cloth, but they went well with their hair, he thought.

The Mass began and followed the proscribed language and rituals. Lee understood Latin well, so he knew what was being said and what they meant. The Mass itself was a deep experience if one took the time to understand its purpose and meaning, but not too many really did.

When it came time for communion, Lee got in line with the rest of the members and waited until it was his turn to receive. He knelt at the rail, received communion and returned down the side aisle to his pew. He never had grown accustomed to the communion wafer which had been made of unleavened bread, or so his mother had told him. It was so dry it would stick to the roof of his mouth and he'd spend five minutes of tongue scraping to clear it off.

The service ended a few minutes later and Lee went outside, mounted Stonewall and headed to the diner for breakfast. Unlike Protestant churches, the priest didn't stand outside after the service greeting his parishioners. Lee didn't know why they didn't because he thought it was a good idea.

He had his breakfast of eggs, ham and biscuits with a lot of coffee and vowed to make this a routine.

After paying for his breakfast, he mounted Stonewall and walked him past the jail and gave a brief thought of stopping in and getting Willie but knew that he needed Willie to make that decision, not himself.

He was back at the canyon by eleven o'clock, and decided it was time to begin the work on some type of shelter.

He dressed in work clothes, but no shirt. He knew how sweaty he would be in an hour. It may be autumn, but it would be warm, if not downright hot.

He entered the canyon and walked to a spot he had picked out earlier. It was close to the stream that began at the spring in the back of the canyon where the horses were. There were plenty of tall pines nearby, and now that he had the mule, he could get the cabin built, Willie or no Willie.

Lee had a rather unusual childhood. It started out normally, growing up with his parents, but when they moved to Colorado and wound up living in Pueblo right next to Chinatown, his education expanded. He was already adept at reading and writing in English, but because he was welcomed by the Orientals, he found that he learned so much more. He learned their language and their different religions. He was passed from family to family to expand his mind and body and learned different ways of fighting, so he could avoid having to use guns.

He learned how to use guns, tactics and how to read men from his father, who had been a deputy sheriff for eight years before a bullet had ended his lawman career. But from the Chinese, he learned how to be patient. Lee was always a quiet boy anyway, but this was much more than just not speaking. He learned how to let peace pass over his mind.

When Lee finally left Pueblo to strike out on his own, he was mature well beyond his eighteen years. He had developed his love of horses because after his father recovered from his near-fatal bullet wound, he worked at the stock shipping area at the railroad depot. He was responsible for loading, unloading and caring for the horses that people would ship when they were going somewhere and taking their horses with them. Sometimes, they'd arrive, and the horses would be left in his care for weeks at a time. Lee had started helping when he was twelve and always had an affinity for the animals.

And now, he was managing his own herd.

But his most immediate concern was the cabin. He started the project by cutting down selected trees and then clearing off the branches. It took him the rest of Sunday and all of Monday and Tuesday to down as many trees as he needed and still had seen no Willie.

On Wednesday, he started cutting the logs to length and cut the notches for putting them in place. He was tired at the end of each day but pleased with his progress. He decided on holding off on putting in a floor until he at least had a roof over his head. The roof would be the biggest problem.

He had the walls starting to go up by the end of the first week, and Willie still hadn't made an appearance. He didn't feel the need to go to confession. All he had done all week that could have merited a visit was a foul word or two over missed cuts or branches that fell the wrong way.

But on Sunday, early the next morning he trotted Stonewall down the decline toward Nueva Luz and arrived just in time and almost snuck in the church and slipped into his pew. No one noticed.

After Mass, he headed to the diner, had breakfast and then thought he'd stop by and see if the sheriff was in.

He was a bit surprised to see the door open when he reached the jail but dismounted and entered the building.

"Good morning, Sheriff Smith," Lee said.

"Morning, Lee. What can I do for you?"

"I was just wondering what happened to Willie. I haven't seen him since he walked into the saloon."

"He left the next morning, stopped over at Phil's, then I saw him leave town heading south an hour or so later. I haven't seen or heard from him since. Didn't come back your way, huh?"

"Nope. I guess he's rid of me. Too much work."

"His kind don't cotton to work all that much."

"I figured that out fairly soon. I only knew him for a few months before we got here. He seemed friendly enough, but the more I got to know him, he seemed like he thought life was all fun and no work."

"You, Lee, seem to be just the opposite. Don't you do anything for fun?"

Lee had to think about an answer before he replied, "You know, I never really noticed it before. I read, but that's not supposed to be fun. I enjoy working, though. I'm building a cabin right now and it gives me real pleasure to see the work progress. So, I guess that makes me a bit of an oddball."

"I wish there were a lot more of you, Lee. It'd make my job easier; I can tell you."

"Well, I've got to get back. I'm getting ready to finish my cabin."

"Good luck, Lee."

Lee returned to his canyon, but instead of working on the cabin, he walked Stonewall down to where the stallion kept his herd. It wasn't really one herd, but there were three. The main herd led by the big gray, then a smaller herd headed by a smaller, but still impressive black stallion, and then a third smaller group of just stallions. He was pleased to see that there were six new foals and three of the mares looked like they were going to drop soon. He was about to return to his cabin when he noticed that one of the yearlings was caught in a bramble. It was a handsome palomino yearling with had a deep gold coat, black mane and tail and a white star on his forehead. Lee dismounted, removed his rope from the saddle and approached the young horse and began talking to it to keep it from hurting itself on the long thorns.

The small horse at first shied away as much as it could, but as Lee kept talking to it, the yearling calmed down and grew curious. Lee finally reached the animal and touched its nose and the young horse pulled its head back. But Lee kept his hand in position, and the yearling finally lowered its head and Lee began rubbing his nose. The colt seemed to enjoy having its nose rubbed and didn't shy away.

After a few minutes, Lee wrapped the rope around its neck and tied the other end around a nearby tree to keep him from struggling against the brambles while he cleared the mess.

Then he put on his work gloves, took out his knife and began cutting the brambles away. It took almost twenty minutes to get enough removed to attempt to free the yearling. He had to make a few more cuts before the small horse was freed, then he quickly started to bolt, but Lee kept talking to him. Then he reached over and began rubbing its neck, still talking in soothing tones.

Soon, the palomino was free, and Lee kept talking to it and rubbing its neck and Lee wondered why the horse was so calm. This was a wild young stallion-in-the-making. They tended to be the most skittish of them all.

He took the rope then led him to the other end of the rope and untied the knot holding it to the tree.

When that was done, he led both Stonewall and the young horse down the canyon toward the cabin and the corral. There were no other horses in the corral yet, so these two would be the only ones in the expansive yard with the mule, of course. It had plenty of grass already since the departure of the sixteen horses to the army two weeks ago. The creek was on its southern edge, so they had plenty of water as well.

He brought them both inside and released the recently saved yearling. Surprisingly, he didn't run at all but just stood in place looking at him. Lee removed Stonewall's tack and let him go, then when Stonewall trotted to the water to get a drink, the palomino went with him.

Lee smiled at the small horse and already had a name for him. He'd call him Jin which was Chinese for gold.

Over the next few days, the walls began to rise, and he made his cutouts for the door and windows. It was Friday when he knew that he'd have to start tackling the roof.

Getting the main beam up for the roof would be the biggest problem in building the cabin, and the most dangerous. It helped that he had left the angle beams in place with extensions. He was able to get a rope over one end and slide the long log through the V-shape and then use temporary supports to keep it straight as the mule slid it into place. Once it was locked down, he could finish the roof.

He went to church the next day. It was becoming routine. He'd slip in the back, take communion, and be the first one out. He'd see the redheaded family show up after him sometimes. He'd smile at them and most would smile back.

His work on his cabin still dominated his time as he used the maul and wedge to start cutting boards for the roof, and overlap them from bottom to top. When it was done, he began collecting stones for the fireplace. It took him two days to find enough. Then another day to assemble the fireplace using adobe mortar. There was plenty of sand in the lower claim. It was about one-third grassy on the top bordering the canyon before giving way to the desert. Lee wondered how this would work. Without Willie, the claim would lapse. He only hoped that no one would notice for five years. Thenm when he satisfied the homestead requirements on his claim, he could file on the other. That was where he could build a real house; a large house built of adobe bricks. He could do it himself, too. It would take a year or two, but he had the time. By then, if the horse sales continued, he'd have the money as well.

He had been so busy making his new home that he'd missed too many Saturdays, so he knew he had to visit Father Kelly in his small, dark booth again.

So, after getting a mild scolding from the parish priest, he was leaving church, and almost ran into the older red-headed girl who was just entering.

He still had his hat in his hand as he quickly stepped aside and said, "Oh, excuse me, miss. I didn't see you there. I shouldn't have been in such a hurry."

"Well," she replied with a smile, "I could understand running away from Father Kelly if he'd just given you a tongue-lashing for committing so many sins."

"No, ma'am. It's just that I'm anxious to get back to work."

"You're going to work? It's a Saturday afternoon. Surely, you can take some time off."

"No, ma'am. I've got things that need to be done, and I'm the only one who can do them. I don't think my horse would do too well wielding an axe."

She laughed as her blue eyes danced and Lee enjoyed the sound. It was no schoolgirl giggle.

She then asked, "I've seen you at Mass every week, but I don't know your name."

"It's Lee Ryan, ma'am."

"And just so you don't have to ask, my name is Mary Flannery. And, as you can probably have already noticed, I have a large family."

"Oh, it wasn't a difficult thing to notice. You all are right-handed and it's a dead giveaway."

Mary laughed again then said, "As much as I'd like to spend some time talking, I'd best be going in and getting my penance from Father Kelly."

"I've found that slipping in some Gaelic into your confession can drop an *Our Father* or at least a *Hail Mary* from his penance requirement. It's just a suggestion, mind you."

Mary laughed, shook her head and said as she stepped into the church, "You have the Irish charm, Mr. Ryan."

Lee waved and pressed on. So, the family's name was Flannery and she was Mary, he thought. Somehow, he didn't think he'd be forgetting it, either.

Lee returned to his cabin and the days rolled past almost without notice except for his visits to the town for either spiritual support or supplies.

He worked every day at the canyon almost from dawn to dusk, always adding and improving, but he never saw Willie there or in Nueva Luz.

He'd see the Flannery family every Sunday, and, if he was lucky, he'd meet Mary on Saturdays and talk to her. Sometimes the talks lasted almost ten minutes, and the more he talked to her, the more he was pleased with her wit and her intelligence. She was very pretty, too, but he had things to do before he could think about doing anything more about it. Yet every minute with Mary added to his normally intense desire to get things done.

———

By spring, the horses in the canyon had become accustomed to his presence. He could even go and pat them on the neck or head, but big gray stallion still seemed to resent him, for good reason, thought Lee.

The cabin now had a floor. It had taken Lee a full week to split and shave the planks with his new plane. He had added shutters and the door, built a simple table and two chairs, added a bed, and purchased a mattress on his next Saturday trip to Nueva Luz.

He built a forge but would purchase standard-sized horseshoes in town rather than try to make them on his own. After he broke horses to the saddle, he would then shoe them, so they'd be ready for sale to the army. It added to his workload, but he didn't mind. He enjoyed the work and the exercise.

He improved the corral and added a second, then moved his young palomino stallion into the second and brought six young fillies to share it with him. He chose the best of the young ladies for his friend and gelded six of the young colts, leaving the best of them intact.

He counted the herd and wound up with seventy-six and thought he might skip a year, but instead pre-selected some older mares for sale to the army. He had a total of twelve that he picked. They were still in good condition, but he deemed them past mating prime.

———

That fall, he made the ride to Fort Grant with his dozen horses and returned five hundred and forty dollars richer. He stopped in Nueva Luz on the way back and deposited five hundred dollars, made another large food purchase and stopped at the diner for dinner before heading back.

As he was leaving the diner, he heard a loud, "Get outta here, you mangy mutt!" and watched as a small black and white dog yelped and was kicked out of the entrance to the livery stable. The dog was barely past being a puppy.

Lee walked over to Jin, pulled a stick of jerky out of his saddlebag, snapped it in two, then he approached the dirty little dog. It looked thin as well and the dog looked at him with hopeful eyes.

"Here, boy," Lee said, offering him half of the jerky.

The little dog ran to Lee and snapped up the jerky, spending all of four seconds tearing it apart and eating it. Then he began bouncing around, looking at Lee for more.

Lee looked down and said, "Well, what am I going to do with you?"

The dog had already made his decision. Lee was his new friend; the one who gave him food.

Lee handed him the other piece and walked down to the dry goods store, the small dog following, but not in a straight line. He zigzagged behind Lee as if he was trying to push him along.

Lee arrived at the store and pointed to the dog and said, "Stay!" The dog sat and looked at him, as if to say, 'Come on, give me something harder to do'. Lee stared at the little dog for a few seconds, grinned and headed into the store.

Lee bought six cans of beef and another two pounds of jerky. Then, after paying, he returned to the boardwalk where the almost puppy still sat, looking at Lee and awaiting further orders.

"Come on, boy!" he called, snapping his fingers, and the dog obeyed instantly, whether he understood or not. Lee figured he could smell the jerky.

Lee arrived at Jin and hooked his new purchases around his saddle horn. Then he turned to the dog and simply clapped his hands and put them out. The small dog leapt into his arms and began licking his face.

Lee laughed and climbed on the young stallion, while Jin was unsure of what to make of the new passenger.

Lee decided to name him 'Hǎo gǒu', or to reasonably Anglicize his name, Hagar. The original Chinese meaning 'good dog'. Hagar turned out to be an excellent companion, and soon grew rapidly to his full size, which wasn't that big. He looked like a border collie, which proved itself when he started running into the canyon to herd the horses. He was good at it, too. If Lee wanted to move a group to a different location, all he had to do was to point Hagar to where he wanted them to be, and he'd take care of it.

———

And so, it went for another year. The herd now numbered eighty-six. A younger stallion had begun to challenge the older one and had taken some of the mares forming a fourth herd. Jin had sired six foals out of his six mares this past year and Lee's bank account had swollen to more than fifteen hundred dollars.

And then there was Mary. He saw her as much as he could, which usually only meant a few minutes after confession, and that was only every other Saturday. It was like they had set aside the time for a rendezvous. He wished he could go and see her more formally, but he didn't think he had enough to offer her yet. Besides, she was a very popular young lady. Whenever he chanced to see her in town other than at church, she was invariably in the company of another young man. He was ashamed to admit he was jealous, so he would convince himself that he had no claim on her. In fact, she hadn't expressed any interest in him other than to enjoy their conversations and laugh at his stories. Maybe that's all he would ever be to her, a source of amusement.

What he didn't understand was that Mary thought of Lee a lot. She wondered why he never came to the farm like the other boys. When she saw him after confession, he was so enjoyable to talk to. She wanted to spend more time with him, but whenever she was in town, she was usually accompanied by one of her many suitors. She would see Lee look at them and just turn away and she just didn't understand why, yet she knew it wasn't her place to invite him to come and visit her. She couldn't be so bold.

———

Another year passed, with their Saturday talks and Sunday smiles, but suddenly one Sunday, Lee noticed that Mary wasn't among the Flannery family and wondered if she was sick. But the following Sunday, she was still missing, and he began to worry about her. He couldn't approach her family to ask about her because he had only a casual relationship with the rest of the family. It was surely not enough to go and ask the whereabouts of the elder daughter.

After that second Mass where Mary was missing, he sought out Father Kelly, and found him in the rectory.

"Father, can I ask a question about one of your other parishioners?"

"You may ask, but I may not be able to answer."

"I understand. I noticed that Mary Flannery wasn't with her family for the past two Sundays, and I was concerned about her welfare. Is she all right?"

Lee could see Father Kelly musing his response. He was more aware of the couple's mutual interest than they were themselves.

Finally, he said, "Aye. Mary's fine. She'll probably return to weekly Masses soon."

"Thank you, Father. It was just that I enjoyed talking to her and she seems like an exceptional young lady. I was worried that she might be sick."

"She is that, Lee. But even good people sometimes make mistakes. Make sure you understand that when you talk to her again."

"I understand that, Father. We all make mistakes in our lives. I've made some huge ones, but without forgiveness, life wouldn't be able to go on."

"You have the right of it, Lee, but sometimes, the last one to forgive a mistake is the one who made it themselves."

"Thank you, Father."

Lee left the rectory wondering what mistake Mary had made and why she couldn't forgive herself. He knew that she had a good heart and deserved any forgiveness, but it wasn't his position to offer it.

————

The next time he saw Mary was coming out of confession the following week. He waited for her and tried to talk to her, but she didn't even smile. She just said a quick 'good afternoon' and walked to her mule to ride back to her farm. Her coldness hurt more than her absence. This wasn't the Mary he knew and had let take possession of his heart.

————

Another year passed, and Mary still stayed aloof. She'd be with her family on Sundays but wouldn't pay him any mind. It was also difficult to not notice the physical change in her appearance. She was more rounded than she had been before. It was most noticeable in the size of her breasts. Overall, she seemed more mature, but he still wished she was the same happy person he recalled from two years earlier. Despite the attention of many of other young women he'd see in his brief visits to Nueva Luz, he paid them no mind. Coldness or not, Mary owned him, and he would be patient because that was his nature. He would wait until his Mary returned.

His cabin was still his only living space, but he was just days away from fulfilling his homestead requirements. He even had the obligatory 'farming' requirement satisfied with his large vegetable garden. Once the homesteading was fulfilled, he could file on Willie's property. No one had claimed it yet; probably because as far as anyone knew, Willie was still there.

Lee had put on more muscle than he had when he was only eighteen. His weight had gone past two hundred and ten pounds, but he still appeared to weigh less. His arms looked like they belonged to a blacksmith, which he was part of the time.

Then came the big day when he could take ownership of his canyon without strings. Lee rode Jin down the slope toward Nueva Luz. Hagar was back in the canyon watching the herd as he usually did.

Lee and Jin were now the best of friends, to the point where Jin could almost read his thoughts. Lee barely had to use the reins at all. He'd just apply a little more pressure with his left or right leg. Both legs would bring him to a stop and leaning forward would cause Jin to accelerate; and could he accelerate! Lee had never found a horse that could match his speed and endurance. His chest was enormous. As a bonus, he had produced large crops of foals every year. Together with their canine friend, they made a perfect team: Lee, Jin and Hagar.

Lee reached the land office and stepped down. He never even bothered hitching Jin, as he would just wait for Lee. He walked into the office and saw the land office clerk behind the desk filling out some forms.

"Good morning!" said Lee.

"Good morning to you, sir. How can I help you?"

"I just completed my five years on my claim and needed to complete the paperwork."

"Congratulatons. What is the name?"

"Lee Ryan."

"Just a moment."

The clerk went to his files and located Lee's folder then returned to the counter.

"You're very punctual, Mr. Ryan. The homestead requirements were satisfied two days ago. I'll just need you to sign here and here and the property is yours."

"Wonderful," Lee said as he signed the two forms and the land clerk signed and dated them, then handed Lee the deed to the property.

Lee then asked, "This was worth the hard work. Can I ask about the quarter section that was filed at the same time under my friend's name, Willie Thompson?"

"Let me check," he said as he returned to the files and pulled out that folder.

"It seems that it has been completed as well."

"He hasn't lived on it for the past five years, so I was wondering how that worked?"

"He hasn't? Well, that makes a difference. Do you want the property?"

"That's why I asked. I was going to file for homestead on that quarter section after the homestead was completed on mine. I've been living on mine for five years raising horses, but I had planned on building a nice adobe house on the lower claim when the upper claim was done."

"Well, to be honest, Mr. Ryan, we don't pay a lot of attention to the homesteads. Unless we get a complaint, we simply issue the deed after five years. The county is anxious to get them onto the tax rolls as soon as possible. Now, as this homestead property was filed five years ago, and no one has complained, I can issue the deed to you right now."

"That would be outstanding. I could begin work next week."

"Perfect! When you make improvements, the land value goes up and the county gets more tax dollars, and that's of paramount importance to the county," he said, finishing with a smile.

The clerk had Lee sign on two more forms, stamped the deed twice and handed it to him.

"May I ask one more question?" Lee asked.

"Certainly."

"Can Willie Thompson come back later and say he had filed, so it's his property?"

"No. He forfeited all rights when he failed to comply with the homestead requirements. The deed is yours legally and is registered as such. I'll be sending both forms to the county later today."

"Thank you, sir." Lee said as he reached over and shook his hand.

He rode back to what was now his permanent and expanded property; two full quarter sections, three hundred and twenty acres, and it was his.

CHAPTER 2

Three days later, Lee was in Nueva Luz on a rare Monday visit. He realized he was out of coffee and didn't want to wait five more days. He was in the dry goods store paying for his coffee and a few other food items when a deep voice came from behind him.

"That your horse out front?"

Lee turned to see a man he'd never noticed before. He was taller than Lee and looked a lot heavier. He looked to be around thirty and needed a shave.

"There are a lot of horses out front. Could you be more specific?"

"The palomino."

"Yes, he's mine," Lee replied then went back to paying for the food.

"Miss Richards wants to talk to you."

"Fine. I'll talk to Miss Richards as soon as I take care of this transaction."

"Miss Richards don't like waitin'."

Lee didn't look at the man, but said, "I'm sorry, but she won't have to wait long. Tell her I'll be out in two or three minutes."

"Mister, you'll get your ass out there now!"

Lee turned and looked at him, more out of curiosity and said, "I didn't get your name."

"My name is Rafe Henry and if you don't get movin', you're gonna wish you never heard it."

"I'm already regretting hearing it. Now, please just go outside and ask Miss Richards to wait just a minute or so."

The big man put his hand on Lee's shoulder and yanked him toward the door.

Lee reached over with his left hand and squeezed the big man's elbow.

Rafe let go of Lee and cursed as he grabbed his elbow.

"Mister Henry," Lee said conversationally, "don't ever touch me again. It appears that Mr. Enright has completed my purchase, so we can go out and see Miss Richards. Now, I ask you, what has your aggressive nature accomplished? Absolutely nothing."

He reached over and accepted his bags of groceries from the disbelieving Harry Enright. Then Lee stepped out of the shop into the bright sunlight, escorting a still wincing Rafe Henry out the door.

He found himself looking at a beautiful young woman astride a magnificent black gelding. She had light brown hair and bright green eyes like his own.

Rafe returned to his horse, rubbing his elbow and glaring at Lee.

Lee looked up at her and said, "Can I guess that you are the same Miss Richards that sent this obnoxious messenger into the store to demand I respond to your immediate summons?"

She laughed and said, "My, my! Aren't you a fancy talker? Yes, I sent Rafe in to find the owner of the palomino. I'd like to buy him from you. Name your price."

"Miss Richards, if Mr. Henry had bothered asking in the first place, he'd have been told that Jin is not for sale. Period. I've raised him from a yearling. We are symbiotic."

"I don't know what symbiotic means, but everything has its price. I'll give you two hundred dollars for him. Surely, even you wouldn't turn down that much money."

"Of course, I would. I don't say things I don't mean, Miss Richards. I have many other nice horses that you could buy for a reasonable price, but Jin is a very special friend. How much money would you sell a friend for?"

"You'll come around, Mister…?"

"Ryan. Lee Ryan."

"Another Irishman. Just what this town needs," she said as she laughed, "Well, Mr. Ryan, you should come and visit me at the Diamond R sometime. Maybe I can change your mind."

"I may visit at some future date, but I won't change my mind. Irish are stubborn that way."

"So, I've heard. But let me ask you this. If you like the animal so much, why did you name him after cheap liquor?"

"He's not. He's named Jin, the Chinese word for gold."

"Well, I stand corrected. Good day, Mr. Ryan," she replied as she smiled at him.

"Good afternoon, Miss Richards," he said, smiling back.

She turned her horse and waited for Rafe Henry to get on his horse, but he was staring down the street. Lee followed his gaze and saw a wagon being driven by the Flannery family's father and his youngest son next to him in the front seat.

"It's that Flannery," growled Henry.

Miss Richards said nothing as Henry walked across the street to intercept the wagon.

The wagon kept coming, and Mr. Flannery was watching Rafe Henry intently as he approached their wagon. Lee had no idea what was going to happen or why, but it sure looked confrontational.

As Rafe got close to the wagon he reached out with his left hand and yanked the reins out of the Mister Flannery's grasp. Then he walked up to the wagon and grabbed him by the collar, then as the redhaired man reached back to knock his grip away, Rafe yanked him free from the seat and sent him flying to the dusty roadway.

Lee had seen enough and quickly walked quickly to the scene.

Rafe started warning Mister Flannery, "You ever gonna listen, Flannery? Here's something to clear your ears!"

Then he reached back and kicked Flannery hard in the ribs. He was setting up for a second kick when he felt a hand on his shoulder. He turned to strike the interloper and found himself on the ground without knowing how he had arrived in that position.

He looked up and saw Lee staring down at him. "Rafe, I suggest you get up off the ground and get on your horse and escort Miss Richards home."

"You bastard! I'll make you wish you hadn't done that!"

Rafe climbed to his feet rapidly and shot his right fist at Lee. Lee blocked the fist, took his right wrist, twisted it and sent him flying into the rear wagon wheel, stunning him as Rafe's head banged against one of the hardwood spokes.

Lee looked down at him and said, "Rafe, take my suggestion, then just stand up and get on your horse. It's only going to get worse."

Lee then heard Miss Richards say, "Rafe, let's go home."

Rafe moaned as he stood and then glared at Lee as he dusted himself off and returned to his horse. He stepped up into the saddle, maintaining his glare until he turned and trotted behind Miss Richards who smiled at Lee and then turned back down the road.

Lee leaned over Mr. Flannery and said to him, "Ceart go leor?"

Flannery opened one eye and said to him, "You'll be askin' if I'm all right in the Gaelic?"

"Well, are you? He put a vicious kick into your ribs."

"I've had worse, but I'll be okay."

"Let me help you up," Lee said as he held Flannery's right arm as he slowly stood.

When he finally made it to his feet, he looked at Lee and said, "I've been seeing you at the Mass on Sunday, but not be knowing your name."

"The name's Lee Ryan, Mr. Flannery. Glad to meet you."

"The name's Ian, Mr. Ryan. And that's my boy Conor."

"Call me Lee, Mr. Flannery."

Then Lee looked over at Conor, who was still looking at Lee with awe and offered him his hand which he shook.

"Nice to meet you, Conor."

"How did you do that, Mr. Ryan? Nobody whips Rafe Henry."

"I didn't whip him, Conor. I just tried to get him to stop kicking your father."

Ian asked, "So, Lee, how is it that all these years we've seen you at church and you've never come and introduced yourself?"

"Well, Ian. I just don't like to intrude."

"Well, I'm mighty glad you intruded today. I think he may have broken a rib or two."

"What are you here for today, Ian?"

"I have to pick up our monthly supply order."

"Well, you won't be loading much today. I'll come along and help."

"I appreciate it, lad. I surely do."

They drove over to the dry goods store that Lee had just left. When they entered, the owner looked at Lee wondering the same thing that Conor had. *How had Lee simply walked Rafe Henry out of the store?*

The Flannery order was large. A full barrel of flour, sixty pounds of sugar, thirty pounds of coffee, and a bunch of other items. Lee noticed that there was no meat in the order, which meant that they must have a farm.

They brought the wagon around back and Lee loaded all the heavy items as Conor continued to be amazed. Lee was picking up large items easily, but when he lifted the hundred-weight barrel of flour and placed it on the wagon, Conor's mouth dropped open. Lee didn't seem that strong just to look at him.

When the wagon was packed, and the bill settled, Lee asked, "Ian, I know you have two older sons at home, so will you be able to get this all unloaded okay?"

"Aye, Lee, it'll be fine. I can't thank you enough."

"No problem. Ian, why did Rafe Henry do that? I couldn't see the motivation."

"It's a queer thing, it is. We have a farm about two miles southeast of town. We grow only one cash crop: hay. For a while there, we tried wheat, but it didn't work out in our soil. Then I noticed that everybody was raising cattle. Now, I figured that with grass being not as good as it is in other parts of the land, they'd be needing hay. So, I begin growing hay. I have about four hundred acres in hay now. I sell the hay to six different ranches. Now, Mr. Richards is my neighbor to the south and has a lot of land and cattle. He was buying half of my crop.

Well, he has too many cows now and wants more hay. He needs all my hay to keep his cattle from getting too skinny but I have agreements with the other ranchers. He says because it's not written down, it doesn't matter. But to me, my word matters. Well, now my crop is ready for harvest in a few weeks and he's getting desperate. This was the first time he's done something like that, though."

"Why doesn't he just put in some hay himself?"

"He has a water problem. He has four sections of land but only has good water on one, so he uses the others just for grazing. If he were to try to grow hay, it would use his water and his cattle wouldn't have a place to drink."

"Why doesn't he just cut down the size of his herd? Sell off a third while they're fat?"

"The reason for that, son, I haven't a clue. Lee, why don't you follow us home, so you can meet the family? I know they're all curious to meet you. They see you every Sunday and don't know anything about you."

Lee thought about it. He really didn't have anything immediate going on and Ian wasn't in condition to fend off another confrontation. Besides, maybe he could get to talk to Mary again. Maybe he could see a glimmer of the old, happy Mary.

"Alright. I'll come along."

Ian smiled at him and started the wagon heading south. When he left the town, he turned slightly east following his own wagon trail as Lee kept Jin at a walk alongside the wagon. Lee noticed that neither Ian nor Conor had a firearm. That was unusual in these parts, even for a farmer.

As they walked along, Ian talked about his farm and his family, having to almost shout over the racket of the wagon. He told how they had lost their farm in Arkansas during the war, had come west looking for a new home and were traveling through Arizona heading to California when their wagon broke its second axle and they reached the town of Nueva Luz on a patched-up wagon and homesteaded there. He and his Maggie homesteaded two quarters and after they had met the requirements, homesteaded two more, with good water on all four. So, now they owned a full section of land tucked under the Gila Range; the same mountains that provided Lee with his small canyon home.

He was immensely proud of his six children. His oldest son, Patrick was nineteen now and a great help on the farm, Mary, whom he knew and yet didn't know, had just turned twenty-two and could do anything around the farm in addition to the cooking. Then came Sean, seventeen; his other daughter, Katherine, who was sixteen, and his last two sons Dylan, thirteen, and Conor sitting next to him, who was eleven. His wife, Maggie, had taught them all to read, write and to do their cyphers, in addition to being the rock for the family, which Ian freely admitted.

Lee could see his parental pride as he talked and smiled. His parents had only one child, which was a rarity among Catholic families. Lee attributed it to the difficulties his mother had in giving him life. He always treated her with great reverence for that, if not for being the wonderful person she was.

Ian rambled, and the wagon rumbled for almost an hour when they finally turned onto a drive toward a large, but modest house. By the time they were in sight of the house, Lee felt he knew every member of the family.

"There's the family estate, Lee," shouted Ian as he pointed.

Lee could already see the sea of hay beyond and realized that it must be a serious amount of labor to get it all cut and bundled. He'd stick to horses. He looked toward the house and could see patches of red hair on the porch. The Flannery clan were all waving at Ian as the team plodded toward their home.

On the porch, the waiting Flannery family noticed the rider accompanying the head of the household. Mary knew exactly who it was when she spotted the palomino, and she was a butter churn of emotions. She liked Lee so much but was also so fearfully ashamed that he would find out.

Katherine guessed who he was quickly as well. She had a crush on Lee just from looking at him at church. The boys were guessing who he was but figured it out when he got closer and they saw the rider clearly.

Ian steered the wagon to the back of the house, where the supplies would be unloaded.

Then, when he pulled it to a stop, the crowd of redheads gathered nearby.

"Welcome home, husband," said Maggie, "And I see you've brought a guest."

"Aye, Maggie. That I have," replied Ian. "I'd like you all to meet Lee Ryan, a fine Irish lad who helped me through a wee spot of trouble I had in town."

Maggie knew that it was probably far from 'a wee spot of trouble' and would get the full story when he got inside.

Instead, she smiled at Lee and said, "It's a pleasure to meet you, Mr. Ryan. Let me introduce you to everyone."

"I'd be happy to, ma'am, and, please, call me Lee," he said as he stepped down from Jin and walked over.

Maggie had a look of alarm and said, "You'd be forgetting to tie your horse, Lee. He'll be running for sure."

"No, Mrs. Flannery, he'll stay wherever he wants to be. I can always call him back, but he usually never goes very far."

Maggie was amazed that anyone trusted his horse that much and said, "He must be a good horse, then. And please be calling me Maggie."

"Thank you for that, Maggie, and yes, he's an exceptional horse."

Lee noticed that the boys were unloading the wagon and thought they might need help with some of the heavier items, so he signaled to Maggie that he'd be back in a minute then walked quickly to the wagon and hopped into the bed.

He moved the heavy flour barrel to the edge of the bed, hopped to the ground, then lifted it and carried it over to the porch where it could be rolled into the kitchen. Then on his second trip to the wagon, he retrieved the sack with the sugar and coffee and carried it up the stairs to the kitchen, setting it down where Ian indicated.

Then Lee walked back to the remaining family and said, "Sorry for the interruption, Maggie. I thought I'd make myself useful."

"Aye. That was quite useful. It's always a chore getting those into the house. But let me introduce you to my passel of troublemakers. Patrick you'll meet later, he's helping Ian unload. My older daughter is Mary."

Lee reached over to shake her hand, wondering how familiar he should be. He and Mary were the only ones who knew about their Saturday conversations, so he decided to let her make the choice.

"Nice to meet you officially, Mary."

She took his hand and said, "And it's good to meet you again, Mr. Ryan."

When he released her hand, he said, "Will each of you please call me Lee?"

They all nodded and murmured their consents.

He was then introduced to the remaining members of the family and Katherine seemed especially anxious to meet Lee.

When the introductions were complete, they all entered the house and Lee noticed that the main room, or family room as they called it, was filled with chairs in front of a large fireplace. He figured with eight family members, they'd need the space.

"So, have a seat somewhere, Lee," Maggie directed.

Lee looked over at the rapidly filling chairs and waited until one was available. When everyone was seated, he walked to one on the end and took his seat.

"Lee, before my husband comes in, tell us about his '*wee spot of trouble]*."

"*Talk about being put on the hot seat!*" he thought.

Lee thought about it for a second and figured he may as well be honest.

"Ian was driving his wagon in the street, and Rafe Henry — for reasons unknown to me at the time — walked up to the wagon and pulled him onto the ground. He kicked Ian before I got there, so I just persuaded Mr. Henry to leave. He got on his horse and rode off with Miss Richards. It wasn't that serious."

"*He kicked my husband, did he?* Well, that no-account has gone too far now," Maggie steamed.

Lee could see the fire in her eyes as the famous Irish temper was engaged.

Ian entered the room with Patrick and heard his wife's angry comment.

"Now, Maggie, it wasn't that serious, like Lee says."

"You men haven't got the sense of a chicken. Of course, it's serious. That Ed Richards is pushing us, Ian."

"I know, Maggie, but it'll be fine."

Maggie decided to let it go for the moment. She'd talk to her husband later – at length.

"So, Lee, tell me. where do you live?" Maggie asked.

"I have sort of a ranch about ten miles north of here. I only have a cabin on the property now, but I'm still building things."

"You raise cattle?"

"No, ma'am, horses."

That got Conor Flannery excited as he quickly asked, "Horses? How many do you have?"

"At the moment, not including Stonewall and Jin who's outside, I have about a hundred and twenty. I'll be culling out twenty or so to run over to Fort Grant. It keeps the herd from getting too big and makes me some money."

"Gin? Why did you name your horse after liquor?" asked Patrick.

Lee laughed and said, That's the same question Miss Richards asked. His name is Jin, with a 'J'. It's Chinese for gold."

"You talked to her?" Katherine questioned.

"Yes, ma'am. Mr. Henry came into the store where I was buying some supplies and told me that Miss Richards wanted to see me immediately. I told him twice that I'd talk to her after I had finished paying for my supplies, but he said she didn't want to be kept waiting, so he grabbed my shoulder. I persuaded him not to do that, and we went outside. It seems that she wanted to buy Jin. I told her that he wasn't for sale, and she offered me two hundred dollars. I told her 'no' again, and she said I should come over and see her so she could persuade me."

"*She offered you two hundred dollars for a horse, and you turned it down?*" asked Ian incredulously.

"She could have offered me a thousand dollars and I would have turned her down. As I explained to her, Jin is my friend as much as he's my horse. What price do you put on a friend?"

"Are you going to go and visit her?" asked Katherine.

"I said I might, but if I do, it'll just be to find out what's going on."

"But she's a very beautiful woman," she argued, "Won't you be tempted?"

"Yes, she's beautiful, but very callous too," replied Lee, "She watched as Rafe kicked your father and wasn't about to stop him, either, although I'm sure she had the power to do so. I wonder how people get that way. I can't see any decent person allowing that to go on. There are things we do that are just mistakes. No matter how bad the mistake may be, they can be forgiven if the person who made the mistake has a good heart. What happened on the street was not a mistake. It was an intentional act of cruelty. Miss Richards, in allowing it to continue when she had the power to stop it, showed that she doesn't have a good heart. She deserves no forgiveness for what she did. After listening to Ian for over an hour wax eloquently about everyone here, I can't imagine anyone in this family doing something like that. You all seem to have good hearts."

Lee had to twist his answer to let Mary understand what he thought about whatever mistake she had made.

"So, Lee, can I be guessing that you're named after the River Lee in the old country?" asked Maggie.

Lee smiled, glad to be onto a different subject.

"No, ma'am, my father had a different reason for the name, although he was happy that it was an Irish name as well. I was born in '64, and my father was a great admirer of Robert E. Lee. It could have been worse, you know. I could have been a Beauregard or something. I'll settle for Lee."

"And what do you think of General Lee?" asked Patrick.

43

"In all honesty, I thought he might be the best general this country has ever produced. They asked him to command the Union Army, but he resigned and took command of the Army of Virginia. He was a very emotional leader and his men would do anything for him. On the battlefield, Lee was a great tactician, but made a strategic blunder by invading Pennsylvania, but I don't think that the politicians gave him any choice. Even then, if he'd had Stonewall Jackson with him, I believe he would have beaten Meade at Gettysburg and everything would have been very different after that."

Now, Grant and Sherman weren't as good as Lee in tactics, but both men were the ultimate in strategy who really understood how war had to be waged when you had a numerical and material superiority."

"Are you a student of war, then?" asked Sean.

"I'm a student of many things, especially history. War is intriguing because throughout history, nothing else can alter history so radically. Over the long term, religion can, but in a very short period, war can make dramatic changes in the flow of history."

"Do you enjoy fighting, then?" Conor asked, recalling Lee's confrontation with Rafe Henry.

"Just the opposite. I think violence is never productive. There are always better solutions that don't result in harm to someone. If I can avoid violence, I will."

"Then why do you carry a pistol and a rifle?" Katherine asked.

"For protection mostly and hunting sometimes. We live in a violent society out here. There are men that will shoot you as soon as look at you. Take Rafe Henry for example, he carries a pistol, and he impresses me as the kind of man that will shoot an unarmed man. My Colt will give him pause because he doesn't know if he can outshoot me. He won't risk it because he's afraid of dying himself."

"Are you good with it?" asked Sean.

"I'm okay," Lee replied, not wanting to sound braggadocious about his skills that had been honed by years of practice.

"Lee, how did you whip Rafe Henry?" asked Conor, not wanting the subject to fade away.

His question raised some eyebrows.

"I didn't whip him, Conor. I just kept him from hurting your father. Once he realized that he couldn't win, he left."

The family then looked at clarification from Ian.

Ian said, "I was on the ground and didn't see anything. The next thing I know, Rafe is leaving and Lee is asking me if I was alright in the Gaelic."

"So, how did you persuade him, Lee?" asked Maggie.

"I just dropped him to the ground a couple of times. It wasn't difficult. He's a big man and quite clumsy."

"You hit him and knocked him down twice?" asked an astonished Katherine.

"No, I didn't hit him at all. I just sort of invited him to have a seat. Not much more than that."

"But how?"

Lee sighed and replied, "When I was twelve, I began to visit Chinatown outside of Pueblo. I became friendly with many of the families and the more I visited, the more I learned. First, I learned Chinese, so I could talk to them better. Then, I listened as they talked about their different religions."

"How many religions do they have?" asked Ian.

"Well, there was Confucianism, Taoism, Buddhism, and quite a few were Christians. There weren't any Catholics among them, though.

That was a bit surprising with as many Jesuits that are in China. What was interesting, though, was when I talked to the Christian Chinese, they asked about my religion and they were surprised to find that Protestantism was broken away from Catholicism because of excesses of the Church at the time or differences in dogma. We got into many discussions about that. Anyway, after I had been there a year, one of the men began teaching me martial arts. It's a way of defense that involves balance and motion. It also uses pressure points on the body to control an opponent. It takes years to fully understand and use. The other aspect of the training was to control my own mind. To be able to calm my emotions when I needed to, and to control how my body is functioning; my heartbeat and my breathing, for example. It also showed me how to bring peace to my mind when it might be in turmoil. It was an uplifting experience when my teacher finally told me that he had taught me all that he knew."

Patrick asked, "Could you show me?"

"How to control your emotions?" Lee asked.

"No, how you made Rafe Henry fall to the ground."

"I really don't want to hurt anyone. I'd rather not."

"How about just a demonstration?" asked Conor.

Lee knew it wouldn't go away.

"Alright, stand in front of me like you're going to hit me," he said to Patrick.

Patrick smiled and stood up. He assumed the classic boxing stance. Obviously, someone, probably Ian, had taught him how to fight. Lee stood and walked until he was three feet in front of Patrick as the rest of the family watched intently.

"Okay, Patrick, give me a shot."

Patrick snapped his right at Lee in an effective jab.

Lee caught the wrist in his left hand and pushed his thumb into the joint.

Patrick winced as Lee slipped his left foot behind Patrick's right foot which was tilted forward for the punch and pulled him off-balance. He started to fall when Lee caught him and sat him down in his chair.

"Are you all right, Patrick?" he asked.

"I'm fine. I didn't even see you move. All I felt was the pain in my wrist and then I was sitting down."

"The reason for the pain was that I pressed on a pressure point. I avoided pressing too hard or it would have hurt a lot more. But once you felt the pain, you lost concentration, which gave me the chance to unbalance you."

Conor asked, "How come all them Chinese wear ponytails?"

"They call them queues, Conor. They wear them because the emperor in China demands they wear them to show their loyalty. They think that the emperor has spies everywhere and if they see them without their queues, he will have their families in China killed. Realize that most of them are here alone. They left families back in China. That's why there are so few Chinese women. I think of the two hundred Chinese in the Chinatown that I knew, there were twenty women."

"Don't they smell funny?" he asked.

"No, they're very clean. In fact, when I first started visiting, they asked that I bathe more often. So, now I take a bath every day. It's what I'm used to."

Lee wanted to talk about something other than himself, so he changed the subject.

"Well, enough about me. Tell me about your family. Ian has already explained how you got here. I was curious how you could harvest that much hay. It looks like oceans of the stuff."

"We have two combine harvesters. That's why we have ten mules," explained Ian, "The harvesters are pulled by four mules and cut the hay and then a bundle of hay comes out the back. It just goes along leaving hay bundles behind it. We can cut two acres an hour per machine. We'll be able to get the whole farm cleared in less than a week."

"I'm glad you don't have to use a scythe."

"We couldn't do it. We could only cut maybe two acres a day with four people working."

"I have one question for Maggie," Lee said as he turned to the family matriarch.

"And I'd imagine I can guess what it is, Lee, but you go right ahead."

"How in blazes did you do it? I mean, I drove my mother crazy and I was all she had. You raised six children and still you seem quite normal and they all seem to be model citizens."

"It was a chore; I can tell you. It's getting better now that they're almost full grown. Pretty soon we'll probably be losing Patrick. He's courting Elsie McDermott in town."

Patrick blushed and started to say something but thought wiser of it and held his comment.

"You were an only child?" asked Maggie.

"Yes. I think it was because of the difficulty my mother had when I was born. She always wanted another baby, but never did. I always felt guilty for depriving her of that. I know it was pointless to think that way. My mother was a lot like you Maggie. She was a strong woman, but she was very kind and loving. She would do anything for me as I'm sure you would do anything for any one of yours. And, just like you, she wouldn't put up with any foolishness."

"Well, thank you for those kind words."

"Just saying what I believe, Maggie."

Conor asked, "Lee, did what the Chinese taught you give you all the strength you have? You picked up that barrel of flour like it was empty."

"No, Conor, they didn't do that. They helped with the balance but being able to pick that up comes from hard work. I'm sure you can do it too."

Then he turned to Ian and asked, "Ian, what else do you have on the farm. I noticed that you didn't buy any meat today."

"No, we don't need to, except when we buy some beef from the butcher. We have two milk cows, four dozen chickens, eight hogs, and a vegetable garden."

"No wonder. I didn't smell the hogs, though. How'd you manage that?"

"They're on the other end of the farm, about a mile away. The smokehouse is on this end, though."

"Wise man."

"Lee, are you married?" asked Katherine with a smile.

"No."

"How about girlfriends?"

"No."

"So, you live alone?"

"No. I have company staying with me in the canyon."

"And who is this company?" Katherine asked with a twinkle in her eye.

"Hagar. I found him in town a few years ago. Someone had kicked him out of the livery, so I gave him some jerky and he's been with me ever since. He's very smart and enjoys herding the horses, even if they don't like it. His real name is *Hǎo gǒu*, which is Chinese for 'good dog'."

"Oh. He's a dog. Is he friendly, like if one of us were to visit, would he bite?" she asked.

"No. He's very friendly to people he thinks are my friends. He seems to sense when someone is there for bad reasons. I had a couple of men show up last year that were probably thinking of relieving me of a few horses, but Hagar began growling at them and they changed their minds. It's really kind of funny that even real tough hombres get really nervous when they see a dog's bared teeth. It was a greater incentive for them to move on than the Colt on my side."

Lee felt a bit uncomfortable talking about himself so much and didn't see any way out, so, he took the easy way.

"Well, it's been nice meeting everyone, but I've got to head back."

"Mr. Ryan, you'll do no such thing. You'll be staying for dinner."

"Maggie, I'd love nothing more, but I do need to return."

"Well, you'd better not stay a stranger then."

"No, I'll stop by some time when things aren't so busy."

Lee stood as did everyone else, then he smiled, turned and walked out the front door and looked for Jin. He had wandered off someplace that he must have found interesting; probably the mules. The redheaded crowd noticed the absence of his horse.

"Jin!" he shouted in a loud voice.

He didn't have to wait long. The palomino stallion came trotting around the corner and stepped up before the porch and looked at him.

"Have a nice visit, did you?" Lee asked him.

He stepped down and patted the horse on the neck before setting his foot in the stirrup as the Flannery clan watched in amazement at the comradery between horse and man.

"Good-bye, Flannery family, it's been a pleasure meeting you all," he said as he tipped his Stetson.

Lee didn't touch the reins, but lightly touched Jin with his left knee and leaned forward ever so gently. Jin turned and headed out as Lee waved.

"What a remarkable young man," said Maggie.

"Aye, I'm thinking the same. He'll make a good friend," replied Ian.

————

As Lee and Jin began their homeward journey, there was tension in the Richards household just two miles away.

Edward Richards, the scion of the family, was berating Rafe Henry as his daughter Stella and his son Frank sat nearby.

"What did you think you were doing, Rafe? I didn't tell you to assault Ian Flannery."

"You said you needed to have more pressure put on him to sell his hay," said the normally self-possessed Rafe Henry with downcast eyes.

"Pressure does not mean beating someone on the main street of Nueva Luz. What if the sheriff had been notified? You could be in jail right now," Richards groused.

"It seemed like a good idea at the time."

"Since when have you had a good idea?" he shouted, then turned to his daughter.

"And, Stella, why didn't you stop it?"

"Dad, it wasn't that bad. Just a good swift kick."

"And were you going to stop it after that? Or did you think a few more good swift kicks would make Ian more likely to sell us the hay? I'm surrounded by idiots," he fumed.

Stella added, "Well, it didn't go too far anyway. There was some young man named Ryan that made Rafe stop. He was quite handsome, too."

"Leave it to you to notice that. How'd you know his name, anyway?"

"I tried to buy his horse."

"You have the best horse in southern Arizona. Why do you need another one?"

"I think this one was better. He was a magnificent palomino stallion. The odd thing was that he wasn't even hitched. He was just standing there."

"It doesn't matter. I'm going to have to go and try to smooth this out with Flannery somehow."

"You know, Father, I offered him two hundred dollars for the horse, and he wouldn't sell."

"I'm glad he didn't. That's way too much for some boy's cow pony."

"Maybe it was too much money, Father, but that was no cow pony, and he most certainly was no boy," she replied with a coquettish smile.

———

Lee arrived at his cabin a little over an hour later. Jin had trotted most of the way, so Lee estimated the distance to be about ten miles.

It was a straight trail, and hadn't had to avoid any major obstacles like ravines.

Hagar sensed his return long before he arrived, recognizing the sound of Jin's gait. He waited impatiently for Lee's return, and when he saw him astride Jin, he began barking a welcome.

Lee smiled at the sound. He had grown immensely fond of that dog. He sidled Jin next to the entrance gate, opened it and trotted Jin inside before Hagar trotted behind him and closed the gate. None of his horses would escape while he was in charge.

Lee stepped down and stripped Jin, brushed him down and released him to go where he wanted to go. Usually, he'd go back to his ladies. Then he turned to shut the gate, saw it was already closed, smiled at Hagar, then returned to his cabin. Hagar trotted behind him and sat down on the small porch.

After putting his saddlebags inside, Lee returned to the porch, and sat down in one of the two chairs he had on his porch that he had added to the cabin the second year. He looked out west, knowing it would be sunset soon. Hagar had joined him and curled near his feet. He knew he really didn't have to leave the Flannery farm, but he didn't want to intrude, not on his first visit. At least, that was the excuse he gave himself. Deep down, he knew the real reason was that he understood that if he was around Mary much longer it would be before he'd say something stupid.

She was definitely not the old Mary that he remembered and began to wonder if she was even there anymore. He had noticed how little she had said, like she didn't even know he was there.

———

But Mary most certainly had noticed and had done more than just notice. She lay in her bed that night wondering why he had said what he did about people making mistakes? *Had he known about her horrible, painful mistake?* It seemed like the whole town knew, but he hadn't treated her badly or even differently than he had before. He seemed to want to talk to her again, *but why? Was he ignorant of what had happened or did he really forgive her for her error?* An error she wished she had never made. If she had just asked him into coming to visit her, it would never have happened. But it wasn't her place to ask. She fell asleep with silent tears in her eyes, wondering, *what if –*

CHAPTER 3

The next morning, Lee still couldn't forget Mary, even if she didn't want to talk to him anymore. He wouldn't let that change his plans for his permanent home, either. He would start on the adobe house. Now. Today. He had been making bricks all year and had over two thousand already stacked.

In typical Lee Ryan fashion, he decided first to add more brick forms. He built two more eight-brick molds, so he could make thirty-two bricks at a time. He would continue making bricks as he built to avoid eating into his supply as much. He would fill the molds in the morning and build the rest of the day, then fill them again when he stopped.

He leveled the ground for the house first. It was such a gradual slope, that it wasn't difficult. He purposefully leveled a larger area than he expected to build. His bricks were fourteen inches long, eight inches deep, and four inches thick. He thought the smart thing to do first would be to lay the outline of the walls with one row of bricks. He also knew that the mortar would add to the size. As he contemplated what he was about to do, he finally decided that he may as well go all out. He would use sixty bricks on the front and back walls and thirty-six on the sides. With the mortar adding to the length, it would be a big house requiring a lot of work, and a lot of bricks.

He had a piece of wood that was a half-inch thick. That would be his spacer for the mortar. He laid his first brick just after breakfast on Tuesday. By the time he broke for dinner late in the evening, as it was getting too dark to do any more work, he had laid the first row of front and back walls which were over eighty feet long, and the side walls, which were more than fifty feet. The house would be a massive building, but as he was accustomed to saying; he had the time.

The next day, he mixed more mortar, laid it down and began the second row. He had made two molds for creating half bricks and used his half bricks to create the strength of an offset. He left gaps for the front door and the back door and also began laying bricks for the interior walls. By the end of the week, he had all interior and exterior walls three bricks deep. He planned for three fireplaces and marked them off with bricks as well.

He was following his much-modified plans that he had drawn up before he began. Sometimes, he would modify on the fly as he came up with a new idea. But the house would be different, too. Even as he was putting his first visions to paper, he had many ideas that were incorporated into the design.

The inspiration for those ideas was back at her family farm ten miles southeast. He never for a second thought he would live in the new house by himself. He could live comfortably in his cabin if he imagined living the rest of his life alone. This was going to be Mary's house, or it would remain empty.

He took a break and walked back to visit the herd, searching for a specific filly. She was three years old and was one of Jin's first crop of foals. He found her at last and culled her out, talking to her constantly. She had a pleasant disposition. He and Hagar brought her to the breaking corral. She was a beautiful palomino like her sire, Jin. The only apparent difference other than her sex, was she didn't have a star on her forehead, but she did have four white stockings. She was also a lighter gold than Jin and was easily the prettiest filly in the herd. The rest of the day, he spent breaking her to the saddle. She was easily trained, one of the easiest he'd ever had. She responded to commands and seemed to enjoy his company, but he'd leave her naming to someone else.

The next day, he returned to brick making and building. He had maintained his supply to around a thousand, despite his high daily usage because he'd sometimes go four days just making bricks.

But this was Saturday, and he hadn't been to confession in a few weeks, so he cleaned up after filling his molds and rode Jin into town.

He rode in from the north and left Jin behind the church as he usually did, then walked around front to go inside.

As he did, he thought he caught a glimpse of red hair going into the dry goods store and wondered which Flannery was headed into the mercantile as he entered the church.

As usual, Father Kelly chatted more than chastised. Lee really did have a problem making up offenses, stretching things like saying 'Good God!' into taking the Lord's name in vain.

Lee said his minimum penance and genuflected before leaving the church.

He was going to return to Jin when he figured he'd head over to Harry's store and see who had been visiting. There was a mule in front, so whoever it was came alone, which was not a good idea, usually.

He entered the store and noticed that Harry must be in the storeroom, then he saw a red head a few aisles to his left. It was a short Flannery, so it was probably Mary or maybe Katherine. There was another head next to her. It belonged to a young man that he had seen in town periodically, but never met.

"Come on, Mary. I know you like me. We can have a good time," he was saying in a low, but clear voice.

Lee waited for Mary's response.

"Leave me alone, Jimmy Avery! I'm not that kind of girl!"

"Sure, you are, Mary. I'm that kind of guy, too," he replied with a lecherous grin.

Lee thought it had gone too far and stepped into the aisle.

"Mary, is he bothering you?"

Mary's head swiveled to see Lee standing not three feet behind her. She felt relief and still more shame that he might have heard what Jimmy had said.

"No, Mr. Ryan, I can handle this."

"Alright, I was just trying to help."

Lee turned to leave and heard Jimmy say, "You'll just have to get in line, mister."

It was both an unnecessary and unwise thing to say.

Whether Mary asked for help or not, that was beyond insulting.

He stepped past Mary and faced Jimmy and said. "Mister, you just insulted Miss Flannery. Now, I suggest you apologize immediately, or you'll do so on your knees."

Jimmy made another profound error in judgment by laughing and saying, "Apologize to Merry Mary? You must be joking!"

Lee reached out and pinched his neck, just at the junction of the neck and the shoulder.

Jimmy's mouth flew open, and he dropped to his knees.

Lee released his grip and repeated, "Now, you're on your knees. You will beg for her forgiveness, or you'll be begging lying flat on your back."

Jimmy's shoulder still was numb as he looked at Lee's burning eyes and knew that Lee was capable of doing it.

"I apologize, Mary. I didn't mean it."

"Now, one more thing, Jimmy. If I ever hear you or anyone else talking about Mary that way, you'll wish you had never been born. Mary is a good woman with a pure heart. To say otherwise would be to incur my wrath. Is that understood?"

"Yes, sir."

Mary was stunned. Lee had heard what Jimmy had called her and still said she had a pure heart.

Lee turned his back on Jimmy and gently took Mary's elbow. He escorted her from the store and marched her across the street to the front of St. Mary's church. When he got her to the steps of the church, he turned her around and faced her with a stern face.

"Mary, I am tired of you being so morose and distant. I don't know whatever you think you did that was so horrible that you felt you had to withdraw into a shell, but it will stop now. You are too good a person to let that change you. I want my Mary back. The one I could talk to and make laugh. I know she's in there."

Mary began to sob as she dropped her eyes and choked, "No, she's not. That Mary is gone."

Before he could say another word, she turned and raced down the steps, mounted the mule, turned him south and rode quickly away while Lee just watched in stunned disbelief.

Lee sighed. Maybe she was right. He wouldn't give up, though. He needed to bring his Mary back.

He returned to Jin, mounted and headed home.

Mary rode the mule faster than she had ever ridden him before. *What was the matter with her?* Lee had defended her and had tried to tell her that she mattered to him. He had even said, *'my Mary'*, but she couldn't accept it. The Mary she was and always would be was the Merry Mary that some of the boys called her and expected of her. The so-called 'good boys', would have nothing to do with her. One mistake and she had been categorized. She was now a loose woman. But still, the very best of the good boys, really the very best of the good men, had treated her like the old Mary; the good Mary. He seemed to know about her mistake and forgiven her. *Had he really? Or was he just trying to make use of the Merry Mary of the rumors.*

Then she suddenly was more ashamed of herself for even thinking that of Lee than she had been about her mistake. He had never done anything to deserve that kind of thought.

———

Lee rode into his canyon, thinking it was time to check on the herd. Hagar trotted behind them.

He saw the main body of the herd and thought about where he was now compared to when he had arrived. The herd had been so long in the canyon that more than half had been born there. His arrival and Hagar's arrival no longer caused any sense of alarm.

Lee dismounted and began to examine the main herd. He was happy to see fourteen mares with foals, not including the four in Jin's harem. So, he'd need to cut out twenty horses for sale.

He had marked a dozen when Hagar began to growl and ran toward the mouth of the canyon. Lee couldn't figure out how he could detect anything from that distance, but he quickly mounted Jin and let him take off. They had almost caught Hagar when he could see movement near the front of the canyon. It looked like one man.

Lee pulled his hammer loop from his Colt and slowed Jin to a walk. When he got closer, he saw it was Willie Thompson. This couldn't be good, he thought.

Willie waved, and Lee just looked at him before asking loudly, "What're you doing here, Willie? I haven't seen you in five years."

"Just come to see how you was doing, partner," Willie replied loudly with a grin.

Lee bristled at the use of the term. Willie was far removed from being his partner, but suspected it was going to cost him to keep Willie away.

"I'm making out. Where have you been all this time?"

"I've been over at the Diamond R. They pay me to do some cattle work and act as kind of security guard, too."

Lee had dismounted and walked closer, so he didn't have to shout.

"So, what brings you out to my ranch?"

Willie chuckled and asked, "Don't you mean our ranch, good buddy?"

"No, Willie. You gave up all rights to it when you got drunk and never returned. I've done all the work and have the deeds, so you have nothing here."

"Now, that's no way to treat your partner. Seems to me, that seeing as how I helped trap that herd, you'd owe me half the money for it. Now, I figure there were seventy horses in there, so half were mine. That's thirty-five horses, so you owe me over a thousand dollars and it's time to pay, Lee, old friend."

"Willie, your math is way off. First, there were sixty-six horses total, and you already got half the money from the first sale. Second, you didn't do a damned thing but sit on your ass while I broke them. I built the corrals to hold them while you were off doing whatever you did. But I'll tell you what I'll do. I'll make you one offer and one offer only. I'll give you three hundred dollars for not doing anything. Take it or leave it. You won't get a second offer."

"Why that's right kind of you, Lee. I'll take that offer," Willie immediately agreed.

"And you'll sign a receipt saying all debts between us are gone, the partnership is dissolved."

"Not a problem. Meet you at the bank on Monday morning around ten o'clock?"

"I'll see you there."

"Bye, buddy!" Willie said as he smiled and offered his hand.

Lee shook it just to avoid Willie leaving in anger. Willie mounted his horse and turned, tipping his hat as he left.

"Bastard!" Lee said under his breath, knowing he'd just added a *Hail Mary* to this Saturday's penance.

He shows up here after five years of doing nothing and demands money. Well, at least he didn't ask about the other quarter section.

Lee took a series of deep breaths. It hadn't been a good day. First, the incident with Mary and now his bank account would take a hit, but he should make it back and then some when he took the twenty horses to Fort Grant.

He returned to the cabin, but before he entered, he walked over to Jin and removed his saddle and brushed him down, then let him trot back to his ladies for the night.

————

Mary arrived at home and put the mule in the corral with the others. She walked to the house and went inside, entering the kitchen where her mother and Katherine were preparing dinner.

"So how was Father Kelly today? Did he lay on the penance, or did he let you off light this time?" Maggie asked.

"He was fine. Just three *Our Fathers* and one *Hail Mary*."

"That's because you're a good girl, Mary," she said as she smiled at her daughter, then added, "You seem upset, Mary."

"No, Mama. I'm fine. Do you need some help now that I'm back?"

"We're almost done. You can start setting the table."

"Okay, Mama."

She took some plates and walked to the large table.

Maggie knew something was wrong but didn't want to open any more wounds for her daughter and just let it go.

———

The next morning, the Flannery family boarded the wagon and headed to Nueva Luz and Mary was anxious to see Lee.

Lee decided to skip Mass for the first time since he had arrived. He knew he'd have to confess to Father Kelly, and maybe he'd talk to the priest on Monday after he paid off Willie. But today, he'd spend working on the adobe house to sweat out the anger and frustration from yesterday's debacles.

———

The wagon pulled up next to the church and the redheads began to climb down from the wagon. They filed into church, dipping their fingers in the holy water as they entered. Mary surreptitiously glanced at the last pew, but Lee wasn't there yet. The Mass began, and Mary again took a quick look, but Lee still wasn't there. She wondered if something had happened, or he had simply gone somewhere. She had a sinking feeling that he may never be back. She went through the motions of the service, not hearing a word.

———

Lee was ten miles to the northeast, filling his brick molds with adobe before laying on the dried bricks to the walls. He had a good rhythm. Mortar, brick, mortar. All with his trowel following to level and clean off excess. After laying the fourth row, meaning the walls were about eighteen inches tall, he decided it was time to build the frames for the doors. The window frames wouldn't be needed for another five or six rows.

———

The Mass was over, and Mary walked out with her family, giving a hopeful glance at the empty pew that was left unfulfilled. Her imagination created all sorts of disastrous reasons for Lee's absence, some of which she had caused. She was miserable as she climbed into the crowded wagon for the trip home.

———

Lee worked right through lunchtime, which was not an unusual occurrence for him, but today it was because he wanted to work harder than usual. He had his shirt off and the sweat dripped off him, as he was cutting and splitting boards. Then he planed the boards to the correct thickness and width. He had the door frames for the main entrance and the back entrance completed by the time he was ready for dinner.

Lee made himself a quick dinner, if one could call it that. He ate a can of cold beans and was not looking forward to tomorrow, but at least he'd be rid of Willie.

———

The next morning, Lee was up early. He made coffee but skipped breakfast. He tried all his techniques to restore his feeling of balance, but they failed. Maybe he wasn't a good enough student after all.

He mounted Jin around eight o'clock and rode down to Nueva Luz, arriving a little under an hour later, having kept a slow pace to allow the bank to open. He dismounted in front of the bank, the doors having just been opened for business. He entered and approached a clerk he had dealt with in the past.

"Excuse me, are you a notary?" Lee asked.

"Yes, sir. We all are."

"Good. I'm going to meet someone shortly. I'll give him a bank draft and ask him to sign an agreement that I'll need to have notarized. Could I borrow a sheet of paper?"

"Certainly. We have an empty desk that you could use if you'd like. It has a pen and an inkwell," he replied, motioning to a nearby desk.

"Thank you. I'll do that."

Lee sat at the desk and began to write.

I, Willie Thompson, and any other aliases I may use, upon receipt of three hundred dollars, do hereby relinquish all claims against Lee Ryan.

Then he wrote out a bank draft payable to Willie Thompson for three hundred dollars. He replaced the pen and waited for the ink to dry, then waited for Willie to show up, not looking forward to the meeting.

Willie showed up early and grinned as he saw Lee. Lee did not smile in return.

He walked up to the table, saw the bank draft and grinned even wider. He hadn't seen that much money since they had sold those horses five years earlier.

Lee stood and walked over to the clerk, noting his name on the plaque on his desk.

"Mr. Harrison, this is Willie Thompson. I made out this draft payable to him. After he signs this agreement, could you notarize it for us please?"

"Certainly."

Lee half expected Willie to demand more money, but he didn't. He looked at the draft and signed the statement. The clerk notarized the paper and Lee picked it up.

"Pleasure doing business with you, Lee," he said, smiling as Lee handed him the draft.

Willie offered his hand, but Lee made a show of blowing on the notarized statement and ignored him.

Willie shrugged and walked to the cashier and presented the draft. The cashier handed him the money, and Willie whistled as he left the bank, staring at the currency. Lee watched him leave, hoping never to see him again, then turned to the clerk.

"Just in case you're wondering what this is all about, Mr. Harrison," Lee began before Mr. Harrison interrupted.

"I have no need for such information, Mr. Ryan."

"Nonetheless, I think it would put your mind at ease somewhat to know. Five years ago, when we arrived here, I had known Mr. Thompson for three months. We trapped some horses in a canyon northeast of here. That was his total investment in the enterprise. He got drunk and disappeared after the initial sale. He arrived yesterday demanding an equal share of the value of the current herd, which I have more than doubled over the period of his absence. So, I paid him that money, so he can't bother me any longer. I felt like a fool for ever trusting him."

"All that aside, Mr. Ryan, having him sign that form and having it notarized was a wise decision. Would you like to rent a safe deposit box here for the document?"

"How much does that cost?"

"Ten cents a month."

"That's a good idea. Let's set that up."

After doing some paperwork, Lee received a key for the box and paid for two years in advance. He placed the paper in the box, shook Mr. Harrison's hand and left the bank.

He walked out of the bank somewhat poorer but feeling better. He had worried more about Willie claiming the land than taking the money. The land was now home to the partially completed Mary house.

He decided to walk to the church to see Father Kelly rather than ride. Jin just walked behind him, making an odd sight.

Willie was happy. He hadn't expected to get this much. He walked into the bar and ordered drinks for the house, which wasn't expensive as he was the only one present. He began to drink and enjoyed every glass.

Lee entered the church hoping to find Father Kelly. He didn't see him, so went outside to see if he was in the rectory.

———

Back at the Flannery farm, Mary was still glum. She wanted to believe that Lee still liked her as he had before the mistake, but she found it difficult to trust any man. They all lied. Except her father and brothers, of course. She just wanted her normal life back again but knew it could never be.

Then, she chastised herself again for her pettiness about Lee. *When had he ever lied to her?* All he had ever done, even now, was to treat her with respect and concern.

But she remained moribund as she convinced herself that she may never even see Lee again. It was a deserved punishment for her sins. Her many and unforgiveable sins.

———

Lee found Father Kelly. He was very understanding about his missing Mass but chided him about missing next week. He told him that he had made an excellent decision in dealing with Willie. Lee hadn't mentioned the Mary-Jimmy Avery episode in his confession because he didn't believe it to be a sinful act on his part. Father Kelly absolved him of the mortal sin of missing Mass and sent him on his way.

Lee did feel better having that behind him as he climbed aboard Jin, and they headed back to his canyon.

He arrived at the cabin and let Jin return to his horse family and was greeted by a happy Hagar. Then, he set to work making himself a hot meal. He'd decided to just press on. If Mary wasn't meant to be part of his life, then he wished her well, but that didn't mean he'd go and seek new female companionship, either. It was Mary, his old Mary, or no one. He knew he'd never find any woman who could fill his soul as Mary had.

After lunch, he returned to the adobe house. He emptied the thirty-two dry adobe bricks and filled the forms with thirty-two wet ones. He made a large pail of mortar and began laying bricks. Tomorrow, he would put his door frames in. He had made special bricks to keep the door frames in place.

And so it went the rest of the week. He made bricks, and he used them, but the brick pile was growing lower. He was down to half the height there'd been at the start, so he decided that next week would be all about making bricks. The walls were now almost four feet high. Soon, it would be time for the window frames. And there were a lot of window frames he'd have to make. The six internal door frames had been a lot easier than the two outside frames to build and mount.

———

It was Sunday morning, and time to fulfill his promise to Father Kelly to attend Mass. He cleaned himself up and saddled Jin. The ride to Nueva Luz was pleasant with the cooling temperatures. The days would still get hot sometimes, but not as devastating as July or August.

Mary joined the family for the ride to church and wondered if Lee would still be gone. She was anxious as the wagon trundled across the rough trail to Nueva Luz.

Lee arrived early, so he entered the church, genuflected and sat in his last pew. There were only four other worshipers in attendance so far.

The wagon full of redheads rolled down the main street, and Mary strained her neck as she looked ahead to see if she could see a palomino waiting outside. She didn't know that Jin was usually behind the church, just that Lee wasn't going to be there and began to slip into the doldrums again.

Lee was sitting in his pew, watching the church fill and wondered if the Flannery family was going to make it. He knew that harvest was close, and they might be busy.

Maybe if he prayed, he thought as he knelt on the kneeler and closed his eyes.

The Flannery clan had entered the church. Mary was walking in front of Katherine and glanced to her left, seeing Lee in prayer. She suddenly stopped, causing a chain reaction of redheads.

She turned and whispered to Katherine, "Sorry, I forgot something. You go ahead."

She made an instantaneous decision and would soon discover if Lee was really the man she hoped he was.

Katherine had no idea what Mary could have forgotten that she could retrieve this close to the start of the Mass but walked around her. As soon as the last Flannery passed her, Mary slipped back two steps and slid left into the last pew. She stepped quietly to where Lee was still on his knees with his head bowed. Mary sat for a moment, then knelt next to Lee.

Lee felt the presence of another worshiper, so he ended his prayer and sat back, glanced to his right, saw the red hair and green bonnet and smiled. He did much more than smile; he was dancing inside. *But was it the new Mary or the old Mary?* The fact that she was sharing his pew gave him hope.

Mary had felt the kneeler move, so after an appropriate amount of time, she sat next to Lee, but of course, no words were exchanged.

Father Kelly stepped onto the altar and began the Mass.

In the Flannery pew, Ian was wondering what had become of his older daughter, but Maggie didn't have to turn around to look. She knew exactly where Mary was, and hoped that she would finally forgive herself.

When they went to the altar to receive communion, Lee followed Mary and knelt next to her at the rail. Then after communion, they both returned to the last pew.

Now, at least Ian knew where she was, and was pleased about it. He knew how much his little girl had been suffering these past two years and knew there was nothing he could do about it, but maybe Lee Ryan could.

After the Mass, Mary left the pew and exited the church in front of Lee. Once outside, she turned to Lee and said, "I was worried when you weren't here last week, Lee."

"I had to see Father Kelly and to confess that omission on Monday. I was a bit upset on Saturday."

"I hope I didn't have anything to do with that, Lee."

Then the rest of the Flannery family exited the church and saw Lee and Mary standing there talking. Katherine was not pleased. One look at them, and she could see that Lee was smitten with Mary. She had suspected it for some time, but seeing them together, she realized the truth.

Oh, well, she thought, there were plenty of boys already interested in her. She did love her sister, and after some thought, she was happy for her. Katherine had just grown up and didn't realize it.

"So, Lee, how have you been?" asked Ian.

"Fine, Ian. Just fine. Things are looking up," he replied, smiling.

"Lee, why don't you come and join us for breakfast?" asked Maggie, aware of the change in Mary and the reason for it.

"Well, I'll tell you what. I'll do that if you'll let me treat you all to a breakfast at the café. It'll give the ladies the morning off, and it'll fill those rumbling stomachs earlier. I know how long fasting can seem."

"No, Lee. There's eight of us and that's too much!" complained Ian.

"Nonsense. I'll explain why during breakfast. Let's go. It's only a short walk."

Ian acquiesced, and the rest of the family thought it was a marvelous idea, especially Maggie.

The diner had to move some tables together to accommodate the nine arrivals but did so happily. Mary too the seat beside Lee, making for a very pleasant morning before the first plateful of eggs was delivered.

And it was a mammoth amount of eggs, bacon, ham and biscuits that made their way to the tables. There was a pile of flapjacks as well with lots of syrup and butter along with three pots of coffee.

As the family of redheads and demolished the food, Lee told them about Willie and his shakedown. They were appalled at the idea, but Lee explained that he had Willie sign a paper relinquishing all future claims against him, and how it gave him a great sense of relief to get the whole episode behind him.

Throughout the extended breakfast, Lee would steal glances at Mary, who was doing the same and when his green eyes met her blue ones, he wasn't quite sure if they were quite the same as he recalled from those before her absence, but it didn't matter at the moment. He was sitting next to Mary and it had been Mary who'd come to his pew in the church.

They finished the breakfast in high spirits and Lee took care of the bill, leaving five dollars on the table, making one waitress very happy.

Once outside, it didn't take a lot of persuasion from Maggie for him to agree to return with them to their farm, so once the wagon was moving, Lee rode behind the crowded wagon, listening to the happy chatting and laughter.

Mary would glance back at the trailing rider and find him already looking at her and they'd exchange a short smile. When she did, Lee wondered about the power of prayer and if it was his Mary taking those short, furtive looks. He would only know when he could talk to her alone, as he had all of those Saturdays before she changed. He wasn't going to bring up the Jimmy Avery incident, either, expecting it would probably send her back into her shell.

When they arrived at the house, their normal Sunday schedule had been disrupted, as no one had to make or eat breakfast, so they adjourned to their family room, taking whichever seats were available, but Lee made sure that he didn't sit with Mary on the couch because it would be too obvious.

After he sat in the hard, straight-backed chair, Ian asked, "So, how's the new house going, Lee?"

"Faster than I thought. I've already got the door frames in place. I had to make eight of them; two for the main and back entrances and the others for inside doorways. I did get a bit carried away, though."

"How's that?" asked Maggie.

"It's a lot bigger than I had first envisioned. I thought I'd start small and add on, but once I started, I changed my mind and thought I may as well start big and get it finished the way I wanted it done. It's over eighty feet by more than fifty feet. I've been doing interior walls for four bedrooms, a library, a large kitchen, dining room and a huge family room. I even made a separate bathroom for a tub."

"My goodness, Lee! That sounds enormous," said Maggie.

"You should come and see it some time."

"Aye, we should," replied Ian.

Maggie then glanced toward her older daughter and said, "Perhaps Mary can go and see how it's going and report back to us."

Lee replied, "That would be nice, but to be honest, I'd be a little worried having Mary or anyone ride out there alone with the problems that you told me you were having with the Richards."

"Speaking of him, he came over the next day and apologized for what Rafe did and that surprised me," said Ian.

Lee said, "It shouldn't have, Ian. Think about it. I'd bet that he may have said something like 'we've got to get Flannery to change his mind about that hay', and Rafe just took it on himself to do something that he believed was what his boss wanted. When Mister Richards was told that he pulled you from the wagon, and I'd bet that he wasn't too happy about it. I think as it comes closer to harvest and distribution, he'll up the ante. I believe he just made that apology to buy him time."

"That sounds right to me, Ian," said Maggie, "I never have trusted that man."

Lee then said, "Maybe I should take a ride over there today and see if I can get a read on their mood. After all, Miss Richards did invite me to visit."

Mary felt a surprising twinge of jealousy that she couldn't understand because she had no rights to Lee and maybe, she didn't deserve any.

Lee continued, "I'll head over there now and stop back when I'm done and fill you in on what I find. How do I get there?"

"Just turn left at the end of the drive, and their entrance is two miles due south," replied Ian.

"Okay. I should be back in an hour or so."

Lee stood, gave a short wave to everyone and another smile at Mary before turning to leave the main room. The whole family rose en

73

masse and followed him out the door as he pulled on his hat and crossed the porch.

Lee found Jin right where he had left him and guessed he had lost interest in the Flannery mules.

He mounted and did the same thing he always did without even thinking as he wheeled Jin to the left and trotted down the road.

Maggie slid next to her first daughter and asked quietly, "So, my darlin', how are you feeling?"

She turned to her mother, smiled and replied just as quietly, "Better, Mama, better."

"Good. Let's go inside and before Lee returns."

Mary took her mother's arm and returned to the house, not quite sure how much better she was feeling now that Lee was going to see Stella Richards.

Lee headed south, letting Jin find the way. He was in a great mood for a reason that was pretty obvious. He didn't have to delude himself at all. It was Mary that had put him into the optimistic and hopeful mood that maybe there was now a good chance that his new house wouldn't be sitting empty after all. He knew had to be careful if he was able to spend that private time with her, though. One wrong word could destroy his growing hopes and send her away, never to return.

Twenty minutes after leaving the Flannery farm, he saw the entrance to the Diamond R, which was easily identified by the very impressive sign hanging over the access road. He turned Jin down the access road and traveled another half mile before he was close to the large ranch house. It was even larger than his partially finished adobe house, and it had two floors, with a porch on the upper floor as well. It was an imposing dwelling.

There was someone on the porch watching him walk Jin down the road, but Lee couldn't make out who it was at first, but it sure looked like Willie, and as it turned out, it was Willie.

When he was close, Willie grinned and said loudly, "Morning, Lee. What brings you out to the Diamond today?"

"Miss Richards told me to visit, so I'm visiting."

"She did? Well, that's a fine howdy do. I kinda had my eye on that pretty little filly myself."

Lee asked Jin to stop as he reached the porch, then said, "You misjudge my intentions, Willie. This is strictly business."

"Well, then I guess that's all right. Go ahead and light. I'll let Stella know you're here."

Lee couldn't help but miss his casual use of her Christian name and wondered if Miss Richards allowed him to use it. He stepped down and left Jin standing as he climbed the four porch steps.

Once he was on the porch, he just stood near the door and waited. A minute later, Stella Richards appeared with a big smile on her face. Willie was nowhere in sight, which bothered him a little for obvious reasons. He didn't trust Willie at all and would rather be able to see him.

"Come in, Mr. Ryan," Stella said as she continued her smile.

"Thank you, ma'am," Lee replied as he removed his hat and stepped past her into a well-appointed parlor.

Stella followed him into the room after closing the door and said, "Call me Stella."

"Then feel free to call me Lee."

"See," she said, "It's not so difficult to be pleasant."

"I've always preferred to be pleasant, Stella. The unpleasantness in Nueva Luz wasn't of my doing."

"No, I guess that it wasn't," she replied.

He scanned the parlor as she indicated one of the brocaded chairs, then took a seat herself. The room was decorated with high-end furnishings made of velvet and dark woods. It looked too ostentatious and a bit depressing for Lee, but each person had his own tastes.

After taking his fancy, but comfortable seat, she asked, "So, have you come to sell me your horse?"

Lee laughed lightly, then replied, "No, ma'am. As I told you, I never would sell Jin. I'm just taking you up on your offer to stop by and visit. I was curious about your ranch and thought I'd come to see what it was like. I have to admit that I'm impressed. It's a nice spread."

"Thank you. We like it."

"I was told you have four full sections so I'd guess you could run about five or six hundred head with that much property."

"We've got over a twelve hundred head, Lee. That's more than twenty-five thousand dollars on the hoof."

Lee nodded and said, "I'm surprised you can run that many. The grass in these parts is kind of sparse. You must need a lot of hay from the Flannery farm. After that little incident in town, Mister Flannery mentioned that your father was one of his customers."

"That's right. We'll need all as we can get and it's critical that we get it, too."

"So that's what caused the violence was in town a few weeks back? Just getting his hay?" Lee asked on an unexpected fishing expedition.

He didn't believe that she would answer his question and was surprised when Stella Richards continued the conversation without hesitation rather than shunting it aside.

"It's not just hay, Lee. It's what we need to ensure our survival. Obviously, you've talked to Ian Flannery about it, so what do you think is a solution to our problem?"

Lee pretended to have to think about it as he scratched the right side of his neck, then, after a few seconds, answered, "It's pretty simple really, you sell off a third of your herd and the need for a lot more hay goes away and you've got a healthy deposit for your bank account to boot."

"That's not the problem. We need those cattle to be fat for a while. The problem is that stubborn Irishman."

Lee smiled and said, "I'm a stubborn Irishman, myself, Stella. I must be not too bright to understand it or I'm missing something. You need hay. Mr. Flannery sells you hay. You want more hay. He doesn't have any more to sell. So, how can that be his problem? He just doesn't have any more."

"But he does have more; a lot more. He sells hay to some of the small ranchers, almost half his crop. We offered him more money for the hay than he's getting, yet he claims that he's under contract with the other ranchers even though he hasn't done any such thing. So, now you can see how it's his problem."

Lee was stunned by the arrogance in her logic, which wouldn't be logical to anyone not named Richards.

He shook his head slowly as he said, "No, I still don't see how it's his problem at all. It's still his hay. What he wants to do with it is up to him. What if he decided to burn his whole crop to the ground? It would be stupid, but within his rights to do so. It's the same thing if he decides to sell his hay for less because he feels honor-bound to those he agreed to sell it to."

She leaned forward and looked at him, saying, "You're getting wrapped up in legal talk. This is simple, Lee. We need the hay and he won't sell it to us, so we'll do whatever we need to do to get that hay for our cattle."

If Lee had been stunned before by her arrogance, he was shocked by her willingness to express her belief in the Richards' absolute right to take what wasn't theirs.

"Sounds kind of harsh. Surely, you're not talking anything violent."

"Why not? It's the way of the world. Especially out here."

"I'm sorry to hear that you think that way."

She leaned back into the chair and stared at him as she said, "My father thinks the same way, Lee. It's time you grew up."

"I've been told many things in the past year, but to grow up wasn't one of them."

She was about to say something else when there was a scream out in front of the house, and both Stella and Lee leapt to their feet then rushed to the front door.

Once the door was opened, they saw Willie on the ground, his arms out in front of him. Jin was on his hind legs, his front hooves reared high into the sky as his wide eyes focused on Willie.

Willie was about to die and the terror in his eyes was evidence that he understood his end was near.

"Jin!" shouted Lee, knowing it would calm the horse down, and for that flash of a moment, thought that maybe he shouldn't.

Jin almost instantly, set his hooves down calmly just a yard away from the cowering Willie.

Lee then hurried across the porch and leapt onto the ground as Jin stepped close to him, snorting at Willie as he passed.

As he rubbed Jin's neck, Lee turned to look at Stella who was still near the doorway, and asked, "Willie wasn't trying to steal my horse, was he, Stella?"

"Of course, not. The horse must have attacked him on its own."

Lee read the lie in her eyes easily and said, "You know better than that. Jin is the most well-behaved horse I've ever seen. He doesn't like strangers on his back unless I tell him it's okay, and I'd bet that Willie was trying to mount him without my say-so."

Willie had scrambled to his feet and passed Lee and Jin as he stepped into the porch where he turned and glared at his former partner as he dropped his hand to the Colt on his right side.

"That horse is insane and needs to be shot," he snarled.

Lee glared back at him and said menacingly in a deep growl, "If you even think about pulling that hogleg near Jin, I'll shoot you so fast that you'll never know what happened, Willie. Do not doubt me on this."

"Just get him outta here!" Willie shouted as he whipped around and shot past Stella into the house.

Stella still hadn't moved but said, "I'd appreciate it if you'd forget this whole incident, Lee. As a personal favor."

"I'll let it go, but just remember what I told Willie," said Lee as continued to stroke Jin's neck.

Stella watched as Lee mounted and without touching the reins, had the horse turn left and trot down the access road. She didn't know if she was more impressed with the rider or the horse but was still miffed that Willie hadn't just led the horse away instead of trying to ride him.

In the barn two hundred yards away, Ed Richards heard the commotion and watched the last minute of the confrontation. He wondered why a friend of the Flannery family had come to the ranch in the first place. He was aware of the connection, even if his daughter obviously was not, although she should have been. If he found out what she had told him, there would be hell to pay, but he never did. When he asked Willie about it later, he told him it had to do with that horse again, and he dropped the subject.

———

Lee kept Jin at a walk on the way back so he could think. The whole visit had been nothing but bad news. He still found it hard to believe Stella's thought process which probably mimicked the rest of her family. He had hoped to meet the father, but he never made an appearance, but it was unnecessary now, anyway. He was convinced that Stella only mouthed what her father believed but was still in disbelief that any rational human being could think that way. Maybe that was the problem in the first place; they weren't rational any longer. *But why did they need to hang onto their fat cattle 'for a while', as Stella had said?* He let his mind clear from the confused, angry conversation so he could look at it from their perspective, which he knew would be difficult because it didn't make a lot of sense.

He returned to the Flannery farm fifteen minutes later, stopped Jin at the porch steps and stepped down before climbing onto the porch and knocked.

"Maggie, Lee's back!" shouted Ian as he opened the door.

Maggie hustled back into the main room and sat down, but the by the time Lee entered, the only spot available was beside Mary on the couch, and he wondered if it was designed that way.

After sitting down, Lee began to explain what had happened at the Diamond R, extremely aware of Mary's proximity.

He started by telling them of Willie's welcoming and then reached conversation with Stella, which had them all in stunned silence.

"I was really taken aback by how readily she spoke of the hay problem. Either she was totally ignorant of my connection to you or she was using the opportunity to deliver a not-so-subtle threat. I would tend to believe it was the former because I can't think that her father would want you to know"

I told her that despite their needs for the hay, it was still your hay. Even if you lost your mind and decided to burn the crop to the ground, you could do it because until you sell it, it belongs to you. She didn't see it that way. She felt that their need overrode your right of possession. That's crazy thinking. I guess that when you are isolated in your views, you can make anything sound right. If her father believed it to be true, then it must be right. That kind of thing."

He finished with the last incident, when Willie tried to take Jin, which had no real bearing on their problem, but was more indicative of the whole mindset of the Richards family and obviously, their hired hands who would so whatever they were asked to do.

When he finished, Ian sighed and said, "It's worse than I thought."

"Can the sheriff do anything?" asked Lee.

"His jurisdiction ends at the town limits. We'd have to get the county sheriff involved, but we really don't have anything to hang on him yet."

"I wonder why he thinks he's going to get more for his cattle? Stella said as much when she said it was imperative that they held onto the herd for a while and kept them fat. That line as much as any other gave me something to think about."

"Well, I for one have no idea what they do with those annoying creatures," said Ian.

"I wish I knew what they were going to do next. How do you deliver the hay, Ian?"

"It depends. Most of them come and pick it up themselves, including the Diamond R. I have two ranch customers that are too small to afford the help, so I deliver their loads myself. But each one only takes two wagon loads, so it's not too bad."

"Could they come in and take the whole lot after it's harvested? You know, sneak in at night and grab it?"

"Not that much. It'd take the best part of two days to move the lot, even with a large crew like he has."

"But, unlike the other ranches, he'd know ahead of time when you'd start harvesting because he's next door."

"Aye. I only notify the ranches when the entire harvest is in."

"So, he'll have to move before then. When do you start?"

"A week from tomorrow."

"Well, I'll make it a point to be here then. I need to make a run to Fort Grant this week with some horses, but I'm usually only gone three days, so I should be back in time."

"I think we can handle the issue, Lee. You don't need to get involved."

"You'll all be busy with the harvest. Besides, I'm more suited to defense."

"Aye, it takes the whole lot of us to drive the harvesters and take care of the mules. Alright, your offer is accepted and appreciated."

"I do have a price, though."

"And what might that be, Mr. Ryan, as if I couldn't guess?" asked Maggie with mischievous eyes.

"Would it be all right if I showed Mary my new house this afternoon?"

Maggie replied, "She's a grown woman now, so it'll be her that'll be doing the answering. But looking over at her, I think I know what her answer will be. Or am I wrong, Mary darlin'?"

"That's fine," Mary answered quickly.

Lee noticed her lack of enthusiasm and guessed that he still wasn't fully trusted, not understanding that Mary it wasn't him that she was worried about; it was herself. She was deeply concerned that if she and Lee talked alone for a while, he'd ask what had happened when she was in her self-made prison and that might ruin everything before it started. She needed time; time to really understand if it was even possible that she could live a normal and happy life.

"Well, then, with that settled, let's get into the kitchen and prepare lunch," Maggie replied as she slapped both of her thighs and stood.

After the Flannery ladies had gone, Lee turned to Patrick and asked, "Patrick, do you or your brothers know how to shoot?"

"No, sir. I've taken a few shots with the squirrel gun, but without any measure of success. It's mainly used to scare off varmints."

"I think it's too late to remedy that, so I'll go with what I originally planned. Ian, I do have one concern that I need you and your sons to understand. It involves the ladies, so I'm glad they're in the kitchen. The biggest vulnerability you have is the women. I've been giving this a lot of thought to try to see things from their viewpoint. Primarily, what could they do to force you to give them all the hay and still remain untouchable from the law? The only thing I could come up with that made any sense was if Ed Richards had a couple of his miscreants try to kidnap one of the women to force you to sell him the hay that he wants."

Ian was shocked by the idea and exclaimed, "Surely, even he wouldn't do anything so devilish!"

Lee shrugged and replied, "If he thinks like Stella does, then he's willing to do anything. If he comes riding in here with guns and threatens you, he'd anger the other ranchers and risk retaliation. But if he takes Maggie, Mary or Katherine, and tells you that they'll only stay safe if you sell him the hay. He'd offer you a contract that you would sign. Then, after he has the hay, he releases the hostage. What can you say? It's your word against his. He'd probably have all his hands and family lie about it. No one would be harmed, and he'd have his hay."

"That would be diabolical."

"Yes, it would. So, what you need to do is make sure that either you, Patrick, Sean, or I are always with them. They can't take them with you there."

"Do you think we should let the women know?" Ian asked.

"I'm inclined to say 'yes.' That way they'll be more wary as well. I think I'll do one more thing if I can, so I might stop by tomorrow. Other than that, I need to get ready to head to Fort Grant."

"I'll think about what you said," Ian replied, troubled by Lee's concern, but seeing the validity of it as well.

The male side of the group talked further about the topic of the Richards until lunch was announced and they all went in for a light meal. After their hefty breakfast, it was more than enough.

After lunch, Lee walked with Mary back to the barn where they kept half of their mules. There were six saddles on a wide shelf. Lee asked which she used, as he knew Mary and Katherine's stirrups would be shorter than the men's, except for Conor's. After she pointed out her saddle, he had her mule saddled and ready to ride in ten minutes while Mary had returned to the house and hurriedly changed into a riding skirt and a white blouse, which made her red hair even more pronounced with the contrast.

When he first saw the changed Mary in the bright sun, the sight caused Lee not a small amount of discombobulation, but he recovered and walked to the front of the barn as Mary climbed aboard the mule, pulling on a tan sombrero to keep the sun off her face.

Lee called for Jin and he trotted up to the barn seconds later as Mary sat on her mule nearby.

"I don't know if I'll ever get used to seeing him do that," she said.

"Mary, you have only seen a small portion of what Jin can do," he replied as he stepped into the saddle.

They set out, waving to the assembled redheads on the porch as they passed.

As they watched Lee and Mary leave, Ian turned to his wife and said in a low voice, "We are very lucky parents, Maggie. I hope that Mister Ryan can help our Mary."

"I believe he already has begun to help her, Ian. Now let's just hope he can bring her all the way home to us," she replied as they all turned to go back inside.

———

After they had cleared the property and turned slightly northwest, which surprised Mary, she asked, "So, Lee, what else can Jin do?"

"I'll show you. Now you just keep the mule walking straight ahead, okay?"

"Alright."

Lee let his reins drop and stretched his arms out to the side. Then he began using his knees and shifting weight to have Jin turn, trot, stop, walk backwards, wheel and then rear up with his hooves clawing the air. When he had finished the display and lowered his arms, he turned Jin and had him trot into position beside the walking mule and his stunned rider.

"Lee, I wouldn't have believed it if you had just told me. That was astonishing!" Mary gushed.

"You haven't seen him run yet. Mary, I've never seen another horse with his endurance and speed. Some are fast, and some can run a long way, but I've never heard of one that could do both. But more importantly, he's my friend. I know it sounds kind of stupid to refer to an animal as a friend, but I feel that way about him."

"No, it's not stupid at all. I can understand it. Do you feel that way about your dog?"

"Absolutely. But I don't spend nearly the time with him as I do with Jin."

Lee spotted the landmarks that marked the land near his canyon then said, "We're almost there. You can see the creek that leaves my canyon. Right where it hooks is where I'm building the house. You can just about make out the tops of the walls already."

"Maybe you can, Lee. But I'm way down here," she said as she laughed.

Lee was almost stunned to hear that laugh again, but it was a good feeling.

"Sorry. Maybe we can remedy that."

"What, are you going to make me grow a few inches?" she asked, smiling up at him.

"In a manner of speaking. Now, even you should be able to see where the house is going to be."

She swiveled her head back to the front and found that she could just see it, too. Even though it was still a tan color from the sand, she could make out the straight walls and kept facing in that direction as they approached, watching the house grow larger in her eyes.

"Lee, it's enormous!" she exclaimed.

He grinned down at her and asked, "I did get carried away, didn't I?"

Ten minutes later, when they were fifty feet of the semi-structure, they dismounted, and Lee just tied Mary's mule's reins to Jin's saddle.

"Shall we go inside?" he asked offering his hand.

"Okay," she replied.

She took his offered hand with some trepidation, and Lee could sense her hesitation.

He led her through the large double-wide front entrance as she asked, "Why so wide?"

"To bring in furniture easier. I've also made the hallways and inner doors a bit wider than normal for the same reason."

He led her through the door, releasing her hand because she still seemed uncomfortable, and into the first room, where she noticed that Lee had begun to build interior walls that divided into two large rooms.

"What will this be?" she asked when standing in the large main room.

"This is the family room. The other half is the dining room. I'll have an open archway rather than a door between them. Then adjoining the dining room, if you'll follow me, will be the kitchen."

He showed her the big dining room and the equally large kitchen. It already had two walled in pantry walls. Then they walked, into the library and four bedrooms. Finally, he showed her the bathroom before they returned to the family room.

She turned and looked at him as she said, "Lee, this is an amazing house. There is so much room to breathe. I also notice that there are a lot of windows to let in the light."

"Did you notice anything odd about it yet?" he asked.

Mary looked around and couldn't see anything particularly different, but asked, "Is it the three fireplaces?"

"No, something else. Follow me."

He took her hand again, noticing that she seemed to be more comfortable, and led her to the kitchen, and continued to a large doorway that looked like an inside door.

Lee said, "Through here is the most interesting part of the house. I've included an atrium."

"What's an atrium?"

"In Roman houses, they left a central area open. It gave them a private place to talk and still enjoy having the sky over their heads. They could plant flowers inside or lilac bushes to provide a flowery scent. They'd have a fountain as well. This, Mary, is our atrium."

Mary noticed instantly that Lee had said *our atrium*, even if he hadn't noticed and wasn't sure if he really intended to use the plural possessive pronoun. In one respect, she desperately was hoping that he had, yet her overwhelming sense of fear of his rejection once he found out the truth of what she had done, made her pray that he'd just made a simple grammatical error.

He had not only noticed; he had carefully used the words while hoping that she didn't feel he had overstepped some invisible boundary.

They stepped out into the large open space and stopped.

"The beautiful flowers, maybe even some birds fluttering inside the atrium; can you see it, Mary? Can't you smell the soft fragrances and hear the rustling of the wind inside the atrium?" he asked as he turned and gazed into her blue eyes.

Suddenly, his vision was transferred to her own imagination and it was a stunning revelation that pushed her fears aside for the moment.

Mary was excited when she replied, "Oh, yes. I can see it, Lee. I can even smell the lilacs."

Lee was relieved and incredibly happy with her reply, and said, "Then that alone is worth the trip. Come on out back and I'll show you why I selected this spot."

Mary walked with Lee out of the atrium where Lee anticipated building an arched doorway. Once outside she could see immediately why this spot was just right for the exit from the atrium. Just a hundred feet beyond the doorway, the creek made a small bow behind the house before leaving to the south. There was still grass behind the house all the way to the creek, but to the west, the desert was ever-present.

Lee was staring at the landscape as Mary was as he said, "This is where we can plant a nice vegetable garden, Mary."

This time, she knew he had said *we* and meant it, and suddenly, what had become a delightful, imagination-filled day had crashed back into reality and her worries slammed back into her mind as she yanked her hand free, then quickly walked back into the atrium.

Lee was stunned by her hostile reaction after hearing her excitement over his description of the atrium and hurried behind her.

Mary had stopped in the middle of the future atrium, wrapped her arms around herself and stared at the dirt near her feet as she said sharply, "Lee this isn't right. You make it sound like this is going to be our house and that can't happen. I'm sorry, but it just can't."

Lee knew he was entering dangerous territory, but he had to know what was so horrible to her to make that statement.

He answered quietly, "Why can't it happen, Mary? I thought we were almost meant to be together. I built this house because I thought it would be your home as well as mine. Why are you acting this way? This isn't the Mary that made me want to build this house."

"Because it can't. I'm not... I can't..." she said as she stumbled trying to find the right words.

Lee was still a few feet away from her, knowing how upset she would be if he did what he wanted to do and hold her in his arms.

Instead, he said, "Mary, let me tell you something. I have no idea what happened to you that caused this change. But whatever it was, it's in the past. This house will be your future; our future. I know that you've been deeply hurt, and I wish I could help make that hurt go away. If you'd rather not tell me, I'll understand. But, know this, Mary Flannery. I love you as you are. I'll wait for you as long as it takes for you to understand that. This house may be reduced to dust, but I'll still be waiting. One of these days, when you think you can tell me about it, I'll listen and then I'll tell you the same thing no matter what it is. I'll tell you that I love you, Mary."

Mary felt an emotional dam burst inside her and she took two steps toward Lee, wrapped her arms around him and began to cry. Lee held her as she continued to shed volumes of tears and began to shudder. She cried without saying a word for almost five full minutes.

Lee's shirt was soaked where her tears had fallen, but he said nothing as he held her; waiting for her to let out the terrible secrets that had been weighing on her spirit and keeping the real Mary locked away.

Finally, she began to talk in little more than a whisper, as she pressed the side of her face against his chest.

"I was nineteen years old and a man named John Everett came to visit the farm. He was a handsome man, asked to visit me and we began to go for long walks alone. He told me that he loved me, and I was thrilled by his words. We went on a picnic and he told me that he was going to marry me, then he began to kiss me and then touch me in places where no one had touched me before."

I was overwhelmed, Lee. I knew it was wrong and that I was sinning by letting him continue but I didn't stop him. I still went on walks with him, further and further from the house and let him touch me because I enjoyed it so much. I was ashamed of myself when I returned to the house, but I couldn't wait for him to return so we could go on another walk. Then, despite my confidence that I could stop after letting him feel me, I succumbed and let him take me. I didn't fight. I didn't even say 'no'. I actually wanted him to take me. I asked for him to do it!"

She shook again after almost shouting the last words, but then even as she slowed to a shiver, continued in her whispering tone.

"Then he just left and I was shocked because he said he would marry me. He never returned to the farm and I never tried to find him. I thought I could hide my shame, but my mother knew right away. She had me confess to Father Riley, and I did, but didn't feel forgiven because it was too much of a sin. Then, almost as a final punishment for what I had done, I discovered that I was pregnant with his child, and if that wasn't obvious enough to everyone that I had relations with a man, I found that he had been bragging about his conquest before he left and it seemed like all the boys in Nueva Luz knew that I had not only given myself to him, but had done it willingly."

Her voice had grown stronger as her confession continued, and her tears had stopped, but suddenly, they reappeared as she buried her face into Lee's soaked shirt.

"Just four months after he'd gone, leaving me in my shame and my condition, I…I lost my baby and I thought I would die. I should have died for all that I'd done."

Lee continued to hold her and hoped that she was finished, because he didn't know if he could bear to hear her sorrows any longer. *What could he possibly do to help her?* Her sorrow and shame were so deep, he desperately wanted to take them all away, but he also had a deep, simmering disgust for the name John Everett for taking advantage of his sweet, trusting Mary.

Mary's tears subsided as did her shaking when she reached the end of her story, "After I'd lost my baby and I felt my life was over. I believed that I couldn't trust any man ever again. What made it even worse was after I was pregnant, my breasts got bigger, so the boys got worse and wouldn't leave me alone. What you saw in the store was only one example, and not even a bad one. I was nothing more than a whore."

She took a deep breath before finally ending her darkest confession to the man that she had hoped to marry before she met John Everett.

"Now you know why I can't marry you, Lee. I'm not fit to be your wife. I'm sullied. I'm spoiled. I'm nothing but a harlot who would shame your life and make you the laughingstock of Nueva Luz."

Finally, Lee felt he could talk to her as he continued to hold her gently against him.

"Mary, that's where you're so very wrong. You not only can marry me, you must marry me. Nothing that happened to you changed who you are inside. You are still my Mary and I will always love you with all my heart for the rest of my days. If you don't marry me, Mary, then I'll spend my life lonely and miserable and that would be cruel. What good will it do for the two of us to spend our days being lonely and miserable when we can spend those same days together and be gloriously happy?"

"But…but I'm impure and they'll all talk. I am nothing but a cheap, wanton woman who isn't good enough to marry anyone, much less you."

"They'll always talk, Mary, but Father Kelly and your family still think of you as a wonderful person, don't they? And you know how I think of you, Mary. So, whose opinion do you value? Those mindless, faceless gossipers or those of us who love you? I know I don't care one bit of what they say. As to the impure part, I find that to be almost laughable if you didn't believe it so strongly. You are my Mary, and what happened to you doesn't shake my opinion that you are the purest heart I have ever met."

Mary paused for a moment, her doubt, shame and fears washed away with her tears and Lee's comforting and almost unbelievable promise.

She raised her blue eyes and sought out his green eyes as they looked down at her and asked softly, "You still want to marry me?"

Lee smiled down at her and answered softly, "Mary, I have loved you for years now. I knew that I did from almost the first Saturday that we talked and was waiting until I could offer you the home that you deserved. Now, as I look back, I realize what a terrible mistake I made by not telling you how I felt, and I believe that it was much worse than yours. You are such a loving, and compassionate woman and were looking for someone to return your love. When John Everett showed up and told you that he loved you, it was what you needed to hear, and he took advantage of you. Mine was a mistake that will bother me for the rest of my days, because think that if I had pursued you years ago, or at least told you how I felt, would you have accepted me?"

Mary sighed and answered, "I would have been overjoyed if you had even said that you liked me and wanted to see me more. I was wondering why you never came visiting, and I'd see you when I was in town, but you always seemed to be afraid to come and talk to me if one of those boys were around, even before John Everett found me. Why would you always run away as if you were afraid?"

"I wasn't afraid, Mary, but I thought that you had already found someone, and I didn't want to intrude. It's silly looking back at it, but that was how I felt at the time. Then, when you disappeared, I was terrified that I'd lost you."

"Whenever one of those other boys was with me, I wanted you to come and chase him away, but I felt it wasn't my place because I'm a woman."

"And that, Mary, is the horrible mistake that I will have to live with to the end of my life. My mistake caused your mistake. So, all we can do to rectify these blunders is to push them into the past and create a wonderful life together; a life that will include this house, with its atrium and flowers. I want to spend it with you, Mary. I love you so very much. You're my life and I want to share it with you."

Mary looked up at the sincerity in his eyes, exhaled softly then said, "I love you, too, Lee. I'm sorry I was so cold to you. I should have trusted you but was terrified that if you knew what I'd done, you'd reject me and then my life would truly be over."

Lee finally released her, but still put his hands on her shoulders as he stood before her, his eyes focused on her as he said, "Mary, none of this was your fault. You are the most wonderful person I've ever met, and I can't wait to have my Mary back and then to make her my wife. Can we dispense with the formal 'calling on you' thing, and just agree that we should be married and go from there?"

"I would find it a bit annoying myself," she replied with a slowly growing smile.

"So, now that you've agreed to come and live with me after we get married, what do you think of your house?"

She turned her eyes to the partially built house and said, "Lee this place is going to be heaven when it's done. When do you think you'll finish it?"

"Well, the roof and the flooring I'm going to contract out to someone who knows how to work with tile. It'll set me back a few hundred, but it'll be worth every penny. I think this time next year, it'll be completed and shining in a nice coat of whitewash."

"I can't wait, Lee. It'll be so beautiful," she replied as her blue eyes danced and her face displayed none of the anguish that had been there just minutes earlier.

"Now, Mary, can I show you the rest of our place, including the herd?"

"I'd love that."

He then took her hand as they walked out of the atrium, crossed through the future kitchen and front room, to the waiting animals. Without even looking at her, Lee could feel his Mary returning to him by the almost electric excitement he felt in her fingers and hoped that just one more nudge would bring her all the way back.

Lee mounted Jin, and Mary mounted her mule as they trotted the quarter mile to the edge of the canyon where they were met by Hagar who was bouncing at the sight of Lee and Jin but wasn't sure about the mule.

They dismounted and Lee said, "Let me introduce you to Hagar."

The border collie was already beside Lee, as he looked at Mary curiously.

"Hagar, this is Mary," he said, looking at the dog, as he put his arm around Mary's shoulders.

Hagar stepped up to Mary and sat in front of her with his tongue hanging out.

Lee turned to Mary with a smile and said, "Go ahead and rub his head. He's waiting."

Mary laughed and scratched Hagar behind his ears, which he thought was better than a head rub, any day.

He barked once and then walked around Mary twice before approaching Lee and sitting down again.

"He likes you a lot. Not too many people scratch him behind his ears. The only thing he likes better is a good belly rub."

Mary laughed and smiled at Hagar and then back at Lee and he could see his Mary returning minute by minute.

After Lee had opened the gate, they remounted and rode the animals through the gate and Mary was astonished to see Hagar close the gate behind them.

"Does he always do that?"

"If I leave it open, he does. Those herds are his horses as far as he's concerned, and he doesn't want any of them to get out."

She laughed again as Lee led them to the first corral where they dismounted.

"Are these the horses that you'll be taking to Fort Grant?" she asked.

"Most of them. We'll be taking seven of them with us when we head back to your farm."

"Why?"

"Because I'd feel better if you all had faster mounts than the mules. Some mules can run fast, but if they've been trained as work animals, they tend to be a lot slower. So, you and I will trail seven of these horses back to the farm when we leave. You certainly have enough hay to feed them."

"Why only seven?" she asked as she did a fast computation.

"Because, Miss Flannery, you won't get one of them."

"I won't?" she asked in surprised disappointment.

"No, Mary, I have a special one for you. Come with me."

Mary couldn't believe that Lee had just said he had a special horse for her. *How would he know that she was even coming, much less that he would have already picked out a horse for her?* Just minutes ago, she was despondent and thought she would spend the rest of her life as an old maid, and now she had Lee walking next to her, and after showing her their future house, he already had a special horse for her?

She followed him across the grassy canyon. If she didn't see it, she wouldn't have believed that such a place could even exist in the desert country. But it must be the very narrowness of the canyon and the presence of the stream that allowed it to happen.

Before they had reached the halfway point, she could easily see the smaller corral with another golden palomino inside and her heart began to race as she saw the beautiful creature.

When they reached the smaller corral, Lee looked at her and said, "This is your new horse, Mary. She's been saddle broken and I can tell you right now, she's the gentlest horse I've ever come across. Come and meet her."

Mary approached the corral's fence and the filly walked right up to Lee, who rubbed her nose.

"Good afternoon, lady. I'd like you to meet your new best friend, Mary."

Mary stepped closer and ran her hand along the horse's neck as the filly looked at her and nodded her head.

"Does she have a name?" Mary asked as she looked at her new friend.

"No, Mary. That's up to you. I didn't want to give her a name because she's your friend now."

"She's lighter than Jin. How do you say light gold in Chinese?"

"Qing Jin."

"Then that's what I'll call her. It sounds like King Gin, but I'll know what it means, and so will she and it's all that matters."

"That's exactly what I said when I named Jin. Did you want to take her for a ride?"

She quickly turned to face Lee with excitement in her eyes as she asked, "Could I?"

"Of course, she's yours now. Let's walk her to the cabin. I have her saddle in there."

"Don't you need it?"

"I bought a new one for Jin. The other one used to belong to Stonewall, who's out there with the rest of the herd. I have a third saddle I use for breaking the horses. I've already adjusted yours for your height."

"Lee, how long ago did you do all this?" she asked as she met his eyes, "I wasn't even talking to you just a few days ago."

"I finished training Qing Jin just a couple of months ago, but I adjusted the saddle over a year ago."

"But you hadn't even seen me much, so how you did you know that I wasn't already betrothed or something?"

"I'll admit that it was a gamble. If you were, and I found out about it from Ian, then she would be my wedding present to you. When I first saw her, there wasn't a doubt in my mind that she was going to be yours."

"You would have given me Qing Jin even if I were marrying another man?" she asked in astonishment.

"Yes, Mary, I would. I wouldn't have been very happy that you were doing it, but I'd still be happy to see you riding her."

Mary was rendered speechless. If nothing else, Lee had just told her just how much he really loved her.

She watched as Lee just opened the gate, and said, "Come along, Lady," then took Mary's hand and walked away as the golden filly stepped out of the corral and followed them.

As they walked to the cabin, Hagar zigzagged behind Qing Jin in case she decided to go somewhere else, although Lee knew that she wasn't going anywhere.

When they reached the cabin, Lee handed went inside to retrieve her saddle and Mary took the opportunity to talk to the horse and rub her nose and neck. Qing Jin responded and seemed to bond with Mary quickly.

Lee soon exited the cabin with all the tack, and they saddled the Mary's new mount. Qing Jin was a lot taller than the mule and it took Mary a few attempts to climb into the saddle, while Lee considered helping her for more than the obvious reason; or perhaps, it was the most obvious reason. He hadn't been close to spending time with a girl or woman since he'd set eyes on Mary and, despite the daily amount of excessive labor, was already well aware of Mary's physical gifts and attraction. But if he ever needed to restrain his urges, it was with Mary. Her story had reinforced that belief and then anchored it with massive anchors.

Once in the saddle, Mary was astonished at the difference just a few inches made in the view and felt incredibly tall. Tall in the saddle, she guessed would be a more appropriate description. Either way, she felt empowered.

Lee mounted Jin and said, "Ready to go, Mary? I figure we can head to the back of the canyon and see the rest of the herd. Now, what I want you to do, instead of using the reins so much, just nudge Qing Jin with your left knee and lean forward just a little. If you lean too far forward, she may break into a gallop. Of course, she'll have to adjust to your weight and feel but she should appreciate the weight change, though. That's an extra hundred pounds of lummox she won't have to drag around."

Mary smiled as she looked at Lee. Lummox, indeed. Lee was as far removed from the term as any man she had ever met and those same urges that had been freed by John Everett had suddenly and almost violently resurfaced when she'd been with Lee in their future home. In fact, she was afraid that as she'd been holding him while she made her confession, her growing desire to be with him might divert all that she was trying to tell him. She knew that he was excited to have her pressing against him, but that only made it more difficult and distracting. She needed to control herself.

She quickly refocused on her horse and tried nudging Qing Jin with her left knee and was stunned when the horse turned that direction. She tried it with her right knee and the palomino quickly responded. Then she turned her horse once more to the left and simultaneously rocked forward and was surprised when Qing Jin began trotting forward. Mary was exhilarated as she began to laugh.

"Lee, this is amazing! It's like she knows what I'm thinking!"

"When I first saddle broke her, I began trying the same muscle commands that I use on Jin and she responded. I was surprised myself, then I remembered she's Jin's daughter."

"That would explain a lot. Lee, I can't tell you how much I'm enjoying this!"

"Then let's enjoy it!" he shouted then leaned forward and Jin leapt into full gallop.

Mary was hesitant for a moment and then trusted Qing Jin and did the same. Both palominos were soon racing toward the end of the canyon; Mary's red hair flying behind her as she had long since lost her sombrero.

Lee was in front and glanced behind him to see an ecstatic Mary with her bright red hair streaming behind her. It was a sight and he knew now; *his Mary was back!*

The end of the canyon was coming up quickly when Lee leaned back, bringing Jin to a smooth halt. Mary had seen his actions, did the same and was pleased enormously when Qing Jin slowly returned to a walk.

"Lee, that was the most exciting thing I've ever done. I've never gone faster in my life!"

"You know, I've ridden on trains, and I know they're faster, but the sensation of having the wind hitting you in the face, watching the ground shoot past and the thunder of the hooves all add to a feeling of total speed. I don't think I've ever experienced anything like it either."

Lee stepped down followed by Mary, who walked over and took his hand.

"Lee, I can never thank you enough. I thought my life was over and that I'd never be happy again. But now I have so much to be excited about in the future and I can't imagine ever not being together with you. I have one question, though."

"And what's that?"

She looked into his eyes and asked softly, "Why haven't you kissed me?"

"I've wanted to kiss you and hold you from almost that first day we talked, Mary. But after hearing your story, I didn't want you to ever think I thought of you as simply some pretty woman that I wanted to bed. I was afraid to hurt you, Mary and that was something that I could never do. I love you too much."

"Lee, ever since those Saturday afternoons, I've dreamed and hoped that you'd be the one to kiss me, hold me, and yes, even touch me. I asked that question because it sounded as if you were seeing me almost as a saint, even after I'd told you what I'd done. I needed to tell you that I still want you to treat me like a woman who has needs as much as you do. I already know that I make you feel that way yourself from when you were holding me. Please don't deny me any longer."

Lee's years of restraint dissolved in an instant as he pulled her close to him and kissed her well beyond what she had expected as he let every bit of love and passion flow into her.

She put her arms around his neck as she felt her knees weaken and pulled herself closer. This wasn't some reaction to being told that she was loved; this was love and she hungrily accepted his passions and returned them with all of her heart.

When the long kiss finally ended, Lee lifted Mary easily from the ground, still wrapped in his arms, until her eyes were level with his.

He then said quietly, "Mary Flannery, will you give me the honor of becoming my wife?"

Mary knew she wouldn't have been able to stand as she replied in a whisper, "Oh, yes, Lee Ryan. I agree with all my heart."

They shared another long and impassioned kiss before Lee finally gently lowered her to her feet.

Mary and Lee kept their eyes locked for another fifteen seconds, exchanging so much, before Lee sighed and said, "I suppose we'd better go back and tell your parents."

Mary smiled and said, "Lee, I believe my parents have been hoping for me to start seeing you, so I don't think they'll be shocked. I'm sure that, if anything, they'll be relieved. I think they thought, as I did, that I'd live to be an old maid. At least they didn't ask me to become a nun."

Lee laughed and said, "Now that, Miss Flannery, would have been a waste. Sister Mary Mary, now that sounds odd. Anyway, that will make our announcement easier, then. Let's go and get the other seven horses stringed up for the ride back and we can't forget the mule, either."

"No, we can't. But I'll tell you one thing. I'll never ride one again. Not after that experience. Qing Jin and I will be great friends."

"I know you will."

They mounted their equine friends, then trotted back to the holding corral with its twenty horses.

"Won't this leave you short for your ride to Fort Grant?" she asked as they stepped down.

"Not at all. I have another dozen that I've already saddle broken. I was sending these first, so I'll just replace them with the others. Let's go and pick them out."

It took twenty minutes for them to decide which horses would go to the farm and once they were ready to leave, Mary asked, "You know who's going to be most excited?"

"Conor would be my guess."

"How'd you guess that?" she asked with a smile.

"I've talked to him a few times and he gets excited when he talks about horses."

"Well, Mr. Ryan, it seems that you know the family pretty well already."

"You have a wonderful family, Mary. And I'll be honored to be part of it after we're married."

"I think they'll be thrilled to have you join us."

"You go ahead and get on Qing Jin and recover your sombrero. I'll get the horses ready to go."

"Okay, but I'll be back soon."

Mary returned to the saddle, and inadvertently started to pull the reins before she remembered where she was, released them and turned Qing Jin back toward the canyon as Lee watched her depart with a greater appreciation of his Mary than he'd had before, which was already quite impressive.

She found her headgear just a hundred yards away but couldn't resist running her new palomino down the canyon and back. Qing Jin seemed to love to run and Mary was so exhilarated when she did. *Such a gift!*

Mary thought there was only one gift she could give to Lee that was this important, but she had decided that it would have to wait until they were married, despite what had already happened. For some reason, she wanted their life together to start out right. But even as she made that decision, she made a second that their wedding had to happen pretty damned soon, despite the long delay for the new house. Even as she headed back to the cabin, she began to examine the simple structure and thought it would still be good enough for a home until the bigger one was finished. Now, she'd just have to convince Lee, but didn't think it would be difficult. Not after he'd had her in his arms again.

Lee had the horses lined up and waiting when she returned with the sombrero on her head.

"I'd better get used to using the chin string, so it doesn't fly off again," she said as she brought her filly to a stop.

Lee smiled up at her as he mounted and said, "That would be wise, ma'am. Let's head back to the farm."

"Wait a minute," she said before she walked Qing Jin alongside Jin, then leaned as Lee leaned toward her and kissed her one more time before leaving.

"Keep this up, Mary, and I don't know how much longer I can wait. The house won't be ready for at least a year," he said as he grinned at her.

Mary couldn't believe that he'd broached the very subject that was on her mind, and replied, "Lee, we can live in the cabin while it's being finished. Remember, I lived for years with my parents, four brothers and a sister and it's always been crowded. The cabin will be almost empty in comparison. That shouldn't be a reason for a delay in our plans. I want to be with you much sooner than a year and for the same reasons."

Lee didn't want to admit that he'd been hoping that she'd make the offer, but said, "Why that's a wonderful idea, Mary, and now that we have all that ironed out, let's get moving and we can talk more on the ride back."

Mary smiled broadly as they started their horses toward the gate, while Hagar remained behind to guard his herd.

———

Once they started on the return ride, Lee enjoyed the time talking to his Mary again, just as they always had, only now the conversation had much more interesting topics because any walls that had been built between them were gone. After all, they were going to be married soon and they had a lot to talk about.

The ride back was slowed by the trailing horses and the one mule, and by their desire to spend as much time as possible alone, so it took another hour before the horse train came in sight of the farm.

Ian was in the yard and saw them coming but had no idea what had happened to precipitate the arrival of so many horses. It wasn't long before he realized that Mary was riding another golden horse and Mary's mule hanging onto the end of the line.

"Maggie, come on out here!" he shouted.

Maggie stepped out of the porch less than a minute later and immediately witnessed what had caused her husband's summons.

"Well, I'd say there was a story in there somewhere," she said, smiling in the hope that the sight of Mary riding the tall, golden horse indicated that something wonderful had happened.

"More than just one story, I'd imagine," replied Ian.

The only other person in the house was Katherine. She was busy in the kitchen and hadn't heard her father's call over the clatter of the pot that she was placing on the cookstove.

Lee and Mary entered the yard with their equine entourage, and both waved at her parents as Mary's teeth reflected the sunlight from behind her enormous smile.

"We're back!" shouted Mary needlessly.

Maggie spotted the enormous change in Mary and wished that her hopes and prayers for her daughter had been filled by Lee.

When they reached Ian and Maggie, they both stepped down, and quickly took each other's hands as they approached her parents.

"And what's all this, I wonder?" asked Maggie, her smile matching her daughter's.

Mary turned her head slightly to face her new filly and said, "Mama, this is Qing Jin, my new horse. Lee had picked her out and trained her just for me. Isn't she beautiful?"

"Aye, daughter, she is a pretty horse at that," commented Ian.

"And what are these others?" asked Maggie, still smiling as she saw Mary and Lee's clasped hands.

Lee replied, "I wanted you each to have faster transportation if you needed to get somewhere quickly. These horses are all saddle broken and are very pleasant. I brought seven and I'm sure Conor will be pleased."

"Lee, we can't be accepting such charity," complained Ian.

"It's not charity at all. I'm desperately trying to get on your good side," he said, feeling Mary's hand squeeze his.

"And why would you be needing to get on our good side?" Maggie asked with hopefully raised eyebrows.

Lee glanced over at Mary who nodded with a big smile.

"Because, Mr. Ian Flannery and Mrs. Maggie Flannery, your wonderful daughter Mary has accepted my offer of marriage. I thought I'd try to ingratiate myself with my future in-laws."

Ian and especially Maggie, were overwhelmingly happy at Lee's announcement. Even Maggie had expected that he might just ask if he could visit Mary, but this was so much better.

Ian said, "Well, Lee, in that case, we'll accept your gift, although tradition is that it is the bride's family that must provide a dowry."

Lee smiled and said, "Ah! You'll be forgiving me, then, father of the useless daughter that I've so generously offered to take off your hands. If it pleases you, then, Mister Ian Flannery, I'll be most grateful to accept a dowry for accepting her into our new home. I'll be thinking that perhaps a fitting offer to satisfy this need for propriety might be some of that hay that graces your fields beyond."

Ian took up the spirit of Lee's whimsy and replied, "Aye. It's a wise lad you're turning out to be. So, just how much of my hay would make a proper dowry for my excessive female child?"

Lee could hear Mary's stifled laughed as he glanced at her dancing eyes and then looked back at Ian and answered, "Why all of it, of course. I'm thinking that this woeful lass will need at least two or three seasons worth of hay to make up for my wonderful loss of my bachelorhood. What say you, father of Mary Flannery?"

Lee could feel Mary's fingers shaking under his own as she was getting ready to explode as her father, answered, "Nay. Alas, but I cannot be agreeing to such a bounty. Begone, scoundrel, and if you'll be leaving those poor wretched animals behind, then so be it."

Mary finally broke into a full belly laugh as she bent at the waist and Lee and Ian joined in as Maggie grabbed a porch support pole as tears of laughter rolled down her cheeks.

Lee wanted to hold Mary again, but let her laugh join her family's as he just let the joy flow over him. He hadn't enjoyed this much family warmth since he left home, and suddenly missed his own parents.

When he finally stopped laughing, Ian stepped down to the ground and said, "Lee, I'm sure I speak for my precious wife, that we would be very pleased to welcome you to our family."

Lee shook Ian's hand and received a hug from Maggie who had followed Ian and desperately wanted to talk to Mary when she could get her alone.

"Let's get these creatures into the barn so we can talk," said Lee.

They all agreed and led the horses to the barn, and after unceremoniously ejecting the five mules to join their fellows in the corral, settled them into their own stalls.

Once the horses were happy and the mules were irritated, Lee and the three Flannerys entered the house and a startled Katherine turned her head to the doorway when they entered. As soon as she saw Mary's face, she knew that something big had happened and was sure that it something to do with Lee because they'd left together, and she wasn't all that happy when she had ridden away. She hadn't seen Mary so obviously happy in years and could see her parents smiling as well. Katherine was sure that she'd soon hear the news.

Katherine asked, "Mary, what happened? You look like it was Christmas and Easter all rolled up into one."

Mary turned to Lee and asked, "Should I tell her?"

"About the horses or the other thing?" Lee asked, sure that she was asking about the other thing.

Mary laughed, and replied, "The other thing, of course."

Lee replied, "As if she wasn't going to hear it from your mother in another ten seconds."

Mary smiled, then turned to Katherine and semi-whispered, "We're going to be married!"

Katherine was stunned at the surprising news, which, just as her parents had thought, was going to be little more than she and Lee would be visiting but smiled at her sister's exultant face and gave her a well-meant hug.

"I'm so happy for you, Mary."

Mary then said "That's not all, Katherine. Come out with me to the barn."

Mary took Katherine's hand, and they walked swiftly to the barn, leaving Lee and her parents in the kitchen.

Lee wanted Mary to have the joy of presenting a horse to Katherine, having already suspected that Katherine might have been fond of him. She might be a bit hurt or even jealous from hearing the news, although he'd never given Katherine the slightest indication that he was interested, and hoped she'd understand.

When Mary and Katherine reached the barn, they stopped at the open door and Katherine was astonished at the fine-looking horses that had magically appeared in their barn. She turned to Mary, looking for an explanation, hoping that it would involve her and one of the horses, but thinking it was too much to ask. But still...

Mary still held Katherine's hand and looked into her sister's eyes.

"Lee gave me the palomino filly. He had picked her out for me a year ago. Do you believe that? She's so perfect. I named her Qing

Jin, which means light gold in Chinese. She's Jin's daughter. He also sent these other horses over for the family. There is one for each of you, but I wanted you to be able to pick out yours first."

Katherine squealed and shouted, *"I get my own horse?"*

Mary nodded as Katherine turned and began looking at the animals. Mary let her hand go as she walked to the line of horses.

Katherine examined each animal. *It was so hard to choose!* She liked them all.

After two minutes, she made her choice. She selected a dark gray mare with three stockings and a light gray mane and tail with a star on its forehead.

"I like this one the best. Do you think I can ride her?"

"As Lee told me when I asked that question about Qing Jin, she's your horse."

Katherine was giddy as Mary helped her saddle her new mount with one of the mule's saddles.

Katherine was practically bouncing, or more accurately, just bouncing as she exclaimed, "I'm going to name her Blaze for that star on her forehead. Mary, I have a horse of my own!"

Mary was very happy for her sister and said, "Katherine, why don't you go into the house and get changed and I'll finish getting Blaze saddled."

She looked down at her dress and said, "Oh. I hadn't thought of that. I'll be right back."

Katherine pulled up her skirt and scampered back into the house, leaving a cloud of dust in her wake. She burst into the kitchen and almost ran over Lee, grabbed Lee in a bear hug and kissed him on the cheek.

"Thank you, Lee! Thank you for my Blaze! She's beautiful!" she said excitedly, then kissed Lee once more before bolting into the bedroom to change.

"It seems like you've won over both Flannery girls, Lee," said Maggie as she smiled.

"I hope Conor doesn't kiss me, too," Lee said with a laugh.

"I wouldn't be shocked," she replied.

"Of course, that'll leave us three saddles short," said Ian.

"I can take care of that, Ian. When I go to Fort Grant, they always have saddles for sale. Most of them are in good shape, too. I can pick them up for a song. You know how the government is."

"Aye. It is true. When it comes to spending the folks' money, they're very good at it."

Two minutes later, Katherine went zipping back out the door wearing a riding skirt and blouse, flew to the barn and saw Mary leading Blaze to her.

She climbed on her new horse and before she could ride off, Mary said, "Why don't you go out to the field and have the fun of telling the boys that they each have a surprise waiting for them in the barn. And, Katherine, make sure that Conor is told first. He'll need the head start with those short legs."

"I'll do better than that. I'll give him a ride on Blaze."

She was wearing a grin that split her face in two as she turned Blaze toward the fields and set her mare off.

Mary stood there and watched her sister gallop off with a smile then heard the kitchen door close and saw Lee striding toward her and just changed her smile's direction from her sister to her future husband.

"I take it Katherine was happy with Blaze?" Lee asked.

"She told you the name she gave her?"

"After she locked me in a hug and gave me a big wet kiss on my cheek. Twice, in fact."

"You sure have a way of making Flannery girls happy," Mary said as she walked toward Lee.

They heard yells off in the distance, and Mary turned her head.

"And it seems that the Flannery boys are pleased as well," Mary added.

A few seconds later, Katherine came out of the fields atop Blaze with Conor sitting behind her as they engaged in a grinning contest.

Blaze came to a stop and Conor jumped off and hit the ground running, after stumbling for the first four steps. He entered the barn and Lee and Mary followed.

"Wow! I can pick any one I want?" he asked as he studied the animals.

"All except the palominos," Mary replied.

"That's okay. Katherine said Lee gave you the palomino because Lee loves you and is gonna marry you."

Lee just looked at Mary and shrugged. *What else could be said?*

Conor settled on his choice quickly. It was a black mare with a brown tail and mane and four white stockings. Soon after, the other three boys arrived and made their choices. They ran afoul of the saddle issue but decided to hold off riding the horses until after dinner.

Lee was soon surrounded by grateful Flannery males who shook his hand and pounded his back. In addition to thanking him for the

111

horses, they each added their congratulations and said they were really happy that Mary had chosen him for her future husband.

Mary stood in the corner and wore a permanent smile and couldn't recall any other day, including Christmases past, where there was such universal happiness in the family.

They all finally returned to the house and soon the boys and Katherine were chatting continuously about their new mounts. Other than Conor, none of the boys had named their horses yet.

Ian stood and watched his happy sons and daughters, then said in a loud voice, "I take it that your poor, neglected mother and I get no choice in which horses we get, then?"

Suddenly the kitchen went silent as none had realized that they had forgotten their mother and father in the excitement.

Before it could go too far, Maggie said, "That's not true, husband I still get a choice. It's you who'll not be doing any choosing."

The guilt was forgotten, and the room resounded with laughter as Maggie knew it would and Lee admired his future mother-in-law even more. He knew that Ian had fully intended to let the children pick out their horses first but leave it to Maggie to come up with the perfect way to make them all return to their merry mindset.

"Just to let you know, lads, Lee is going to be going to Fort Grant this week and will be returning with saddles for the rest of you. Mary already has one, and that means Katherine already has one because it was the short stirrups."

Again, the boys all thanked Lee. Then they were all kicked out of the kitchen while the three ladies prepared to make dinner. They went out to the barn to talk horses and Lee could tell them more about their selections.

———

Just a few miles south, Ed Richards was having a meeting with his foreman, Rafe Henry, and six of his selected hands. Also, in the meeting were his son, Frank, and daughter Stella. His wife was not privy to the topic being discussed, nor any other meetings and had been restricted to her room upstairs.

"Now, we know that Flannery is going to begin his harvest in a few days. We need to get the kinks smoothed out before we go forward. Our primary target is the younger Flannery girl. She's the best option. She'd be more susceptible to temptation, I think."

He looked at one of the hands and said, "Now, Jonesy, you're sure she doesn't know you work here, right?"

Pete Jones was five feet and seven inches and weighed a hundred and thirty pounds with horseshoes in his pockets. But he was handsome and had a boyish face that looked younger than his twenty-one years and could easily pass for seventeen.

"Yes, sir. I've seen her a couple of times and she always looks at me real close. I've said howdy and smiled at her a few times, too. I think I've got her on the hook."

"Good. Now, if we're able to get her on her own and then hold her someplace, we let them panic for a few days, and then I can ride in and suggest that I've heard rumors about her location. But ask him why should I help him if he wouldn't help me with my problems? Once we get the signed contract for all the hay for the next ten years, we let her go. Nobody's hurt and we get the hay and then sell the cattle when we get that army contract."

"What do you need me and the other boys to do?" Rafe asked.

"Rafe, you and your boys will do nothing more than rotate guards, two at a time, where she'll be held."

"Did you want me to do something different, boss?" asked Willie.

"No, Willie. You'll stay here. I still need protection in case something happens."

Willie nodded, pleased at his own self-importance and being able to stay in the house with Stella.

"Okay, then, I think we make our move on Saturday. The young lady will be around the church by herself for at least a few minutes. Let's make this work."

What Ed didn't tell them was that he wasn't sure he was going to release the Flannery girl at all. Frank had been watching her for the past few months and had become infatuated. Ed knew that his son had always liked them young, but maybe this one would be permanent and not likely to get him hanged or blasted by some angry father's shotgun.

———

Lee had said his good nights to the family and was allowed a few private moments with Mary on the porch before leaving.

They stood face to face, holding each other's hands.

Mary said softly, "Thank you for the most wonderful day of my life, Lee."

"Mary, this is just the start. They may not all be so wondrous as today, but I'll do everything I can to make sure they all make you happy. I love you, Mary Flannery."

"And I love you, Lee Ryan."

Lee gave her a long kiss before leaving, then called Jin who came trotting out of the barn.

Mary watched to make sure that Qing Jin didn't follow as she was following Lee's lead and not tying her reins. Also, at Lee's suggestion, she began calling her by her new name, so she could realize its significance.

He mounted Jin and waved to Mary as he rode off into the darkening evening, his new life now much more real and exciting now that Mary was going to be part of it.

That night, as he lay atop his bed in the cabin, all he could think about was Mary. She dominated his mind now even more than she ad before, but this was much different. His Mary was back and soon, she would really be his Mary.

CHAPTER 4

The next morning, Lee moved the other twelve horses he was going to sell to the army into the corral with the original remaining thirteen, which was more than he had originally planned to take, but now, he thought it might be wise to add even more to his healthy bank account. He packed his necessaries into the saddlebags and took the lead of the first horse and left the canyon. It was just after dawn when he left his canyon and knew he could make it to Fort Grant within five hours if he kept going, but he always took at least one break to water the horses and let them feed for a while. He had found a spot just past halfway that suited the purpose.

––––––

He rode into Fort Grant just past noon and after leaving the horses in an empty corral near the quartermaster's office that were there for the purpose he dismounted and entered the office of the quartermaster, whom had already become a friend.

"Good evening, Sergeant O'Malley. How are you doing this fine autumn day?" he spoke loudly, announcing his presence.

Sergeant O'Malley's face lit up as he stepped out from behind his row of shelving. He was always happy to see his young Irish friend. In addition to being a personable lad, he always brought the best horseflesh they had gotten over the years. Some of the less scrupulous horse sellers tried to slip unbroken mustangs into their herds, or even diseased animals, but Lee Ryan never brought them anything but fine, well-mannered horses that were prized by the troopers.

"Well, welcome back, laddie. Did you bring us more of your fine horses on this trip?"

"Aye, that I did. Come and see them," Lee replied as he waved him outside.

The sergeant quickly followed Lee out to the corral and once again, wasn't disappointed by the horses that he spotted inside.

"That's a fine lot that you have there, Lee. But I'm afraid I can't be paying you forty-five dollars a head for them anymore."

Lee was a bit surprised because he hadn't heard that the fort was closing.

"I'm sorry to hear that, Michael. So, I'll be taking them back now, I guess."

"No, my lad. I was just pulling your leg a bit. Seems that the army was getting sold too many old flea-bitten nags, so the Department of the Army authorized an increase to seventy-five dollars per head for good horses. Now, it doesn't take a smart man to realize that those are all first-class mounts. So, I'll be writing you a voucher for $1,875 you can take to the Disbursement Office."

Lee grinned and said, "Now, Michael, that's the best news I've heard in two days, but not nearly as good as the other news."

"What could be better than this, Lee?"

"Because, my fine Irish friend, I've been fortunate enough to win the hand of the bonniest lass in the whole country. A fine, red-headed sweetheart by the name of Mary Flannery."

The sergeant's face lit up as he said, "Well, isn't that as fine a thing as I've heard! Congratulations to you, Lee. I'm sure that you'll be a happier man the next time you come to visit."

Before he could reply, Sergeant O'Malley grabbed Lee's hand and shook it for a good minute.

When he finally let go, and because of the unexpected largesse, Lee said, "I'll tell you what, Michael. How about I treat you to a nice steak dinner to celebrate."

"Ah, I wish I could, Lee. It turns out that we're on low rations as far as beef goes now. They're slowing down shipments. We'd been getting our beef shipped in from Omaha in faraway Nebraska, but the cost of shipping was going up and the beef critters didn't fare that well on the long trip. So, the Quartermaster General tells us to start buying beef locally. We should get the authorization in the next few months. Before spring, for sure. Of course, that's easy for the forts on the plains, but tougher for us out here. So, they told us we could pay up to thirty dollars a head for any cattle we can get locally, which is still cheaper than they'd have to pay for buying it and shipping it from Omaha."

The light went on in Lee's head. Ten dollars extra a head was an enormous increase. If Richards sold the army five hundred head, it would result in an extra five thousand dollars, which was nothing to sneeze at.

But Lee had another question for the quartermaster sergeant and asked, "While I think about it, Michael, I have a request for you. I just gave eight horses to my future bride's family, but they were short a few saddles. Do you be having any for sale?"

"Of course, we always do. Come along."

They returned to the large offices and he led Lee to another section of the warehouse.

"Here's where we keep all of our excess saddles. Now here are four that I have no idea what to do with, so I'll just let you have them, as they're for your lady's good Irish family. Let me give you the receipt."

Lee noticed that the condition of the saddles was far from used.

Sergeant O'Malley handed him a receipt for four saddles and had to work to get them to fit into two huge, heavy burlap bags. He then tied a leather strap between them. It was a heavy load, but Lee handled it without any problem as he and the sergeant walked out to his horse where he placed the bundled saddles over the back of his own saddle.

"Michael, one more thing. You haven't confiscated any derringers since my last visit, have you?"

Derringers were strictly contraband as they were only used in arguments between usually drunk soldiers and led to unwarranted deaths.

"Aye. Would you be willing to take them off my hands? I have six of them with six boxes of cartridges, too."

"That's perfect. I'm worried about the ladies in my wife's family and I'd like to give them protection."

"You're a wise man, Lee," he said as he walked to the back and returned with another burlap sack.

Lee didn't look inside.

"Well then, Michael, I'll get that voucher and treat you to a wee drop over at the sutler's store in an hour."

"Now, that will be worth having more than any steak, Lee. Let's go up front and we can do the paperwork that the army loves as much as an Irishman loves his whiskey."

After filling out the forms, Lee took his unexpectedly large voucher to the disbursing officer and received his payment, put it into his money belt and returned to Jin.

He was getting hungry, so he went to the sutler's store. They had four tables inside and no guests at the time, so Lee ordered some chicken and roasted potatoes with lots of coffee, of course.

He ate his dinner and when he was finished, he heard the greeting of Sergeant O'Malley.

"Well, there you are, Lee. Why didn't you eat in the mess?"

He replied, "I felt like chicken," he said before signaling to the bartender to come over.

When he arrived, Lee asked, "Now, my good Irish friend here has a birthday wish for some fine Irish whiskey. I'm buying, so you don't have to worry about the cost. Do you have anything that would make an Irishman proud?"

As he finished his query, he slid a ten-dollar gold piece across the table as incentive.

The bartender smiled and answered, "I just might."

While an anxious quartermaster sergeant looked on, the man returned to the bar, shuffled around some other bottles until he produced an unopened bottle of real Irish whiskey, returned to Lee's table and set it down.

"You're a fine man. Keep the change," Lee said as he tossed him the ten-dollar gold piece.

Lee figured the bottle was probably no more than three dollars but making sure it was real and not watered down was important. The seal attested that it was still unopened.

He looked up at Sergeant O'Malley and asked, "Well, Michael, will you be needing a glass?"

"No, Lee. I'm just amazed that this even existed within a thousand miles."

"You'd be surprised, my friend."

Sergeant Michael James O'Malley was still standing as picked up the whiskey and reverently opened the bottle. As he took a long swallow, then gently placed the bottle back on the table, a single tear traced across his right cheek.

"Tis a bit of heaven, Lee. Are you not wanting some yourself?" the sergeant asked, hoping for a negative reply.

"No, Michael. I am the shame of the Emerald Isle. I never developed a taste."

"Not to worry, my lad. I'll do the tasting for ya," he said with a big grin before tipping the bottle to his lips and took a much longer swallow.

Lee smiled before he said, "Michael, as much as it pains me to leave your company, I have my lovely lass waiting for me at home and I'm anxious to see her again."

He lowered his whiskey, and with quickly replied, "Sure. Sure. Lee, I understand. I can't thank you enough for this."

Lee stood and shook Michael's hand and hoped he didn't finish the entire bottle at one sitting. He'd hate to return on his next visit and find him as Private O'Malley, although he suspected that it had happened before.

He went outside, boarded Jin and headed north to go home. At least the reason for Richards' desire to hold onto his cattle was discovered. That and having made extra money for his horses made the trip worthwhile.

He only traveled another ten miles back before setting up his cold camp. He never packed for anything but a cold camp when he made the trip. It was only one night after all.

As he lay atop his bedroll, he wondered how he could stop Richards — if he could at all, still not believing that they would do anything so terrible just for five thousand dollars. But mostly, he spent his remaining conscious hours thinking about Mary.

———

He awakened later than usual, and after taking care of his morning needs and just grabbing some jerky for breakfast, saddled Jin and then hung the heavy bag of saddles across the back of the saddle. It was an awkward thing, but he knew Jin was getting the worst of it and apologized. He hooked the derringer bag over the saddle horn and started Jin heading north again.

After another three hours of riding, which included riding past the Diamond R, he neared the Flannery farm.

He arrived just a little after lunch time, making it a very quick trip. He knew why, too. He had a red-headed, blue-eyed incentive and hadn't dallied at Fort Grant.

Jin walked down the short road to the house, but Lee didn't see anyone out and was getting worried when he heard horse hooves behind him, and for just a second thought that the Richards were mounting some kind of offensive and quickly pulled his Winchester. But when he turned around, he saw a golden palomino and three other horses racing down the road. The palomino was being ridden by a certain red-headed girl with no hat who was waving and smiling at him as she approached, no reins in her hands. Katherine was behind her on Blaze with a big smile on her face as well. Conor and Dylan made up the rest of the happy entourage.

Lee held Jin and waited for the Irish posse to reach him as he slid his Winchester back in the scabbard.

Mary slid close and said, "Welcome back, Lee. You didn't take as long as you said it would."

He smiled at her and said, "For some reason, I was anxious to return as quickly as possible. I can't imagine what it might be"

"Would that be for the same reason I wanted you back just as quickly?" she asked with a grin.

"I would assume so, ma'am. Let's go to the house. I have some information for everyone. But first, I need to drop these off," he said, pointing at the large bags.

"What are they?" Katherine asked.

"Saddles"

"Oh, that's right. You said you were going to buy some old saddles," said Mary.

"Yes, ma'am. That's what I said I'd do."

He then winked at her, but Mary had no idea why.

By the time they reached the barn, Maggie had joined them. Ian, Patrick, and Sean were preparing the harvesters for use, so they were nearby. They needed greasing and had to be loaded with steel wire.

Lee stepped down from Jin and was joined by the Flannery riders. Mary was practically glued to his left side as he lugged the heavy sacks to the barn. Lee estimated they weighed over about a hundred and a half pounds.

Once there, he pulled the knife from his scabbard, cut the rope, then pulled the first saddle from the bag.

"Lee, that looks almost new!" exclaimed Mary.

"There are three more like this. Sergeant O'Malley thought that my future Irish family should sit their Irish behinds on good leather."

His future Irish family laughed as he began to remove the other saddles and tack from the bags. As each was removed, they would be placed on nearby shelves.

"What's in the other bag?" asked Katherine as she pointed at the one still hanging on Jin's saddle horn.

"That's something I'll need to explain to the entire family. So, if Ian, Patrick and Sean can join us, I'll fill you all in."

"Lee, did you get any lunch at all?" asked Maggie.

"Well, not exactly," he admitted.

"That's what I thought. We'll march you right inside and get something to fill your stomach. Mary take this future husband of yours inside and feed him. Katherine, go and tell your father that Lee is back and needs to talk to all of us."

Lee took the bag of derringers with him as he followed Mary into the kitchen. She quickly made him a ham sandwich and gave him a pickle and a quick kiss to go with it. Then she sat down next to him as he ate.

"Want to hear some good news, Mary?"

"Good news is always worth hearing, Lee."

"I took those other twelve horses that I had saddle broken along with the thirteen I had in the corral. When I got there, I was told that the Army was tired of getting stuck with old nags and changed the price to get better mounts. So, instead of forty-five dollars, I got seventy-five per head. That netted me $1,875 for the trip."

Mary smiled and said excitedly, "Lee, that is good news. That makes up for what Willie did to you."

"And quite a bit more. It'll make getting our house done faster, too, so you won't have to live in a cabin very long."

"It doesn't matter, Lee. As long as you're there with me."

"You know, we still need to buy all that other stuff. Dishes, pots and pans, and all those things and a nice cook stove."

"Don't forget, Mr. Ryan. I have all my things, too. I've been collecting them for years now. You'd be surprised about what a propertied woman you'll be marrying," Mary said as her eyes danced.

"It doesn't matter if you came to me without a stitch of clothing on your back. Wait a minute," Lee said as he closed his eyes, "I'm trying to picture that in my mind."

Mary leaned forward and whispered, "Soon, you won't need to be imagining anything as my husband. I'm ready, Lee. I'm so very ready."

Lee opened his eyes and let her know with his eyes just how ready he was before he finished his lunch. It was just in time, too, as the rest of the Flannery clan came flooding into the kitchen.

"Lee, that was fast. Did everything go okay?" asked Ian.

"Better than okay. I got more for my horses than usual and have some information that will explain why the Richards want that hay so badly."

Ian glanced at his wife then said, "Let's head into the family room. It's more comfortable."

They all trooped into the main room with Lee and Mary bringing up the rear. After they had all seated, Lee took his now standard seat on the couch next to Mary as he lowered the bag of derringers at his feet.

"First, the news about why Richards isn't selling his herd. I learned from Sergeant Michael O'Malley, the fine Irishman who sent the saddles along, that the army was initiating a new program that allows them to buy beef locally rather than through their own procurement channels. It won't be effective for a few months, maybe March or April next year. So, Richards needs to keep his cattle till then, because the army is going to pay ten dollars more per head than he can get on the open market, as long as he delivers them there. I don't know how he found out about it, but that's why he's holding out. It'll mean an extra five thousand dollars to him."

"No wonder he wants to keep them here and fat, too. I'm guessing the army isn't going to pay that for skinny cows."

"You're right, they have to meet standards of quality. Now, the second thing that I need to talk to you about and it involves what is in the bag. After my discussion with Stella, I realized that there is a chance they may pull some fool stunt. Now, when I was at Fort Grant, I asked Sergeant O'Malley if they had recovered any number of a certain contraband. He said they had, and he asked if I'd take them off his hands. It was what I was looking for."

He reached inside the bag and pulled out a derringer.

"I have six of these with six boxes of ammunition. With your permission, Ian, I'd like to see each of the Flannery women to have one as well as three of the men. They aren't meant for shootouts or any real defense. They're solely to be used for close-in defense against someone who means you harm. I'll have to check each one to make sure they're in good condition and fire well. Ian, Maggie, what do you think?"

Ian was undecided, so he turned to his wife and asked, "I'm not sure. Maggie?"

"I know I'd feel better having one. How about you, Mary?"

"I know I would."

"Me, too," echoed Katherine.

"Well, I guess that answers that question, Lee," replied Ian.

"Alright. It's going to take me about a half an hour to go through the guns and makes sure they're safe to use and functional. After that, I'll show those that are going to use them how to do it. More importantly, I'll tell you what to do if you need to use it. Because these are last-ditch personal weapons, it's different from using something like my Colt."

"Can I watch as you check them out?" asked Mary.

Lee looked away from the derringer and at her as he replied, "Sure. It's really kind of boring, though."

"Not if you've never fired one before," she replied.

"Okay. I'll do it on the front porch where there's more light."

Lee then stood, took the bag and walked out to the front porch. He called Jin, who trotted to the porch moments later, then stepped over to his friend, reached into his saddlebag and removed his gun cleaning kit.

Lee then sat on the steps and after Mary joined him, pulled the first derringer from the bag. It seemed in good condition. In fact, it almost looked new. He opened the tiny gun and looked down its rifled barrel and found it immaculate. Then he dry-fired it and was pleased with the action.

He set that aside and removed the second one, then instead of cleaning it removed them all and found each was in the same excellent condition. He wondered why they were all so clean and guessed that some gun salesman had shown up, unloaded a few to the soldiers and then immediately after he left, the commander ordered a shake-down inspection looking for the illegal firearms.

"Well, Mary, it looks like these are all just about in new condition. There are six boxes of ammunition, too. After loading each one, that still leaves a lot of rounds. I'll test fire each one and let the user test fire a shot. Then I'll load them again and that will be that. Hopefully, none of you has to use one."

"Let's go back inside," Mary said as she took his hand.

Lee and Mary walked back into the room, Lee's right hand in Mary's and his left carrying the bag of Remingtons.

He looked at the family and asked, "Okay, aside from the three ladies, who gets the guns?"

"Patrick, Sean and Dylan," said Ian.

"Alright, now in a few minutes, I'm going to take you all outside and I'll load each gun with two rounds. I'll test fire one and show you how to get it ready for the second round. Then you'll test fire the second round. There aren't too many pistols that are easier to use than this Remington."

"That's the easy part; knowing how the gun works. The hard part is knowing when and how to use it. These guns aren't very accurate past thirty feet, but they still pack a surprisingly powerful punch. There are some rules you must follow with these as you would with any firearm."

Never point a gun at someone unless you have the need to kill them. If you shoot to try to wound them, you'll probably miss, and because they were there to hurt you, they'll hurt you worse. So, you need to know that going in. If you are in such a horrible situation that requires you to pull this out of your pocket, it is to stop someone from killing you, hurting you badly, or hurting someone you love. This isn't a time to be noble and worry about the sanctity of human life. The man who is there trying to kill or hurt you doesn't care a bit about such things. He's already made that decision. You pull out the gun and aim it straight at his face. Not his belly or his chest. He knows that may not kill him, but if he's looking down the barrel of a derringer from six feet, he knows he's going to die if you pull the trigger."

But just having the gun on him isn't enough. You have to mean it. You need to have that look in your eyes that says you will pull the trigger and kill him. If you look at him with fear or doubt, he'll call your bluff. I need you to look at him with hate for what he is planning on doing. Let your Irish temper run free and make him drop his weapon and back away. Never let him get close. Never listen to him. He will always lie, and never fall for the attempt at distraction. If you can, have your back against a wall, so if he yells, 'Shoot her, Mac,' you know he's bluffing. All these things may make it sound like I want you to be some cold-blooded killer, but I know you're all better than that. But if you ever find yourselves in one of those situations, it will be your only chance to survive. Does everyone understand that?"

There were nods and grunts of understanding.

"Okay. Enough of the morbid stuff. Let's go shoot these things, because, believe it or not, it's fun."

He loaded all six derringers while they watched, then they returned to the front porch, then crossed the front yard toward a tree stump. Lee stopped about fifteen feet away and took the first small gun.

"The gun can't go off in your pocket by mistake, so don't worry about shooting yourself accidentally. You need to cock the hammer and then pull the trigger."

Lee aimed at the stump, cocked the hammer and squeezed the trigger. The Remington fired, blasting its .41 caliber bullet out of the short barrel with a cloud of gunsmoke and a loud crack. The sound wasn't as loud as they'd expected, but the hole in the stump showed how much power it had.

He fired each gun once to make sure they were all good, then showed them how to set up for the second shot, which was just a repeat of the same actions as the first; nothing more than pulling back the hammer and then the trigger.

He handed the first one to Mary then stepped aside as she cocked the hammer and fired at the stump, then turned and smiled at Lee when she knew that she'd hit the target. Then Katherine and Maggie. Patrick, Sean and Dylan each took a single shot, and all hit the stump.

Lee then asked, "Great shooting, folks. So, what do you think?"

"It was very easy to use," said Patrick.

They all agreed with his evaluation and Lee quickly collected each pistol then returned to the porch with Mary where he cleaned each pistol, before loading each one with two more rounds then returned them to its new owner with one more important instruction.

"Now it won't do you any good if it's in a drawer or on a table. Keep it in your pocket."

Then once the family was armed, Lee took Mary aside.

"Mary, I've got to run into town and deposit this money. Then I'm going to head over to the cabin for the night, but I'll be back tomorrow. When do they start the harvest?"

"Next Monday."

"Okay. You take care of yourself, Mary. I love you, sweetheart."

"I love you, Lee."

The others had all gone in to give them some privacy, so Lee kissed her before he climbed on Jin, then waved to Mary as he trotted down the lane and headed to town, never letting her out of his mind. She had been almost constantly living there since that day at the halfway completed house, as she should have been.

He made it to the bank ten minutes before closing and made his deposit to a smiling cashier and got a receipt. He felt better having that large balance that meant that he'd be able to provide for Mary much more easily.

He rode past the church and headed back to the cabin.

As he was passing his incomplete house, he stopped, dismounted and walked into the house with its four-foot-high walls. *Had it only been a few days since he stopped working on it?* It seemed so distant already. Then he recalled how Mary had told him of her disgrace and how it had made her feel, and then the catharsis after which his Mary had been returned to him. He'd always remember the spot where it happened; in the atrium in Mary's house was where their lives were changed forever. Mary's house, where he knew they would live and raise their own family.

But then the recent realization that he missed his parents resurfaced and he wondered how his parents were Pueblo. He hadn't written to them in months and knew it was overdue, especially with all of the wonderful news. So, he'd write them a letter soon and tell them about Mary and his plans and let them know that he'd send a wire when they had set a date for the wedding.

He felt a nudge and turned to see Jin standing behind him in the house, then smiled and rubbed his friend's nose.

"Jin, so many things have happened so fast, but it can all come crashing down if we let that greedy rancher cause the Flannery family grief, and all for just more money."

Lee thought it wasn't even that much in the big scheme of things. Even he had nearly five thousand dollars in the bank. Sure, this would be like free money to Richards, but at what cost? *Alienating your neighbors? Possibly causing harm to an innocent?*

Lee shook his head. Maybe Richards' plans went beyond just getting a contract for the hay, maybe he wanted the farm that produced the hay as well. If it hadn't been for the conversation with Stella, he wouldn't have believed that they would try anything illegal, but now, he was convinced they'd stop at nothing.

He and Jin walked back out of the house and Lee just kept walking with Jin stepping beside him as they headed for the cabin. As they neared the cabin, Hagar left his perch on the porch and raced down to Lee.

"Hello, Hagar," he said as he rubbed the dog's head.

The three friends of different species returned to the cabin after the walk. Lee took off all Jin's trappings and let him go visit his ladies and his new foals. That open corral was turning into a nursery.

Lee thought it would be wise to increase his practice time with his Colt and Winchester now that it was more likely that he would be using them. So, after entering the cabin, Lee snatched up a box of the .44 caliber Winchester cartridges that fit both guns, then left the cabin and walked down in the direction of the new house but turned east along the long wall of rock and stopped fifty yards away.

This was his target range where the tall edge of the plateau served as a backstop for his bullets.

For almost an hour as the light faded, Lee practiced with his pistol first at fifty yards, then moved to a hundred yards for the Winchester. He knew that his accuracy hadn't suffered at all, but practice never hurt.

Two hours after leaving the cabin, he sat at his table with his newly cleaned weapons sitting before him, still troubled by his lack of knowledge of what Richards was planning to do and hoped that he was wrong, and he'd just buy his hay and sell the damned cattle.

He tried to think of some way to avoid any kind of problems at all by simply going to the Diamond R and just talking to the man. But that short stop at the big ranch told him that there wasn't much of a chance to get him to change his mind. He'd learned very early in his still short life that men like that, who believed themselves better than others and above the law, never changed their minds. They knew that they were right and everyone else was wrong.

After sitting there for two hours, he finally put away his guns, washed up and climbed into bed.

———

Early the next morning, Lee felt rejuvenated and felt that he should take the offense in the Richards situation, at least becoming more noticeable to keep them from trying to take Ian's hay. He left Jin in the corral as he jogged down the canyon to the pool where the spring pushed water from the mountains into the stream, stripped off his clothes and dove into the cold water. He stayed in the pool for ten minutes before stepping out and shook his hair, realizing he probably needed a haircut. When he felt he was reasonably dry, he dressed and walked back to his cabin, where he shaved and ate a quick breakfast of beef jerky and cold beans.

Then he left his cabin, he called Jin, and after two minutes, he finally trotted to the cabin and Lee wondered if he had been busy with one of his mares, because other than the clue provided by the long delay, Jin didn't look happy. But after a minute of rubbing and talking to him, he accepted the saddle without complaint.

Lee rode down to Nueva Luz, arriving just after eight o'clock and entered Enright's Dry Goods.

"Morning, Harry," he said to the proprietor as he entered.

"Howdy, Lee. What can I get for you?"

"Do you have any field glasses?"

"There seems to be a sudden demand for them this week, so I only have one pair left, but it's one of the new ones."

"Great. And give me that scattergun, will you?"

"Aiming to do some hunting, Lee?"

"Yup. Give me two boxes of shells, too. One number two or three and one double aught."

"Whew! You're looking for some big beasties."

"Yes, sir. Saw some tracks up in my place. I need to find a sling for that, so I can hang it on my saddle. Do you know where I can find one?"

Harry Enright turned to where he had taken the shotgun and reached to a lower shelf and pulled out a box.

"Do you mean like this?"

Lee couldn't believe his luck.

"Perfect. All I need now is another box of .44 cartridges and that should do it. I've been doing too much practice shooting these days."

"Okay, Lee. Your total is $38.40."

Lee pulled out two gold double eagles and handed them to Harry, then accepted his change and said, "Thanks, Harry, you've helped a lot."

He took his purchases and returned to Jin, took the sling for the shotgun and fixed it to the saddle, then loaded the shotgun with two rounds of double aught shells. He slid the shotgun into the sling and put the spare shells, cartridges and field glasses into his saddlebags, glad that the field glasses were new. The case was sturdy, too. Usually the problem with used ones was that the case was in such bad repair that it provided no protection whatsoever. He had just put his foot into his stirrup when he remembered something Harry had said.

He removed his boot, walked back into the store and asked, "Harry, you said there had been a run on field glasses. Who bought the others?"

"Rafe Henry bought two used pairs. He didn't want to spend the money for the new pair you bought."

"That's interesting. Thanks, Harry."

Lee returned to Jin wondering who Rafe was watching at the farm, or whether he was watching more than one place. Now he was really glad he had the field glasses.

He neared the farm a little while later and scanned for Mary as he turned down their access road. There was no one out front, but that wouldn't be unusual with the harvest only five days away. It turned out he was right for the lack of visible movement. The entire Flannery family was either in the barn getting the harnesses for the mules cleaned up and repaired or they were out in the corral behind the barn getting the mules fed. They fattened the mules up for the week before the harvest, so they could handle the extra work that would be demanded of them in a week of pulling the harvesters.

After he dismounted, he found Mary in the corral, just as she saw him coming and waved. He waved back and headed her way as she worked with Katherine and Dylan.

"Getting them ready for work?" Lee asked.

"I think they suspect something, too. They're all giving us the evil eye."

"Maybe they're not as stupid as I thought," he said, drawing a laugh from his intended.

He waved Mary over, and when she was close, he said, "Harry Enright told me this morning that Rafe Henry bought two pair of field glasses this week. That means he's watching the farm."

"Why?"

"That's the question, isn't it? When are you going to be done for the morning?"

"In about half an hour, why?"

"I was wondering if you'd like to go for a ride."

She grinned and replied, "I think I can spare the time to spend with my fiancé."

"Good. Where's your mother?"

"She's the only one exempt from harvest preparation. She's in the kitchen baking bread. We go through a lot of sandwiches during harvest."

"I'll see you when you're done, Mary," he said, before he smiled at her, then turned and headed back for the house.

He entered the kitchen and saw Maggie mixing something into a large mound of flour in a large bowl.

"Good morning, Maggie. I thought I'd come by and let you know something. I know that Ian is busy, so I thought you could pass it on to him when he takes a break."

Maggie put down her spoon and asked, "What is it, Lee?"

"I stopped by Enright's this morning to pick up a pair of field glasses, and Harry told me that Rafe Henry had bought two pair this week. That means he's watching the farm at least. Why, I don't know. It's just a good thing to be aware of."

"Aye, it is. So why did you buy some field glasses?"

"For the opposite reason. I want to find the watchers. I thought they'd be out there, but not for just observing, and that surprised me a bit. I thought they might be nearby ready to cause some mischief at the best opportunity, but learning this throws a whole new wrinkle into the situation. It's like they're planning something."

"So, Lee, what will you be doing this morning?"

"I'm going to take Mary riding shortly. I need to get my head cleared of some things that are rattling around."

Maggie smiled with her eyes twinkling and asked, "Are you sure that's only thing that's got something rattling around?"

"Normally, Maggie, I'd agree with you. But in this case, I really do need to see if I can get some things clarified in my mind. Having Mary with me always seem to clarify my thinking. Talking to her and bouncing ideas off her helps a lot."

"Why, Mr. Ryan, I do believe you love my daughter as much as I love that husband of mine," she replied.

"Maggie, every day I don't think I can love her any more than I do, but then the next day arrives and it proves me wrong. You have a very special daughter, Maggie. "

"Yes, she is. I think that you are both suited for each other, and, Lee, I can never thank you enough for bringing my Mary back to me."

Lee leaned over and kissed Maggie on the cheek then said, "Maggie, you are a marvelous mother and a wonderful woman. Ian is a very lucky man."

Maggie picked up the spoon and waved it at him, unable to speak.

Lee smiled at Maggie, turned, left the kitchen and stepped onto the back porch where he waited until he saw Mary come around the corner of the barn. He smiled as he watched her, very aware of how special she really was.

She hopped up to the porch and gave Lee a quick kiss, then hurried inside to change into her riding clothes, although Lee didn't think it was necessary. She had been wearing her bib overalls and he thought she looked quite fetching.

Ten minutes later the two palominos were stepping out of the farmyard and headed east.

———

About nine hundred yards south, lying on a blanket spread across a large boulder, Rafe steadied his field glasses and watched them leave. He guessed who the man was easily enough. It was that no-account cowboy who somehow tricked him and made him look like a fool in front of Stella. It still rankled him. *But which Flannery daughter was with him?* He doubted if it was Katherine. Her parents weren't about to let their young daughter go riding with a cowboy. Frankly, he was surprised they allowed the older daughter to go, but then again, understanding her reputation, maybe they didn't care. It didn't matter, though, he had to keep an eye on the younger one. When the two women were together, it was easy because she was shorter. But when they were with one of the brothers, it was tougher. One thing he did learn, though; it seemed like they were never alone. Not that they could grab her on the farm, he just wondered if that was going to make the operation more difficult. He finally just forgot about who he was watching and just continued observing the riders as they rode into the distance.

Lee and Mary rode for ten minutes and then Lee stopped Jin and said, "Mary, let's step down. I need to do something."

"And I'll bet I can guess what it is, Mister Ryan," she replied with a grin.

"Normally, you'd be right, Miss Flannery, but this time your guess is probably wrong."

They both dismounted, then Lee reached into his saddlebag and took out the field glasses and removed them from the case.

"Mary, stand with your back to the farm while I'm going to get close to you."

"I thought you said I was wrong."

"Only for a few minutes and then I'll probably prove your guess to be accurate."

Lee stood directly in front of Mary and began scanning the farm with his field glasses, hoping to disguise what he was doing from any watchers. He had almost reached the end of his sweep when he saw something on the top of a large granite boulder about a quarter of a mile south of the farm's southern edge. It was easy to spot because it was a large dark square on the light gray rock. He kept watching then saw a flash as the light reflected off a lens.

"Gotcha!" said Lee.

"What do you see, Lee?"

"I'd guess it was our good friend, Rafe Henry or one of their other ranch hands."

He put the glasses back in the case and returned them to the saddlebags.

"And now, Miss Flannery, I will prove you right," he said before he scooped her into his arms and kissed her.

Two miles south, Rafe Henry, assuming he wouldn't get any more information, quit for the day and slid from the rock, taking the blanket with him. He was annoyed that he'd been given such a simple task and that damned Willie was staying on the ranch. Rafe knew that Willie had his eye on Stella and that didn't sit well with him.

After a few minutes of precious private time, Lee and Mary reluctantly mounted their horses, and headed back to the house, returning fifteen minutes later.

He explained to the family what he'd seen and that he'd return each day to keep an eye on the farm while they harvested the hay.

———

The following days repeated the same pattern: preparation for the harvest, a ride with Mary, and seeing an observer on the rock, but nothing dramatic ever seemed to come of it. Each day he'd return to his cabin, take some time for target practice, and return the next day.

It was Friday, then they'd go to Mass on Sunday and begin the harvest on Monday. Lee began to hope that maybe his premonition of violence was just a product of an overactive imagination and they'd just sail through the harvest without any problems at all.

His hopes of a quiet harvest were dashed before it even began when his premonitions of violent disaster were realized on Saturday.

CHAPTER 5

Lee had awakened that Saturday morning in almost a giddy mood. For some reason, his worries seemed to be put away with the bright morning sun, but it wasn't the blinding daylight that had chased away his concerns. He'd had wonderful dreams about his Mary, and in a little while, she would join him in his cabin and those dreams would become real.

He jogged to the stream with Hagar, bathed, and then shaved as his canine friend wondered what he was doing, before returning to the cabin.

He decided to skip breakfast and have it at the café this morning to almost celebrate his good mood. Even as he had hoped that it wasn't going to be necessary, the constant observation by someone on the Diamond R, confirmed his belief that Richards was going to try something. But that didn't dampen his cheerfulness as he knew he was ready to face the challenge of Richards and his crew. He felt as ready as he ever was, and having his Mary back made all the difference. It was knowing that he'd be seeing her later today that was the real source of his restrained joy.

He called Jin, then readied him to take him into town and then to the Flannery farm. Ten minutes later, he rode past his half-completed house and trotted down the slope, arriving in Nueva Luz by before eight o'clock and dismounted at the café.

After taking his now customary table and placing his customary order with the waitress, who already brought him his pot of coffee, he sat drinking his first cup when he noticed he was the object of a prolonged stare from a young man, but Lee wasn't sure of his age. He could be anywhere between sixteen and twenty-two with that baby face. Baby face or not, he was sitting with Otto Krueger, who was anything but a baby face. Lee had seen him before and asked the sheriff who he was because he seemed to be trouble in boots. The sheriff had told him he was one of the 'ranch hands' on the Diamond R that didn't seem to do much cow punching and agreed with his perception that Otto was a possible problem but seemed to be under the control of Ed Richards.

Otto was about four inches taller than the kid, but Krueger probably outweighed him by almost a hundred pounds. Otto's size and blonde hair made him stick out.

Lee assumed that the younger man with him worked in some capacity at the ranch, but he was sure that it wasn't cow punching, or any other manual labor. The fact that he was chummy with Otto Krueger placed him into the non-ranch hand category.

The waitress brought him his breakfast, and smiled at her before beginning to eat, paying minimum attention to the kid or Otto. After a few minutes he noticed that the kid suddenly jerked and then immediately shifted from his glare to intently ignoring him. Lee smiled inside, understanding that he must have gotten a kick from Otto under the table, and it wouldn't have been any love tap either.

He had no idea why the kid was interested in him, or why Otto didn't seem to like that he was being so obvious, either. He suspected that his visits to the Flannery farm were behind it somehow, but he didn't know the exact reason unless he walked over to their table and introduced himself, which would probably be an exercise in futility.

He finished eating, then decided to ignore the pair, so he left a quarter on the table, then rose, picked up his hat and headed for the door.

As he exited, Otto said, "The boss wanted you just to lay low until that girl shows up, so don't make yourself so obvious. I'm gonna follow that cowboy out of town. Just hang around and be friendly."

"Alright," Pete Jones replied before Otto hastily stood, then left the diner and the payment for his large breakfast to Pete.

Lee had already mounted Jin and turned him south toward the farm when Otto mounted his animal and had him at a slow trot down the main street, two hundred yards behind Lee.

Lee had noticed the big man when he had exited the diner soon after he had set Jin to a medium trot down the main street. As the Diamond R shared the road with the Flannery farm for a while, it wasn't any sign of hostility yet. Lee figured he'd just ride along and pretend that he wasn't back there. He knew that he had a good two-hundred-yard safety cushion behind him and concentrated his hearing for any approaching hoofbeats. He didn't believe that Otto would be stupid enough to take a shot at range.

He wondered why Otto would leave the ranch this early on a Saturday. Regular ranch hands would be out working the cattle already, but even those non-working hands wouldn't be in town paying for breakfast instead of chowing down at the ranch. *And who was that kid with him?*

The questions remained unanswered as he rode along, still listening for any sudden approach by Otto.

Ten minutes later, Lee made the turn to the Flannery farm and then glanced to his right just a minute after that and spotted Otto Krueger as he continued down the road toward the Diamond R.

When he neared the farm, he was pleasantly surprised to see Mary waiting on the porch waving at him and waved back. He didn't understand why she wasn't already working to prepare for Monday's harvest.

He reached the house and stepped down as Mary walked off the porch.

"Good morning, Mary," he said as she approached.

"Good morning, Mister Ryan," she replied with a smile.

Lee was astonished how rapidly she had returned to her musical self and never wanted anything to happen to her that would make her change again, and hoped it was no longer possible.

When she was near enough, he pulled her close and kissed her warmly. If anyone was watching from either the farmhouse or that rock, then it was just too bad.

"Well, Mister Ryan, that was somewhat unexpected," she said as she leaned back slightly.

"I just want the world to know that I love you, Miss Flannery."

"Well, I think they know now."

Lee freed her from his grip, then Mary hooked her arm through his and they walked up the porch steps. The morning chores had been completed an hour earlier, so Mary ushered him into the kitchen and sat him down at the kitchen table, walked to the cold room and took out a steel pitcher and filled a tall glass of buttermilk. She set it on the table before him and took the closest seat.

"I remember that you once told me how you always loved buttermilk," Mary said.

"I did tell you that, and I'm happy to tell you that I still do."

As he was sipping his milk, Ian walked in and joined them at the table, and Lee was again surprised that he wasn't working.

So, he asked, "So, what's the Flannery plan for today? It seems to be different than before."

"That's because we're ready to go for Monday. The harvesters are in great condition and we have plenty of steel wire. To tell the truth, we're ahead of schedule. We could start today, but that would run us into Sunday, so we'll begin early Monday morning as we'd planned."

"Do you want some free labor?"

"I might take you up on that offer, Lee. But for now, I'd be more comfortable having you watching the house and the farm for any trouble."

"I understand. It's what I planned to do today. I wanted to ride the perimeter."

Ian smiled and said, "That sounds like a military operation, Lee."

"It's just for a few more days, Ian. Then everything can go back to normal."

"I hope so, Lee. I just don't know how that's possible. Richards will either be mad or sulking, unless he gets his way."

"Well, I'd rather he was sulking than mad or angry, Ian," he said as he raised his glass and said, "Here's to a sulking Edward Richards."

Mary and Ian laughed as Lee finished off the buttermilk.

"Did you want me to come when you make your ride?" Mary asked.

"As much as I'd love to have you with me, Mary, I need to be able to hear anything and be aware of any movement. I'll be back for lunch, though."

With her father just a few feet away, he limited his brief farewell to the visual and looked deeply into her blue eyes. They held the look for a few seconds, each understanding what the other meant.

The silent goodbye ended, then Lee smiled and left the kitchen, walking through the main room and out the front door to a waiting Jin. He stepped up and swung his leg over the saddle, then rode south across the front of the property.

He had Jin walking slowly as he scanned the horizons for anything that didn't belong there. He had the field glasses around his neck, but they stayed in place until he spotted something that piqued his interest. He took his time, stopping every few minutes to inspect the area, but found nothing out of place. He reached the southern boundary soon and turned east, finding another mile of serenity. The only thing he saw of interest was a large diamondback rattler about ten feet to his left. It was going its way and ignored the horse and rider even as Jin's eyes widened when he saw the reptile, but the stallion didn't react otherwise.

After riding the eastern border, Lee turned north. There was a shallow rise as he went north, and when he finally reached the northeastern corner, he glanced back, expecting to find someone watching him. He checked with his field glasses, but no one was there. He exited the farm and kept walking Jin as he headed for what would be a good lookout point.

A few minutes later, he arrived at a large cluster of boulders, dismounted then climbed onto the smallest and began leapfrogging to the next higher rock until he reached the top. Once he was at its highest point, he was pleased with the vantage point.

He scanned the entire area, beginning with the farmhouse just eight hundred yards away, where could see male redheads doing various tasks, but no females. He couldn't make out their faces at this distance. He looked at the far side of the farm and could see the Richards house, which was no surprise as it was so large. It was too far to pick out any individual movement, though.

Just for curiosity, he swung his glasses in a complete arc but didn't see anything until he was looking northeast and saw a lone rider where there shouldn't be anyone. He couldn't make out the rider, but the horse looked familiar and that made the identification possible. It was Rafe Henry. *Now what was he doing that far out of the picture?* The town and his ranch were both miles to the west and south respectively. Then he realized that Henry was heading his way, and not wanting to be noticed, he quickly hopped down and mounted Jin, heading directly to the farm. This information was only necessary to him. It may not have any value at all, but it was peculiar. Between seeing Rafe out there and Otto and that new kid in town, Lee found himself getting a bit twitchy and as Jin trotted, he closed his eyes to use meditation to calm his mind.

Lee reached the farmhouse almost simultaneously with the Flannery boys. He walked Jin into the barn, stripped him of his tack, then brushed his friend and let him take his feed and water. He patted Jin on the rump as he left, then headed into the house, entering through the kitchen door.

The family was all sitting around the large kitchen table and looked at him en masse.

"Find anything, Lee?" asked Ian.

"A good-sized diamondback, but that was about it. For a Saturday, it was pretty quiet. Is anything going on here?"

"Nothing at all. It's really kind of boring. That will all change on Monday," Ian replied.

"Come Monday, I'll be staying here until the harvest is done and the hay is all moved. I'll stay in the barn, if that's all right."

"Lee, you will do no such thing. We have room," protested Maggie.

"It's not a question of room, Maggie," Lee explained, "I want to be in the barn in case they try anything at night. Anyone who does that won't be expecting any problems from the barn. I'll be in the loft with my Winchester and just feel better being up there. I just lay my bedroll in the loft near the upper doors and lie there with my Winchester and a spare box of ammunition."

"Alright, then. But that's the only excuse you could have gotten away with," Maggie said, "Now, come and sit down and have some lunch."

Lee sat in the only open chair which was conveniently next to Mary. After he sat, she slid her hand over his and smiled at him. He gave her hand a squeeze before starting to eat one-handed.

After lunch, they all went about various light chores that still needed to be done while Lee went to the barn and spent the time cleaning his guns and checking out his new shotgun. He had it cracked open when Mary entered the barn.

"When did you get that?" she asked.

"The same time I bought the field glasses. I saw it there and realized that I didn't have one. It's something that every farm and ranch should have. For what we might be facing, it will be a serious calming influence. Bad guys will get jelly legs when they see this pointed at them. Once this whole Richards thing is done, I'll give it to your father. He could use it on varmints like that big old rattler I saw today."

"Is it hard to use?"

"No, ma'am. You just point it and cock one or two hammers. Then pull the trigger. It has a nasty kick, though. It can make a real mess of things with the size shot I have in here right now. Tell some miscreant that you have it loaded with double aught shot and, unless he's a total moron, he'll do whatever you tell him."

"Why would you give it to my father?"

"Because he would never think of buying one. I'll just go and buy another. Mary, come and sit down, if you please."

Mary sat next to Lee wondering why he had even asked.

"I'm sure that you know how ecstatic I am to have my Mary back, so now I need to ask you an important question. After this is all done, how long do you want to wait until we get married? You know what I'd say if given the opportunity to set the date."

Mary smiled in relief if nothing else as she asked, "Which date would you choose?"

"Let's see. Your father said he'd be done with the harvest by Saturday, so I thought twenty minutes after it was finished."

Mary laughed and replied, "Strangely enough, I was going to suggest half an hour."

"Well, that's settled. Seriously, though. How about the fifteenth of October?"

Mary sighed, then answered, "That would be perfect, Lee."

Lee smiled at her and said, "I'm happy that we settled that big problem. Now, sometime before then, I'll need to buy a suit and the rings and even fix up the cabin. I'll make a bigger bed, for some mysterious reason. I'm not going to go all fancy until I have our house finished. We'll need some furniture, but that can be added as we go. The cook stove will be the biggest expense. That and the tub for the bathroom, but you'll have things to do for our new home as well."

"And what will that be?" she smiled, expecting a different answer than the one she received.

"Your atrium, sweetheart. That will be all yours; the lilac bushes, the flowers, all of it will be yours. I would like something to sit on out there with my lady love. Outside of that one requirement, however you want to make it, it's yours. It will forever be Mary's atrium to me as it was even before I laid the first brick. It was where my Mary returned to me."

Her eyes misted as she looked at him and she whispered, "Lee, you've made me happier than I could ever have hoped for."

"If there is one person in the world that deserved that happiness, it's you, Mary."

He pulled her close and gently kissed her, then after they separated, Mary sighed.

"I suppose I need to go back and help with dinner," Mary said.

"Who's off to confession today?" he asked.

"Katherine and Dylan. How about you?"

"I went last week, and Father Kelly can tell I'm running out of things to make up. Last week, I had to say that I had bad thoughts about a scorpion I saw crawling near the new house."

Mary laughed, and said, "I suppose he gave you a Hail Mary for that one."

"He was getting exasperated with me and asked me if I was trying for sainthood."

Mary laughed, then stood, gave him a short kiss and left the barn. Lee watched her walk away, admiring those feminine curves and saying he'd probably have to confess that immoral thought next week. It was better than that scorpion curse.

He closed the shotgun and leaned it against the wall after reloading it with double aught shot then began moving his things into the loft for the night.

———

It was getting near twilight when Katherine, mounted on Blaze, and Dylan, sitting atop the horse he had named Paddy just to irritate his oldest brother, left the farm. They were starting later than usual, but with the horses, that cut down the travel time immensely. They could ride the two miles in less than fifteen minutes, and even less if Katherine let Blaze run; and she did love to let her run.

That night, they both kept it at a trot, so it was after five o'clock when they arrived at the church knowing that Father Kelly would only be hearing confessions for another few minutes, depending on how many were in line. Katherine and Dylan dismounted at the side of the church, tied their horses to a hitch rail, then went inside, Katherine putting on her green bonnet as she entered. She slid into the pew next to the confessional pew first pleased that there was one other person waiting.

Dylan knew he would have to wait for two plus the person in the confessional and hoped the other two weren't big sinners. He knew his sister wasn't going to take long.

Outside in the growing darkness, Rafe Henry stepped out from behind the church and unhitched Blaze, then walked the horse to the back of the church and waited.

Pete Jones stood near the hitch rail and waited, pretending to be worried, hoping that the girl would be the first to leave the church. It would be a lot easier that way.

Katherine finally entered the confessional, thinking that the previous penitent must have had some whoppers.

She only took a few minutes of Father Kelly's time, and he spent longer admonishing her than she did in telling him of her transgressions, which she didn't think were all that bad in the first place.

She received her absolution and left the confessional, went to the front of the church, knelt at the altar rail and said her penance. She was finished in two minutes, and after genuflecting, stepped quickly down the side aisle and left the church.

Pete Jones saw her leave and waited until she drew close and prepared to begin the show.

Katherine turned the corner and didn't see Blaze where she'd left her, and a sudden panic took control before she saw that handsome boy who had been paying attention to her nearby. She forgot about her horse when he began to step closer to her and her heart began to race.

He stopped a few feet away with a worried look on his face and said, "Miss, do you own a dark gray horse with a white star on its forehead?"

Her mood suddenly shifted back to concern as she asked, "Yes, that's Blaze. Where is she?"

"She was sick, miss. I had to move her to the back of the church where those trees are. I thought maybe if she ate some leaves she'd do better."

Katherine glanced at the trees, then began to walk quickly to see her poor horse, not noticing that the young man walked behind her. *Blaze was sick!* As she turned the corner, she was stunned when she saw Blaze standing before her, with Rafe Henry holding her reins. Blaze looked fine, but that evil Rafe Henry looked menacing.

"Give me my horse!" she exclaimed as she reached for the reins.

Then she heard a sound behind her, and as she turned, she caught a glimpse of that handsome young man and then a pistol barrel before everything went black.

"Quick! Load her onto her horse!" said Rafe.

They picked up the unconscious Katherine, laid her across the saddle then Rafe tied her hands and feet together before they mounted their horses and rode away, trailing Blaze behind them. They walked due east out into the desert past the trees as the darkness descended.

———

Dylan exited the church five minutes later, walked to Paddy and noticed that Blaze was already gone. He was annoyed with Katherine for leaving him alone. She was probably racing home just to enjoy the ride. Shaking his head, he untied Paddy, mounted, and after one last look around, began walking the horse home at a reasonable pace.

———

Rafe and Pete were already two miles east of town when Dylan left the town limits, then they shifted to a slightly more northeasterly direction. Rafe had been riding this route several times during both the day and night to familiarize himself with the landscape. Even with the moon only a weak crescent, he was comfortable with the trip.

By the time Dylan was arriving home, Katherine had been carried two miles due north of the Flannery farm and was more than halfway to her destination.

Dylan rode into the barn, took the saddle from Paddy and brushed him down. He didn't notice the missing Blaze in the darkness, before he left the barn and walked into the kitchen for dinner.

In the kitchen, Maggie had set the table and was awaiting the arrival of her two children when Dylan entered the door.

Dylan said, "I'm home, Mama. Where is Katherine? I want to yell at her."

"Now, Dylan, why would you want to yell at your sister?"

"She left me again. I came out of the church and her horse was already gone. I had to ride back by myself."

Maggie's stomach dropped when she feared what might have happened. *No, surely not!* Katherine must have come in the front door.

She stopped stirring the stew, turned and quickly strode to the main room, almost shouting, "Katherine! Katherine Margaret Flannery, where are you?"

Everyone in the main room could hear the panic in her voice and stood as she entered.

"Maggie, what is the matter?" Ian asked.

"Dylan came home without Katherine. He thought she had gone off on her own, but she's not here."

"Let me go and check the barn," said Lee as he ran past her and out the kitchen door.

He raced into the barn and immediately noticed the empty stall that Blaze usually occupied, then turned and found Ian right behind him.

"Those bastards took my darlin' Katherine! Let's go get her back, Lee!" he exclaimed, his voice rising with each syllable.

Lee put his hands on Ian's shoulders and said, "Ian, she won't be there. If we go over there, they'll act sympathetic and concerned but all it will do is to make matters worse."

"Then what will we do, Lee?"

"Let's go back and get everyone together," he replied in his calm, controlled voice, which settled Ian's nerves somewhat.

After removing his hands from Ian, he turned and walked beside the visibly shaken Ian. Even though he had suspected that they might do something like this, the actual event was very unsettling. Even before they reached the house, he was thinking of how he could find Katherine.

They walked into the main room from the front porch and everyone's eyes were on them.

"Blaze wasn't in the barn, so we have to assume that Katherine's been kidnapped," began Lee.

Then, he quickly continued before anyone could interrupt.

"Now isn't the time to panic. We know who is responsible, but I'm positive Katherine is not being held anywhere near the Diamond R because Ed Richards needs to be seen as innocent of any wrongdoing. It would be impossible to track her in the dark, which is why they waited. Ian and Maggie, this is your decision, but I will tell you what I'd recommend. In the morning, I will see if I can track them from behind the church. They probably have at least two that took her, so that means three horses. I want you to stay here and that means skipping Mass, but I'm sure Father Kelly will understand. They will probably leave a ransom note pretending it is a kidnapping that is unrelated to the hay harvest, but I don't think that they will harm Katherine. That would be the last thing they would want to happen. I think within twenty-four hours of the ransom note, Ed Richards or maybe Stella will show up and claim to have some information as to her whereabouts, but then ask why they should help you with their problem if you wouldn't help them with theirs. Then, it will be your call, Ian. If you sign the contract, they'll return Katherine to you unharmed. They'll get their hay and you'll get Katherine back. They would get what they want, and they'll think you'll let it go."

He paused, took a breath and continued.

"Now, I'll spend that time trying to find her in the interim. If I find her, I'll bring her back as soon as I can. Ian and Maggie, this is your call. Katherine is your daughter."

Maggie replied in a strong voice, "I know, Lee. It hurts me to admit that you're right. There's nothing we can do until tomorrow and you're the only one who can go out there and find her. What happens here when the Richards show up is up to us."

"How come we all can't come and blanket the area?" asked Patrick.

"Because you'd be too easy to spot coming. Secondly, they're probably watching the house right now. When it gets late, I'll slip out of here and head to my cabin. I'll be in town at sunup and see if I can find the tracks. I'll need to stay out of sight as much as possible. I don't want them to know I'm out there. I need to find where they're holding her and take care of her guards."

"Can you do that, Lee?" asked Mary.

"Easily. It's a question of whether I'll need to kill them or not. Everything will depend on how they're positioned and how many there are. I think there will be two, but I can't be certain."

Mary was very distraught. First, her sister had been taken, and now her future husband was going to go out and face danger to bring her back.

As the tension in the room began to rise, Maggie stood and reminded them that they still had to eat, then ordered them into the kitchen.

———

Ten miles northeast of the farmhouse, Katherine had regained consciousness and was bewildered. She had no idea where she was or why she was there. It was so dark. For a few foggy seconds, she couldn't remember what had happened, then it struck her. *That boy had told her that Blaze was sick, but then she saw Blaze being held by Rafe Henry!* It suddenly dawned on her that she had been kidnapped and realized with almost painful certainty that she had left her derringer in her room. She didn't think it was right to take a gun into church, and now thought how naïve she had been. But the question still remained: *where was she?* She felt around, and her hands ran across a crude cot beneath her. She swung her legs off the cot, started to stand but quickly returned to her seat with a rush of dizziness, then felt her Irish temper rise. *That damned Ed Richards and Rafe Henry! And that damned cute boy that she thought liked her!*

Just a few feet behind the shack, Rafe and Pete sat on some rocks chewing on grass.

Pete glanced to the shack and said, "Sounds like the missy is awake in there."

"'Bout time, too. I'm gettin' hungry and all the food is inside. Let's get a fire going back here. Ain't nobody going to be looking for her tonight and the shack will block the light anyway."

"Okay. I'm hungry myself," Pete replied before he rose to gather some firewood.

Rafe walked around to the front of the shack and opened the door.

Katherine heard him coming and as soon as the door swung wide, launched herself at him. She slammed into him, but it wasn't much of a contest. Rafe was a foot taller and almost a hundred pounds heavier and simply wrestled her to the ground and shoved her back onto the cot.

He pointed at her and snarled, "You'd better behave, missy. Now we're not gonna hurt you, but if you want to fight like that, I won't be concerned much about knocking you around a bit of maybe enjoying myself with you."

Katherine tried to appear fierce, but the thought of being assaulted by Rafe made her shrink back against the wall in horror.

Rafe nodded at her new meekness, then walked over to the wall and took down a coffeepot, a frypan and cooking grate before grabbing a couple of cans of beans and the coffee. He found a can of beef and added that to his stack.

Katherine thought briefly that she might be able to bolt past him now that he had his arms filled, but that passed almost immediately when he turned and glared at her.

"You behave yourself and you'll be back home with your mommy and daddy and all the rest of them redheaded brats in a day or two. I'll even feed you, but not if you give me a hard time."

Katherine's anger suddenly overrode her fear as she snapped, "You and Ed Richards can go to hell! Lee is going to find you and make you wish you were never born."

"Who the hell is Lee? Is he that wimpy cowboy that's trying to bed your floozy sister?"

Katherine wanted to scratch his eyes out but surprising herself, she calmed down and spoke more calmly when she said, "Lee is going to marry Mary. But before he does, I can guarantee he'll kill you, Rafe Henry."

Henry stared at Katherine for a few seconds before he laughed, turned and closed the door. Once outside, he set his things down, swung the newly added bar across the door locking her in, then picked up the food and cookware to walk to the back of the shack.

When he arrived, he found a good fire already blazing, handed the tins to Pete to open, then began to set up the cooking grate. Once it was in place, he put the frypan on top, accepted the opened cans of beans and beef and dumped them in. He filled the coffeepot with water from the water bag, then added it on the grate.

When he took his seat on the rocks, Pete grinned and asked, "It sounded like that little girl gave you a hard time, Rafe. You enjoy putting her back in her place?"

Rafe didn't even bother looking at him, but replied, "She ain't gonna give us any more trouble."

Pete snickered as they both stared at their bubbling supper.

After they ate, Pete took the remaining food and a cup of coffee to the shack, flipped open the bar, then opened the door more cautiously.

Katherine had no intention of getting close to him again, so when he entered, she was pressed with her back against the wall.

Rafe set the plate and spoon on a small, rickety table, then left the cup of coffee beside it and backed out of the shack, closed the door and returned the bar into its locked position.

Katherine may not have wanted their food, but was famished, so she quickly ate the bean and beef mix in the dark, drank the coffee and returned to the cot.

She didn't call out to them to come and take the empty plate and cup but assumed one of them would show up soon anyway.

But after an hour, Katherine realized that they probably wouldn't be coming again, and even worse, she had an urgent need to pee. After searching in vain for a chamber pot, and disregarding the idea of using the coffee cup, she began to pound on the door.

Rafe turned to the back of the cabin and shouted, "What do you want?"

Katherine was surprisingly embarrassed as she yelled through the wooden wall, "I have to pee."

Pete looked at Rafe and giggled, as he stood, then walked around to the front of the shack, slid the bar off, then opened the door and when she walked out, pointed to a small alcove carved into the rocks. She ran to the spot and after glancing back to make sure they couldn't watch, relieved her bladder. She returned a few minutes later and entered her small, dark prison.

Rafe then joined Pete, and after the fire began to die, slid into their bedrolls for the night.

Katherine curled up on the cot feeling lonely and miserable, and hoped that Lee would not only find her, but make those two men suffer for what they did.

CHAPTER 6

Lee woke with a start the next morning, and quickly slid out of his homemade bed, stood and opened the door. It was still dark outside, and the predawn hadn't even arrived, so he looked at the sky. The moon had already set, so he guessed it was around four o'clock in the morning, and it was time to get moving. He washed but held off shaving to save time, but still made himself a hot breakfast. It might be the last food he'd be able to eat for a while. He would stay out in the field until he found Katherine and those bastards who had taken her. He packed three cans of beans and a lot of jerky to keep him going so he could eat something to keep his energy up. He took three canteens of water and made sure his Winchester and shotgun were fully loaded. He even added a sixth round to his Colt's load.

As he was preparing to leave the cabin, he reached down and rubbed the alert Hagar, saying, "I've got to get this right, Hagar. These bastards can't get away with this sort of thing."

Hagar was dancing around his feet, trying to herd him out of the cabin as he pulled his Stetson on, walked out the door, and called to Jin. He wasn't sure the horse was awake yet, but the palomino had heard him stirring and quickly trotted to the front of the cabin, nickered and waited for the saddle.

After saddling his friend, he mounted, patted his neck and said, "Let's go, Jin. I'm going to need you at your best today."

He reached the gate, swung it wide from the saddle, and let Hager close it as he began the smooth descent into Nueva Luz. The predawn still hadn't arrived when he left, but by the time he reached town, the dawn sky was breaking. He thought he'd need more light to find the tracks, but didn't want to be seen, so he headed behind the church, then dismounted and checked the ground.

Even in the weak light, he could make out a group of hoof prints, so he began walking, peering at the ground as Jin naturally followed behind matching his pace.

———

At the Flannery farm, they had been up for an hour as no one had slept well, and when Ian opened the front door, he found a folded sheet of paper lying on the porch. He picked it up, opened it and found a child-like scrawled print that read:

WE HAVE YOUR DAUGHTER
WE WILL SEND DEMANDS LATER
DO NOT TRY TO RESCUE HER
OR WE WILL KILL HER AFTER WE USE HER

Ian blanched, then turned and walked quickly back inside with the note and handed it to Maggie. Despite the note's arrival being exactly has Lee had predicted, the wording of the threat was unnerving, and all they could hope was that Lee's other prediction, that they wouldn't harm Katherine was just as accurate.

After letting Mary and the boys read the note, the family all took seats to discuss what they would do when they heard from the Richards.

———

At the Diamond R, Rafe was briefing his boss on the successful venture, after he and Pete had been relieved by two other hands.

"So, she's behaving herself?"

"Except for the initial half-hearted attempt, yeah."

"Good. Who's up there now?"

"Otto and Chili."

"Good. I think I'll send Frank up there. He might convince her that we can be friends after all this is over. I don't think Flannery will do anything about it anyway. After he gets her back, it would help if she says she likes Frank. When you go back at four o'clock, take Frank with you. I'll fill him in what I expect him to do."

Rafe thought his boss was delusional with that idea. Frank liked all young girls, and suspected that the Flannery girl might be too old for his tastes, and not only that, if Frank was in the mood, things could get out of hand and the whole plan could blow up in his face. But despite his concerns, he let it go. It wasn't his business. Besides, he wasn't the boss.

———

Katherine's morning hadn't been any better than her night. They'd fed her some cold beans and a lot of water and then let her use the rock bathroom again, but even the sun didn't lighten her feelings of despair. She'd expected Lee to show up right away to rescue her, but he hadn't arrived.

Now, she was dirty, hungry and even more afraid.

———

Lee had been following the trail after leaving Nueva Luz. The sun was up now, and he could see the tracks clearly, and wondered how far they'd go before they started hiding the tracks. He would have been shocked they led to the location where they were holding Katherine. They must have been planning this for weeks now and surely had a path that made tracking almost impossible. He was familiar enough with the area to have a good idea where they'd be headed now, too.

It was eight o'clock when he lost the tracks. They tracked down into a gulch, and when they came exited, they crossed onto an enormous lava bed almost a mile across. He dismounted and stepped onto the lava bed. He wasn't really good at tracking and the hard surface of the lava bed was emphasizing that deficiency.

He began slowly looking around the lava bed for any signs of scratches or displaced rocks, but saw nothing to indicate where they were going, so he decided to follow the direction that they had been headed when they entered the lava field.

He stayed trapped on the lava bed for two hours and his feet were almost blistered by the time he exited, having never picked up even a single sign of horses, not even any droppings, which made him believe that they had exited the lava bed earlier than he'd suspected.

Once on dirt again, he began his search for the lost trail and found nothing on the side of the lava bed for a half mile in either direction. He as getting frustrated as the sun passed its zenith and began its downward path toward sunset.

He reached behind him, took a canteen from Jin and took a long drink before letting Jin finish the canteen's contents from his hat.

After replacing the empty canteen, he took a piece of salty jerky from his saddlebags and grabbed it with his teeth just to help his mind work as he looked south and the Flannery farm that was beyond the horizon. He decided to head toward the farm, but he knew there was nothing there, but might be able to pick up the tracks.

He walked for another hour with Jin patiently following and found nothing. So, he mounted Jin and turned north again, slowly scanning further out from the flow. It was past two when he reached the spot where he had begun his southern search, dismounted again, lifted a second canteen and took out more jerky. He chewed on the jerky, then took a few swallows of water before he filled his hat again and offered it to Jin. The palomino quickly emptied the hat and a severely frustrated Lee continued to walk and search for that damned trail.

———

As Otto and Chili played cards in front of Katherine's prison shack, they suddenly heard the horses in back snorting and rearing and had no idea what was causing the ruckus. Just as they dropped the cards and stood, they heard a large crash as the old timber rail that Rafe had used to tie all of the animals disintegrated.

As they raced around the shack, they found all the horses in panic and in the midst of all the noise and confusion, they heard the distinct sound of a threatened rattlesnake, stopping them in their tracks as they tried to find the source of the terrifying warning, and soon spotted the large reptile as it lay coiled on a nearby rock.

As Otto and Chili moved to avoid the snake, they were almost crushed by a lunging Blaze as the mare made her escape. Otto quickly turned to try to catch the terrified animal, but it was no use; she had her head up and was gone in a flash.

They started to panic that the horse would leave prints all the way back to the farm, but when they chased her to the mouth of the small canyon, they were relieved to see her turn northwest, directly away from the farm. As they watched her run into the distance, they quickly went back to see to their own animals. By then, the snake had moved on and their horses had calmed down, so after tying them to a nearby mesquite bush, they went back to their cards.

Inside the shack, Kathrine had heard the horses panic and even the sound of the snake and hoped that Blaze was all right. Then she laughed at herself. Here she was being held captive in a small shack, and she was worried about her horse.

———

Blaze continued to run, heading northwest to her ancestral canyon.

Pete, Rafe and Frank were almost halfway to the canyon shack and Frank was smiling. He had been given instructions by his father to sweet-talk the Flannery girl but had already decided to do more than just that. A little sweet-talk and some good Frank loving would bring her around. Rafe saw the smile and wasn't happy about it, but it wasn't his call. He wasn't the boss.

———

Lee had maintained his northern path. It was after four o'clock and he would be losing the sun in another hour and was about to turn west, when he heard hooves approaching from the east; but not running hooves, walking hooves. He turned to the sound and almost started laughing in relief when he saw Blaze walking toward him. Jin nickered at Blaze, who responded and gladly trotted toward them.

Lee couldn't believe his luck when he'd spotted her. Blaze would have left an easy trail to follow, but when she was close, he noticed that the horse was both winded and sweating and wondered why she had run.

He grabbed a canteen, dismounted and walked up to Blaze, talking to her as he went. Blaze knew the voice and walked to Lee as he removed his hat and poured the entire canteen into the large crown and let Blaze drink every drop as he rubbed her neck.

"Blaze, you are one outstanding girl and I thank you for showing me the way."

————

Back at the farm, Ed Richards, who had arrived just as Blaze had made her dash, was explaining his position to Ian. Inside, Ian was seething at the duplicity of the man, but he remained externally calm, which was somewhat of a miracle for an Irishman.

"Look, Ian, I know we've had our differences, but I think I can help you find your daughter. One of my hands was out riding and saw three horses and one of the horses had someone draped over the saddle."

Ian shook his head and said, "Explain to me why you think hay is as important as my daughter's life."

"I'm not saying that. I'm just telling you that signing the contract is a good way to establish a solid working relationship between your farm and my ranch. Now, you'll admit I'm offering you more money than you're getting from those other ranchers. You'll make an extra two hundred dollars for this year's crop alone. What do you say, Ian?"

Ian was conflicted. He knew that Lee was out there and may have already found Kathrine, but he also knew that if he signed the contract, he could be sure that she'd be home safely.

"Alright," he finally agreed, "I'll sign."

Ed Richards was ecstatic but tried to hide it. Maggie, who stood nearby, could see the greed in his eyes as Ian signed the contract, so she stood, turned and left the room.

————

In the shack canyon, Rafe, Pete and Frank had arrived, and he had no sooner stepped down when Rafe noticed was the damage to the hitchrail and the absence of the girl's horse.

"What the hell happened to her horse?" he asked angrily.

Otto replied, "Rattlesnake panicked all of 'em. The girl's horse pulled apart the old hitch rail and took off. We chased it, but it was racing away too fast. The good news is that it turned northwest, away from the farm. We watched it disappear. You didn't see it, did you?"

"No, I didn't see the horse. I guess it couldn't be helped, but I don't like it," Rafe said as he wiped his hand across his brow to clear the sweat.

Otto and Chili were anxious to leave, and quickly mounted up and left the shack and the canyon as the other three men began to remove their horse's tack and get their bedrolls out.

————

It was closing in on sunset, and the light was fading, but Lee was tracking Blaze's trail easily. He hoped he would be able to find its starting point before the light was gone when he stopped and looked straight ahead, and thought he saw something about two miles away. He quickly took his field glasses out of his saddle, snapped them to his eyes, and as he peered through the lenses, he saw two riders who had just exited a small canyon. He was sure that the canyon must be where they were holding Katherine.

With his goal set, he mounted Jin and trailed Blaze's hoofprints to the southeast. He moved at a good clip, knowing that the low light left only the sound from Jin's hooves as a warning of his approach, and that would only become an issue if he were in front of the canyon mouth, and wouldn't reach it for another six more minutes. His only questions now were; *how far into the canyon were they holding Katherine and what was the setup?*

————

Rafe and Pete were settling in for another boring night behind the shack and already had stoked the fire for their dinner which had to be shared with their guest.

Katherine was getting hungry again but didn't want to talk to them unless she had to but could hear them talking and knew one would come through the door within ten minutes.

But just a minute later, she heard the bar being removed and when the door opened, she was surprised to see the grinning face of Frank Richards. She knew who he was and even at her tender age, understood what he was just by the leering look in his eyes that was obvious even in the low light.

Frank continued to smile as he said, "Well, good evening, Miss Flannery. I hope you're comfortable. I thought I'd see if I could help you pass some of your lonely time."

Katherine didn't answer but suddenly wished for one of the other men to come inside as she backed to her cot.

Frank reached behind him and closed the door.

————

Lee had pulled up about a hundred feet from the canyon mouth, then dismounted and let Jin control Blaze with the trail rope. He took the shotgun, pulled back both hammers and stepped quietly toward the canyon's mouth. As soon as the opening began revealing its secrets, he could see the light of a fire reflecting off the walls and then picked up the shack just fifty yards or so into the canyon, but he also could see three horses standing behind it as well. That meant there were three kidnappers he would have to eliminate which taking a delicate approach off the table. He was formulating a plan as he began a stealthy walk toward the shack, keeping his eyes on the horses, waiting for the guards to appear. He felt he had little time as something in his head told him to hurry.

———

Inside the shack, Frank had done all the sweet-talking he thought was necessary and the girl still hadn't looked at him with anything less than a mix of disgust, hate and fear.

He stepped even closer to her and said, "Well, you little sweet thing, I think you need to learn what it's like to be a woman. How'd you like Frank to show you how to do that?"

Katherine snapped, "Go away, you bastard!"

Frank didn't reply but slapped Katherine across the face hard, sending her crashing into the wall. Outside, Rafe and Pete heard the commotion and Rafe knew what Frank was doing, but it wasn't his business.

———

Lee had gotten within fifty feet of the cabin and had heard the commotion as well, so his time was up. He had only one choice, and that was to eliminate the two that must be behind the cabin near the fire and the horses, so he stepped quickly and as quietly as possible toward the cabin.

———

Katherine hand was against her pained cheek and her terror was engulfing her. *Why wouldn't those two other men help her? Were they going to come in and abuse her after Frank was finished with her?*

Frank's grin had been replaced with a malevolent stare as he stepped forward, then suddenly grabbed her blouse, ripping it apart and exposing her.

She hurriedly tried to cover herself, but he grabbed her ankles, throwing her off balance and onto the floor, then yanked off her riding skirt, snapping the buttons free.

"Now, I'm gonna give you what you need, even if you don't want it. I like it when you girls fight," he said in a low, ominous voice as he began to unbutton his britches.

———

Lee was so close to the small building that he could hear the cloth rip and Frank's threats and he knew his time was almost gone, so he forgot about being quiet as he trotted past the wall and almost immediately spotted the two silhouettes outlined by the fire.

Rafe had his back to him, but Pete spotted Lee when he appeared, but neither had even heard his last dash as they'd been listening to what Frank was doing in the shack.

Before Pete could cry out, Rafe saw Pete's face and began to turn, but it was too late.

Lee had brought the shotgun level at twenty feet, and pulled the trigger, just as Pete was beginning to rise. Both barrels exploded in a massive display of flame and smoke that was followed by the awesome sound created by the gunpowder's ignition.

The massive, close impact of dozens of lead pellets did their lethal work almost instantly, as Pete absorbed no less than a dozen of the bullets in his chest and gut and Rafe caught eight on the side of his head and neck. Neither man lived to hear the roar echo through the canyon.

Lee paid no attention to the two victims of the blast, but as soon as the shotgun blast left the barrels, he dropped the gun, whirled and ran ten steps to the front door and yanked it open.

Frank had jumped away from Katherine at the sudden blast that sounded close enough to be in the room, and wondered for a moment what Rafe had done to Pete, knowing that the two didn't get along, but just seconds later the door was suddenly yanked open and there was someone there that wasn't Rafe or Pete. Frank barely had a chance to see the man's eyes as his hands grabbed him.

Frank still had his shirt on, but his trousers were around his ankles as Lee grabbed him by the scuff of his neck, and after pulling him from the small dwelling, lifted him like a toy over his head as he screamed and squirmed to no avail and hurled him the ten feet to the side wall of the canyon.

Frank continued flailing his arms as he flew through the air before he slammed into the granite wall, his head crushed in the impact, then slowly slid to the ground.

Lee didn't even look at Frank after he had seen him hit the wall of unforgiving granite, but quickly turned back to the shack, saw a naked Katherine cowering in the low light with a look of horror still on her face.

Katherine was in a state of shock at what had just happened and hadn't even recognized Lee in the low light. All she knew was that Frank was going to rape her and suddenly, Frank was gone.

Then her eyes blinked as she recognized that it had been Lee that had pulled Frank from the shack and she felt an unusual mixture of intense relief and embarrassment for her nakedness as he walked closer to her.

Before he said a word, she saw Lee begin unbuttoning his shirt, and Katherine's eyes grew wide in disbelief. *What was he doing? Not Lee, too!*

Lee still hadn't spoken, but when he removed his shirt, he held it out to Katherine and said, "Katherine, you can put this on. Are you all right?"

"Are they all gone?" she asked in a shaky voice as she reached out and took Lee's shirt.

"They are all gone to hell where they belong," said Lee in a reassuring voice.

Then inexplicably, she asked, "Is Blaze all right?"

Lee smiled at her and said, "Yes, sweetheart, she's fine. You get dressed and then when you're ready, we'll go and get her."

Lee then left the shack and walked around the back to retrieve his shotgun while Katherine dressed.

Katherine quickly donned his large shirt, which almost covered her completely, but then had to tighten it around her waist to make room for her riding skirt. Without the buttons, it was a bit loose, but Lee's shirt helped to keep it in place.

When she was dressed, she left the shack walked up to Lee who was waiting outside the door and was going to say, "Let's go," but instead, wrapped her arms around him tightly and began to cry.

Lee held her and let her release the pain and terror that must have filled since they'd taken her from Nueva Luz and wished he could shoot every one of them again.

After a minute or so, Katherine stopped and released her death grip on Lee, looked up at him and smiled as she said, "I'm better now. Thank you, Lee. I knew you'd come."

"I wish I had made it sooner, Katherine. Do you know why I was able to find this place at all?"

"No."

"I was a few miles northwest of here and had lost the trail. I was going to lose the light when I saw Blaze come trotting up to us, so I was able to follow her trail back to you."

"Thank you for giving me Blaze, Lee. I'll always treasure her."

"I know, Katherine. Now, I need to do some grizzly work. I want you to just sit over here on this rock. It'll take me about fifteen minutes to get this done. Did you want me to call Blaze?"

"She'll come to you?"

"No. But she's attached to Jin."

"Yes, please. I want to thank her and give her a big hug."

"Jin!" Lee shouted, then turned back to Katherine and said, "I'll be right back."

Lee went around back and picked up Frank first. He wasn't very heavy. Earl pulled up his pants first. He didn't cotton to seeing Frank's naked butt or any other things. He lifted him and took him to the horses. Miraculously, none of the horses were hit with his shotgun blast. Lee looked at the angle and saw that the horses were off to the right of the line of fire. It had just been their luck to be kept safe. He really hadn't cared at the time. He guessed Frank's horse was the one with the gun belt looped around the saddle horn, so he took the gunbelt and placed it near his empty shotgun then threw Frank unceremoniously over the saddle and used Frank's own rope to lash him down.

Lee removed the gunbelts from the other two and put them in the pile. Then he threw pretty Pete Jones over his saddle. *Not so pretty anymore*, Lee thought. He used some pigging strings on Pete because he had no rope.

Rafe was a bloody mess, but Lee couldn't care less. He was heavier than the other two, so it took more effort to get him over the saddle. Then he tied down Rafe and tied a trail rope to the three horses, put the three gunbelts around his shoulder, picked up the shotgun and led them around the front of the cabin. Lee glanced at the dying fire and let it go rather than waste any water.

He walked the horses up to Jin and tied the trail rope to the three body-draped horses around his saddle.

Katherine was already mounted on Blaze and was focusing her attention to the south where her family waited for her and away from the three bodies.

Lee stepped up on Jin, looked at her and said, "Let's go home, Katherine."

She smiled at Lee, then nodded before they started the horses south. Neither talked about the bloody cargo.

Once they were underway, Lee said, "Now, Katherine, I know you're anxious to get home, gut don't go racing off on me. I demand the right to watch their faces when you walk in the front door and surprise the hell out of them."

"I can't wait, Lee," she replied, feeling giddy already, "And, Lee, I'm really happy that you're marrying Mary. She was so hurt by what happened to her and we thought she'd never come back us as her normal, happy self. Now she's not only back, but she's happier than any of us can recall."

"Well, Katherine, she's helped me, too, and I have to admit I am impressed with all of the Flannery women. You showed a lot of courage back there, Katherine, and I won't even bother to ask where your derringer is."

Katherine grimaced, and confessed, "It's in my room."

Lee looked over at her and laughed, "Well, so much for that."

Katherine laughed at her own failure to keep the small pistol, not realizing that it had almost cost her a world of pain.

Twenty minutes later, they could see the lights of the farmhouse and Katherine began to smile in earnest.

"We're almost home, Lee!" Katherine exclaimed loudly.

"And I don't know about you, Katherine, but I sure could use some hot food."

"And a hot bath!" she cried.

Five minutes later, the five horses stopped in front of the house, but no one inside had heard them approach. They were all in the main room talking about Katherine and the contract, so they didn't hear the footsteps on the porch, either. But they did hear the door squeak on its hinges as it swung wide.

Lee had let Katherine go in alone, so he stayed on the porch and watched through the screen door. He wanted her to have the attention she deserved.

"I'm home ..." was all she said before bedlam broke loose.

The first to reach her was Maggie, who quickly wrapped her in her arms as tears flowed everywhere.

Lee was enjoying watching the joyful reunion until Katherine turned and caught his eyes on the other side of the screen door and said, "Lee, please come in. I need to get changed and give you your shirt back."

As Lee walked into the room, Katherine scampered away to get changed and he was suddenly aware that he was shirtless as everyone was gawking; especially Mary.

"What happened, Lee?" asked Ian quietly.

Lee gave a short version of everything that happened, ending with the three bodies outside.

No one had asked a question yet as Katherine entered the room to give Lee his shirt back.

She smiled as she held it out to him and said, "Here you are, Lee. It was a little big for me anyway."

She hadn't noticed her family's stunned silence until she looked at Lee with a curious look in her eyes.

"I just told them how you got out of there," he said.

"Oh."

Katherine then looked at Lee and suddenly realized in the lamplit room that he was still shirtless and understood at least why her sister was sitting with her mouth open.

The first question any of the family asked wasn't about Katherine's rescue and came from his fiancée.

"Lee," Mary finally asked, "Can you do me a favor?"

"For you anything, Mary."

"Can I give you a hug," she asked, "before you put your shirt back on?"

He smiled, then walked to his future wife as she stood and hugged her and could feel her hands sliding over his muscular back.

"Enough of that, you two," interrupted Maggie, "You're not married yet."

Lee leaned over and kissed Mary before stepping back and putting his shirt on as both Katherine and Mary watched. So, did Maggie for that matter.

"Now I know how you moved those barrels," commented Conor.

"Just work, Conor. Maggie, could Katherine and I persuade you to get something to eat. I know Katherine needs the food more than I do."

"Of course, I should have thought of it. I'll fix something," she said as she stood, then walked to the kitchen.

Lee said, "Before I eat, I've got to go outside and take care of Jin. Katherine, I'll take care of Blaze, too. I'll be back in ten minutes."

After he stepped outside to take care of the horses the remaining members of the Flannery family all clustered around Katherine to ask about her experience.

After the preliminaries about her abduction, she told them of the tiny shack they'd held her in and and how she was sure Lee would come for her and then when it was getting dark, she had given up. She said how she had prayed for her deliverance, but instead, Frank Richards had entered the shack and was going to molest her when she heard the shotgun blast and she knew it was Lee. Then the door opened, and he was there. At first, she said, she didn't realize it was him until she watched him pick up Frank and hurl him away as if he was a rag doll. Then she said how he had seen her naked but when he offered her his shirt, he turned his back, so she could dress in privacy. Mary was so proud of Lee she was ready to burst.

Lee then walked back into the room just fifteen seconds after Katherine finished the story and asked, "Now, for the Richards. What do you want to do, Ian?"

Ian hung his head and replied, "It's too late, Lee. I signed the contract. Richards still wins."

"Nonsense, Ian. The contract doesn't mean a thing. Besides, after I have something to eat, I'm going over there to deliver those three bodies. Then, I'm going to take that contract back."

Ian's eyes widened as he said, "Lee, you can't do that! There are too many of them over there. They'll kill you."

"No, they won't. This is going to end, Ian. Tomorrow you'll harvest your crop with a clear conscience," Lee replied as he walked toward the kitchen.

Mary caught up to him as he began to sit down at the table and said, "Lee, you can't do this. It doesn't matter anymore."

He waited for her to take a seat and took her hands as he said, "Mary, it most certainly does matter. That bastard has been intimidating, threatening the family, and then kidnapped Katherine. His son was going to rape her, and his father probably knew it. No one can get away with that. Sooner or later, he'd decide he'd want more. Maybe he'd try to take the farm itself instead of paying for the hay. Men like him never stop by themselves. They have to be stopped, and I will do it tonight."

Mary knew she had lost the battle, and said, 'Then I'll come with you."

Maggie heard her stubborn daughter and hoped Lee could talk her out of it.

"No, sweetheart, this is going to be very fast and possibly very deadly. I need to be sure there are no people around that I don't want to hurt. I will only hurt those that are there to hurt this family. If they choose to leave, then they can go. I need to eat something, then I'll ride over there."

Maggie was grateful for his victory but knew how dangerous it would be for him and all they could do was pray for his safety.

After Katherine arrived, she gave Lee some hot stew and biscuits, then poured some coffee into a cup and set it next to his bowl of stew. Katherine was on the other side of the table as her mother gave her a bowl as well and even as she dipped her spoon into the thick beef stew, she stopped to watch Lee calmly devour his stew. This was like something out of a fairy tale – a violent fairy tale.

Lee finished his food, stood and said, "Thank you, Maggie. You never cease to impress me."

He took one step forward, gave her a hug and a kiss on the forehead, then smiled at his future mother-in-law as if he was just going out for a Sunday ride.

Katherine began to rise to give him a farewell hug, but quickly returned to her stew, understanding that it had to be Mary's moment.

Lee turned to Mary, who rose and took his hand, then they walked out the kitchen door, crossed the short back porch into the back yard and headed for the barn.

Once inside, Mary said nothing as he saddled Jin, but simply watched as he loaded the shotgun with two more shells, then dropped two more into his jacket pocket. He checked his Colt, returned it to its holster, then he levered his Winchester, catching the ejected cartridge before releasing the hammer and reinserting the cartridge into the loading gate.

He slipped the Winchester into its scabbard, then turned to Mary who slowly stepped close to him.

"Come back to me, Lee," Mary finally whispered.

He framed her oval face in his big hands and said, "I'll always come back to you, my Mary. I love you too much not to."

He then held her close as he kissed her deeply to seal the promise before he released her from his arms and led Jin out to the front yard where the three body-laden horses stood.

Mary followed as he took the cache of pistols he had taken from the dead men and placed them on the porch along with their rifles from their scabbards.

He then turned, looked into Mary's eyes once more, smiled, mounted Jin, and turned him toward the road. Mary didn't shed a tear as she watched him leave. This was her man going to make things right, but her pride was tinged with an all-encompassing fear that he may never return to her.

CHAPTER 7

Lee turned south at the end of the farm road and walked Jin and the three carrion carriers toward the Diamond R and set his mind into a peaceful state. Violence should only be used as a last resort to solve a wrong, but this was probably going to take a lot of violence before it ended. He silently thanked his father for all the other skills he would need to get this settled.

———

Inside the ranch house at the Diamond R, Ed Richards was in his office celebrating by himself and Stella was up in her room getting changed after riding. He didn't care where his wife was, or even if she was still alive, for that matter. The only other person in the house was that Willie character. Why he kept him around, he couldn't remember but it didn't matter now. He was in a good mood as he stared at the contract on his desk, and even as Lee had suspected, was already making plans to take that Flannery ranch and avoid having a recurrence of the issue. It hadn't been just about the one-time sale of the cattle, but with a willing buyer, he could expand his herd much larger than it was now with the added water and all that hay.

That Willie character who was no longer needed, was upstairs. He had been in the front room when Stella came in wearing her riding clothes and had watched as she began undoing the top button on her blouse to change. Willie had seen her look at him as she passed, and he took the glance to mean she was inviting him for a fun night. *Why not?* There was no one else around and she seemed obviously willing.

He gave her a minute to prepare for his arrival, then he unbuckled his gun and left it in the chair before he walked upstairs quietly already anticipating what lay waiting for him in her bedroom. He walked to her room finding the door already ajar and Willie recognized it as a second invitation. He looked through the opening and saw Stella half naked already. *What a sight!* He quietly opened the door and then closed it behind him.

Stella looked up suddenly and was startled to see Willie walking towards her with a big smile on her face.

"Get out of my room, Willie!" she ordered, making a feeble attempt to hide her nakedness behind her hands.

Willie was surprised, but not in the mood to be denied as he said, "Now, Stella, you know that you invited me here. Come on, admit it."

He then took two more steps toward her where she stood near her dressing table.

Stella turned, dropping all pretense of modesty and reached for her scissors, and once they were firmly in her grasp, swung them at Willie, catching him on the arm with the sharp edge.

Willie was stunned by her reaction and rejection, and snapped, "Why, you bitch! Look what you did!"

He reached at her and wrapped both hands around her thin neck and squeezed.

Stella desperately tried to stab him with the scissors, but she was rapidly losing consciousness as she was exerting herself and no more oxygen was entering her system. She was jabbing ineffectively as Willie continued to squeeze her thin neck, his anger fueled by his initial desire. Then, Stella gasped loudly as her eyes rolled back into her head.

Willie felt the weight of her lifeless body in his hands, then quickly released her and hurriedly bent over Stella, thinking she might have just passed out, but soon realized that he had murdered her.

He quickly stood over her body, still breathing heavily from the brief struggle, and realized what had resulted from his uncontrolled anger and a panic overtook him and he knew he had to run, but just as he turned, the door suddenly opened.

Mrs. Richards entered the room, saw Stella's inert body on the floor and then whipped her head toward Willie, shouting, *"What have you done?"*

Willie had no idea who she even was but didn't care, as he had to escape and without saying anything, he rushed to the door, throwing the small woman eight feet to the far wall as he passed her, then raced down the stairs, grabbed his gun belt and blasted out the door. He quickly crossed the porch and stumbled down the stairs running to the barn. He was going to look for his horse but found Chili's already saddled and didn't want to waste the time. He needed to get out of there fast, so he leapt on Chili's horse and rode quickly out of the barn, out the access road and northwest toward town.

Chili was in the chow house when he heard Willie's panicked escape, and he and Otto, who had just finished eating, walked toward the barn.

"What was that, you reckon?" asked Otto.

"Don't know. But he came out of the house pretty fast. I think we should go check."

Ed Richards had heard Willie come charging down the stairs and waited to hear if anything else happened. It hadn't, so he shrugged it off and continued to run the numbers on the pending sale of a significant part of the herd next year and then began projecting future profits after he acquired the Flannery farm.

Up in Stella's room, Lucy Richards had gotten to her feet and walked to where Stella lay, still half-naked, but found no remorse for her death. Stella wasn't even related to her, but just was the product of her husband's philandering. He only took her Stella into the house to put Lucy in her place, saying 'Here, you can be a mama to this'. She was twenty-three when Stella had been given to her and had just finished nursing Frank.

She glanced back at Stella once more, then turned, walked down the hallway and then down the stairs.

Lee had entered the access road and picked up the pace, somehow missing Willie's escape in the low light. The steady clopping of the four horses on the hard dirt was loud enough to be heard by Otto and Chili at the front of the house, and they stepped toward the sound. Lee had his shotgun in his hands and didn't need any reins.

When he was within a hundred feel he spotted the two figures walking slowly away from the porch as they were outlined by the lamps from the house. Jin continued his pace as Lee cocked both hammers.

Otto and Chili stopped. They could make out a rider and three other riderless horses coming toward them and at first, they thought that the rider was bringing packhorses. Then almost simultaneously, they saw the shotgun in his hands and started to go for their pistols.

"Hold it right there!" shouted Lee as he swiveled the shotgun toward them, "I don't have any quarrel with you two yet. Drop those hoglegs and start walking. My argument is with your boss. If you want to be useful, you can bury your pals Rafe Henry and Pete Jones as well as Frank Richards. If you want to join them, by all means, go for those Colts."

Chili was smarter than Otto. Unfortunately, he was also close to Otto, so when he started to unbuckle his belt, it didn't save him when Otto, whose right hand was already on his pistol, thought he had an edge because of the distance. He thought it was one hundred feet but had seriously overestimated the gap in the dim light. It was less than forty feet, so when Otto pulled his pistol, Lee pulled his trigger. The roar of the double barrels shattered the silent night as the long flames temporarily lit up Jin's face.

Inside the house, Ed Richards jerked when the boom echoed against the house and pellets struck like powerful hail. He had started to leave his library and office when he stopped and turned back into the room. He looked out the office's door to the hallway and thought about closing the door, but then he heard footsteps on the porch, and he knew he didn't have the time. He quickly took his seat behind the desk and slid the top drawer back and saw his Colt revolver. He put his hand on the revolver and his finger on the trigger as he waited. Ed had already guessed who would be coming through the door, and he would surprise him when he did.

The footsteps approached and Ed moved to the front edge of his seat as he watched the front door. He glanced one more time at the side door, but didn't think that he would be coming that way, then turned his eyes back to the front and licked his lips, more out of fear than anticipation.

Lee saw the open library door and heard some noises inside the room, then unhooked his hammer loop and slowly walked to the doorway, until he saw Edward Richards sitting behind his desk.

Lee made a mistake in leaving his pistol in his holster, even though his hammer loop was off. He should have had it pointing at Ed, but for some reason, didn't believe that he was a threat.

"*What do you want?* You weren't invited here!" Richards growled.

"Yes, I was. You sent the invitation when you ordered the kidnapping of Katherine Flannery," Lee replied calmly.

"I did no such thing. I even offered to help them find her."

"You are one lying bastard, but I'll give you one thing, Richards, you stick to your lies. The problem for you is that Katherine is at home with her family right now and I have three horses out front, all wearing the Diamond R brand. Each one of them has a body draped across its saddle; three men I'm sure you'll know: Rafe Henry, some kid I don't know and Frank Richards."

Ed was sent into a rage as he screamed, "You killed Frank! You bastard! I'll have the law on you for this!"

"It's a funny thing about the law, Ed. They don't cotton to men trying to rape a young girl. You sent Frank there to do that, didn't you, Ed? I had to shoot Rafe and the other one to get to the shack fast enough to keep Frank from assaulting that sixteen-year-old innocent girl. Now Frank didn't get shot. I pulled him away from Katherine picked him up over my head with his naked behind facing the moon and threw him against the canyon wall where he met up with some hard rocks. But he didn't suffer enough as far as I was concerned."

All this grief, Ed. All for what? Some extra hay and some more money? Don't you have enough? You try to destroy a family just to get what you want, and it probably wasn't going to stop there, either. This ends tonight, Ed!"

Outside in the hallway, Lucy Richards was listening as Lee threatened her husband and gripped the pistol she had carried for years then slipped forward silently.

Lee walked up to the desk and put his hands on the surface.

"Ed, I was going to come in here and shoot you, but that's too good for you. I think maybe if all this was just taken from you that you'll learn what it's like to be an honest man. I'm going to bring you into town, Ed. They'll try you and then they'll hang you. You'll have all that time to wonder what it will feel like when they put that noose around your neck."

Lee started to stand straight when Ed Richards pulled the Colt from the desk and Lee finally understood that he had made a fatal error. He reached for his Colt, just getting it clear of his holster as Ed Richards just smiled, knowing he had won as he cocked the hammer. But before he could pull the trigger, there was a loud gunshot to Lee's left, and Ed Richards head jerked sideways.

Lee snapped his head to his left and saw Lucy Richards standing with her hand outstretched holding a smoking revolver in her hand. As he watched, she lowered it slowly and dropped it to the floor.

Then she turned and looked at Lee as said calmly, "Lee, I believe I'm going to need your help."

Lee was perplexed, to say the least. *Who was this woman? She just shot Ed Richards, and she knows who he is?*

Lee was still trying to understand what had just happened, but recovered enough to say, "Yes, ma'am, I'll be glad to help, but I don't believe I've had your acquaintance."

"I was Lucy Richards. I may still be that legally, but I won't be living here any longer. You told him that you killed Frank?"

"Yes, ma'am. I'm sorry, but he was about to rape Katherine Flannery and I couldn't allow that."

"I listened to the whole story, Mister Ryan. Do you know how Frank was conceived? That bastard that I just shot raped me when I was nineteen. My father, for the sake of family honor, forced him to marry me. Then he arranged for us to move out here as far away from his family as he could send us. In one violent action, that worthless excuse for a man made me an outcast. He took me away from someone I genuinely loved; a man who offered to marry me despite my being deflowered. But my father wouldn't allow it. He wanted me out of the house, out of the state, and out of his life. So, we came here. Ed never even took me to bed after that, which suited me fine. But his womanizing was his life back then. That's how I got saddled with Stella. She wasn't even my daughter, you know. Frank had just finished breast feeding and that piece of trash who called himself my husband gave me the daughter of one of his conquests and told me to feed this one, too. They both grew up just like him. Did you know that Stella is dead, too?"

Lee was stunned as he asked sharply, "How? I would never shoot a woman."

"I understand that, although I might disagree with your reasoning for not shooting women. She was strangled just before you arrived by a man you know well, Willie Thompson. As I don't intend to stick around, Mr. Thompson may get away with it as there are no other witnesses."

Lee was being hit by one stunning revelation after another by the remarkable woman standing before him and almost felt obligated to match her incredible aplomb.

"No, ma'am, he will not escape punishment. I won't rest until justice is served."

Lucy smiled at him and said, "I expected nothing less from you, Lee. You impress me as that rarest of men, Mister Ryan. One with honor and decency which are as important to you as your strength of character and mind. You see, Lee, you are a true oddity. You try to help those that need it, even if it means risking your own life like you did tonight. Well, Mister Ryan, I am leaving this house in the morning. I am taking the train back to Philadelphia and I'll empty the bank account before I return east. Do you have any money, Lee?"

Lee was using every bit of his control to try to keep up with Lucy Richards as he replied, "Yes, ma'am. I have quite a lot in the bank. I need it though because I'm building a home for me and Mary Flannery."

"So, I've heard. Congratulations on that, by the way. I have many sources of information and I knew about that poor girl and how she'd been treated. You really do love her, don't you?"

"I really can't explain just how much to anyone, even to her. I'll just have to go through the rest of our lives showing her."

"Back to the subject of money, Lee. I was asking if you had any money in your pockets."

"Yes, ma'am. About eighty-five dollars."

"Give it to me, will you, please?"

Lee had no idea what was going on. Maybe she needs money for her train ticket. He reached into his pocket and pulled out four gold double eagles and three silver dollars.

He handed it to her and said, "I was wrong, ma'am, all I have is eighty-three dollars. Will that be enough for your needs?"

She smiled at him and replied, "I think this is sufficient. Would you please take a seat?"

Lee sat down as she walked past her dead husband's body, pulled open the bottom drawer and removed a metal box, then opened the center drawer, took out a key, opened the box and searched through some papers. She found what she was looking for, dipped a pen into the bottle of ink.

She wrote for a minute and then let it sit to dry before walking past her husband's corpse again and standing near Lee.

"Mister Ryan, I believe we have seven bodies to clean up. Would you be able to do that?"

"Yes, ma'am. Did you have any specific instructions?"

"Yes. Find a hole and put them in it. If you can do that and then return, I'll wait for you in the parlor."

"Yes, ma'am. It may take me some time to get the hole dug, though."

"The tools are in the barn, but the good news for you is that they had already dug a hole just on the left of the access road for bodies they thought they'd be producing."

"Bodies?" he asked, stunned by what she had said.

"I don't believe that creature that called himself my husband was going to stop at just getting his hay."

"I thought he might do something more heinous, but not so soon."

"Evil follows no calendar, Lee. I was counting on you to stop it. If you had failed, I was going to put an end to it soon, even though I knew it would probably result in my death."

Lee was having a difficult time absorbing the information but was totally taken by Mrs. Richards and her extraordinary behavior.

"Well," he finally replied, "having the hole already dug will save a lot of time. I'll be back."

Mrs. Richards nodded with a smile on her face as he stood and for just a few brief seconds, their eyes met. That short shared gaze told Lee a lot about Lucy Richards and astonished him even more. *What an extraordinary woman!*

Thoroughly flummoxed, Lee set about the cleanup. He started with the closest body belonging to Ed Richards. Disregarding the damage that would be done to his own shirt, he picked up Richards, threw him over his shoulder and walked him outside. He just tossed him over the same horse that held Pete Jones, then he went back inside. He didn't bother asking Mrs. Richards where Stella's body was, but figured the bedrooms were on the second floor, so he climbed the stairs and headed for the only open door. He saw the semi-naked dead body of Stella and pulled a quilt from the bed. He wrapped her in the quilt and took her downstairs and added her to the horse holding Frank, then led Jin down the road, looking for the hole. There was enough moonlight available to find it easily and after stopping beside the gaping blackness in the earth, just dropped Ed in without ceremony. He did the same with Jones and Rafe. He treated Stella with more reverence, simply because she was a woman, yet still a woman without conscience. Then he dropped Frank in before he walked the horses back to the yard and tossed Chili on one and had to strain to get Otto on a horse, but he did. He walked into the barn and picked up a shovel then returned to the burial site. The hole was a large one, and he wondered who they expected to bury but the thought made him shudder. After he slid the last two bodies into the pit, he began shoveling dirt into the hole. It took him almost an hour to finish covering the bodies, but it still was all done in a lot less time than if he'd had to dig the hole. He knew he should say something once the job was done, but he couldn't find any words that he could say.

He returned to the big house, sweaty, dirty and bloody and found Lucy Richards sitting quietly in the parlor. She smiled at him when he entered, and Lee realized how handsome she still was and wondered just how pretty she was when she was younger.

"Done already?" she asked.

"Yes, ma'am. Having that huge hole there made it a lot easier."

"Lee, if you don't mind, please call me Lucy. And would you take a few minutes to tell me about Mary? I feel as if I know her already, although we've never met."

Lee found a seat but didn't lean back to avoid transferring his dirt and mud to the chair, then said "I'd be only too happy to, Lucy. She's the one topic I never get tired of discussing. Besides being a physically beautiful woman, she is a spiritually and emotionally beautiful woman. Before I knew how much I loved her, I would just spend as much time as I could just talking with her. I found that no matter how much I discovered about her, there was always more. She had such depth, and her intelligence and levels of compassion were almost overwhelming. But there was always the joy and laughter, until she was lost to me after a stranger named John Everett took advantage of her innocence."

She told me that she did so willingly, but I know that a good part of it was that she believed she was in love and hungered for it. Unfortunately, the man took her, then left her lying on the picnic blanket as she went from a euphoria of imagined love to the very real pain of rejection and shame. She was like that for two years. She wouldn't even talk to me during that time and was hounded by a number of boys because that Satan incarnate was not only satisfied with taking her, he had to go into town and brag about how easy it had been. She went into a deep shell that I thought she would never leave."

"But you brought her out of it. Didn't you, Lee?"

"I had to, Lucy. I was miserable, and she was worse. I knew I loved her completely, but I needed my Mary back; the happy Mary, the real Mary. So, I showed her the house I had been building for us near my canyon. It was a large house and as we walked through the unfinished rooms, she was still quiet and distant. But when we made it to the atrium, the one I had designed just for her, she stopped and asked why I had built it for her. Then, she finally opened her heart and poured out her worries and shame over what had happened and how she was being treated. I told her how much I loved her and wanted to marry her. She came back to me, then, Lucy. My Mary was returned to me."

Lee didn't understand why he was being so open to Lucy Richards. It was as if he'd known her for years after that one tiny glimpse into her soul.

Lucy sat back and looked lovingly at Lee.

"Her story is not so different from mine, Lee, except she had a loving family that accepted her. My father rejected me like I had done something wrong. But Mary had you and I had Jefferson. Now, I'll be able to go back to him."

She sighed and said, "Well, Lee, I have only one more request of you."

"Yes, ma'am?"

"Tomorrow morning at eight o'clock, could you come here and hitch up my buggy and take me to the bank and then the train station?"

"I'd be happy to do that, Lucy."

"Perfect. What will you do about the law?"

"I'll explain to the sheriff what I did and why. If he chooses to arrest me, I'll live with those consequences."

"You are truly a remarkable man, Lee," Lucy said with a warm smile.

"Thank you, Lucy, and may I honestly say, you are an extraordinary woman."

She expanded her smile and said, "Coming from you, Lee, and knowing of your firm belief in honesty, that is a very high compliment."

He stood and offered his hand, then she rose shook it and said, "I'll see you in the morning then."

"Yes, ma'am. I'll be here."

He waved to her as he left the house, still trying to understand all that had happened since he'd arrived at the Diamond R. It had been the most unusual experience of his lifetime. He mounted Jin and led the three empty horses to the barn where he stripped them and brushed each one down before letting them eat and drink. He put them in stalls and remounted Jin.

After Lee had gone, Lucy Richards had things to do besides packing for her journey – so many things.

Lee trotted Jin down the access road, glanced at the large mound of dirt in the moonlight, and headed for the Flannery farm. He couldn't wait to see Mary and tell her of the night's extraordinary events.

Mary was beside herself as she stood on the dark porch. Lee had been gone almost six hours and she'd heard gunfire in the distance. It was past midnight when she heard the trotting of a horse in the darkness. *It had to be him! Please! It had to be Lee!*

There was only the moonlight, but when she could see the lightness of the horse, she shouted, "Lee!" and was rewarded with, "I'm home, Mary."

Mary ran from the porch and met Lee and Jin as they neared the house. Lee had seen her coming and quickly dismounted just in time to catch a flying Mary Flannery, despite his need for a good bath.

Soon, they were wrapped into one chaotic bundle as Jin stood by patiently while they let their emotions run amok. Finally, he set her down.

She asked breathlessly, "What happened, Lee? You were gone so long."

"More than you can imagine, sweetheart. Let's go to the house and I'll cover everything. To be honest, I can't believe some of it myself. First, we need to stop at the barn and take care of Jin and I really need to get clean."

Mary walked with him, holding his hand as they headed for the barn in the moonlight, just exulting in having him returned to her alive and well.

After making sure Jin was comfortable and complimented, Lee and Mary walked back to the house through the kitchen door where the lamps were still lit, and they were soon greeted by a wave of redheads anxious for news. In the light, they all could suddenly see the blood stains on Lee's shirt.

"*Lee, are you hurt?*" asked Maggie, with alarm in her voice.

"No. Maggie, this belongs to someone else. I don't know whose, though. Do you have some coffee?"

"Of course, I do. You go and sit in the family room and I'll bring you some."

They all made it to the family room and sat in their now accustomed positions as Lee sat next to Mary on the couch. Maggie brought Lee his coffee and then sat with the others, all waiting to hear the story.

Lee took a deep swallow of the warm, but not hot liquid and began to tell them of the extraordinary night.

"First, Ian, you don't have to worry about the contract. It is null and void."

"Bless you, Lee," Ian replied.

"Don't go thanking me too soon, Ian. I may have created another problem for you. By tomorrow morning at eight o'clock, the Diamond R will be empty. There will be no more Richards on the ranch and I think all of the real ranch hands had already deserted the place."

"You killed them all, even Stella?" asked a shocked Katherine.

"No. Let me explain. Like I said, it was a most unusual night. I showed up leading the three horses. As I got close, I could see two men near the front of the house walking toward me. I had my shotgun cocked and when I got close enough, I warned them not to do anything and to drop their weapons and leave. One was smart enough to start dropping his gun belt, but the fat guy, Otto, went for his gun. It was the other man's bad luck to be within six feet of Otto when I touched off the scattergun. Then I left the shotgun in the sling and went into the house. It was eerily quiet and I found Ed Richards at his desk, sitting there. We had a few words, and then I made a real blunder and put both hands on his desk. He pulled a gun out of the drawer and had me dead to rights. My Colt was barely out of its holster when I heard a shot and watched Ed Richards fall over dead with a shot to the head. I was shocked, and I looked to my left and saw a woman of about forty, standing there with a pistol in her hand. It was Lucy Richards."

"*She shot her own husband?*" asked a disbelieving Maggie.

"She did, and that was my introduction to one of the most remarkable people that I've ever met."

After he explained her personal story and her marriage to Ed Richards, he continued.

"She is a truly remarkable woman. She seems to have a network of informants that keep her apprised of local events. Mary, she knew we were getting married, and even about what happened to you two years ago. She said to tell you that she thought very highly of you."

They were all so mesmerized that no one asked any questions.

"She told me how Stella had died when Willie Thompson, my erstwhile partner, had entered Stella's bedroom and Willie strangled her before running out. He's still out there, but I'll find him."

But then it got even stranger, if you can believe it. She told me that she was leaving on the train in the morning for Philadelphia and asked me to pick her up at eight o'clock in the morning, so I could take her to the bank where she would empty the account and then I could take her to the depot to catch the morning train. I told her I would, then she asked me how much money I had. I had eighty-three dollars on me, and she asked if she could have it, so I gave it to her. I guess she needed it for the ticket, although that didn't make any sense if she was closing out the bank account."

Anyway, she asked if I could bury all seven bodies. I said I could, but it would take some time. But then she told me that they had already dug a large hole to get rid of some other bodies. She didn't know whose but told me that she didn't believe Ed Richards was going to stop at just getting the contract for your hay. When I returned after burying the bodies, she asked me about Mary. I talked for a while, because that is my favorite subject, then she said as she was the only witness to her husband's and Stella's deaths, and as she was leaving for Philadelphia tomorrow, how would I explain it to the law? I told her I'd just go tell the sheriff what happened and just see how the law handles it."

He paused, then took one long, deep breath to conclude the story.

"So, tomorrow morning, I'll be taking Lucy Richards to the bank and train depot. Then I'll go and talk to the sheriff. If I'm not in jail after that, I'll come back here by eleven o'clock and let you know what happened."

"So, what happens to the ranch, then?" asked Ian.

"That's the other problem I created for you Ian. If it's abandoned, and it sounds like it will be, the ranch will go to auction in a couple of years unless Ed Richards had a brother or sister and they could claim it. That means that although your contract is gone, you'll still have a lot of hay with no market."

"Ah. That's not true, Lee. I have plenty of market. I have customers waiting in line, so don't worry about a thing."

"Have I left anything out?" asked Lee.

"How did your shirt get so bloody?" asked Katherine.

"Moving the bodies. Speaking of that, I'm going to go and wash my shirt out and then get some sleep. I think everyone else needs to sleep, too. It's been an overly exciting day."

"I'll take care of your shirt," said Maggie.

"No, Maggie. You all need your rest. You have a harvest to get in. I can handle this. I'm going to clean up and get some sleep and suggest that you all get some sleep yourselves."

Lee could barely keep his eyes open any longer as he was emotionally drained by the day's events, so he stood, then walked out of the house to the front porch,] but wasn't surprised when Mary soon exited the house to catch him.

"Lee, I'm very worried. They won't put you in jail, will they?"

"I hope not, Mary, but it's up to the sheriff. All of this happened outside of his jurisdiction, so he should notify the county sheriff or the U.S. Marshal's office. We'll see what he does. You go and get some sleep, Mary. You look tired."

"I am. But I'm more worried than tired, Lee."

"Mary, I understand, but I don't believe I've done anything wrong. The five men that I killed tonight were committing serious crimes or about to shoot me. If I felt differently, I'd be worried myself. But you just need to know one thing, Mary. That I will always be here for you. You are my Mary."

"I love you, Lee. I'll see you before you go."

"I'll look forward to that, Miss Flannery," he replied with a gentle smile.

She gave him a quick good-night kiss, then turned and entered the house as Lee stepped down from the porch.

Lee spent ten minutes scrubbing out his shirt in the trough, then washed off his own grime before walking with his wet shirt into the barn where he hung it from a hook. He was exhausted and thought he'd fall asleep seconds after sliding into his bedroll, but he didn't find sleep easily as he worried about what would happen tomorrow. Despite what he had told Mary, he was very concerned about what the law would do. There were no living witnesses to most of the killing. It would just be his word, and while that might hold sway with the sheriff, it might not have any worth at all with those that would be responsible for crimes in their jurisdictions.

He slipped back out of his bedroll, then walked to the front porch and sat in one of the three rocking chairs where he started rocking, and let his mind ponder other things than his possible legal troubles. He wondered about what he could do about Willie. Lucy had expected him to find Willie and bring him to justice and for some obscure reason, he felt he owed her that. He owed Stella that too, despite her faults. Then he speculated about Willie's whereabouts. As far as he knew, Willie didn't know a lot about the area, so maybe he'd head for Lee's canyon and his unoccupied cabin.

After a while, he began to nod and fell asleep around three o'clock in the morning, then woke up with a start three hours later when he heard noise behind him. There was someone awake in the house. He noted the predawn and guessed it was around six o'clock, and he needed to get ready to visit the Diamond R and meet Lucy Richards again.

He stood and stretched, feeling a lot stiffer than he had expected. Then again, burying seven bodies and then sleeping in a rocking chair would do that.

He answered nature's call and then washed outside before he went to his saddlebags, took out his shaving kit and shaved before he removed his dry shirt from the hook in the barn and put it on, then left the barn and headed for the kitchen where he found Maggie and Mary cooking breakfast.

"Good morning, ladies," he said on entering.

"Where did you sleep last night?" asked Maggie.

"Um, I fell asleep on the porch in a rocking chair," he admitted.

Maggie just shook her head and muttered, "Men," then said to Lee, "Well, at least you look better. Sit yourself down and I'll feed you in a few minutes."

Lee looked over at Mary and smiled as he said, "I guess I'd better do what the fine Irish lady just said."

The men folk came drifting in and Lee could tell they were dressed for heavy work today. The harvest would start in just a few hours and Lee greeted them individually as he sat with his coffee cup.

Mary began doling out platters of scrambled eggs and ham as Mary put a large plate of biscuits on the table with a bowl of butter, and they began to eat. Lee assumed Katherine would be sleeping in a bit after her ordeal yesterday.

He waited until all the working men had filled their plates before taking some eggs and a slice of ham. He took one biscuit before Mary joined him and put some food on her plate. As she ate, she reached under the table and took his hand, looked at Lee and smiled. He smiled back and gave her hand a gentle squeeze.

The Flannery men all filed out to begin harvesting the hay, leaving Lee with Mary and Maggie.

"Maggie, how's Katherine this morning?" Lee asked.

"She's sleeping like a baby. We all felt that it was the best thing for her. You know, Lee, you've become a hero to her. She told me that she always knew you'd come and get her and then when you did, it was like a knight in one of her tales that she likes to read."

"I'm no hero, Maggie. I'm sure that when she's been around me more after I marry Mary, she'll discover I'm just another ornery Irishman. It'll be up to Mary to smooth out the rough edges."

"Well, you can say what you'd like, but we're all very grateful to have you around, Lee Ryan. And we're even happier that you'll be joining our family."

"Not as happy as I'll be."

He turned toward Mary and said, "This bonnie lass has stolen my heart and everything else. She is all that matters to me."

Mary simply stared into his eyes and smiled.

It was after seven o'clock, so Lee stood and said, "I'd better get going. Today should prove an interesting day."

He gave Mary a kiss and followed it with another kiss for Maggie.

"Tell Katherine I owe her a kiss, too. I'll be back by eleven o'clock."

He stepped out of the kitchen, into the back yard, then stepped quickly to the barn, and on the way, he saw the two harvesters being harnessed to their teams of mules and waved at the Flannery men. They waved back as he entered the barn and saw Jin.

"Good morning, Jin. I hope you're ready for some work. This won't be difficult as yesterday, but it could be just as interesting."

He saddled Jin and led him out of the barn and found Mary waiting by the barn door.

"I wanted to see you once more before you left, Lee. Can you hold me for a little while?"

Lee dropped Jin's reins and stepped over to her, then cradled her in his arms gently. No crushing hug this time. He knew Mary was crying as she pressed her head against his chest. Not the deep shuddering tears of her confession in the atrium, just a quiet discharge of fear and worry.

He leaned over to her and whispered, "I love you, my Mary. I'll be back to tell you that again soon."

She didn't answer, but just nodded and wiped her tears as he released her. Then she stepped back to let him go.

He climbed aboard Jin and rode out of the farm, stopped at the end of the short entrance and turned to see Mary watching. He waved to her and she returned the wave, then he turned Jin back around and headed south to the Diamond R.

Mary felt almost a feeling of doom overtake her as she returned to the house.

Lee set Jin to a fast trot. He would get there in ten minutes, leaving him plenty of time to harness the buggy.

As he turned into the long access road to the ranch house, he glanced to his right and saw the fresh dirt on the gravesite in the bright morning light, shivered as he thought of what lay under the blanket of soil, then rode on. He swung Jin toward the barn and when he dismounted and walked inside, he found the buggy at the back of the barn, and the harness hanging on the wall nearby. He wasn't sure which horse was supposed to be used for the buggy until he started taking the harness off its hooks and noticed that one black gelding seemed to be getting antsy. He took the gelding from its stall and backed it up to the buggy, attached the harness and led the gelding out of the barn pulling the buggy behind him.

He stepped into the buggy and drove it to the front of the house, set the brake, stepped out, tethered the horse to the hitching rail and stepped up onto the massive porch. Lee knocked on the screen door, noticing that the main door had been left open.

Lucy's voice echoed from the back of the house, when she said loudly, "Come in, Lee."

Lee opened the door entered the house and looked for Lucy but didn't see her.

That was clarified when she said, "I'm in the kitchen," and he headed down the long hallway.

Lee smiled as he stepped along, anticipating another conversation with Lucy.

He found her at a the nicely polished kitchen table drinking a cup of coffee and was stunned at her appearance. Now that she had some time to rest and then get ready, she was quite an attractive lady, and looked much younger than her forty years.

"Have a seat, Lee. I'm feeling my age this morning."

Lee smiled as he sat down and said, "Lucy, I never even thought of you as being anything but a very attractive woman."

She smiled at him broadly and said, "Well, thank you for that, Lee. Would you like some coffee?"

"That would be great. I'll get it."

Lee rose again, took a cup from a nearby shelf and filled it with hot coffee from the pot before he returned to his seat at the table.

"Are you ready to get rid of me, Lee?" she asked, smiling.

"Lucy, I'd wish you'd reconsider, or at least delay your departure. You are one of the most remarkable persons I have ever met, and it would be a real pleasure having you around."

"Be careful, Mister Ryan, if I were twenty years younger, I'd give that Mary of yours a run for her money," she said with a lively eye and a smile.

"Lucy, you wouldn't need twenty years, but my Mary is the only woman for me. You, on the other hand are simply an amazing lady that could spice things up around here."

"If there were more people like you here, I might take you up on that suggestion, but you are one of a kind, Lee. What I would like to do is for you to engage in correspondence with me after I've gone. Would you do that?"

"Lucy, it would be a great pleasure to do that. I haven't known you for a day, and I find that I will miss you immensely after you're gone."

"And I will miss you, Lee. Now, I suppose we must be going. I have a trunk upstairs. Would you be able to bring it down? It's rather heavy."

"It's not a problem. It can't be as bad as Otto Krueger."

She laughed, and replied, "True. I'll wait for you here."

Lee walked up the stairs and past Stella's room, then saw another room further down the hallway with an open door. He went inside, found Lucy's large trunk, and picked it up. It wasn't too heavy, at least not to Lee.

He put it over his shoulder, walked down the hallway and then down the stairs. Lucy watched as he effortlessly carried the trunk down.

"Are you ready to go, Lucy?" he asked when he reached the bottom floor.

"I'll follow you out the door, Lee."

Lee carried the trunk out the front door and heard Lucy close it behind her before he stepped down the porch and walked to the buggy. He set the trunk on the ground, flipped down the short shelf on back and placed the trunk on it. The same straps that held the shelf in place when it was not in use were used to secure the trunk, so he tightened them down and walked back to front of the buggy.

He stepped into the seat as Lucy was already aboard. In the brightness of the day, Lee was astonished to see that Lucy looked even more beautiful than she had in the dimly lit interior.

He looked at her and said, "Lucy, you amaze me again. If you hadn't told me your age, I would have not guessed you to be more than thirty. And a beautiful thirty at that."

"Is this more of that famous Irish blarney I've heard about, Lee?" she asked, smiling.

"Lucy, I have never lied in my life and I don't indulge in false flattery. You constantly surprise me. Maybe it is better that you go. I can't have you tempting me. As it is, I will look forward to writing to you and receiving your letters. I'll have to share them with Mary, though, for obvious reasons."

She laughed again before she said, "I understand, Lee. Now, let's start moving before I learn to blush all over again."

Lee laughed and started the carriage, keeping the horse at a slow trot to extend his time with Lucy as long as he could.

But the three-mile drive seemed all too short for them both as they engaged in lively conversation during the entire trip.

Eventually, they pulled up to the bank. Lee stepped out and Lucy surprised him by waiting until he came around to help her exit. She smiled at him as she took his hand. Lee hadn't been exaggerating about her appearance as other men stopped and looked at her as she stepped down. Lee noticed and cringed inside, knowing that he'd have to explain this to Mary.

As she took his arm, she said quietly, "I apologize, Lee. I thought you were just being nice. I hope I don't get you in trouble with Mary."

"I was thinking the same thing, Lucy."

He led her to a clerk's desk, and he held out a chair for her.

After she had taken a seat, he pulled a chair from a nearby empty desk and sat down next to her.

"How can I help you, ma'am?" asked the clerk.

"My name is Lucy Richards. I'll be returning to Philadelphia on the next train, and unfortunately, must close my account."

She produced two papers from her purse and handed them to the clerk. He looked at them and then looked back at her.

"How would you like this disbursed, Mrs. Richards? Realizing, of course, that we don't have sufficient funds to cover a full withdrawal."

"I understand. I'd like two hundred dollars in cash and a draft for the remainder."

"Very well."

Lee watched curiously as the clerk walked to the cashier's cage, wrote some notes and had the cashier sign a piece of paper. He signed it, accepted some currency from the cashier, and then returned.

"Here is your cash, Mrs. Richards, and your draft. We hate to lose you as a customer, but I'll need you to sign these forms and this receipt, please."

Lucy took the pen and signed all the papers before sliding them back to the clerk.

"Will there be anything else?" he asked.

"Yes, I'd like to get something notarized, please."

"Yes, ma'am," he answered.

Lee was still thinking about what Lucy Richards had given the clerk that would allow her to empty the account when it was probably in her husband's name. If her name was on it, then she could, but he couldn't imagine Ed Richards letting that happen, especially in light of what she had told him last night.

She pulled another packet of papers from her purse and signed the back of one of them and handed it to the clerk.

The clerk looked at the paper his eyebrows raised, but in good banking tradition, said nothing. He simply signed it as a notary and dated it. Then he waited for it to dry and handed it back to her.

"Will that be all, Mrs. Richards?"

"Yes, thank you. You've been a great help."

They shook hands and she stood, and Lee stayed sitting for another three seconds before he suddenly realized she was finished, then quickly rose from his seat, offered his arm, which she took, before they walked out of the bank.

The clerk watched them leave, still very curious about what had just happened.

Once outside, Lee helped her into the buggy and walked around the front. He untied the horse and stepped inside. It was 8:30, and the train had already arrived, and was scheduled to depart in thirty minutes.

"Well, Lucy, do we head to the depot? We can still chat a while before you leave."

"Don't you want to just kick me out of the buggy and be on your way?" she asked with a mischievous smile.

"Now, Lucy, that was almost mean-spirited. Here I was trying to convince you to stay, and you make it sound as if I want to be rid of you. You know I'd rather take up every second of your time before you depart. You just wanted to hear me say it."

She laughed then replied, "You have me there. It was a cheap theatric, wasn't it?"

"And totally beneath the normally razor-sharp wit that I've come to expect."

Lee started the buggy rolling toward the depot when they heard the whistle of the train announcing that it would be leaving soon.

When they reached the station, Lee hopped out and trotted around in back to help Lucy from the buggy.

"You know I'm only doing this so I can get to hold your hand," she admitted.

"I suspected as much, but you didn't hear me complain, did you?"

Lucy smiled and replied, "No. And thank you for that, too."

Lee then went to the back of the buggy, unlashed and lowered the trunk to the ground, and after restoring the flatbed to its stowed position, carried it to the station as Lucy walked next to him. Lee put the trunk down and waited as Lucy bought her ticket.

When he heard the cost of the first-class ticket to Philadelphia, Lee was impressed. It was eighty-three dollars and he wondered how she knew or if she knew. Nothing about Lucy Richards would surprise him anymore.

The stationmaster tagged her trunk and a freight attendant took it away as Lucy turned back to him, regained control of Lee's arm before they walked to a bench and sat down.

Lee looked at her and said, "Lucy, I hope that when you get to Philadelphia, you find some good man who can make a happy life for you. You're too good a person to go through life alone. You should find someone that appreciates all those incredible qualities that you possess. It's been a delight sharing the few hours we have spent together, in spite of the rather drastic way it started."

Lucy smiled and said, "As it happens, Lee. I do have someone in mind. When I was a young girl, before Ed Richards ruined my life, I was deeply in love with a young man not unlike yourself. Maybe that's why I've taken to you so quickly. I found that he is now divorced and living alone. I'm as nervous as a teenaged schoolgirl with the prospect of seeing him again."

"I really hope it works out for both of you, Lucy. When you get situated, write to me, so I can write to you in return."

The train's bell was ringing, and the conductor was shouting for all the passengers to board. It was time for Lucy to leave Nueva Luz.

Lucy stood, and Lee could see her eyes misting. He tried to control his own emotions as he had become very fond of Lucy in such an enormously short amount of time and sincerely wished he'd see her again.

He escorted her across the platform to her first-class car and then stopped before the car's entrance.

Before she boarded, Lucy turned to Lee and asked, "Lee, could I ask one last favor before I go?"

"Anything, Lucy."

She was looking into his eyes and said softly, "Kiss me."

Lee leaned forward to give her a kiss on the forehead and was surprised when Lucy put her arms around his neck, pulled him to her lips and kissed him like a fiancée leaving her beloved. Lee thought he owed it to her somehow and put his arms around her and continued the deep kiss.

Finally, she stepped back and smiled, as she sighed and said, "Thank you, Lee. I needed to do that and I'm so happy that I did and that you let me know how you felt."

The conductor was crying for all to board the train, and Lucy opened her purse, extracting the sheet of notarized paper. She pressed it into Lee's hand and said, "I hope you and Mary find more happiness there than I did. Give my love to Mary, and you will always have mine, Lee."

She stepped on the car's platform and waved as she entered. The train began rolling and Lucy was soon gone. and Lee missed her already. *What an incredible woman!*

He had almost forgotten the paper he held in his hand as he watched the train disappear over the horizon. When he did finally look at it, he was stunned. It was the deed to the Diamond R.

He stared at it for a few moments in disbelief, then he opened the deed and found a note from Lucy folded inside.

My dear Lee,

For too many years, I have lived in this house and been miserable and alone. Then I began paying attention to my surroundings and watching events unfold, living my life vicariously through others. I knew when you had arrived and how you felt about Mary almost before you did.

It was just happenstance what happened last night, but it freed me, Lee. You freed me. I know that you will make it all right. Take the ranch and make it a happy place rather than the miserable home it has been.

Tell Mary that I think she is a lucky woman. She must be an exceptional woman for someone like you to love her.

Now, take that deed to the land office and get it registered.

Love Always,

Lucy Ford (My maiden name. I will never use that other name again.)

P.S. I left many of my clothes that should fit your Mary perfectly and something else that you would have bought for her if you could. Tell her to wear them for me. And you, Lee, enjoy the library. My favorite is "Great Expectations."

To say that Lee was dumbfounded would be an understatement. He was expecting to go to the sheriff first but decided that he would take Lucy's advice and stop by the land office.

He got into the buggy and turned it to the land office, arrived just minutes later, tied off the horse and went inside.

The clerk was at his desk and saw Lee enter.

"Welcome back, Mr. Ryan. What can I do for you?"

"I don't know how to put this. I was just handed this fifteen minutes ago by Lucy Richards. She's returning to Philadelphia."

He handed the deed to the clerk. As he read it his eyebrows rose incrementally.

"This is astonishing, Mister Ryan. She even wrote 'as I am now a widow', before signing it and having it notarized. What's even more amazing is the sales price. Did you really pay her eighty-three dollars for the ranch?"

"I wasn't aware of it at the time. She asked me for some money and that was all I had on me. I thought she needed it for a train ticket or something."

"Well, bizarre it may be, but it is legal. If you'll wait a second, I'll get the transfer completed."

He pulled out his files and began writing and stamping then he annotated the map and issued him a fresh deed as well as the one Lucy had given him.

"Here you go, Mr. Ryan. And let me be the first to congratulate you," he said as he shook Lee's hand.

Lee thanked him and returned to the buggy, still trying to comprehend everything that had happened in the past twenty-four hours.

He then stopped again at the bank and opened his safe deposit box, then placed the deeds in the box, closed it and handed it to the clerk. Then he withdrew a hundred dollars to replace the eighty-three dollars he'd given to Lucy for the Diamond R and pocketed the money.

Now, it was time to visit the sheriff, so he took a deep breath and walked to the office, leaving the buggy.

It only took a few minutes to reach the jail, but Lee felt like it had taken ages.

Finally, he arrived at the open door and walked through, seeing the sheriff sitting behind the desk.

"Good morning, Lee. What can I do for you?"

"Ernie, I need to sit down, and you need to listen. This has been a very unnerving twenty-four hours."

The sheriff looked at Lee and wondered what could have shaken him so deeply.

"Go ahead, it couldn't be that bad," he said as he sat on the other side of the desk.

"No. It's worse. It begins with, of all things, hay…"

And Lee began recounting the events leading up to the previous day before he finally told of the kidnapping, his finding the kidnappers, discovering Frank Richards rape attempt, his arrival at the Richards and what happened at the house. Then he told him about what had transpired that morning.

Finally, he blew out his breath, and said, "I knew it was outside your jurisdiction, and I didn't want you to get hurt, so I took care of it. Willie is still out there, but if you want to arrest me for any of that, I'd understand and wouldn't hold it against you."

The sheriff sat back and looked at Lee as he said, "I have to admit, Lee. That's a hell of a lot to digest. Let me think about it for a minute."

He closed his eyes and ruminated for a good minute and a half, then opened his eyes, rose from the chair and said, "Alright, Lee, stand up."

Lee was expecting handcuffs, but instead Sheriff Smith said, "Raise your right hand."

Lee did so with a puzzled expression on his face.

The sheriff continued, "I, Lee Ryan, do solemnly swear…"

Lee repeated the oath, not fully realizing why the sheriff was doing it.

When he finished, the sheriff handed him a badge and said, "Now, pin that on. You are now an unpaid deputy sheriff. I'll send a report to the county sheriff and the U.S. Marshal about the situation. I'll let you know what they say in a little while. Do you have anything else you need to do in town for about an hour?"

"Yes, I do, in fact."

"You go ahead. Stop back before you leave."

Lee shook his hand, knowing that Ernie was trying to help.

He left the sheriff's office and went back to the buggy. He unhitched the horse, stepped in and drove to the other end of town.

He tethered the horse and began walking towards St. Mary's to unburden his soul, but before he began to climb the steps into the church, he saw parish pastor heading back to the rectory.

"Father Kelly!" he shouted.

The priest turned, and upon seeing Lee, turned and began to walk towards him.

Lee swallowed and took the last few steps to meet the priest.

"Lee, I didn't see you or the Flannery family at Mass yesterday. Was something wrong?"

"Yes, Father. Very wrong. Do you want to walk while I explain?"

"That's a good idea."

Starting as he had when he confessed to the sheriff, he said, "It began with hay…"

They walked almost a mile before turning back. Lee hadn't stopped talking, and Father Kelly hadn't asked a single question.

They were almost back when Lee finally said, "So, you see, Father. That's why I needed to see you. I killed five men. I know I should feel guilty, but I don't. I actually feel guiltier for kissing Lucy Richards than that. I can't get over feeling that I'm flawed somehow."

Father Kelly stopped and looked at Lee before saying, "Lee, what you did wasn't murder, nor was it a violation of God's commandment. Too many read the words literally. *Thou shalt not kill* really means that you will not commit murder. What you did was to save others from harm. You didn't do it out of anger or jealousy or greed. So, no, the only sin I need to absolve you for is missing Mass, which I will do gladly and not even assign penance. I'm proud of you, Lee Ryan."

With that he absolved Lee of the only sin he was sure he had committed and Lee felt a huge weight lift from his soul and his shoulders.

"Thank you, Father. Now I need to return to see the sheriff. I hope the law enforcement community can be just as forgiving."

"Go ahead, Lee. The badge looks good on you, by the way."

Lee smiled at Father Kelly, then turned and trotted to the buggy and released the reins. He climbed on board and drove it to the sheriff's office, finding it empty when he arrived, so he sat and waited. It was after eleven when the sheriff finally appeared with some papers in his hand.

"Okay, Lee, here's what I sent."

He handed Lee a sheet that read:

SHERIFF JAMES LIPTON GILA COUNTY ARIZONA
U.S. MARSHAL CHARLES TRACY PHOENIX ARIZONA

NOTIFIED OF KIDNAPPING IN NUEVA LUZ
DISPATCHED DEPUTY LEE RYAN TO INVESTIGATE
TRACKED KIDNAPPERS TO ABANDONED MINE SHACK
ENGAGED TWO GUARDS IN FIREFIGHT KILLED BOTH
HALTED ATTEMPTED RAPE OF KIDNAP VICTIM
RAPIST DIED WHEN FELL AGAINST ROCK
DEPUTY RYAN WENT TO HOME OF ONE WHO ORDERED KIDNAPPING
WAS INTERCEPTED BY TWO ARMED GUARDS
BOTH DREW AND WERE KILLED BY SHOTGUN
ATTEMPTED ARREST OF KIDNAP INSTIGATOR
HE PULLED GUN ON DEPUTY WHO SHOT AND KILLED SUSPECT
FOUND A HOMICIDE VICTIM IN HOUSE
SUSPECT WILLIE THOMPSON STILL AT LARGE
FIVE FOOT FIVE INCHES ONE FORTY BLACK BROWN AGE TWENTY-FOUR
WILL PROVIDE MORE DETAILS ON REQUEST

SHERIFF ERNIE SMITH NUEVA LUZ ARIZONA

Lee looked up at him and almost laughed in astonished relief.

"Here's what I just received in reply."

He gave Lee two more much shorter messages.

SHERIFF ERNIE SMITH NUEVA LUZ ARIZONA

GREAT JOB BY DEPUTY RYAN
WILL LOOKOUT FOR THOMPSON
NO DETAILS NECESSARY

SHERIFF JAMES LIPTON GILA COUNTY ARIZONA

SHERIFF ERNIE SMITH NUEVA LUZ ARIZONA

EXCEPTIONAL WORK
CONGRATULATE DEPUTY RYAN FOR ME
WILL ADVISE ON THOMPSON
NO MORE DETAILS REQUIRED

U.S. MARSHAL CHARLES TRACY PHOENIX ARIZONA

The sheriff grinned at Lee and said, "And that, Deputy Lee Ryan, is that."

Lee shook his hand, then removed his badge and held it out to the sheriff.

"Oh, no, you don't! You have to wear that now. I hate to do all the work now anyway, so I may be asking you to go do some more lawman work now and then."

"I told you a long time ago, Ernie, that I'd always be willing to help. My father would be proud to know I was wearing a badge."

"I remember, Lee. And I was glad I could help, too. That really was some great work, by the way. One of these days you'll have to stop by and fill me in on all of the details."

"Will do, Ernie. I'm going to go back now and surprise Mary."

"You do that."

They shook hands again and Lee bounced out of the office and climbed aboard the buggy, giddy with excitement and anxious to tell Mary all the incredible news.

He set the horse to a fast trot and after he bypassed his new ranch he pressed on to the Flannery farm, swung the buggy on to the access road and was pleased to see three red-headed ladies on the porch waiting for him.

The buggy slowed to a stop in front of the house, Lee loosely wrapped the strap around the hitching post and stepped up to the porch. Mary didn't care who was watching as she left the porch flooring, threw herself onto Lee and hung onto his neck as she gave him a kiss, then suddenly leaned back, ran her tongue over her lips and then dropped down.

Maggie and Katherine saw her actions and wondered what was going on.

"Mister Ryan, you have some explaining to do!" she exclaimed, her slumbering Irish temper awakened.

"I have a lot of explaining to do, my love, but I need to take you for a ride. Maggie, tell Ian not to sell the hay that he had promised to sell to Richards. We'll be back in about an hour."

With that, he scooped up Mary and carried her protesting into the buggy, jogged around the front and sat next to a sulking Mary. He quickly turned the buggy and rolled down the road leaving two very perplexed Flannery women on the porch.

Lee turned the buggy south and slowed the horse to a slow walk.

A seething Mary asked, "Now, Mister Ryan, did I or did I not detect lipstick when I kissed you?"

"You did, Miss Flannery. A very astute observation."

"Here I was worrying myself sick about you and you were out philandering with other women."

"I most certainly did not. I was with one other woman, Mrs. Lucy Richards."

"It was she who kissed you, then?" she asked as she fumed.

"Aye. Before she got on the train returning to Philadelphia. She asked me to kiss her goodbye, so I leaned over to kiss her on the cheek, and she surprised me by doing, well, doing what you just did."

"And I suppose you're going to tell me that you hated it, too."

"No, I quite enjoyed it. Lucy is an extraordinary woman, Mary. You would have liked her if she hadn't had to leave. She told me before she left that she had been in love with a young man when she was just nineteen and was raped by Edward Richards. Lucy's father made Richards marry her, and he hated doing it but was afraid not to. Lucy lived a lonely existence ever since. So, she began having people fill her in on the happenings in town. She told me that she lived her live vicariously through others. She even told me that she knew I loved you before I did. Now, my beloved Mary, I want you to know that Lucy is a very special lady and I intend to write to her often. I expect you to read everything that comes and goes. In fact, it would please me greatly if you two would become friends."

Mary didn't say a word as she stewed in her jealousy as Lee turned the buggy down the access road of the Diamond R.

"Why are we going here?"

"Why not?"

"Can't you get in trouble?"

"You never noticed my badge?"

Mary realized that she hadn't. After seeing his eyes, she forgot about everything else until she tasted the lipstick.

She turned and looked at his chest and asked, "You're a deputy?"

"Aye, my fine lass. Ernie Smith heard my story and sent a telegram to the U.S. Marshal and the Gila County Sheriff outlining what happened. He told them I was his deputy. They both replied with a 'good job' and that was all."

"So, sou're not going to jail?" she asked in astonishment.

"No, Sweetheart, you're stuck with me."

He glanced over at her and saw that she was still fuming over his obvious enchantment with Lucy and knew he had his work cut out for him. It was the first time he'd witnessed an angry Mary and had to admit that the look wasn't bad at all. He thought it made her look cute.

They arrived at the house. Lee popped out and tied the reins to the hitching post, then he walked to the other side and offered his hand.

"What are we doing here, Lee?" she asked as she stayed sitting with her arms crossed.

"Inspecting, my love."

"Inspecting?"

"Exactly. Please come with me."

She reluctantly took his hand, left the buggy, then walked with him toward the big house.

"I've never been here before. This is a very big house."

"You should see the inside. Come on in."

"Are you sure it's okay?"

"Positive."

Mary kept a tight grip on his hand as they entered the house. Once inside, she was struck by the beautiful hardwoods. Like Lee, she didn't care for the furniture, but it was a nice house. He led her into the library where she momentarily set aside her jealousy.

"Look at all these books, Lee. I could live in here for years!"

"I'm looking for one in particular right now, Mary. I want to find Dickens' *Great Expectations.*"

"And why is that?"

"Lucy told me to enjoy the library and that her favorite was *Great Expectations.*"

"She did, did she?" Mary snapped as her jealousy was reactivated.

Lee turned to Mary, pulled her into his arms and gave her a deep kiss.

"Mary, my Mary, you must understand how much I love you. You are now and always will be the only woman in my life."

Mary's jealousy evaporated before she replied, "Well, all right. Let's find out why it was her favorite."

It took them a few minutes, because the books had been placed in random order. Finally, Lee found the leather-bound volume and slid it from the shelf.

"Here it is, Mary," he said holding the book aloft.

Mary walked over and watched as Lee opened it.

It wasn't really a book at all. It was a box. Inside the box was currency; a lot of currency.

"Lee, how much is in there?" she asked with big eyes.

Lee took out the cash and began counting. When he finished, he had $3,340 in his hand.

"Well, this is interesting ..." was all Lee said as he pocketed the money.

Mary was stunned. *Lee was stealing the money!*

"Lee, for the first time since I've known you, I'm ashamed of you. You have no right to that money. It belongs to the next owner of the ranch."

"Yes, I suppose you're right. I'll just give it to the next owner, all right?"

"You'd better if you ever plan on being my husband. First you kiss another woman and now this!"

"I'll tell you what, I'll give the money to the next owner right now. Okay?"

"And how would you be doing that?" she asked.

"Like this," he answered, as he pulled the wad of bills from his pocket, turned Mary's hand upside down, then placed the money in her palm and closed her fingers.

"Now, the owner of the ranch has the money. Or, more correctly, the future wife of the new owner has the money."

"Have you gone daft, Mister Ryan?" she asked, her eyes growing as large as billiard balls.

"No, my Mary, when Lucy asked me for my money last night and I gave her eighty-three dollars, she wrote on the ranch's deed 'sold to Lee Ryan for eighty-three dollars'. She had it notarized and then I took it to the land office. It's been recorded, and the new deed is sitting in my safe deposit box at the bank."

Mary was beyond stunned and after a few seconds of silence, quietly asked, "You mean the whole ranch is yours? Even the cattle?"

"Yes, Mary. Even the cattle."

"And the house and furniture?"

"Yes, but I need to talk to you about that."

"You do?"

"Yes, but that's later. Until then, there's one more thing I need to check out."

Mary handed the cash back to Lee and said, "You'd better take this. I don't have any pockets."

Lee smiled at her, stuffed the currency into his pocket and said, "Let's go upstairs, love."

He took her hand and they walked up the broad staircase, then led her down the hallway to Lucy's room.

"This was Lucy's room, Mary. She said you and she were the same size and she wanted you to have her clothes. She wrote me a note that I want you to read in a minute. She said you'd make her happy if you wore them."

Mary stepped forward slowly. There was a large closet built into the far wall, so she slowly opened the doors and saw a row of beautiful dresses. None were too fancy, as Lucy couldn't go out, but the dresses were all in nice fabric and well-tailored.

"Lee, these are beautiful. Did she really say that, or are you making this up?"

"Like I said, Mary, I'll let you read her note in a second. But before I do, I want to find something that she mentioned in the note. You go ahead and look at the dresses. They're all yours now. I have a feeling that you and Katherine will be spending some time on that sewing machine downstairs adjusting some for her. Am I wrong?"

Mary turned slowly to Lee and asked, "Did I just hear you say that there is a sewing machine downstairs?"

"Uh-uh. Saw it when I was moving things around, to be polite."

"A real sewing machine?" Mary asked in astonishment.

"Yes, Mary. A real sewing machine."

Mary was having a hard time digesting all this news.

Lee meanwhile was doing some searching, but not finding anything until he looked at the dressing table. On the table was a blue box with a small note on it that read simply: *For Mary.*

He took the small box and while Mary was looking at the dresses, opened it. Inside was a beautiful emerald necklace and two matching earrings. Lee quietly closed the box and walked to Mary with the note in his other hand.

"Mary, I found the other thing that Lucy wanted you to have. She even left a note."

Mary slowly rotated toward Lee, almost afraid to look as she saw his smiling eyes.

Then as his hand came up, she looked down and saw the blue box with the note on it.

"Lee, what is it?"

"In her note, she said it was something that I would have bought for you if I could, and she was right."

He put the blue box into her shaking hands. She spread her fingers apart and pulled the box open. When it was open, the hand that had just opened the lid, flashed to her mouth.

"Lee, I can't take this. This is too expensive."

"Sweetheart, Lucy wanted you to have it. That's why she left the note. It's a perfect necklace for my Irish lass. Now, if you still think that I am making this up, take a look at this."

He handed her Lucy's note. Mary, her hand still trembling, read it through twice.

Lee said, "Now you know what an exceptional woman Lucy is, as you are. She recognized it in you, and I believe it was through you that she lived her life vicariously. It was in you that she saw herself twenty years ago. That is why I liked her so much, and why she felt compelled to kiss me before getting on the train. When she kissed me, it wasn't her as Lucy, it was her as Mary. You were even the same size. That's why I want you to write to her and be her friend. She needs you, Mary. She needs you to be happy, unlike her past twenty years, and she knew I could do that for you, Mary. So, let me put this necklace on you. We'll worry about the earrings later."

Mary was already beginning feel tears filling her eyes as she handed the box to Lee. She lifted her hair as he removed the necklace from the box and slid it around her neck. Then he fastened the clasp and she let her hair back down and turned back to face him. The dark green of the emerald set off the red of her hair and the blue of her eyes as she looked up at him.

Lee looked at his future bride and fell in love all over again.

There was nothing else to do but to hold her tight and kiss her.

When the kiss ended, he said, "Well, Mary, my love, now you know the whole story. We can go back now and tell the others. But as we ride back, I'd like to propose something."

"Lee, before we go, I need to apologize. I was petty and jealous when I had no right to be. You've never shown me anything but kindness and love, and I should have trusted you. From now on, I don't care if you come home with a woman's garter on your head, I will never do that again."

"Thank you, Mary. I'll never give you cause to doubt me again."

He took her hand and they entered the hallway and stepped down the staircase. When they stepped out on the porch, Lee suddenly stopped Mary.

"Mary, could you stand here for a second?"

She stood where Lee indicated as he descended the steps to the yard and turned around to look at Mary. The bright Arizona sun reflected off her bright red hair and now, the emerald in the necklace dazzled at the top of her chest where the neckline of her dress ended. Add in her brilliant blue eyes, and Lee stood there just taking in the sight of Mary. His Mary.

"Lee, are you all right?" she finally asked.

"Mary, you have no idea how beautiful you are. I had to burn it into my mind. It'll be there forever, my Mary."

Mary smiled as she stepped down and let Lee help her into the buggy.

Lee went out to the barn and saddled Jin, then walked him out of the barn and when he got close to the buggy, he dismounted, then dropped his reins and hopped into the buggy. There was no need for a trail rope with Jin.

He started the buggy down the access road. Then he began explaining what he wanted to do and to ask her advice. When he told her, she was more than just agreeable, she was ecstatic. It was like he had read her mind.

The buggy made good time and soon turned into the farm. It looked like everyone was at lunch after the morning's harvesting, so their timing was good.

He pulled the buggy up to the trough to let the horse drink. Jin walked right past into the barn to make his hellos to Qing Jin.

Lee and Mary walked arm-in-arm into the house. Neither could be happier.

As they entered the house, it was Katherine who noticed the emerald necklace on Mary's neck.

"Mary, that is gorgeous! Where did you get it? Did Lee buy it?"

"I'll tell you in a minute. But first I need to ask Lee something."

She turned to Lee and whispered into his ear.

He turned and smiled. "I'd be surprised if you hadn't thought of that. I think she'd be pleased."

"I'm glad that you approve, almost husband," Mary said before she gave Lee a quick kiss on the cheek.

Lee handed the blue box to Mary.

"Katherine, these are for you," Mary said as she handed her sister the blue box.

Katherine's reaction at being handed the blue box was the same as Mary's when Lee handed it to her.

Her hands shook as she slowly opened the box and Lee thought she might pass out when she saw the emerald earrings.

"Are they really for me?"

"Of course, Katherine. You're my sister and I love you."

Katherine slammed the box shut and embraced her older sister.

Then she stood and asked, "But what about Mama?"

Lee answered Katherine's question when he asked Mary, "We have that taken care of, don't we, Mary?"

"We most certainly do, Lee."

They walked into the kitchen where the Flannery men were eating their lunch and all of them noticed Mary's emerald.

Maggie said, "Mary, I suppose there is a story behind the necklace that involves Mister Ryan."

"Mama, it's a story that you won't believe."

"After the past two days, I'd believe it if you said he was going to fly to Phoenix."

"Lee, do you want to tell them?" she asked.

Lee nodded and said, "Okay, then. I'll get to the big thing first. I am now the owner of the Diamond R."

That caused a general chaos to around the table, but when it calmed down, Lee continued.

"After the deaths of Ed, Frank, and Stella, that left only Ed's wife, Lucy. Her name was on the deed. She didn't like the place, so when she asked me for the eighty-three dollars last night, she was actually selling me the ranch."

"*She sold you the entire ranch, cattle and all for eighty-three dollars?*" asked Ian disbelievingly.

"That's not all. She left everything in the house as well, including over three thousand in cash that she told me where to find and the emerald necklace and earrings. She left a note on the box that read, *For Mary*. Mary asked me a few minutes ago, as I knew she would, if she thought Lucy would be happy with her for giving the earrings to Katherine. So, Katherine now has the matching earrings. Naturally, Katherine's first question was, 'What about Mama?'. Mary has the solution for that, as well."

Mary had been smiling as she watched Lee, then turned to her mother and said, "Mama, there's something in the house that I know you would value more than the most priceless piece of jewelry, and Lee and I want you to have it."

Maggie was nervous as she asked, "And what would that be?"

223

"A sewing machine."

Maggie's mouth dropped as she exclaimed, *"Are you joking with me, Mary? A sewing machine?"*

Her hands went to her mouth as the thought of having her own sewing machine struck home.

Mary had told Lee how much her mother had always spoken reverently of having her own sewing machine, so she knew what an impact it would have.

"Yes, Mama, but before we do any moving, Lee has some more things to talk about."

She turned and beamed at Lee, having seen her sister and mother so taken by their gifts.

"Well, while I think of it, I'm going to spend some of Lucy's money on having those bodies moved out of the hole I had to put them in last night and bury them in the town cemetery. That aside, here's what I propose. Now, Mary and I are going to be married on October 15. We'll move into the big house, but I'm going to contract out to have the adobe house on my ranch finished. When it is done and all the furniture we buy is there, we will move to our new home. It will be our permanent home. Now, the big house can't stay empty. So, I would suggest that the remaining Flannery family move into the house. I'll turn the deed over to Ian and Maggie. Then, when Patrick marries Elsie McDermott, he can take over the farmhouse."

Lee and everyone else turned in time to watch Patrick's face shift to match his hair color.

"Now, where you all choose to live is up to you. Both houses will be owned by the Flannery family. The other good news is the cattle. I propose that we form a cattle company called the Shamrock Cattle Company. Each of us in the room gets one share. So, when we sell cattle, we'll all profit. I'd recommend that we initially trim the herd size down to about four hundred. That means if we sell the six hundred to the army, we'll net eighteen thousand dollars. That's two thousand dollars to each person in the room. Then we manage the others, so the herd grows, and we can sell them as it does. What do you think?"

Ian spoke first. "Lee, that's just not right at all. It's your ranch now. You should have the money and the house."

"Ian, I paid eighty-three dollars for the ranch. Lucy wrote me a note and said that she hoped that we would turn the ranch into a happier place than it was when she was there. I can think of no other way to make it any happier than if the Flannery family moved in. Now, it'll take some work and you'll have to hire some cow hands. But just driving them to Fort Grant shouldn't be difficult at all. It'll be two days out. I'll talk to them and ask when they want to start getting deliveries. I think a hundred a month would suit them well. In case you're wondering why we plan on living in my adobe house, it's for one very special reason."

Lee turned to his adoring fiancée and said, "It's where I got my Mary back."

Then he looked back at the rest of the family and continued.

"So, we need to work out details as soon as the harvest is done. The other part of this is that all the legal issues involving the Richards are taken care of. I'm now an unpaid deputy sheriff. And Katherine? Mary has another surprise for you later. And, I need to ask what happened to the weapons I left on the porch."

Patrick answered, "They're wrapped in a tarp in the barn, Lee."

"Good. Let's leave them there for a while. If anyone would like to learn to use them, let me know."

He had been talking so much, he was out of breath. So, he paused for a few seconds.

"Now, I know this is a lot of change for everyone to deal with. We have a lot of details to work out, but I think that we can do what Lucy asked and make the Diamond R a happy place. The money from the sale of the cattle will ensure security for everyone. I know you still have a harvest to take in, so I'll let you do that. I'll head back to town with Mary and we can get started on the other things."

Maggie, being a true Irish mother, asked, "Have you eaten, Lee?"

Lee smiled at her and said, "No, Maggie. I was holding back so I could have some of your marvelous cooking."

"And so, you will," she answered as she stood and walked to the stove.

She put some corned beef hash on a plate and gave it to him. He handed it to Mary and waited as Maggie filled another for him. The men had already finished and were heading out the door, waving as they left. Ian stopped by and gave Maggie a kiss.

After they had eaten, Maggie took their plates and said, "Now, you two go and get your things done. You'll come back for dinner and we can all sit around and talk some more."

Then she looked at Lee and said, "Lee, you are an amazing man."

Lee kissed her on the cheek, then took Mary's hand to return to the buggy.

As they pulled out of the farm, Mary slid as close as possible to Lee and said, "That was a bit of a shock for everyone."

"Mary, I'm still not sure I'm over it yet."

"When do we bring them to the house?"

"With the harvest going, I don't think the men can make it until it's finished, but we can bring Katherine and your mother tomorrow. You can show Katherine the dresses that you're going to share wither and Maggie can see her sewing machine."

"Did you see her face when I told her?"

"It would be hard to miss. Now, almost wife, I think we'll head over to the bank first to get rid of most of the money. Then we'll take care of the gruesome reburial at the undertakers. And then, my Mary, we can go to the Macy Construction Company and tell them what we want to do for our home."

"What about furniture?"

"I think we'll have to order that and the cook stove from the catalogs. We'll arrange for delivery and setup as part of the order."

"I'm so excited, Lee. Our own home!"

"And then, sweetheart, you can design your atrium."

They followed their itinerary and made the deposit, bringing his balance to close to nine thousand dollars, then he had to write a draft for two hundred and twenty dollars for the reburial. He had basic markers ordered and described each of the deceased to the undertaker. Initially, he was concerned until Lee gave him the basics of the situation and told him that the sheriff, the county sheriff, and the U.S. Marshal were all aware of the event.

Then they went to the Macy Construction Company which took a good part of the afternoon. Lee told them what he wanted, and they asked if he could take them to the site and show what was needed before they could give an estimate.

So, Lee, Mary and engineer John Gilmore went out to the adobe location.

Lee and Mary stepped down and waited as John Gilmore dismounted, then removed a pencil and a heavy notebook from his saddlebags and followed them to the unfinished house.

They stopped at the entrance and Lee said, "This is what I started, but things interrupted me, so I decided to see if I could have you complete the job."

John had already scanned the site and said, "You did a great job in getting started. This is going to be a magnificent home when it's done. Walk me through it and I'll have a better idea as we go."

"The brick molds are all over there. I can make thirty-two at a time."

"Excellent. We'll probably make another set for thirty-two, so we can produce more of the same size for the walls. We have our own stockpile for other things. Now, do you want a red tile roof?"

"Yes, and I'd like a nice tile floor as well."

He led the engineer through the house and as they walked through the rooms, he made notes constantly. He praised Lee for the design of the three fireplaces and the layout of the house itself and said the rooms were generous without being structurally weak. He asked where they were planning on placing the cook stove and marked it down. He asked about the style of doors he wanted and about a front and back walkway and even the privy, with a stone walkway.

While they were in the kitchen, Lee said, "There's something else I want to show you. This is something that I wanted and has special meaning to us both."

He went to the doorway on the side of the kitchen and they all stepped into the future atrium.

John looked at the sky, and exclaimed, "*An atrium?* Why this is marvelous! We've never built a house with one. This is a very large one, too. It's perfect! What would you like to do in here?"

Lee turned to Mary and asked simply, "Mary?"

He thought she was going to cry but she held back her tears as she said, "I'd like a stone walkway starting from the entrance and following in a curve to the back exit. I need to ask, Mr. Gilmore, do you think this soil will allow me to plant flowers?"

He looked at the ground and bent his knees, scooped up some dirt and rolled it through his hands.

"Bring in some water, and I think it'll be fine."

"Speaking of water, John," said Lee, "come on outside and I'll show you why I chose this location."

They walked through the atrium exit and Gilmore saw the creek not one hundred feet away, curving down into the back area before heading back east. He studied the slope as well.

"Mr. Ryan, if you'd like we can run an underground pipe from the stream and build a pool in your atrium with say, a two-foot-high wall. That would give you about four feet of water. You could use it to water the plants and provide a nice esthetic addition to the atrium. We'd use stones on the floor of the pool, so you wouldn't have any problems with silt."

Lee turned to Mary and looked at her with his eyebrows raised. It was her atrium after all.

Mary's eyes lit up immediately as she said, "That would be beautiful! Can I show you where I'd like to have it?"

She hurried back into her atrium after asking how big the pool could be and John said it could be whatever size or shape that she wished.

Mary marched around the atrium and imagined the walkway and the flowers, giddy with excitement. She decided on almost the center of the atrium, just offset enough to allow the walkway to pass. She asked if it could be eight feet by four feet and John nodded and wrote it down.

Finally, John was satisfied he had enough information and began to crunch the numbers.

"With the additional supplies and things like the doors, the total would be around twelve hundred dollars. It would take about two to three months to complete. Others could do it faster, but we prefer quality work."

"As do I, John. Do you need me to sign a contract or just write you a draft?"

"You don't have to pay the full amount, Mister Ryan. We can start the work on half, and you can pay the other half when it's complete and you're satisfied with the work."

"I'll tell you what, John, I'll swing by in a little while and I'll just write you a draft for the entire job. If I'm not satisfied, you'll be the first to know."

John laughed and said, "I'm already aware of your reputation, Mister Ryan. Trust me, you'll be satisfied."

Lee smiled and shook his hand, then said, "Then I'll stop on our way home."

John took his writing tools and returned to his horse, mounted then waved as he returned to town.

After he had gone, Lee turned to Mary and asked unnecessarily, "Are you happy with our plan, my Mary?"

He knew it was almost silly to ask as her ecstatic face gave him the answer.

"Happy, Lee? I'm well beyond happy. Our home is going to be perfect. The atrium will be our special place. We can even enjoy a nice dip in the pool sometimes."

"If I'm in the water with you, Mary, there are two things I need to warn you about."

"And those are?" she asked as she smiled mischievously at him, hoping the two things were what she hoped they were.

"One, I'll only go in there with you if we're both naked. And secondly, I don't know how long I'd last before I had to take you out of the pool and ravage you."

Mary was glad to see his thoughts were traveling along the same line as hers.

"And why, Mr. Ryan, did you not think that I would have ravaged you before even getting into the pool with you, and you without a stitch of clothing?"

"Why, Miss Flannery! I'm shocked beyond belief. I thought of you as a demure, proper woman and here you are talking like a wanton woman. Why, I'm appalled!"

"Oh, I'm sure you are. I've seen that look on your face for some time now, Mister Lust-filled Ryan. And don't tell me that you don't see it on mine."

He pulled her close and kissed her gently. Then he whispered, "Mary, I've desired you as much as any man has desired a woman for a long time. It's a measure of my love for you that I haven't pressed you at all. I think I can hold off for another three weeks, but, then, my love, I'll take you to bed and make you the most contented woman in the country."

"I'd rather not wait, Lee. But I know why you feel the need to postpone what we both want so desperately. I love you even more for that. And yes, we can wait three more weeks. And then, my love, we'll make each other much more than content."

He kissed her again, a long kiss and then just as a preliminary, he slid his hand down across her back and caressed her curves. She sighed as he did.

"We'd better get back to the buggy before my firm commitment is gone."

She laughed and said, "I lost mine a long time ago."

He clutched her close to his side as they walked out of Mary's atrium and headed for the buggy.

Before they boarded, he asked, "Do you mind if I take a little time to check on the herd? I haven't seen them in almost a week."

"Of course, I don't mind. That's where you gave me Qing Jin. It's as much a part of that day as my atrium."

Lee smiled as he recalled that day; the day his Mary returned to him. He helped her into the buggy and they headed toward the canyon a minute later.

The buggy hadn't gotten within a hundred yards of the canyon when Lee stopped, then quickly turned the buggy around, heading toward the town.

"Lee, I thought you were going to go and visit the herd?"

"Not yet. Later tonight, I think. Right now, we need to get out of here."

"Why, Lee? What's wrong?"

"I'm pretty sure that Willie Thompson is in my cabin."

Mary was beyond surprised as she asked, "How would you know that?"

"I can't get within a hundred yards of the cabin before Hagar would come running down the slope. Never. He's not there, Mary. I hope that Willie didn't kill him. Maybe he just frightened him away, but I doubt it. That was Hagar's home as much as mine. He wouldn't leave. So, now I've got to ferret him out of there."

"Lee, isn't there a better way?"

"No. He'll be on the lookout for the law since he murdered Stella. Now, he's on the lam and he's desperate. The best thing for me to do is go in after it's dark. He'll be cooking something and that'll be my best chance. Remember, I built that cabin. I know its layout. I know where he'll be."

"I hope you're wrong for once," she said as the buggy continued to Nueva Luz.

———

Lee wasn't wrong. Willie had arrived at the cabin shortly after killing Stella. He knew where it was but didn't know about that damned dog. It was dark when he arrived. As he got close, he heard a deep growling noise and the small hairs on the back of his neck went up, giving him shivers. He pulled his gun and first thought it was a wolf. But when the growling stopped and was replaced with a higher-pitched barking, he knew it was a smaller dog.

"Damned Lee!" he muttered, "It's so like him to get a dog!"

Then, he slowed his horse and kept him walking toward the sound of the dog. He had his pistol out but hesitated to use it because of the loud report and wasn't absolutely sure that Lee wasn't in the cabin. He should be at the Flannery Farm, tickling Miss Flannery's fancy. He had to admit that she was a looker. But then he thought back to the vision of Stella and wished she hadn't done that to him. *Why didn't she just let him bed her?* He knew she wanted it. All that pretend stuff with the scissors. He should be in her bed right now feeling he soft skin under his fingers. He was drifting into a pretend world and hadn't noticed that the dog was getting closer.

Hagar had slid behind the horse and rider. Suddenly, he let loose with a series of loud barks that startled the animal and Willie was thrown from its back and Hagar chased the horse to the northeast and kept going. He knew he had done all he could. The horse had run south, probably back to its home barn. Now, Hagar would wait for his human friend to return to get rid of the intruder.

After Willie got up, his left shoulder hurt like the dickens. He could barely move it. *Damned dog!* He figured it had been dislocated, so he hunted around and found his pistol on the ground. Then he walked the remaining fifty yards to the cabin and paused. His shoulder was throbbing, but he waited to make sure Lee wasn't there. He surely would have heard the dog.

Finally, he opened the door finding the cabin empty, so he closed the door and lit a match. The cabin was clean and well-stocked. The problem was that Lee would probably come back sooner or later. First, he had to take care of his shoulder. He looked around the room and found a short, thick log for the fire, picked it up and put it under the armpit of his damaged shoulder. This was going to hurt. He stepped to the side of the cabin and suddenly shoved his elbow against the windowsill. The shoulder popped into place as Willie screamed, and the log fell to the floor. It hurt terribly for a few seconds and then it returned to a much more tolerable ache. He slowly rolled the shoulder around. It worked, but it was still pretty sore.

He wasn't that hungry, but he made a fire and then some coffee. After drinking one cup, he climbed onto Lee's bed and went to sleep.

He had slept through the night and late into the morning, finally waking with a start, as he realized what a dangerous predicament, he was in. He spent the rest of the day with the door opened just a few inches and peered outside down to the desert, waiting for Lee.

He had heard the buggy coming toward him and stayed in the cabin, staring through the gap in the door. He watched it approach and could see the red hair and guessed it was Lee and that Flannery woman. He pulled his pistol and waited. This might work out better for him anyway. If he plugs Lee, he can have himself a fun time with his woman before he killed her, too. He'd have a way out and could carry a lot of food in that thing. Nobody knew about the cabin except Lee and him anyway. Well, and maybe that woman.

He anxiously watched the buggy get closer. Suddenly, it turned and headed back to town and Willie wondered why. He didn't have a fire going so he was sure that he wasn't seen. He figured either Lee forgot something, or the woman had nagged him into heading back. No matter, he was still okay. But it also meant that Lee would probably be back tomorrow.

———

Lee drove the buggy back to Nueva Luz and stopped briefly to write a draft for the construction that they said would begin this week. Then, they headed to the farm.

It was dinnertime and the Flannery men were still out in the fields when they pulled up to the house. Mary stepped down and followed Lee as he led the horse and buggy to the barn. He parked the buggy on the side of the barn, then unharnessed the horse and led him inside where he brushed the gelding down.

Mary stood silently watching her future husband. She wasn't as worried as she felt she should have been and wasn't sure if it was because she was drained of worry or she had gained so much confidence in Lee.

Lee set the gelding into his stall and collected Mary as he left. He held her hand as they walked to the house, entering through the kitchen.

As soon as they stepped into the kitchen, they were greeted by the ever-present Maggie as Katherine was helping with the dinner.

"Welcome back, my two lovelies. How did everything go?"

Mary answered, "Mama, the house is going to be so special. I got to talk to the man who was going to oversee the building and tell him what I wanted in my atrium. Mama, I'm going to have flowers and a walk and a pool of water right there! I am so excited, and it's all because of Lee."

As she said the last sentence, she turned and smiled at her fiancé.

"Well, I'm so happy for you both. Anything else?" Maggie asked.

Lee replied, "We took care of the body removal. They'll take care of it tomorrow. Then, I think I ran into a new problem that I'll take care of in a few hours. I think Willie Thornton is hiding out in my cabin."

That stopped Maggie in the middle of chopping a carrot.

"Is that the heathen who killed Stella Richards?"

"He's the one. And I'm ashamed to admit, I'm the one that introduced him to the area. I should have been able to see what he was before we even got here, but I needed help to trap the horses. That was all that lazy good-for-nothing ever did, too. He helped with the barbed wire and that was all. But now he's back, and I have to go and get him. Besides the fact that he's wanted for murder, he's in my cabin and I can get him out. I just hope he didn't kill my dog."

For some reason, the murder of a dog struck Maggie as especially heinous.

"Surely he wouldn't kill your wee dog."

"He would. To him, Hagar would have been an annoying obstacle."

"So, you'll be going over there to get him?"

"Yes, Maggie. It's the best way. I know the cabin and the surroundings. I'll arrest him if I can, but I think he'll fight rather than surrender. To be honest, if he knew that Lucy was gone, and she was the only witness against him, he might stick it out."

"Will it be dangerous, Lee?"

"Not so much. He probably knows I'll be stopping by, but he doesn't know when. That means he must stay vigilant constantly and no one can do that. If he saw us riding up there today, and he probably did, he will be really nervous for a while, but then he'll have to relax. After sundown, he'll think I won't be back until tomorrow, so I should be able to get close. Then, I'll play it by ear. He's inside my cabin, and I only have one door. If he knows I'm out front, even if he waits, he'll only have one way out. If I need to, I'll wait him out."

"Well, it sounds like you have it planned out as well as you can."

"And once Willie is out of the way, there are no more loose ends. We'll be able to start getting our plans in motion, including, Miss Mary Flannery, our wedding plans. Now, tomorrow, I'll send a telegram to my parents up in Pueblo about the wedding. For some reason, we have plenty of space for them to stay."

Mary looked at her mother and was almost afraid to ask, "But, Lee, our wedding night. Won't that be a bit, um, less private?"

Maggie smiled to herself. She had never known Mary to be so timid. Katherine was on the verge of laughing out loud.

"Ah, Mary, ever so thoughtful. No, Miss Flannery, I was planning on spending our wedding night and a few nights after in our lovely cabin currently occupied by Mister Thompson. After he is evicted, I'll have plenty of time to make it into the romantic hideaway it should be. And besides, during those rare moments when we are not busy being husband and wife, we can walk down the slope and see how our new home is progressing. By then, it should be well on its way to completion."

Mary blushed because her mother was standing three feet in front of her when Lee had more than just suggested that they'd be busy doing 'husband and wife' things a lot. She agreed with him but not with her mother right there. Katherine was doing a good job of holding back her laughter.

Maggie was getting more amused by the minute at Mary's discomfort.

"Now, tomorrow my Mary, we will take your darling smirking mother and your sister, who seems ready to explode, to the big house. She can worship her sewing machine, and you and Katherine can go through the volumes of dresses to see which ones you'll need to adjust."

"And what, Mister Ryan, will you be doing?" she asked.

"Exploring the library. It's much larger than the one I'm having built in the new house, but I fully expect to abscond with some of them for our new home. Then, Miss Flannery, we can go to see Harry and spend an hour or so looking through his catalogs and buy all those things you'll need. Furniture, pots and pans, plates, linen, lamps. You know. Everything."

"It'll take more than an hour, I'm afraid," Mary replied.

"Take all the time you want. We'll have to get the cook stove and the tub delivered early so the contractor can put in the pipes and flue. Mary, I'm going to let you and your sainted mother discuss things while I go and check on some things I'll need for tonight."

The casual way that Lee mentioned going into a possible gunfight sent a chill through her body, so she took a deep breath and nodded.

He gave Mary and then Maggie a kiss on the cheek and not wanting to leave Katherine unsmooched, added another quick kiss to her cheek before he left to go to the barn.

After he'd gone, Mary said, "Mama, I'm not as worried as I was before, but it still gets me nervous. I'm sure he'll be fine, but there's always that chance."

"Mary, in our lives, there is always that chance. Right now, my husband and my sons are out there just mowing hay. They could trip and fall into the blades or have a mule step on them. They could get bitten by a rattlesnake. At least Lee knows what he's up against and is planning to avoid being hurt."

"Thank you, Mama. You always know what to say."

"And, Mary? One more thing. Spending a lot of time with your husband in bed isn't such a bad thing, you know. If you've noticed, we have a lot of proof that your father and I did the very same thing."

Mary glowed a deep red at the imagined vision of her own mother admitting to...

Katherine's previous mirthful mood vanished, and she had a look of horror on her face.

Maggie smiled as she watched her daughters realize what they had just been told, as if they didn't notice the noises coming from their bedroom even in the past few days.

CHAPTER 8

Out in the barn, Lee was examining the weapons he would need for the night. He wanted to wear moccasins rather than boots so he could make a quiet approach. He'd take his knife and Colt for sure, but the Winchester he'd leave on Jin. He'd take the shotgun and loaded it with #4 shot. It wouldn't hurt the cabin, but it would surely hurt Willie. He was wondering about ammunition, though. He'd need a box of .44 caliber cartridges and another four shotgun shells. He was wondering where he should put them and then decided that he'd leave the box of cartridges in his saddlebag on Jin. If he needed that many more shots, it would be a disaster anyway. The shotgun shells he'd just put in his pockets, and maybe eight or ten cartridges, too.

It was almost approaching sunset when he had everything ready to go. He had decided on approaching from the northwest. He'd swing wide to avoid being detected. There was almost a full moon, which was bad luck, but it couldn't be helped.

He walked out of the barn and saw the Flannery men walking in from the fields. They had already done almost half of the work. He waved, and they returned the gesture then walked toward them.

"How's it going, Ian?"

"No, problems at all. We scared a few critters out of their homes, but they'll be back. How did everything go with you?"

"We got the housing contract done. Arranged for the removal of the bodies. And then I think I discovered the whereabouts of Willie Thompson. I'll go get him after sunset, and it shouldn't take long."

"Can't be happy with just a normal life, can you, Lee?" Ian asked.

"This *is* my normal life lately."

"Where is he?" asked Conor.

"In my cabin in the canyon."

"He's in your cabin?" asked an astounded Dylan.

"I'm not surprised. He knew about it. It's out of the way, and he didn't have a lot of options. As far as he knows, every law enforcement agency within five hundred miles is looking for him. He's not too far wrong, either."

"Do you need some help?" asked Patrick.

"No. This is a one-man job. I can sneak in and get close. I just hope he didn't kill my dog."

"No real man kills a dog," commented Sean.

"That is the truth," replied Lee.

The Flannery males stopped at the outside sink and all washed before dinner and Lee followed their example.

After a typical Flannery dinner, Lee went out to the barn with Mary following.

He saddled Jin and added his chosen weaponry and was soon ready to head to his cabin to evict its unwanted tenant. The sun was already down, and the ride would take two hours as he was taking a long loop around.

He saw Mary's concerned face and cupped his hands around her chin and kissed her softly. So softly she barely felt his lips brush hers.

"Mary, my darling Mary. After tonight, I look forward to spending relaxing hours with you in our new home. No more nighttime shootouts, and no more bad surprises. We can just enjoy being together."

Mary sighed and said, "Then go and do what I know you must do. Just come home safely to me."

"I always will," he said then gave her a warm hug before he turned and just left the barn with Jin following.

Mary watched him mount and then disappear into the darkness.

———

Ten miles to the northwest, Willie was relaxing. After watching the buggy head toward Nueva Luz, he had been on a razor's edge for an hour, then began to calm down. Now it was dark, and he'd have to get some sleep soon so he would be ready in the morning. But it was time to fill his stomach before getting to bed, so he began rummaging through Lee's stores. He had quite a selection, so he chose some beans and a can of beef. He was going to add tomatoes and onions but decided to save them for tomorrow.

He soon had a good fire going and began to cook his dinner.

———

Lee had Jin moving at a trot as he passed north of Nueva Luz by about two miles. Then he would make a wide loop, putting him a mile north of the canyon, before turning back south toward the canyon's mouth. When he got within a quarter mile of the cabin, he would dismount and walk the rest of the way in his moccasins.

It took him another hour to reach the point where he would turn east toward the canyon, then once he made the turn, he slowed Jin to a walk. After another forty minutes, he stopped Jin, stepped down and told the horse to wait.

Two hundred yards away, Hagar smelled Jin and Lee. He knew his friends would come, so he stood and began trotting toward the scent.

Lee hadn't walked fifty yards when he was startled by a wet tongue licking his left hand. He automatically jerked his hand and spun away before he looked down and saw Hagar looking at him, his tail wagging. Lee was relieved and exhilarated as he dropped onto his heels and was reunited with his canine companion.

"Good boy, Hagar! I thought that bastard might have shot you."

He rubbed Hagar's neck and then he remembered that he had a stick of jerky he had brought along in case he had to stick it out for a while. He thought the dog's needs were greater than his and reached into his pocket and handed the meat to Hagar, who almost swallowed it whole.

"Now, Hagar, let's go kick this bastard out of our house."

Lee stood, then began walking toward the cabin at a normal pace. Even though he wasn't going slowly, the moonlight provided enough light, so he could avoid stepping on anything noisy.

———

In the cabin, Willie was enjoying the last of his meal, then belched loudly and laughed at himself.

Lee saw the smoke rising out of the cabin. For some reason, even though he knew that Willie was there, knowing he was eating his food and burning his firewood irritated him immensely, and he didn't bother using any Oriental techniques to achieve peace, either. He wanted to be angry this time.

He and Hagar approached the cabin quietly. Hagar went through his personal opening in the fence as Lee went through the gate a little further along. They converged about twenty feet from the front of the cabin.

Lee pulled back both triggers on the shotgun, then pointed the gun at the doorway. He was wondering how to get Willie to open the door when Hagar solved the problem for him when he began to bark.

Inside the cabin, Willie heard Hagar's loud barking and twisted to face the closed door.

"That damned dog is back! I'll teach that mutt to drive off my horse," he snarled as he tossed the tin plate he had been using and stood up.

He unhitched his hammer loop and pulled the Colt from its holster, then yanked open the door and saw the dog still barking twenty feet away. He didn't see Lee sitting to the right also twenty feet away and began to raise his Colt.

Lee knew that he could have blown him away right then, but he knew he couldn't do it. He needed to offer him a chance to surrender.

He shouted, "Drop the pistol, Willie! I've got a shotgun on you. Drop it!"

Willie was startled and almost turned his pistol toward Lee's voice but knew he didn't stand a chance if he did. He didn't want to be hanged, either, so he gambled that Lee wouldn't shoot him if he turned away, so he whirled and slid back into the cabin, but had to leave the door open.

As he crouched beside the bed, Willie shouted, "Come and get me, Lee! You have that big old scattergun and I only have a Colt."

Lee chastised himself for not shooting Willie. Now, it would be difficult.

"Willie, you've got no chance. I'm here to arrest you for murdering Stella Richards. Lucy Richards saw you do it. You're going to hang, Willie, and I'm going to be the one to get you there. It's my cabin, so if I have to burn it down around you, I will."

"Tell you what, Lee. I'll make a deal with you. I'll come out if you don't use that shotgun. Keep your Colt in your holster and I'll do the same. It'll be a fair contest. It's the best you're gonna get. Either that or come in and get me."

Lee thought it over. He had never seen Willie draw a gun and it was more likely that he was better at this than Willie was but doing it in the moonlight was going to be tricky. The better shooter may not win, but he knew that Willie was right on one count; sitting here waiting wasn't going to solve anything. He didn't doubt that he had more patience than Willie, but Willie had more food and water.

"Alright, Willie, come on out. I'm putting the shotgun down."

"Not good enough, Lee. I want to hear two shotgun blasts."

"Never did trust anyone, did you Willie. That was your second biggest problem."

"Really, what was my biggest?"

"You're lazy, Willie. You never wanted to do an honest day's work."

"It didn't matter in the end," Willie shouted followed by a loud laugh.

Lee released one hammer on the shotgun and then fired. He pulled back the hammer on the second barrel and fired that into the air. He was laying down the shotgun when Willie popped out of the cabin door with his pistol drawn and quickly tried to set his sights on Lee in the moonlight.

"You shouldn't have trusted me, Lee."

Lee had no chance and was ready to jump to the side when a blur of black and white leapt across the front of the cabin, smashed into Willie and knocked him to the ground. His pistol went off and Hagar continued his path, leaving a stunned Willie in his wake.

Lee didn't hesitate, he flipped off his hammer loop and pulled his Colt at the same time, cocking the hammer as he brought it to bear. He saw Willie on the ground, bringing up his Colt. Now, it was too late for Willie. Lee fired and before Willie's brain even registered the hit from the first shot, Lee fired again. Both .44s had drilled through the center of his chest. Willie went into convulsions for a few seconds before succumbing to the inevitable and lay still on Lee's porch.

Lee didn't look at Willie, but put his Colt back into its holster and then he looked to his left and called, "Hagar!"

The collie came running out of the night, and stopped in front of him, wagging his tail.

Lee looked at his faithful companion and rubbed behind his ears. "You are one hell of a dog, Hagar."

He finally looked at Willie's lifeless form and said, "You almost got lucky for once, Willie. That'll teach you to be mean to a dog."

He went into the cabin and was disgusted by the mess Willie had made. He'd have to come back in the morning and clean it up. For now, he walked to his shelves and found a can of beef. He opened it and poured it onto a tin plate.

"Hagar!"

The border collie entered the cabin and was uncomfortable being inside. He changed his mind when Lee set the plate of beef in front of him.

Good human! He thought. *Good friend.*

Lee had to dispose of the body, so he took off Willie's gun belt and put it and the Colt on a shelf in his cabin, then laid his shotgun there as well. Then he walked back to the corral and found the mule. He wasn't going to belittle one of his horses with the likes of Willie.

The mule was led to where Willie lay in an awkward position on the ground, not that it mattered. Lee put him across the animal's back and tied him down. Then he closed the cabin door. Hagar had gulped down his dinner and had already returned to his herd.

Lee walked the mule out the gate and closed it behind him, yelled, "Jin!" and waited two minutes for Jin to arrive in front of him.

He tied the mule's trail rope to Jin's saddle, and they stepped off toward Nueva Luz.

An hour later, Lee led the mule to the sheriff's office, dismounted, then disconnected the trail rope and tied him to the hitchrail. The only lights in the town came from the saloon and he wondered if Ernie was having a beer, so he wandered down that way. He was in luck, because that's exactly what he was doing. An unmarried man of his age didn't have much else to do.

He approached the sheriff's table, pulled out a chair and sat down.

"Good evening, Sheriff Smith."

The sheriff was surprised to see him that late, and in this location and asked quickly, "Lee, what brings you to town and into the saloon tonight?"

"Business, Ernie. Earlier today, I was going to visit my cabin and noticed my dog didn't come to greet me. It dawned on me that Willie Thompson might be holding out there because he knew about the cabin. I went back tonight, found him there and I tried to talk him out, but he would only come out if I fired both shotgun barrels into the air. As soon as I fired the second one, he popped out of there with his pistol ready to fire. I really screwed up, Ernie. He had me dead to rights when my dog flew at him and knocked him down. I was able to get my Colt out and fired before he could get off his second shot. I've got him out in front of your office on my mule. What do you want me to do with him?"

"Leave him there. I'll run him over to the undertakers in the morning and I'll keep your mule here for you to pick up. I'll notify the county and the U.S. Marshal's office, so they can take him off their list of wanted men."

"Thanks, Ernie. I hope this is the last of the excitement for a while. I'm getting married in nineteen days."

"Congratulations, Lee. And I hope you're right about the lack of excitement."

"Thank you for all your help, Ernie. You've been a good friend."

"Just hang around, Lee. I'm sure I'll be needing you."

"Anytime, Sheriff Smith."

Lee smiled at Ernie, stood and headed out of the saloon, mounted Jin and soon passed the sheriff's office where the mule watched him leave and probably wondered what he did to deserve this.

He set Jin at a good trot and arrived at the farm thirty minutes later.

As he entered the access road, he was not in the least surprised to see a lone red-headed girl waiting on the porch, illuminated by a kerosene lamp at her feet and lamplight through the windows. He was thinking of galloping the last two hundred yards, but didn't want to alarm Mary, so he let Jin pick his pace.

Mary could see Lee in the moonlight and smiled as she felt an inner peace wash over her. She walked to the edge of the porch and just waited; each of Jin's hoofbeats a heartwarming sound.

From fifty feet away, Lee could already see her emerald necklace reflecting the moonlight and seemed to be almost as blue as a sapphire.

He pulled up, dismounted with his eyes still on a smiling Mary, then stepped onto the porch and stood before her, the kerosene lamp's light giving the scene an almost ghostly appearance.

"Is it over, Lee?" she asked softly as he took her hands.

"Yes, sweetheart, it's over. Willie is lying across my mule's back in front of the jail. Ernie will take him to the undertaker in the morning."

"Thank God," she said as she exhaled.

He took her arm, then they stepped off the porch and strolled toward the barn in the bright moonlight with Jin following. After entering, Lee unsaddled him, then let him choose his stall and Lee followed, then brushed him down and let him decide when he wanted to eat.

Everything had been so calm and subdued since he arrived, and Mary expected nothing different when he turned to face her, but suddenly Lee snatched her from the barn floor, and held her close.

With her ear just inches from his lips, he whispered, "Now it's all about us, my Mary. No more interruptions. In nineteen days, we'll be married and have our whole lives to spend together."

Mary sighed and whispered back, "That sounds so perfect, Lee."

He kissed her softly and set her down just as gently before saying, "Let's go inside."

He took her hand, and they quietly entered the house through the kitchen where he found it surprisingly empty, even at this late hour.

He asked, "Can I guess the family Flannery is in the Flannery family room?

"That would be a wise guess."

They walked with hands linked into the main room and the sea of redheads turned as they entered.

"Is he gone?" asked Ian.

"Yes, he's gone. Well, technically he's still with us. He's just waiting for burial in town."

"So, it wasn't so bad then?"

"No. But I'm lucky to have my friend, Hagar. He was one heroic canine tonight."

"So, he didn't kill your doggie after all?"

"No, sir. He probably just scared him off and Hagar was just waiting for me to return. He's back at his old job minding the herd now," he replied, then after a pause, asked, "So, how many more days until the harvest is all in?"

"I think we'll be done by tomorrow afternoon."

"That's really fast, Ian."

"Aye, we seemed to be moving along a wee bit faster this year."

"That's great. Now, tomorrow morning I'll stop in around eight o'clock to take the Flannery ladies to the big house. I'll bring the buggy and Jin. The buggy is big enough for all three ladies."

"If it's okay, Lee. I'd rather ride Qing Jin," Mary said.

"And I'd prefer to take Blaze," added Katherine.

Lee looked at his future mother-in-law, who said, "Aye, I may as well ride my new horse, too."

"Well, I'll still be here by eight o'clock. I'll be staying at the big house tonight and spend some time doing a little looking around. There are a lot of places I haven't seen yet."

"Does that mean you'll be leaving us so soon?" asked Maggie.

"It's already late, Maggie, and the Flannery men have another day of harvesting. So, I'll be saying good-night to you all."

He smiled, gave a short wave, then started for the kitchen door as Mary hustled to catch up. He made it to the ground before he heard her running behind him.

"Lee, I need to talk to you," she said as she bounced close behind him.

He had already started to turn before she said anything, so he stopped and asked, "Mary, how can I set your mind at eas?. You seem troubled again."

"The comment about your dog and how lucky you were to have him. What happened?"

He knew the best approach was honesty; especially with Mary.

He took in a deep breath and said, "He had me, Mary. Dead to rights because I made a stupid mistake and trusted him. My gun was still in my holster and he burst out of the cabin door with his pistol cocked and ready to fire. Hagar jumped out of the night and knocked him down giving me time to get my gun out and shoot him before he could get another shot. I didn't want to have to tell you the details, but I'll never lie to you, Mary. No matter what the consequences."

He expected many kinds of reaction, just not the one he received.

She just stepped close to him, put her hands around his neck and kissed him softly, then said, "Thank you, Lee. I know you were just trying to keep me from worrying."

Then she let go and smiled at him before she returned to the house.

Lee was smiling as he harnessed the buggy and instead of saddling Jin, just loaded his tack into the buggy.

Lee arrived at his new ranch barn twenty minutes later, drove the buggy to the barn and unharnessed the gelding. After leaving Jin and the buggy horse in the barn, he entered the front door of the house, closed the door and took a minute to find a lamp. Once he had light, he walked through the house lighting more lamps until the house was lit up as when it was fully populated.

Not surprisingly, his first stop was the library. He sat at the desk, opened the center drawer and saw the revolver that Ed Richards was going to use to kill him. Then he went through the other drawers. There was very little. A bank book showing their balance before Lucy closed it — $32,654.33. That should get Lucy started, he thought with a big smile. Then he left the desk and began surveying the titles on the massive number of books. They covered a wide range of subjects and he wasn't surprised that most of them looked untouched, knowing that they wouldn't stay that way. To Lee, there were few things sadder than an unread book.

After leaving the office and library, he climbed the stairs and entered Stella's room, which looked immaculate. He wondered why Lucy had cleaned it up and made the bed. It looked as if it was ready for Stella to return. There were a lot of dresses and other female knick-knacks in the room and he was sure that Katherine would find a lot that she could put to good use.

Then he examined the other five bedrooms. Three were just generic guest rooms with no personal items, but the same could not be said when he found Frank's room. There was a nice desk in the room that was made of a lighter wood than the massive desk in the library. Lee thought this would be a nice addition to his own library. He began going through the drawers and found a money belt with $225 in it, which he emptied into his pocket. The bottom two drawers were empty. He was thinking that Frank was really boring until he went over to his chest of drawers and began pulling drawers open. The top two drawers held his underwear, socks and shirts, but when he opened the bottom drawer, he was at first puzzled. It looked like frilly underwear, so Lee began to remove them from the drawer and realized he was looking at the kind of underwear young girls would wear. Then after he had pulled them all out, he saw a large envelope lying on the flat wooden bottom. Lee almost was afraid to find what was inside but opened it nonetheless and soon wished that he hadn't when his stomach twisted. The envelope was full of postcards and tintypes. All of them depicted nude girls with small or no breasts at all.

He quickly slid the pictures back into the envelope and then grabbed the frilly clothes. He turned and rapidly left the room, trotted down the long staircase and entered the parlor. He set the envelope and clothing aside, and quickly started a fire in the enormous fireplace. Once he thought the fire was strong enough, he tossed in the clothes first, which burned quickly. Then he emptied the contents of the envelope into the flames which began to emit blue and bright green flames.

Lee stood, tossed the empty envelope onto the fire, and watched the death of the disturbing images. What made him even more disgusted was knowing that Frank had almost hurt Katherine.

When they had been reduced to ash, he sighed, then turned and went back upstairs to Frank's room. He needed to make sure it was clean before allowing the Flannery women to explore the house.

His thorough search uncovered no more evidence of Frank's depravity, which only left one unknown bedroom; that belonging to Ed Richards. After what he'd found in Frank's room, he was nervous about what he might discover in his father's private place.

When he entered Ed Richards' room, he found it almost totally devoid of any human touch and Lee wondered if he brought his women to this room to shame Lucy whose room was next door. He wondered how he could even do that at all in the first place. Ed Richards was married to this remarkable woman who met all of society's standards for an ideal wife. He had this beautiful, well-figured, charming, witty, and amazing woman who lived next to him, yet he preferred to bring in floozies. No matter how hard he tried, Lee simply couldn't understand how any man could have ignored, much less disliked Lucy.

Once Lucy resurfaced in his mind, he thought he should revisit her room again for a more thorough search. As quick as her mind was, he believed that she had left even more for him to find in her room.

He stepped into the room and just absorbed the ambiance of Lucy. She spent most of her time here and could feel her presence, as he walked over to the dressing table where she had left the emerald necklace and earrings. He opened the drawers and found bottles of perfumes and colognes, then closed the drawer and walked to her dresser and began pulling out the much larger drawers. They were mostly empty except for one that had some frilly things that belonged there; unlike the ladies' underwear he had found in Frank's room.

Once he'd found there was nothing else, he felt saddened, having hoped to find another letter or note from Lucy. Even with that emotion still present, he smiled at the recollection of Lucy's smile after she'd kissed him.

He turned to sit on the bed for a while to just think and spotted the large linen chest at the foot of the bed, wondering how he'd missed it. It was probably because it was the same stain as the bed itself.

He stepped before the chest and lifted the heavy lid, which rested on the bedposts.

It was full of bedclothes, and on top of them was an envelope that was addressed simply 'Lee'. He smiled as his fingers grasped the letter and found his heart pounding as he lifted the envelope from the chest. He lowered the top slowly and held the envelope close to his face and inhaled the gentle scent of lilac.

He sat on the edge of the bed but delayed opening the envelop. He knew it would be the last he heard from Lucy in some time and didn't want to rush the moment.

Finally, he let out his breath, slid the single sheet from its protection and unfolded the note. He read:

My Dearest Lee,

I hope that you had the tenacity to fully explore my room before turning it over to Mary. I didn't want to give you this note, because it was important that you find it after I was gone. I am returning to Philadelphia to find my long-lost love as I told you. And I do want so much for you to write to me. I just don't know how much longer I will be able to write to you. I have been having problems with my arms and legs that, quite honestly, frightens me. It doesn't happen all the time, but it seems to be getting worse. There have been times when my hands shake badly, and I don't think the condition will improve.

But I am still happy, Lee. I am going home, and I am free; all thanks to you. I may not have a long time on this earth, but I intend to make the most of it. I will get to love again, something I never thought possible. In the brief time we were together, I found I could love again because I love you. I will ask you to kiss me before I leave and if you grant me this one last wish, and I'm sure that you will, it will be my first kiss since my love kissed me before I left almost twenty-five years ago? That is such a sad thing, but now I will have my opportunity to change that and when you kiss me, it will begin my new life.

So, please write to me often. Tell me of Mary and your life together, and tell her that although I never met her, I love her because we are so very much alike.

If I do not write as often, it will be only because of my impairment. If need be, I will dictate my replies; hopefully to my new husband.

If you look in the bottom of the chest, you will find a photograph I had made two years ago, and I want you to have it. Could you send me one of you and your precious Mary? It would mean so much to me.

Tomorrow I will be leaving you physically, but part of my soul will always be with you and Mary.

With All My Love,

Lucy

Lee lowered the letter slowly, an incredibly feeling of loss filling his soul. Lucy was dying. He didn't know what condition she had, but deep down he knew that she was right. He hoped she'd be able to last years, but the thought of losing her was heart-breaking. He had only spent a single day with her, yet he felt that she owned part of his soul as well.

Once he had her address in Philadelphia, he would write to her as often as possible and keep her in his and Mary's lives where she belonged.

He tucked the letter into his shirt pocket and returned to the linen chest, took out all the bedding and found the photograph on the bottom. It was in a glassed frame and was of the Lucy that had so overwhelmed him when he saw her the morning after the shooting, but he could see the sadness and loneliness in her eyes, which detracted so much from the Lucy he'd known after she'd been freed from her long prison sentence. He would ask her for a new photograph, hopefully with her new husband.

He laid it on the bed as he put the bedding back into the chest, closed the top and took a deep breath.

He picked up Lucy's portrait, took the envelope out of his pocket and left the room. He went down to the library and looked for a place to keep them safe. He found a drawer under the center bookshelf, slid it open and found a ream of maps. After removing them and setting them on a side table, he placed the letter and photograph on the bottom, then returned the maps too the drawer to hide the priceless artifacts beneath.

The letter had drained him, so he walked into the kitchen and removed his shirt, then washed in the cold water and went back upstairs. He chose one of the guest bedrooms for his resting place. He had originally thought he'd sleep in Lucy's room, but somehow it seemed irreverent.

He slid under the blankets and fell into a deep sleep; still disturbed by Lucy's letter.

———

He awoke early to the chimes of the grandfather clock in the parlor, which he hadn't even noticed. Remarkably, he hadn't even heard it before, either. He guessed his timing was always wrong. He heard it strike six times, so it was six o'clock in the morning.

He hadn't slept this well in quite a while, which surprised him because he'd been so troubled by Lucy's letter. He slid from the blankets, remade the bed, then quickly dressed and went downstairs. He needed a bath and thought he had enough time, so he built a fire in the huge cook stove, filled two large pots with water and set them on top. Then he began filling the tub with cold water. It wouldn't be a hot bath, but it'd be better than the cold ones he was used to.

He stripped naked and enjoyed the freedom and privacy to walk through the house without clothing. It was his house, after all. *Thank you, Lucy,* he thought.

He dumped the hot water into the tub and lowered himself into the warm water. He took the soap that was there. It was probably Stella's rose scented soap, but he didn't care. He washed himself thoroughly and shampooed his hair with the same bar of soap. When he was done, he stepped out of the tub and dried himself with one of the many towels in the room. He used the warm water to shave, then drained the tub and used his towel to dry the tub and keep it clean. Then, he had no idea what to do with the towel until he saw a square, covered basket in the corner. He opened it and saw other dirty towels, then dropped his in and decided to go upstairs and see what men's clothing he could conjure up.

He knew Frank was too thin, but Ed Richards should have a shirt that would fit. He found one he liked and tried it on, finding it fit well. Then he found some clean underwear but didn't bother with the pants because he knew that there was no chance that they'd fit, but he did take some of Ed's socks. He felt amazingly clean and smelling a bit flowery as he left the room. The ladies would have to live with it.

He went downstairs to the kitchen to see what was available for breakfast and found some items he had no idea what they were. He found a can of peaches, though, so he opened it and then he put on some coffee and ate the peaches while the water heated up.

He continued his search in the expansive kitchen and hit a gold mine when he lifted a flowered porcelain cover on the counter and found a cake sitting on a plate which soon produced an enticing aroma of brown sugar and cinnamon.

He cut himself a large piece, put it on a plate then poured some coffee into the pot of boiling water and waited a minute. After filling a large mug with the fresh coffee, he sat down at the polished kitchen table, took a bite of the cake and rolled his eyes. *This was amazing!* It really went well with the coffee, too. He thought he'd have to see if he could get Mary to figure out how to make one as he quickly polished it off and was tempted to have a second piece but decided to save it for later.

At 7:30, according to the grandfather clock that he had just wound, he left the house and went out to the barn. He found Jin in a good mood, saddled him and rode out ten minutes later, heading for the farm.

When he arrived at the ranch, he first spotted the men out in the hay fields driving their harvesting combines, but had only ridden halfway down the access road when the three Flannery women, all dressed in riding outfits, popped out of the front door, and waited for him with big smiles. It seems they were all anxious to see the big house and its contents; including the magical sewing machine.

"Good morning, Flannery ladies," he said as he dismounted.

"Aren't you looking grand this fine September morn!" Maggie said loudly as they stepped down from the porch.

Lee stepped forward and gave Maggie a hug.

"And what's that I'm smelling, Mr. Ryan?" she asked.

"That's for you to wonder about, Mrs. Flannery. Shall we go, ladies?"

Lee looked at his future bride who looked amazing in her riding clothes. Then again, he thought, she always looked amazing.

They had already saddled their horses, so after going to the barn and retrieving them, everyone mounted and rode at a good pace out of the farm. Lee watched Maggie, as he didn't know if she could ride at all. She must have ridden in the past, because she handled her horse well.

Fifteen minutes later, they were stepping onto the enormous porch with its polished wooden surface, and after entering, Mary quickly took her mother's hand to show her the sewing machine.

He heard a surprising squeal of delight from Maggie and giggles from her daughters followed by excited chatter and knew that Maggie wouldn't leave that room for a while.

Mary and Katherine then exited the room with big smiles, and Lee followed them as they climbed the stairs to Lucy's room where Mary would show her the incredible dresses.

Once in the room, Katherine saw the closet full of beautiful dresses and was overwhelmed. Mary, being Mary, told her to pick out the ones she liked the best. Katherine, despite her admiration of the clothes, bypassed those she knew Mary would like.

After they had picked out their dresses, Lee said, "Mary, Lucy emptied all the drawers except for one. That's the bottom center drawer. I have no idea what is in there, but I think that you might."

Mary smiled at Lee, turned to the dresser and slid open the bottom drawer and lifted one of the silky garments from the open drawer.

She turned and grinned at him, saying, "Those, my almost husband, are nightgowns. You'll see what they are for in eighteen days."

Seeing the silky-smooth fabric in her hands and imaging Mary inside gave him goosebumps, so all he did was stare, which after a few seconds, made both sisters giggle before Mary returned it to the drawer and closed it.

Lee shook off the image and said, "Mary, I think you may want to show Katherine the last bedroom on the right."

"Alright," she replied then, as she walked past Lee, gave him a quick wink and a knowing smile that made his vivid imaginary vision of Mary in that nightgown resurface.

She and Katherine had already left the room before Lee recovered and trotted behind them to Stella's bedroom.

When they entered, Mary and Katherine found many more dresses and other things in the room, so Mary turned and asked, "Were these Stella's?"

"I think so. By the way, in the drawers in Lucy's dressing table are lots of perfumes and colognes, and I'd be surprised if there weren't more here."

Mary's eyebrows arched as she asked, "You were in her room last night looking around?"

"I checked out all of the bedrooms last night, and I'm glad that I did. You don't want to know what I found in Frank's room; but suffice it to say it was necessary that I burned it all."

"I can imagine what it was," said Katherine quietly.

Lee was sure that she did, but asked, "Katherine, would you mind if I borrowed Mary for a few minutes?"

"As long as it doesn't involve trying on one of those nightgowns," she replied with a light giggle.

"I should be so lucky. Could you come downstairs with me, Mary?"

Mary took his hand and he walked with her down the long staircase into the library, then closed both doors.

He let her sit down behind the desk and said, "Mary, the reason I looked in Lucy's room was that I was searching for a letter. I just felt that she wanted to tell me something, even though she hadn't told me about it. It was just an eerie feeling. I don't know why, but I felt her presence and I was drawn to the room."

"Did you find one?" she asked quietly.

Lee exhaled sharply then replied, "Yes, Mary, I found one and it broke my heart to read it. Stay there and I'll let you read it."

"Alright."

Mary didn't know what to think. It was Lucy again. *Why? And why was Lee so upset about the letter?*

Lee opened the drawer and took out the maps, setting them on the side table before he took out the envelope. He left the photograph in the drawer for the time being.

He stepped over to the desk, pulled the heavy oak straight-backed chair beside her heavy leather chair, sat down beside her and handed her the envelope.

Mary saw the pain in Lee's eyes, before she looked back to the envelope, opened it, slid the letter free, then began to read.

Lee watched her closely, and soon saw her tears forming and sliding down her face as she finally began to understand Lucy.

Mary was just as affected by what she read as Lee had been and understood why he seemed so devastated, especially as he'd only known her for a day. This woman who was so remarkable as to touch Lee's heart in such a short time was dying and she felt ashamed for having such demeaning thoughts of her. Lucy, who had lost her love so long ago and had to live without love for so long had been freed by Lee, so she could go back and find the love she had lost. *Who was she to begrudge Lucy one kiss?* The one kiss that must have meant so much to her.

She looked up at Lee through her watery eyes and asked quietly, "Could I see the picture now?"

Lee smiled at her, stood and returned to the bookcase. lifted the photograph from the drawer and walked back to Mary. He presented it to her and watched her blue eyes look at Lucy.

Mary saw a stunningly beautiful woman with intelligent eyes and a face that spoke of her loneliness and sorrow. The woman who had written that letter to Lee had spoken to her as well, and Mary felt a strong kinship with the woman she had never met.

She stared at the picture and said in a whisper, "I'm sorry, Lucy. I wish I could have met you."

After three minutes, she finally returned the picture to Lee, then gave him the letter. He placed them both back in the drawer and covered them with the maps then closed the drawer and quietly stepped back to Mary.

Lee lifted her from the chair and held her close and saidd quietly, "Do you understand now, my love?"

She was still crying on his chest but managed to answer, "Yes, I do understand, and I'm sorry, Lee. I apologize to you and to Lucy. I didn't understand before."

"I know, Mary. It's such an unusual friendship that emerged from such a difficult time, but we'll do what we can to make Lucy's last years as happy as we can. And do you know how we do that, Mary? We'll make Lucy happy by being happy ourselves. She'll feel our joy and happiness, just like I feel the joy of just having you close. We'll write to her and send her pictures. When the children start arriving, we'll make her their godmother. But right now, Mary Flannery, it's about us. We need to start our lives together beginning with this day."

Mary had one last sniff before nodding and saying, "You're right, Lee. Let's begin now."

She shook her red hair and wiped the tears that still clung to her face before she said, "I'm glad you closed the doors."

"I knew how it would affect you. It was worse for me last night."

"So, tell me, Mister Ryan. Why do you smell like roses?" she asked with her normal, bright smile.

Her smile changed his mood before he replied, "I took a bath this morning and didn't realize the soap was probably Stella's. There are all sorts of flowery soaps in there, but I didn't find any plain white soap. I assume there must be some in the house somewhere. I can't imagine Ed Richards would like to talk to his ranch hands and thugs smelling like roses."

Mary laughed and said, "I suppose that would have been bad for him. On the other hand, sir, maybe I'll try using some myself. That and some of Lucy's fragrances."

Lee smiled at Mary and said, "Whatever you want to do to entice me into your bed faster is fine with me, woman."

"Don't tempt me, mister. I'm awfully close to dragging you upstairs and having my way with you."

"What kind of talk is that?" Maggie asked as she entered the side door wearing an appropriate mother's scolding face.

Lee laughed and said, "From what I hear, Mrs. Flannery, you were saying some pretty racy talk yourself in front of your wee daughters just recently, so you'll not be one to be doing the finger shaking."

Maggie laughed and replied, "It was only the truth, now."

"So, what did you think of the sewing machine?" he asked.

"It's a marvel. I can't wait to try it out. I hear that there are some dresses that need adjusting."

Mary said, "Katherine has some she'll need hemmed and shortened around the top. Lucy was rather chesty."

"And so are you, Mary my love. So, all of the dresses that you chose fit you?"

"Perfectly."

"Well, at least I can use it on Katherine's."

Lee then said, "Mary and I are going into Nueva Luz to start ordering furniture and things. The only two items I've seen in the house that I'd like are the desk in Frank's room and the grandfather clock. Mary, have you seen anything that you'd like?"

"Could I have some things from Lucy's room?"

"Of course, Mary. If we know what we need for our house, we can go and order them now and specify a delivery date. I also need to send that telegram to my parents. We should be back for lunch. Oh, speaking of food. Can we all go to the kitchen for a minute? I found something this morning I'd like to see if my bride could learn to make for her new husband."

After showing them the cake and letting them each sample its sweetness, Mary pointed out a large cookbook on a shelf and told Lee she could bake the cake for him.

———

An hour later, she and Lee were in Nueva Luz where Lee first sent the telegram to his parents. He had already sent a letter but hadn't specified the wedding date. Then they went to the construction company and asked when they want the cookstove and tub to arrive. They checked their schedule and gave them a date.

Then they went to Enright's Dry Goods to place their order for the furniture and other household necessities. He was tickled pink at the huge sale he was going to make and carried out an armload of thick catalogs. They spent three hours ordering all that they needed to furnish the house and when they were done, the bill was a whopping $538.86. Lee wrote out the draft and specified when the various items should be delivered to the house and which had to be warehoused for a while.

When they returned to the big house just after one o'clock, they found it empty. Maggie had left a note that said they had to return to the farm and fix lunch for the men and that she and Katherine wouldn't be returning today.

After reading the note, Lee asked, "Mary, do we want to have a private lunch here? They have a lot of food."

"I'll just fix something quick."

Mary sliced some bread and made two sandwiches with smoked ham and some sweet relish that they found, which turned out to be quite tasty.

"So, Mary," he asked as they ate, "have we forgotten anything?"

She shook her head and replied, "I can't see how that is possible after going through those catalogs page by page."

"We can always add what we need later, I suppose."

Mary popped the last of her sandwich into her mouth, and said, "I'll be right back. I just thought of something."

Lee nodded as she popped up from her chair and walked quickly out of the kitchen.

Lee watched her hasty exit but just shrugged his shoulders as he started on his second sandwich.

He finished the second one, and took the plates to the sink, washed them and set them in the drying rack, but Mary still hadn't returned, and he wondered where she was and what she was doing.

So, he left the kitchen, walked down the hallway, glancing into the empty rooms until he reached the stairs and stepped up to the second floor.

When he reached the upper floor hallway, he asked quietly, "Mary?"

He heard her reply, "I'm in Lucy's room," and walked down the long hall to the open door.

When he turned into Lucy's room he froze in his tracks.

Mary was standing before him wearing one of Lucy's nightgowns and to say it was revealing would be a woeful understatement, but he could see so much in her blue eyes as he slowly stepped closer to her.

She was looking into his green eyes as she softly said, "Lee, I want you in the most urgent way. Can you make love to me now?"

He took another more, long step and wrapped his arms around her silk-shrouded and almost naked body and said, "Even if you hadn't asked, Mary, I don't believe that there was any chance of my leaving this room without making love to you."

She slipped her lips next to his ear and whispered, "Please."

Lee kissed her with as much love and passion as he could release and as he began kissing her neck, she started undressing him.

He continued kissing her in places she'd never been kissed before as she began fumbling with his buttons as she felt weak and goosebumps erupted all over her skin.

But she finally managed with his assistance until his last vestige of clothing dropped to the floor and he took her in his arms and as he kissed her passionately and his hands slid over her smooth, curvaceous body.

Mary had been waiting for this for so long and began exploring Lee's magnificent, masculine body as she returned his kisses with equally impassioned responses.

Lee finally decided that the nightgown had done its job, slipped it over her head and gasped when he saw Mary's perfection.

"Mary, you are magnificent," he said hoarsely before kissing her again.

Mary was already more excited than she'd ever been before as Lee slipped his arms behind her knees, lifted her from the floor, carried her to the big bed and laid her gently on the quilted softness.

He looked down at Mary's marvelous blue eyes that were framed by her sea of red hair and said, "I want to make you happier and feel more loved than you ever thought possible, Mary."

Mary sighed and as she laid her hand on Lee's heavily muscled thigh, said, "I'm already there, Lee."

But she was so wrong as Lee did all he could to make his Mary understand how much she was loved.

Mary's frenetic, lusty responses to his caresses and kisses was no surprise to Lee, nor were her loud, excited verbal demands and cries of pleasure. His Mary was nothing less than a vibrant, fully aware young woman without inhibitions.

For twenty more minutes, they writhed and shouted as they experienced a release of the years of restrained lust and passion.

Finally, when neither could deny the inevitable any longer, they experienced love to its ultimate conclusion, and after they had collapsed onto the quilt in a perspired exhaustion, they laid on the bed clinging tightly to each other as they breathed heavily.

Lee finally had enough air to gasp, "Mary, my Mary, I hope you enjoyed that as much as I did. My, lord, you were amazing!"

Mary had to wait a few seconds to catch her breath before she kissed his chest and replied, "I never knew it could be so exciting, not once in my wild imaginings. I needed you so much. It's almost all I've been thinking about."

Lee kissed her damp forehead and said, "My sweet wife, you have no idea how you affect me. I can think of only one thing better."

"And what could that be?" she asked as she looked into his eyes."

"If we do it again."

C. J. PETIT

Mary laughed and kissed him, thinking he was talking about tomorrow, but when he began do touch her again, she soon discovered it wasn't going to be nearly that long.

———

They enjoyed being with each other for two more hours, before they realized they had to make an appearance at the farm, so they regretfully slid from the bed to dress.

As they dressed, each took time to admire the other as they did.

They finally were fully dressed but spent an extra few minutes kissing and running hands over places that had been forbidden just hours earlier.

"We have to stop, Mary. I want to drag your cute behind back to the bed and ravage you again."

Mary sighed and said, "I suppose we'll have to postpone any more bedding for the moment. You think I have a cute behind?"

"Don't get me started again. You know what I think of that behind of yours and not to mention your…"

She put her finger to his lips and said, "Don't say it. I know where you're going. Let's just go back to the farm."

He laughed, and they walked out of Lucy's bedroom and as they entered the hallway, Lee laughed, then shouted, "Thank you, Lucy!"

Mary joined him in laughter and said more quietly, "Yes, thank you, Lucy."

She wondered if Lucy had left the nightgowns in the drawer just for that purpose and knew that she probably had because she had wanted them to be happy; *and were they happy!*

They went downstairs, left the house and twenty minutes later, rode out of the ranch and headed back to the farm.

———

"Well, you're finally back," said Maggie when they entered, "Did you spend all that time ordering things for your house?"

Lee answered, "No, ma'am. We did spend a frightfully amount of time ordering things, though. Harry kept bringing catalogs and you don't want to know the final bill. After we finished ordering we stopped back at the big house and found your note. We thought it was too late to get back and have lunch. So, Mary made us lunch, and then we spent some time exploring."

Mary glanced at Lee, then stifled her laughter and had to turn away.

"Did you find anything interesting?" Maggie asked.

"Oh, we looked in some new places. There was one area where I found two interesting things on top and something nice behind them, too."

Mary tried. She tried so hard, but she couldn't hold it back, and quickly left the room before she started roaring in laughter.

Maggie watched her go, turned to Lee and asked, "What made Mary feel so jolly, I wonder?"

"She's been that way all day. I say something relatively innocent, and she starts laughing. Maybe it's just a release from all the excitement that had been building up in her the past few days."

"Maybe that's it. I can't recall ever seeing Mary act that way."

"I'll go talk to her and see what's up. Did you want her to help with making dinner?"

"No, Katherine will help. You two have a lot to do."

"Yes, we do. Thank you, Maggie."

Lee walked into the family room. Mary wasn't there which left her in her room with Katherine.

In her room, Mary was still recovering from Lee's answer and not-so-subtle reference to her recently discovered treasures.

"Mary, what is the matter?" her sister asked.

"Oh, nothing Katherine. Lee just said something that struck me as funny."

"So, where were you two all afternoon?"

The question alone was enough to start laughing again and Katherine was confused. *What had she said that was so funny?*

Lee heard her laughing and wondered what Katherine had said.

Finally, Mary slowed down enough to say, "We ordered all of the things and then stopped back at the big house and found Mama's note. So, I made Lee some lunch and then we came here. You'd be surprised how many things we had to order and how much it all cost. It cost half as much as the house."

"Really?"

"Lee sent a telegram to his parents and invited them to the wedding, and we had to go to the contractor again. It was a busy day."

"You do look worn out."

Mary honestly tried not to laugh. She tried deep breathing but didn't matter. She kept laughing until tears began to fall.

There was a knock on the door, so Katherine walked to the door and opened it, all the time watching her now giggling sister.

Lee asked, "Katherine, is Mary okay?"

"She seems to think everything is funny."

"She had a very tiring day. I guess she's just worn out."

Mary finally laid down on her bed and curled up, still laughing.

"You stay here, Katherine. You can be the chaperone while I talk to Mary."

The mention of a chaperone added fuel to the fire as Mary's giggling intensified as Lee sat down on the edge of the bed.

Finally, Mary was laughed out, opened her eyes and saw Lee's face.

He said to her quietly, "I'm sorry, my Mary. I should have been more serious in my replies. You're just hard to get off my mind. I love you, dearly, my Mary."

His tone and words sobered her, and she whispered, "I'm sorry, Lee, I just couldn't help it."

"I know. Let's go and have a seat in the family room."

He led her out to the main room. Katherine followed out of curiosity.

Once everyone was in place, Lee began talking about routine things.

"Tomorrow I've got to go and clean out the cabin. Willie Thompson really made a mess of it, so I'll probably spend all day out there. Mary, why don't you and Katherine go over to the big house and you can put small tags on anything you want to take to our house when we move? I assume that most of the furniture and kitchenware stays. We ordered all of that yesterday."

Mary nodded and replied, "We can do that."

"Good. Now, about our wedding. We both need to see Father Kelly. I think there are some things he is supposed to lecture us on before the big day. Did you want to go and see him Friday?"

Mary answered by turning to Katherine, and asking, "Did you want to go over to the big house tomorrow?"

Katherine replied, "That would be fun. And, Lee, could we bring you lunch? I've never seen your cabin or your canyon with the horses."

"That's right, you haven't. Mary knows the way, so I'll look forward to having the two prettiest young ladies in Arizona coming to visit."

"How about the wedding visit with Father Kelly, Mary?" Lee asked.

"Um, sure. Friday is fine," she replied.

"I suppose you'll be picking out your wedding dress. I need a new suit, too."

Mary had shifted from wild laughing to an almost somber mood.

"I'll see what Lucy has in her closet that will work."

Lee sensed her troubles and wondered if they stemmed from their early afternoon of lovemaking. He'd see if he could get her alone later and talk to her.

There were loud noises from the kitchen as the Flannery men came tromping in from the fields.

"Sounds like the boys are home. Let's see if they're done," Lee said.

They walked out to the kitchen and were met by tired and satisfied redheaded Flannery males.

"It's a record, Maggie! We harvested a full day faster this year!" Ian exclaimed, "I think it's because Conor and Dylan have gotten so much bigger."

Lee smiled at the proud father's comment. The two younger boys were still shorter than Mary and not much heavier.

"Tomorrow we'll send out notes to the ranchers to come and get their hay. We'll start deliveries for the others. Lee, do we want to move the Diamond R hay?"

"For a few days, let's leave it in the fields. Once the dust has settled, we can start moving it into that big barn. I'll be able to help. Now, Ian, I'll be writing a draft for the hay. I'll be setting up an account for the Shamrock Cattle Company and that will be its first expense. When we sell some cattle, the money will be deposited there. So, after the first deposit, I'll move the cost of the hay back into my account."

"Aye, it sounds like a good business plan."

"It means I'll need to ride to Fort Grant and talk to the army. The last time I was there, Sergeant O'Malley said the first local purchases wouldn't be made until March, but he also told me that they were already low on beef. I think they'll find a way to buy cattle to keep the men from grumbling. Does anyone want to come along?"

Ian looked at his boys and saw the two younger lads' begging eyes.

"Well, I suppose I could let Dylan and Conor go for a couple of days," Ian said.

The boys grinned, then thanked their father and Lee. Then they wanted to know when they'd be going.

"Monday morning around seven o'clock is a good time. It's only a four-hour ride. You're both gonna be mighty sore when you get back, but it'll be an experience. We should be back in time for dinner."

Maggie interrupted when she said, "Speaking of dinner, you boys get out of here. Katherine and I are going to start cooking dinner. Mary probably wants to spend some time with Lee. Off with you all, then."

Lee wasn't surprised at all by Maggie's comment, then turned to Mary and said, "Mary, let's go to town and see if there has been a reply from my parents."

"Alright."

He took her hand and led her out the front door and into the barn where they saddled the two palominos in silence, which reinforced Lee's belief that Mary was upset about something.

Once they were walking their horses toward town, Lee turned to Mary and asked, "No secrets between us, my Mary. What is bothering you?"

"Lee, I feel so ashamed of what happened in the house. I wanted you so badly, and I was looking for any excuse for it to happen and when I saw the nightgowns, I was convinced that they were there for just that reason. I was so happy when we were making love and right afterwards that I thought I would be all right. But after all that laughter, I realized that I had done exactly what I had done before, only much more willingly."

I had to be honest with myself, Lee. I'm ashamed of myself for what I did. I'm nothing but a loose woman pretending to be a good one. I shouldn't have dressed in that nightgown knowing that you wouldn't be able to resist. I feel so dirty. How can I see Father Kelly? How can I walk down that aisle in a white wedding dress, even before today? I'm a slut, Lee."

Lee was stunned by her second confession and collected his thoughts for a few seconds before replying, "Mary, you have to be more that just honest with yourself. You have to understand who you really are and in no way are you a wanton woman. When it happened two years ago, you were gullible, and John Everett took advantage of you. He wooed you with words of love to fill your heart and make you susceptible to his advances, but his only purpose was to bed you. You believed you were going to be married shortly. Do you honestly believe that all the couples that are about to be married are chaste? I would imagine that less than half haven't done what we did earlier, and I'll bet that very few of those women think of themselves the way you do. It's just the Irish guilt coming out, Mary. What we did today was nothing less than the physical expression of our love for each other. Remember when I gave you Qing Jin? I could read your eyes, Mary. You knew when I told you how much I loved you, even to the point of giving you that gift, even if you weren't going to be my wife, that there was only one gift you could give me that was its equal and probably much greater; or am I wrong?"

Mary sighed and answered, "No, you're not. It was on my mind."

"Because it was a gift, Mary. It's a gift we gave each other. Now, let me ask you one question. Did you enjoy sharing that gift?"

Mary closed her eyes briefly, recalling the passion and admitted, "Oh, yes, maybe I enjoyed it too much."

"Did you ever wonder why God made it so enjoyable? Why He made it, so men and women wanted to be together? He made it that way because it's right. Mary, can you name one commandment that we broke earlier today?"

Mary had to pause as she ran through the ten commandments in her head before replying, "No. Now that you mention it, I can't think of one, but everyone says that lust itself is sinful."

"Pure lust, perhaps. Like the lust that Ed Richards had for our young Lucy when he raped her. He didn't love her, and she surely didn't love him. But lust drove him to take her, ruining both their lives. Lust by itself is ruinous. But what you and I felt, Mary, and what we will always feel, is a deep love. The desire we felt to be together was just part of that love. I, for one, felt no guilt whatsoever in loving you, Mary. I'd do it again right now if we had the chance. I just don't want you to feel like you are somehow sinful or different from other women. Do you remember what you told me that your precious mother said about how much fun she had with your father?"

"How could I forget?" she replied as she smiled at the thought.

"Do you think your parents are sinners?"

"Of course, not, but they were married."

"Are you sure they didn't do anything beforehand? Your mother reminds me a lot of you, Mary. You're both loving and vital women. I wouldn't be surprised one bit if they didn't succumb to the passion that they felt for each other."

Mary thought about the many times she would see her parents engage in mild teasing and touching each other over the years and realized that it was much more than just a possibility and felt a growing sense of relief.

"Maybe they did, but I can never ask her."

"You don't need to, Mary. I just want to know that what you consider as sinful lust, I am eternally grateful that my wife will be as active in our bedroom as I am. I can't tell you how enormously pleased you made me earlier today. You not only satisfied my physical needs and desires, but you filled my heart and soul with your unbounded love. You, Miss Flannery, have nothing at all to cause you the least amount of shame."

Mary smiled at him and asked, "Lee, how do you do this?"

"Do what?"

"Talk me out of one of my moods."

"It's just that I know you, my Mary. Just as you know me. You've helped me get past some difficult times, too. Now, on Friday, I want to sit with you as we talk to Father Kelly and know that you are as good a woman as any to talk to him about a wedding. Because, my love, it's all so very true."

She stopped Qing Jin and waited for Lee to bring Jin next to her before they mutually leaned over and exchanged a quick kiss in the gap between the horses. Anything longer could have resulted in an equally quick drop to the Arizona dirt.

After they arrived in town, they dismounted and entered the Western Union office and found a telegram from his parents.

LEE RYAN FLANNERY FARM NUEVA LUZ ARIZONA

ECSTATIC AT WEDDING NOTICE
WE WILL BOTH BE THERE ON OCTOBER 10
CAN'T WAIT TO MEET MARY
HAPPY FOR YOU BOTH
LOVE

SEAMUS AND MARY RYAN PUEBLO COLORADO

Lee handed it to Mary who read it, and he could tell when she reached the last line.

Mary's eyes snapped to his and asked, "Your mother's name is Mary? How is it that you've never mentioned that?"

"Because her real name is Maire. She uses Mary most of the time because too many people think it's like a female horse. At home, my father always used the Irish, so I grew up knowing her as Maire."

"Oh. So, there isn't some deep, hidden reason for you not to tell me," Mary asked with a smile.

Lee laughed and said, "No, ma'am, none at all. I'm sure she's tickled pink to find that my wife will be a Mary, though."

It was a much more pleasant and chatty return ride to the farm as Mary had finally forgiven herself and deciding that she wasn't such a bad person after all but wasn't about to change her lusty ways with her husband. After all, he'd told her that he liked her that way.

––––––––

The next day went as planned and Lee spent the whole day fixing up the cabin, and one of the first jobs he'd undertake was to make the bed larger and get additional blankets and a new mattress. But restoring the cabin to its previous well-ordered state didn't take as long as he expected. He had it shipshape when he was outside removing the last remnants of Willie's blood from his porch when he spotted Qing Jin and Blaze making their way across the desert to his cabin.

He stepped off the porch and waved as they approached. Hagar sat next to him watching the two horses. When they got closer, he recognized the horses and one of the riders had a memorable scent, but he didn't know the other one.

Lee opened the gate and let them both in, then let Hagar have the pleasure of closing the gate. Mary had told Katherine about Hagar's ability to secure the opening and she watched in disbelief as the dog promptly closed the gate.

"Lee, this is amazing! This place doesn't even look like it belongs here!" Katherine exclaimed as she stepped down and gazed down the canyon.

Lee was looking at her mount as he said, "Katherine, look at Blaze. She knows she's back where she started and can smell the herd."

When Katherine turned and looked at her horse, she noticed Blaze's nostrils were flaring, her ears were peaked, and she was staring down the canyon.

"Why don't we all go down and visit the herd. The only horses in a corral are Jin and his mares. I won't even saddle Jin."

He called the palomino, then jumped onto his back before they began trotting deeper into the canyon.

"Right now, there are a hundred and eight horses, and almost half now are under three years old. I have a lot of yearlings and foals."

As they approached the herd, Katherine asked, "Lee, do you have a brand assigned to your ranch? What if someone comes and steals them?"

"The ranch is listed as the L-R connected. I don't brand my horses, but if you look just inside Blaze's left ear, what do you see?"

Katherine folded Blaze's ear and saw what looked like a tattoo that read: *L-R 0092*.

"You tattoo them?"

"Technically, no. When they are foaled, I use a special ink and brush to paint that number in their ear. It's the same ink that the Chinese use to create tattoos. I know how to make it and keep a good supply on hand. It never rubs off and doesn't hurt the horse at all. If any of my horses are stolen, those numbers are much easier to trace, and rustlers wouldn't even think of looking. They'd see a naked rump and figure it was safe to steal it."

They soon arrived at the herds and dismounted. There were now four distinct herds, including one of young bachelor stallions.

"Look at the foals!" Katherine shouted, "There are so many!"

She was in heaven looking at all the beautiful animals as they walked among the amazingly well-discipline horses. Even Lee, who saw them often, was always in awe of their majestic beauty.

After twenty minutes, they returned to Lee's cabin and after entering the construction, Mary was impressed that, although it was only a single room, it was a large room and well-built with a good floor and large fireplace. She immediately thought how wonderful it would be to spend their wedding night here.

She saw Lee smiling at her and she smiled back and winked, which pleased Lee more than she realized. Mary was flirting with him and he knew that she had accepted herself as she really was and without guilt.

They had the lunch that Mary and Katherine had prepared, and after they left, Lee began working on expanding the bed. He cut some of the logs he had stored for firewood into posts and trimmed them to length. He attached them to the existing bed and ran rails down both sides and the top and bottom. When he was done, he had almost doubled the size of his narrow bed, then used a rope weave to provide support for the mattress.

There was enough time in the day to finish the project, so he rode down to Nueva Luz and bought a second mattress, larger sheets and more blankets. He loaded them all on the mule he had brought with him and returned to the cabin. He was pleased with his construction and decided to test it first. So, once it was all assembled, Lee stepped back, took a deep breath and leapt onto the finished bed, half-expecting it to crash beneath him, but he just bounced as the ropes stretched and rebounded. He rolled onto his back, laughing at his successful dive, and knew he and Mary would be spending many happy hours testing it even more.

———

The next day he returned to the farm and found the Flannery men loading their wagons full of hay. They had four wagons and Ian told him that two of his ranch customers had already arrived to take their orders. Simon's Livery had also showed up and filled his wagon.

After unsaddling Jin, Lee helped with the loading until all four of the wagons were packed full of bundles of hay and were driven away by Ian and his sons.

He stayed behind because he needed to wash again before he and Mary went to Nueva Luz for their visit with Father Kelly.

So, early in the afternoon, Lee and Mary rode into Nueva Luz to have their talk with Father Kelly before their marriage. Mary was still a bit anxious, but not nearly as bad as she had been.

As it turned out, even her minimized worries were groundless, and she discovered that soon enough when she and Lee were greeted by the priest at the door of the rectory with a stern face.

"I was expecting you two fine young folks soon, and I can't wait to give you a proper chastising about the evils of lust and excessive coupling."

Mary had been momentarily stunned until Father Kelly laughed as his Irish eyes twinkled mischievously and gestured for them to enter.

Father Kelly dispensed with all the formal lectures he was required to give and just amiably chatted with them for almost an hour, which included Mary telling him that she'd confessed to Lee in their new atrium and that was when she realized how much he really did love her. He told them that he couldn't be happier about their marriage and extracted a promise that he'd be able to christen their new home before he baptized their babies.

Before they left, he hugged them both before giving them his blessing.

Mary was beaming as she and Lee left the rectory and walked to their horses.

After they had mounted, she turned to Lee and said, "Lee, was I wrong in thinking that Father Kelly knew we had been together?"

Lee smiled back at her, "No, my Mary, you aren't wrong. I'm sure he did. It's like we had reached a new level of love that can only be achieved until the physical joins the emotional."

Mary laughed and said, "My, my, aren't you the philosopher."

Lee smiled back at her and said, "One of my many hidden talents, ma'am."

Mary was still euphoric as they turned their horses out of Nueva Luz to return to the farm.

Lee left Mary at the farm and returned to his cabin for the night.

———

On Saturday, he returned to the farm to escort Mary to confession. Neither confessed to the sin that Mary was now convinced was no sin at all and on Sunday, they went to Mass, Lee now sitting in the same pew as the Flannery family and receiving a big smile from Father Kelly as he saw them together.

———

Monday morning, Lee, Dylan and Conor headed out of the farm southbound to Fort Grant. The boys were excited as neither had been further than five miles from the farm before.

They chattered almost non-stop along the way asking questions about everything from his herds, to his gunfights and even the cattle on the Diamond R.

When they arrived at Fort Grant, Lee led them to the Quartermaster's office and was pleased to find a still-Sergeant O'Malley behind his desk, the Irish whisky having not caused any interruption in his career. The sergeant was grinning as he approached.

"Sergeant O'Malley, my good man, I'd like to introduce you to two of my future in-laws. This is Dylan Flannery, and this young lad is Conor Flannery."

The sergeant looked at the two redheads and broadened his grin before saying, "Why, there'd be no doubt as to those lads being full of the Irish. Fine looking lads, they are, too."

He shook both their hands before asking, "Are you bringing us more horses already, Lee?"

"No, I've come to ask you about your beef situation. It seems that I've suddenly come into possession of over thirteen hundred head of prime cattle. With the Flannery family, I'm starting a company called the Shamrock Cattle Company."

"Well, you've chosen a fine name and a fine time to be starting, I don't mind saying. I told you just a little while ago that the bigwigs in Washington were deciding what to do. While they were deciding, the commanders of the western forts were all sending messages to the general that their men weren't getting enough to eat. So, the general sent them a message three days ago telling them to go ahead and start procuring local cattle. How many can you sell to us right away? The men are grumbling something fierce."

"How many can you handle in your pens?"

"We can use fifty to start and then fifty more each month."

"I'd only be able to do it for about a year because I don't want to cut the herd too deep. I want to see how many calves we get next spring. But I think we could do that and I can have some of the other ranchers fill the gaps, too."

"Glory be! The commander will be pleased as punch. I'll go tell him and get his okay. You wait here."

Sergeant O'Malley scurried out the door as Dylan asked, "Is that going to work, Lee?"

"I think so. I checked the herd, so it should work out. We'll have eight hundred total new calves by the time the original cattle are all moved, and the timing works out that we should be able to keep bringing beef to the fort indefinitely."

Sergeant O'Malley came bouncing back into the room and said, "Lee, my boy, the commander was as tickled as I was. When can you bring us fifty head? He's authorized me to give you a contract for thirty dollars a head."

"I'll bring some in two days. Will that work?"

"Two days! You're a saint, Lee. A true saint."

O'Malley took out a standard contract form and filled out two copies. They both signed, and he gave Lee one of the completed forms.

"Will you be staying the night, Lee?"

"No, my good friend. I've got to head back and get the cattle ready to move. We'll need to start out tomorrow morning."

They shook hands, and Lee took the boys over to the sutler's for a chicken lunch and began their return ride back an hour later.

––––––

When they returned, the family was pleased with the news, and Lee asked who would be helping on the cattle drive and was paired with Sean and Patrick this time. It was such a small herd and a relatively short move that it didn't require any of the trappings of a full cattle drive. They wouldn't need a chuck wagon or a remuda, either, but Lee thought it might be wise to take a couple of extra horses with them from the Diamond R corrals.

––––––

The next day, it took Lee and his helpers only nine hours to move the cattle; far faster and easier than they thought it would be. They herded them into the Fort Grant pen at four in the afternoon, then stayed the night in the NCO quarters. The next morning, right after a big breakfast, Lee was given a voucher for fifteen hundred dollars and then after a hearty thanks and farewell from Sergeant O'Malley, they made a much quicker return journey and arrived in time for lunch at the Flannery home. It was a happy meal and filled with a palpable atmosphere of optimism.

As much as Mary wanted to accompany him, she understood how much work he had before him, so after a warm kiss, Lee left the farm leading the Diamond R horses with Ian, who had to join him at the bank.

Lee left the horses in their large corral after filling the corral's hay pile and trough then rode to town.

As they rode, Ian and Lee talked about the new cattle company and the need to hire more ranch hands. His boys could handle the animals in the short run, but they really would need permanent help to do the more difficult jobs.

The entered the bank and had to spend some time creating the account for the Shamrock Cattle Company before they deposited the fifteen hundred dollars and then Lee wrote out a draft to Ian for the hay. Ian deposited the draft into his family account and the first sale of the new business was complete.

The next few days were busier than they all expected as they had to move the hay to the Diamond R and hire those ranch hands. It was surprisingly easy to find men wanting to work the ranch as those hands that Ed Richards had driven away hadn't gone far.

Lee let them pick the foreman, and the six men, including the cook were established back in their old bunkhouse. He gave the foreman, Al Compton, authorization to buy supplies at Enright's, so the ranch was back to normal in just a couple of weeks after that horrible, yet incredible night.

Once the ranch was settled and renamed as the Rocking F, it was time for Lee to start his preparations for the upcoming wedding. He finally had to buy the suit he hoped he'd only wear once and found a nice pair of wedding bands in Enright's.

The construction on their new home was going well, as the walls were all up and the windows were framed.

Mary still hadn't picked out her dress yet, and Lee thought she still was hesitant about picking out a white dress but didn't know how to convince her that it was all right.

———

On the tenth of October, Lee and Mary were at the station awaiting the train carrying his parents. Naturally, Mary was nervous and this time, Lee didn't try to mollify her anxiety as he suspected he wouldn't be successful anyway.

The train arrived a little early, and Mary's anxiety increased as the train huffed and clanged to a noisy stop and steam whooshed from the locomotive.

As the passengers started disembarking, Lee began scanning for his parents, knowing that he'd spot his father first.

When he saw the shock of red hair and waved above the other head, he waved. His father saw Lee and hooked his arm around his wife's waist, and they headed toward Lee.

Mary was surprised to see that Lee's father was also a redheaded Irishman, while his mother had light brown hair with some gray. Her eyes, though, were a sparkling blue, like her own. Both parents were smiling broadly as they found Lee with his arm around his future bride.

"It's good to see you again, son!" his father said in a deep, rumbling voice, then he turned to Mary, smiled and said, "And this must be your Mary that you wrote to us about."

He then surprised Mary when he scooped her into his arms in a bearhug and said in his cavernous voice, "I'm pleased to be meeting you, Mary. You're even prettier than Lee said you were, and that is going some."

He gave her a kiss on the cheek, then stepped back, allowing Lee's mother to step close and hug her. She was shorter than Mary and just a wee bit of a woman, but her strength when she hugged Mary surprised her.

She smiled at her future daughter-in-law and said in her melodious voice that contrasted with her husband's bass, "Mary, you're just too perfect for me to compare you to anything but yourself. My son is the most fortunate of men."

Mary looked into her blue eyes and said quite sincerely, "No, Mrs. Ryan, I honestly believe that I got the better part of the arrangement. Your son is the most remarkable man I have ever met. I count myself the luckiest of women."

His mother glanced over at Lee who was in conversation with his father, and said, "Aye, I'll give you that. He is quite a special young man. All the time he was growing up, we waited for him to give us trouble, but he never did. And please, call me either Mary or Maire."

"I read the telegram telling us you were coming, and I asked Lee why he never told me that your name was Mary. He said he always thought of you as Maire."

"Aye. He did. Once, some large lad in the schoolyard made the mistake of telling Lee that his mother was a horse. Lee was much shorter and the boy was stouter as well, but when he was finished the big boy apologized and no one ever made a joke of my name again."

"That sounds like Lee. Did he tell you about all of the excitement we've had the past month?"

"He mentioned that there were some difficulties but didn't go into detail."

"Well, we'll have him go into detail later. Now, we're going to head out to the ranch. Lee brought the buggy for you and we'll ride our horses. It's a short ride, about two miles."

Lee and his father walked over carrying their trunk with them. Lee put the trunk on the back of the buggy and strapped it down and after his parents boarded the buggy, Lee handed them their travel bags.

As they drove, Seamus Ryan looked at the almost matching palominos and noticed that neither Lee nor Mary seemed to be holding the reins tightly. He wasn't surprised at all, either. Lee had always had a way with horses and hoped that Lee would take time to show him his herd.

Ten minutes later, they turned into the access road to the ranch and the large house loomed in the distance.

"This is where you'll be staying, Papa," Lee told him as he leaned closer to the buggy.

"And who owns this place?" he asked.

"Right now, I do."

His father was taken aback and said, "I thought you only had a cabin."

"I still do. It's about twelve miles north of here. I'm having our new house being built right now. We can ride over there this afternoon. The roof is on and they're putting in the tile floor."

"What will you do with two houses and a cabin?"

"Mary and I will be staying in the cabin after the wedding and then we'll return to this house until our new home is ready. When it's finished, and all the furniture is in, we'll move out and turn the ranch over to the Flannery family. They'll run the ranch and the farm. I'll run my ranch and the horses."

"I suppose there are stories behind all of this."

"A few. Maggie and Katherine are making lunch right now. So, we'll all get better acquainted then. The house has a huge table, so there's room for everyone."

They arrived at the house and Lee dismounted, unstrapped the trunk and carried it into the house as his parents exited the buggy and walked behind him and Mary.

Maggie and Ian met his parents at the door and greetings were exchanged and introductions made to all the Flannery young people who had been waiting in the large parlor.

For three hours, with a large lunch included, they talked, and Lee had to fill in the details of the past month. Needless to say, his mother wasn't pleased about getting all of these details a month late, but she was extraordinarily proud of her son's rescue of the pretty Katherine and his subsequent takedown of those responsible.

His father was not only pleased with what he had done, but that he was now a deputy sheriff as he had been before his injury.

———

That afternoon, Lee, Mary and Katherine rode as Seamus and Maire drove the carriage to the new house. Even Lee, who had not seen it for three days, was astonished at how much had been done. The crew was still there, putting in the tiled floor and the windows, while the foreman showed them around. The floors were gorgeous and as impressed as his parents and Katherine had been, it was overshadowed when Lee led them into the atrium. The walkway was already there, as was the pool which was already full of water.

Even though she had expected it, when Mary saw her atrium, even without the lilacs, she almost started to cry, but instead just looked at Lee and mouthed, "I love you."

Lee's mother was awestruck by the atrium and asked, "Is this your idea, Lee?"

"Yes, Mama. When I first designed the layout, I was going to make it smaller, but thought as long as I was going to do it, I may as well do it right. So, I expanded my original design and wondered what I could add just for my Mary. I thought that having her own space that she could design herself would please her. It would become the focal point of the house, and that led to the atrium. The pool and walkway are only her first two steps. She's going to have lilac bushes and flowers everywhere. Without any wind to take away the flower scent, it will add a bouquet aroma to the whole house. If we go out the back, you'll see where we can add a vegetable garden and have a clear view out to the west where we can watch those spectacular Arizona sunsets."

After they finished their tour of the almost completed house, his parents boarded the buggy and Lee, Mary and Katherine mounted their horses to make the short ride to the canyon.

Hagar was still on duty and was happy to see everyone as they all seemed to be part of Lee's family.

They hadn't seen a canyon like his, even in Colorado and were impressed with his cabin, knowing he had built it himself when he was so young. But the biggest impression made on his father was when he saw the magnificent herds in the back of the canyon, and almost had to be pried loose from the horses.

After almost two hours, they returned to the big house. When they arrived, there was a crate on the porch addressed to Lee and Mary Ryan.

Lee looked at the shipping notice. It had come from Philadelphia.

"What is it Lee?" asked his father.

Ian asked, "Are you going to open it? It showed up two hours ago."

Lee looked at them and said, "I don't want to seem rude, but I believe that Mary and I need to open this in private. It's a long story that revolves around the remarkable woman that I told you had sold me the ranch. But it's one that is tinged with sadness for both of us, too. So, if it's all right with everyone, we'll take this inside the office, and we'll open it there."

"We understand, Lee. You go right ahead," said Ian.

Lee picked up the crate and found it not to be nearly as heavy as he'd expected, then lugged it through the front door and headed for the office, then changed his mind and began walking up the stairs. This should be opened in Lucy's room.

Mary understood the reason for the change and followed him up the stairs and wordlessly walked behind him to Lucy's room.

Lee brought the crate inside and closed the door. Mary sat on the bed nearby and felt tightness in her chest as Lee began to open the crate.

Lee took out his knife and pried the crate's top open, hearing the squeaks as the nails released their grip on the wood. They each took a deep breath as he pulled the cover free and set it aside. He removed some cloth packing and found a wooden box on top of more packing, so he opened the box and found a framed photograph.

It was of a radiant Lucy wearing a beautiful white wedding dress. At her side was a tall man with a kind face and an equally shining disposition and Lee immediately understood that Lucy had found her happiness after her long, lonely years and smiled as he handed the wedding portrait to Mary.

Under the picture he found two envelopes. One for Lee and the other for Mary.

Lee took his, gave Mary hers, then opened the envelope, slid the letter out and read:

Lucy St. John
1343 12th Street
Philadelphia, Pennsylvania

My Dearest Lee,

Now that you have my address, please write to me. As you can see in the picture, I've married my lost love, Jefferson St. John. He was as happy to see me as I was to see him. The fire was still there, Lee. It will always be there when it is fueled by true love.

We were married five days after I returned, and I never thought I'd experience the joy of married life. The kiss we shared at the train station was just my first step into in the total immersion into the world of love. A world I'd been denied for so long.

My friends tell me that you successfully cleaned up that horrible mess I left you. I knew you could. I was worried that I might have been subpoenaed for what I had done or witnessed, but leave it to you, my love, to smooth it all out so I can revel in my freedom and happiness.

My health problems are low at the moment, but my physician tells me that isn't unusual and that over time the attacks will worsen. I can live with that. I can live with anything now that I am here with Jefferson. You'd like him and he reminds me so much of you. I told him how I had departed, and he understood my need to act like some hussy on the train platform and I'm sure that your Mary understand as well.

I'm including a letter for Mary and a gift to her. If she doesn't want to share her letter with you, don't be upset. Although I find it hard to believe you would ever be anything but forgiving to your Mary.

So, Lee, write to me often. Send me a picture of you and Mary so I can share it with Jefferson.

Love,

Lucy

Lee took a deep breath and let it out. He looked over at Mary who was reading her letter with tears rolling down her cheeks.

Her letter read:

My Dearest Mary,

For someone that I have never met, I feel I know you better than I have any other woman. It is for that reason that I'm including this gift.

By now, you may think I'm an evil woman for leaving those nightgowns in my bedroom. They were hardly what most women consider decent night attire. I left them for you for exactly the reason that you probably suspected, and I hope you that you put them to good use. I wanted you to experience the joy of being one with Lee.

I know how passionate he is about you. When he talks of you, his eyes are alive. I knew that no man who loves a woman that deeply could neglect the physical part of love for very long. Nor could a woman. Being one with the man you love is something that I dreamed about when I was in love with Jefferson. I wanted to be with him so badly, it ached.

Then, the only time I experienced physical intercourse with a man was the cruel forced action of a heartless man. There was no love, no tenderness. It was a brutal attack and my dreams were shattered.

Then Lee Ryan entered our lives. He really was like the white knight in the fairy tales. I watched as he vanquished one foe after the other and began to fantasize about being with Jefferson again; of being loved as a woman for the first time. I longed for him and my ache returned, even as the promise of Lee's actions made them closer to realization.

When I was free, I was so lost in the possibility that I could be complete and experience what you and Lee shared that I decided to leave the nightgowns. I had ordered them years before in the hope that someday I might be free to wear them for Jefferson. I had four but left two for you.

So, Mary, don't think of yourself badly. I know you probably do. Or did, unless I miss my guess that Lee explained to you why you should be nothing but happy. Recognize that you were doing nothing more than showing Lee how much you love him. I hope you will continue to wear the nightgowns to keep him happy. He deserves it, and so do you.

The gift is the same wedding dress that I wore in the photograph. I had no emotional or moral difficulties wearing the beautiful cream silk dress. Jefferson and I had been together so much before the wedding, it was almost difficult to find the time to set it up. The dress is for you. You will wear it proudly as an announcement that you, Mary Flannery, are a good woman with a pure soul, because you are.

Give Lee a kiss for me, and please write when you can.

Love,

Lucy

Mary closed her letter and turned her head to look at Lee s she clutched Lucy's letter tightly to her chest.

"Lee, would you be mad at me if I kept this letter private?" she asked softly.

Lee smiled at her and replied, "Not at all, my Mary. But you'll understand why it's all right when I let you read her letter to me."

He handed her the letter, and for a moment, she thought she should read it, but then let her eyes drop to the familiar handwriting, and she read each word, understanding why Lee had expected her to keep her letter private and at the same time drifting into an ever deeper understanding of just how remarkable Lucy is.

She handed him back the letter, and asked quietly, "Do you know what her gift is?"

"No."

"It's my wedding dress. Lucy knew. She knew I'd feel bad and explained everything, just as you had. She even knew that you'd make me feel better. She explained why she sent the dress. It's the same one she wore just a few days ago at her wedding and I'll be proud to wear the same dress she wore. And when Katherine gets married, she can wear it, too."

Lee reached with his right hand and touched her face with his fingertips as he looked into her blue eyes and said, "I'm glad to see you finally understand, Mary. You are as innocent and good as any person I know."

She touched his face gently and said, "Lucy is an incredible person, Lee."

"She is, and Jefferson is a lucky man. I just wish she could experience that happiness longer."

"I'm just happy she got to experience it at all. If you hadn't been the way you are, she never would have, Lee. You can't put a value on what you did for her."

They let their hands slowly return to their laps and he said, "Well, at least we can tell them downstairs that the gift was a wedding dress."

"We can do that."

Lee stood and took Mary's hand until she rose and then closed his arms around her and kissed her softly before saying, "I'll be waiting for you at the altar and anxiously waiting for you to appear in that lovely dress, my bride."

She hugged him, and they left Lucy's room hand in hand. Lee had the photograph in his left hand as they made their way down the stairs, but the precious letters were in Mary's dress pocket.

Lee let Mary explain about the wedding dress as the wedding photograph of Lucy and Jefferson was passed among the families. The three Irish women and many of the Irish men were teary eyed as Mary told Lucy's story, including her sad prognosis, culminating in Lucy's marriage and shipment of her wedding gown to Mary.

After the tears were dried, Mary turned to Katherine and said, "And after I've worn it, Katherine, I'll pass it on to you for your wedding."

Katherine smiled and changed the sad mood when she replied, "I think it will need to be taken in. Especially in the top."

The women all laughed, the men didn't dare laugh in fear of what would happen if they did, so they pretended not to understand.

Lee showed his parents to one of the guest rooms and his mother asked the obvious question, "So, where will you be staying after the wedding?"

"We are going to spend a few days in my cabin. Mary loves the idea."

"Then we'll have the whole house to ourselves?" his wee Irish mother asked him, her eyes twinkling.

Lee rolled his eyes, remembering Maggie's comments to her daughters. *Not his mother, too!*

"Yes, Mama, you and Papa will have the house to yourselves."

CHAPTER 9

The day of the wedding finally arrived and the big house was a beehive of activity. Lee was staying at the farm, preparing for the big event. Amazingly, he and Mary had been so busy, they hadn't had any time to repeat their tryst in Lucy's bedroom.

Lee confirmed that he had the rings in his pocket and was surprisingly nervous; not about marrying Mary, but of fumbling some of his very serious vows. He had gotten a haircut the day before and had a long bath in the morning, shaved early in case he wound up with any serious nicks and by nine o'clock, he was ready.

At the big house, Mary was putting the finishing touches on her wedding gown. She always wore her emerald necklace but made sure it was prominently displayed. They had arranged for a photographer to take four pictures of the newlyweds and several family pictures as well.

Mary would be driven to the church by Ian, who chafed in his suit, having not worn it since Conor's baptism eleven years earlier. They had rented a carriage for the other women and Seamus. Ian had wanted to ride but was told by his wife that he'd be taking the carriage, which ended the discussion.

Finally, at ten o'clock, Lee stood at the altar of St. Mary's church, watching as Mary was escorted down the aisle by her father. Lee had expected to be in awe of his bride when he finally saw her in Lucy's dress, but soon realized that awe wasn't even close to describing his feelings.

He had believed that she had been most beautiful when he first saw her wearing the emerald necklace standing on the porch in the Arizona sun, but now, it wasn't even close. His Mary was exquisite in every detail. She was flawless and he wondered how he could ever have been so blessed.

Mary nervously walked down the aisle, hoping she didn't trip. She was concentrating all her attention on Lee as he watched her. She looked into his eyes and wondered how this perfect man had ever fallen in love with her. *How he had seen through all her faults and troubles and adored her the way he did? How did she ever deserve the happiness she knew was upon her?*

She reached the altar without a single misstep and stood before Father Kelly. The wedding Mass had been said, and then the vows were spoken. Lee slid the ring on her finger as he made those last promises before she placed the large ring on his.

Father Kelly said those magic words, "I now pronounce you man and wife," then Lee kissed his Mary as his wife and the one woman he knew he would have waited forever to return to him. For some reason, the much less passionate kiss was unlike all the others; it was sweeter and more meaningful.

They turned and walked down the aisle, arm in arm smiling at family and friends as they strolled past, each feeling the happiness that was almost overwhelming.

They walked to the buggy with Jin standing behind; his reins dropping straight to the ground.

Lee held Mary's train as he helped his bride enter the buggy, the trotted around the front and boarded on the opposite side. They waved at the assembled crowd, and after receiving a loud cheer, Lee snapped the reins and they rolled away heading back to the ranch.

They wanted to go to the cabin right away and be free to unleash their bottled passion, but instead had to return to the big house to meet everyone. A wedding feast had been prepared by the three women not getting married and Lee had hired some help to roast the beef and pork, bake the cake and the other things that would take too much of the women's time. He also had the photographer there to take those all-important photographs.

They all enjoyed the food and family togetherness, but everyone knew that the newlyweds had other, more important things on their minds. So, after eating and accepting congratulations from everyone. They were finally able to make their escape to Lee's cabin.

Mary had changed out of the silk wedding dress into a striking riding outfit that accentuated her impressive curves, probably as a result of her mother's skill with the new sewing machine. As they mounted, Lee reminded himself to tell Maggie she did a great job.

On the ride to the cabin, they stopped dismounted outside their new house. It was ahead of schedule and after entering, they found that stove and tub had been installed and the beautiful tile floor had been completed. The kitchen still needed its pump installed and the counters and cabinets put in, but the house would be done in just two or three weeks.

"Lee, would it be alright if we visited the atrium?" Mary asked, knowing where they both wanted to be.

"Of course, we can. It's your atrium."

They passed through the kitchen and walked inside. Mary walked along the stone pathway and past the pool, running her fingers through the water creating small waves as she passed. She pictured the atrium with blooms everywhere and smiled.

She sighed, turned to Lee and said, "And now, dear husband for real, let's go to our cabin retreat."

"At your command, always, my beloved wife."

They almost jogged from the house, mounted their patient horses and rode the last two hundred yards to the cabin, passed through the gate and let Hagar close it.

They then stopped at the cabin, quickly removed the tack from both horses and just tossed them on the porch. Lee would store them properly later as there were more pressing issues.

The palominos wandered away to the corral, but neither Lee nor Mary noticed.

Lee opened the door and before she could enter, swept Mary into his arms as she laughed then carried his bride over the threshold.

He closed the door with his foot, walked to the enlarged bed and laid her down gently.

"I see you've been busy, husband," Mary said quietly as she spread her arms across the widened bed.

"Not as busy as we're going to be, my Mary."

———

The saddles remained untouched out on the porch for the better part of the day and through the night. By the time Lee finally opened the door the next morning, there was dew covering both saddles, which may have been a cardinal sin in the leather world but would never reach Father Kelly's ears in the confessional.

Mary stepped out behind him, somehow clothed in one of his shirts, but nothing else.

She put her arm around his waist and asked, "Are you going to bring them inside now?"

He glanced at her and smiled as he replied, "I'm thinking about it but seeing you in that shirt is giving me ideas. It's actually even more inspirational than your nightgown, but don't tell that to Lucy."

Mary squeezed her husband and asked, "Those wouldn't be the same ideas you had last night, would it?"

"They could be," he replied, then turned toward Mary, pulled her inside, flipped the door closed with his foot, and reclaimed his shirt.

They ate a late breakfast, and then slept most of the afternoon, curled up in each other's' arms. When Lee finally opened his eyes to see his wife's still sleeping face just inches from his he smiled and just looked at her. He watched her for almost ten minutes until her eyelids slowly opened to see him.

"Is it morning already?" she asked sleepily.

"No, my love, it's actually late in the afternoon."

"I suppose I'd better get out of bed and get dressed. Someone needs to cook something."

"You could always cook dressed as you are."

"Lee, I'm naked, or hadn't you noticed?"

"Oh, trust me, I noticed. So, you go ahead and get dressed. I suppose I need to get moving as well, but I will enjoy the show."

Mary had long since forgotten about those worries about her lusty nature and decided to make it a real show. Putting on her clothes slowly and seductively, as opposed to how they came off. Lee appreciated it, so as soon as she finished, he decided he'd do the same for her, and she appreciated her own entertainment.

Fortunately, they were able to successfully cook and eat dinner before returning to other activities, both grateful for the remote location of the cabin and hoped they weren't spooking the herds a half a mile away.

But the privacy and isolation had to end as Lee's parents were leaving the next day, so regretfully, the newlyweds had to leave their honeymoon cabin and return to the big house.

They arrived in the late morning, having enjoyed their honeymoon one last time. The house was empty except for Lee's parents and Lee had told Mary about his mother's question and its implication.

Mary began to wonder if all women were secret, wanton harlots or just Irish women.

His parents were packed and planned to leave on the train at 3:30 for the trip to Pueblo, so Lee and Seamus rode as Maire and Mary chatted during the short ride to the station.

When they arrived at the station, Lee handed his father an envelope and said, "Papa, here's your tickets and your horse tag."

Seamus glanced at the envelope and said, "I didn't bring a horse."

Lee said, "He's over in the corral. He's the big black stallion. I'll leave his name up to you."

Seamus stared at the magnificent animal as Mary smiled at her mother-in-law, who was almost as stunned as her husband.

"Lee, I don't know what to say. He's the best horse I've ever seen."

"You deserve him, Papa. You and mama gave me everything and let me grow up to be me. Not too many sons receive that gift."

He hugged Lee and smiled at Mary before he turned and watched his horse being led into the stock car.

The whistle blew, and the conductor announced their train's imminent departure, so Lee kissed his mother and hugged his father again before his father hugged the newer Mrs. Ryan then Maire kissed her new daughter-in-law.

The elder Ryans boarded the train and waved through the window as it began rolling.

Lee and Mary remained on the platform as the caboose passed by and Mary said, "I think your father liked his horse."

"When I first saw the black, I knew that he was meant for my father just as Qing Jin would always be yours."

"Well, you are two for two, my husband. I think we need to go to our new temporary home now."

The younger Mr. and Mrs. Ryan returned to the big house driving the buggy while both palominos trotted behind. After they returned to the empty house, they immediately walked to Lucy's bedroom and Mary modeled the other nightgown, but only for a short duration, of course.

It was when she had taken the second nightgown from the drawer that Mary found a short note from Lucy. It told her how she had ordered the nightgowns in case she wanted more.

She showed the note to Lee and smiled.

"Now, that's an idea," he said.

"Why? You never get to let me wear them for more than five minutes."

"I didn't know I waited that long."

———

The next two days passed quietly. They would have to make another cattle run in a few days, so he and Ian had made the arrangements but wouldn't have to make the trip as the ranch hands could handle it.

Lee had discovered that he had two new foals when he returned briefly to check on the herd.

———

On the evening of the second day, Lee was walking into Harry's to order some more lamps for the new house and after he entered, he saw a stranger talking to Harry. He was about thirty and seemed to have an attitude of casualness that wasn't quite right for a stranger.

He was going to head to the back to pick up something for Mary when he heard the stranger give his name, and that changed his whole plans for the day.

"Yes, sir, I've been through here before and have fond memories of your town. Fond memories, indeed. My name is John Everett, and I was wondering if you could tell me something about an old acquaintance of mine."

When Lee heard that name his temper exploded and for a moment, almost did something rash until he remembered his training and calmed down.

He caught Harry's eye as Everett asked, "I wonder if you could tell me anything about Mary Flannery. You see, she and I were very close, very, very close, if you catch my meaning. I would like to look her up."

Then he laughed and said, "Or perhaps, look up her skirt. Not that I haven't seen it before, mind you. As I said, we were very close. Do you know if she's still living at the family farm?"

Lee could tell that Harry was about to smack the man in the head when he started shaking his head slowly at Harry and then Lee put his finger to his lips.

Harry nodded and said, "I don't rightly know. The gentleman who just came in might be able to help, though," then he looked at Lee and crooked his finger to wave him over.

Lee managed a warm smile as he stepped closer to the counter, "What do you need, Harry?"

Harry replied, "This gentleman, his name is John Everett, is asking where Mary Flannery is. Do you know where she is these days?"

"I think so. Say, John, want to go to the saloon and I'll give you the whole story about Mary?" Lee asked before he winked.

Everett broke into a wide grin, and replied, "Now, you're talking!"

Everett turned and started walking out of the store as Lee looked back at Harry and nodded.

Harry smiled and wished he could be there to witness what was going to happen, but even he couldn't imagine what Lee had in mind.

Lee walked down to the saloon with John Everett, who had ruined his Mary, but continued to act jovial and friendly. They walked into the saloon where Lee pointed out a table and told John to have a seat. Lee then walked to the bar and said in a low voice, "Phil, I need you to start giving me tea and bring the man I'm sitting with some hard whiskey. He hurt my Mary, and I'm going to make him regret it. Don't worry, I won't hurt him at all."

Phil nodded and poured two glasses, then said, "Yours will always be on your right."

Lee nodded and took the drinks back to the table, gave Everett the whiskey, and he sat down opposite with his whiskey-like tea.

"I never did catch your name," said Everett.

"Oh, sorry. The name's Jeff St. John."

"Nice to meet you, Jeff," he said as he gulped his whiskey.

Lee was stunned by his ability to empty the glass in one swallow, but asked, "So, where are you staying, John?"

"I haven't checked in yet, but I'll do that when I leave. So, what do you know about Mary?"

"Probably a lot more than you do, John," he replied as he winked again.

"I'm not sure, Jeff," he laughed before leaning forward and whispering, "I deflowered that Irish rose a couple of years ago."

"Really? How did you manage that?" Lee whispered back, having to use every bit of his training to keep his temper in check. He was Irish, after all.

"I pretended I was in love with her and promised her I was going to marry her. It always works with all these farm girls," he said as he smiled.

Lee waved at Phil and finished his tea and the bartender quickly brought over two more drinks.

"So, you've had other girls using that line?" Lee asked as he took the right-hand glass.

"Lots of them. You smile at them, tell them all sorts of flowery expressions of love and marriage, then get them away from their parents and start moving in."

He swallowed his whole glass of whiskey again, and Phil brought him another one without being summoned, but Lee could see the mirth in his eyes.

"Wow! I never thought of that. I always thought you had to call on them and meet with the parents and everything," Lee replied in phony astonishment.

"Nah! That's for suckers. Once you get them alone, start with a nice innocent kiss, then get a little more serious. Then you start sliding your hands around and get them nice and ready. It works every time."

"So, that worked on Mary, too?"

"Pretty much. She was a little tougher than most of them, though. I had to really work on that one. It took me three trips out on the desert before I deflowered her. She was a challenge. That's why I thought of having another go, because I have to tell you, that is one fine young lady under those clothes," John said before slamming back his third whiskey.

"She is a good-looking woman."

"That's why I'm back here in Phoenix."

Phoenix?

Lee noticed he was heading into drunkenness already, which surprised him after only three glasses of whiskey, considering his obvious familiarity with the drink.

"So, where is she these days? I'm really getting to feel the need, if you know what I mean," he asked as he giggled.

Lee noticed his eyes glossing over already as Phil brought his fourth drink and winked at Lee.

Lee said, "I'll tell you what, go ahead and finish your drink, and I'll show you where she is. Maybe we can peek in her window as she's getting ready for bed."

Everett nodded his head vigorously and threw the fourth whiskey down.

Lee left a five-dollar gold piece on the table for Phil.

Everett was still nodding in agreement as Lee stood, then helped him to his feet and led him staggering from the saloon.

"Where's your horse?" Lee asked.

Emerson couldn't talk, so he pointed at a brown gelding and Lee helped him into the saddle and called Jin. He climbed into his saddle, took Everett's horse's reins and led him north out of town.

It was slow moving and as the sun was setting, they arrived at his cabin and Lee helped him down, sure that Everett had no idea where he was anymore. His head was rolling around on his shoulders as his boots touched the ground.

He led Emerson stumbling into the cabin and laid him on the bed and he was snoring just seconds after his head dropped onto the pillow.

Lee then went to work to punish the bastard for what he had done to his Mary. He opened Everett's jacket and pulled his pants down a few inches and as John Everett snored, Lee worked and was finished an hour later. Then he added two more touches and let everything settle while he wrote a note and let it dry.

Two hours later, he redressed Everett, picked him up from the bed and tossed him over his shoulder and walked out of the cabin, closing the door behind him, glad he hadn't vomited in the process.

He tossed Everett over his saddle as if he were dead, then stepped up on Jin and walked them out of his canyon and turned him west. After he'd ridden for almost an hour, he stopped, dismounted and slid Everett from the horse. He tucked the note under Everett's shirt so he could find it when he woke up, then mounted Jin and rode away.

He knew it was late and had Jin moving at a fast trot as they headed for the ranch house where he suspected that Mary would be waiting anxiously.

It was after midnight and Mary was petrified as she paced the upstairs hallway as she worried about Lee. He hadn't been out this late since those bad nights and knew that he really enjoyed their private time together, so whatever had delayed his return must have been serious and probably dangerous.

She was at the far end of the hallway when she heard footsteps on the front porch and as she turned, the front door open and she rushed down the stairs wearing one of the nightgowns, so Lee was greeted with the awesome sight of Mary bouncing down the stairs creating an incredibly arousing vision.

"Lee! What happened? Are you alright?" she shouted as she reached the first floor and rushed to him.

He removed his hat, set it on a table and replied, "Yes, Mary. I'm fine. Come upstairs, and I'll tell you."

"Where were you?" she asked even as she felt his hand tugging at her nightgown.

"I was drinking at the saloon," he replied with a smile, but still let his fingers slide across his bride.

Mary was shocked, ignored his touches as she exclaimed, *"You? Drinking?* Lee, I didn't think you drank at all!"

"I just had some tea. I was buying whiskey for another gentleman, although I would normally not call him that. I wanted to get him drunk."

Mary was confused and said, "Lee, this is so unlike you. Let's go to bed and you can tell me there."

Lee put his arm around his wife and walked with her up the stairs to Lucy's bedroom, which they had used as their honeymoon suite.

She sat in bed with her feet curled under her waiting for Lee's explanation.

Lee glanced at her and looked at her in the diaphanous nightgown and her angelic face, exhaled, and knew that he had to tell her what had happened before he did anything else.

He sat down next to her, resisting the urge to hold her and said, "I was going to the store to order some more lamps for the new house, and when I went in, I saw some stranger talking to Harry. I had never seen him before. Then I heard him give his name to Harry. It was John Everett."

Mary turned white and put her hand to her mouth and in a shaking voice, asked, "Why was he here?"

"He was looking for you."

Mary closed her eyes and wrapped her arms around herself before she whispered, "Is he going to the farm?"

"No, my Mary. He isn't going to the farm and he won't be bothering you or any other woman ever again."

Her eyed exploded as she almost shouted the horrible question that she was almost afraid to ask, *"Lee, you didn't kill him?"*

Lee reached over and simply rested his hand on her shoulder and replied, "No, Mary, I didn't hurt him at all. He'll be able to ride away from Nueva Luz with no pain at all, but I guarantee that he will never bother you again."

Her fear gone, she curiously asked, "Lee, if you didn't kill him, then what did you do?"

Lee almost apologetically replied, "Well, when I finished hearing what he said to Harry about really having known you, I just wanted to beat him to a pulp. But I calmed down and took him down to the bar. I drank tea, and he drank what I guess was some of Phil's special mix. It's basically pure grain alcohol with some coloring to make it look like whiskey. He had four glasses of the high-powered stuff and was as drunk as you can get and still walk, or at least stagger. I took him out to the cabin and, well, I disfigured him."

"I thought you said you didn't hurt him."

"I didn't. Remember when Katherine asked about how I marked my horses?"

"Yes, you said you tattooed them with special ink."

"Yes, ma'am. I use a special and permanent ink. It gets into the skin and can never be removed. Well, I wrote in two-inch high letters on the back of one hand 'LIAR' and on the other hand I wrote 'BAD'. He'll always be marked and can never get away with what he did again."

But before I tell you anything else, sweetheart, I need to let you know something he said before he passed out. While he was in his liquor, he told me that what he did to you, he did to many young women in other towns. He said he'd profess love and marriage and get them away from their parents. Then, he'd start kissing them and move on from there. He confessed that you were his most difficult target, but you were so pretty, he kept focusing on you rather than switching to another girl. He said it took three tries to finally get what he wanted. Mary, you were far from easy, but you were still so pretty that he wanted to see you again. Now, he won't be able to see any other girl or woman without them knowing what he is."

"But couldn't he wear gloves?" she asked.

"I suppose, but he'd lose the touch of his fingers, so he wouldn't have any pleasure when he started groping. But there was something else that I did."

"I almost hate to ask, but what was it?"

Lee exhaled and answered, "I left him in the desert with his horse and a note warning him never to come near this town again. But before I took him out there, I opened up his shirt and pulled his pants down a bit and painted something on his chest and all the way down to his hips."

"And this was?"

"A very large phallus, complete with companions."

"*You didn't?*" she gasped.

"Yes, I did," Lee replied, then asked, "You're not mad at me, are you, Mary?"

Mary's face answered his question before she did when she said, "Mad at you, my wonderful, wonderful husband? I can't imagine anything that would please me more. He wasn't hurt, but you took away his ability to prey on women."

Mary suddenly knelt and pulled Lee down on top of her and Lee guessed he did the right thing.

———

The next day was Saturday, and Lee knew he had to go and confess what he had done.

So, after entering the confessional and the preliminary formalities, Father Kelly asked him to confess his sins.

Lee said, "Father, I disfigured a man."

The priest was no longer surprised by anything anymore, but had to ask, "And how did you do this, Lee?"

So, Lee began his confession of his artwork he'd permanently left on display on Mary's defiler.

When he finished with a complete description of the large drawing on the chest, he waited for Father Kelly's absolution, or at least a comment, but there was nothing but silence.

Lee listened more carefully, and thought he heard stifled laughing behind the screen.

After almost a minute, Lee asked, "Father?"

He heard a rushed, stilted, "Bless you, Lee. You have no penance, nor need for absolution ..." from the other side.

"Thank you, Father," Lee replied before standing.

Lee left the confessional wondering what had just happened, was six feet away and just as the next penitent prepared to enter the confessional, he heard loud laughter break out from Father Kelly's box stopping the sinner in her tracks.

He rode home and told Mary of the unusual occurrence at the church with triggered more laughter from his wife. She hugged and kissed her husband, then set about making dinner. She felt the final chapter of her old life was over now that she had Lee.

Lee watched her walk away and knew he would always have Mary. His Mary.

EPILOGUE

The newlyweds had sent Lucy a package with a long letter a few days earlier, explaining all that had happened and what they had done with the ranch and the cattle. Lee wrote about how he had inflicted just punishment on Mary's defiler and Mary mentioned giving the earrings to Katherine. She thanked Lucy for the wedding dress and included their wedding picture. Mary had ensured that the emerald necklace was visible in the image. She also thanked Lucy for the nightgowns and said they were getting quite a workout, but not much wear. Above all, she wrote that she was most grateful for the letter she had left for her in the linen chest. They didn't mention Lucy's illness because it was pointless.

The monthly deliveries to the army began to become routine; their company's bank account was growing, and the herd didn't look any smaller. After storing the hay in the ranch's barn, they hoped they could get by with only half the crop. They figured they would break the herd up into lots that were going to make the trip in the winter months and give them more feed and it worked out.

The house was finally complete in mid-November. All the furniture had been put into place and those things that they wanted to take with them, had moved as well. For sentimental reasons, they emptied out Lucy's bedroom and it became their bedroom albeit in their new home. They sent one of their new beds and a chest of drawers to the ranch house to take the place of Lucy's furniture.

When they moved into their new house, the change was dramatic. Lee could work with his herd and still come home for lunch. The Flannery family moved into the big house, except for Patrick who stayed in the family home and prepared for the arrival of his betrothed, Elsie McDermott. They were to be married in February.

Katherine was now the focus of almost every young male in the area. She had suddenly achieved the level of physical maturity that she had hoped for; not quite up to Mary's, but noticeable. She had asked Lee if he could make sure she wasn't swept off her feet for the wrong reason. He was flattered and told her that he'd make recommendations, but the choice would be hers.

They continued to correspond with Lucy on a weekly basis, keeping her abreast of all that was happening. They would get letters from her, each with a noticeable degradation in the handwriting.

Not surprisingly, Mary announced she was pregnant just before Christmas and wrote to Lucy before she even had a chance to tell Lee, telling her that she hoped it would be a girl. She didn't mention her wish to Lee, thinking he would want a son, but one night, he was lying in bed with Mary, his hand resting on her stomach and said how he wished they had a daughter. Then she confessed that a daughter was her desire as well, and Lee had just kissed her and told her it was because she was so perfect, and he wanted their baby to be just as perfect.

Mary had been concerned about losing the baby early because of her first loss, but she had a good pregnancy. She went into labor early on the fifth of August and delivered the baby after only four hours. Mary was radiant when they gave her the squirming pink bundle to hold. Lee was allowed in after Mary had settled in with their infant.

She was tired but glowing as her husband entered the room, and she said, "Lee, we have our daughter. Come and meet our Lucy."

Lee was so happy to have his Mary come through childbirth so easily as he looked down at their new baby girl and said, "Welcome to the world, Lucy Ryan."

"Lee," Mary said softly, "when I first held our baby girl, I was smiling at her and then I heard a voice. I looked to my left, and I saw Lucy standing there, smiling, as she was in the picture when she was married. She said, 'We have a beautiful baby girl, don't we, Mary?' I looked down at our Lucy, and then when I looked back to tell her that we did, she wasn't there anymore."

Lee believed everything Mary had just said and wondered if it meant that Lucy was now free of her pain.

He replied softly, "Lucy has been a big part of our lives, Mary, and I know that she'll continue to watch our Lucy grow."

A week later, Mary was nursing Lucy in the large family room. Lee had gone to town for the mail, and when he returned, he had a letter from Philadelphia. It was in Jefferson's hand, just as the last few had been, dictated by Lucy to him.

He sat down, and Mary looked at him as he opened it. She saw his face drop and knew what was in the letter without asking.

His eyes flooding with tears, and his voice shook as he said quietly, "Lucy has passed away. Jefferson said she died peacefully in her sleep in the morning of August 5, and the last thing she said to him was to tell us thank you for letting her see our Lucy."

1	Rock Creek	12/26/2016
2	North of Denton	01/02/2017
3	Fort Selden	01/07/2017
4	Scotts Bluff	01/14/2017
5	South of Denver	01/22/2017
6	Miles City	01/28/2017
7	Hopewell	02/04/2017
8	Nueva Luz	02/12/2017
9	The Witch of Dakota	02/19/2017
10	Baker City	03/13/2017
11	The Gun Smith	03/21/2017
12	Gus	03/24/2017
13	Wilmore	04/06/2017
14	Mister Thor	04/20/2017
15	Nora	04/26/2017
16	Max	05/09/2017
17	Hunting Pearl	05/14/2017
18	Bessie	05/25/2017
19	The Last Four	05/29/2017
20	Zack	06/12/2017
21	Finding Bucky	06/21/2017
22	The Debt	06/30/2017
23	The Scalawags	07/11/2017
24	The Stampede	07/20/2017
25	The Wake of the Bertrand	07/31/2017
26	Cole	08/09/2017
27	Luke	09/05/2017
28	The Eclipse	09/21/2017
29	A.J. Smith	10/03/2017
30	Slow John	11/05/2017
31	The Second Star	11/15/2017
32	Tate	12/03/2017
33	Virgil's Herd	12/14/2017
34	Marsh's Valley	01/01/2018
35	Alex Paine	01/18/2018
36	Ben Gray	02/05/2018
37	War Adams	03/05/2018

51952140R00189

Made in the USA
Middletown, DE
06 July 2019